IT ONLY HURTS A MINUTE

It Only Hurts
A Minute

A NOVEL BY DON M. MANKIEWICZ

G. P. PUTNAM'S SONS

NEW YORK

For Jane

IT ONLY HURTS A MINUTE

1

The coastal foothills run east and west, dividing Los Angeles (and Hollywood and Beverly Hills) on the south from the San Fernando Valley on the north. South of these hills, the real estate advertisements read *N. of Sunset*. North of them, they read *S. of Ventura*. Either line is a proud declaration that the property described lies in the cool-by-summer, warm-by-winter, prestigious-all-year hills, rather than in the smoggy grid of Los Angeles or the treeless grid of the sprawling Valley.

Slithering along the top of the tiny brown range, now a bit to the Valley side of the summit, now hooking coastward, is Mulholland Drive, a road which has probably been seen by more human eyes than any other thoroughfare since time began. This is because extensive stock-footage of its exists, and this film is used, by means of an elaborate process, in nearly all motion picture automobile chase-sequences.

The black station wagon proceeding westward along Mulholland, however, is neither chasing nor being chased, merely moving along in the shimmering late-afternoon heat.

Inside the car, the driver squints as a twist in the road brings the sun into his windshield. His free hand starts for the visor;

then, as the road swings back and the sun no longer shines in his eyes, his hand goes to the air-conditioner control and turns the blower up a notch.

Now the station wagon leaves Mulholland, turning right, onto a narrow road with a long Spanish name; the name, according to the local joke, would be longer than the street if the street ran straight downhill. But it does not run straight, but goes down in a series of eight well-rounded switchbacks, so arranged as to provide the greatest possible number of homesites, each with a view of the valley below.

Halfway down the switchbacks, the car turns off into a driveway which leads to a double garage joined to the house it serves by a breezeway. As the car nears the garage door, it opens; when it is inside, the door closes again.

Inside the garage, the driver gets out, taking with him a handsome briefcase from the front seat of the station wagon. He walks through the vacant half of the garage, through the breezeway, and pauses for a moment at the side door to look to his right, through the breezeway, into the rear yard where the hot air, striking the cool surface of the swimming pool, causes the stone fence that marks the rear property line to appear to shimmer. Beyond the fence, below it, running down the hill, are several similar but not identical houses, all with swimming pools. The man smiles; even in the heat of the afternoon, this is a pleasant sight; anyone, he seems to be thinking, would smile.

Inside the house, the man pauses in the main hallway to turn a wheel which speeds up the action of the air-conditioning unit. Then he carries his briefcase into the study and puts it down on the floor next to a desk. On the desk, held down by the telephone, is a piece of paper on which is written a ten-digit telephone number. The man sits down, takes the paper from under the phone, studies it for a moment, then dials the number.

The conversation is short but, to the man, satisfactory. He tells his wife he misses her already. She tells him the flight was a pleasant one. Her sister has had her baby, a boy, something of a disappointment since her first child was also a boy, but both she and her sister feel guilty at their own disappointment and are prepared to rejoice that the baby is healthy. She will return tomorrow afternoon. He is not to meet her at the airport. He should not take time off from work for so slight a reason. Moreover, her car is at the airport. Something is said about this being the first night they will have spent apart since their marriage; warm farewells are exchanged. The man hangs up.

Now the man moves from the study into the bedroom and begins changing his clothes, taking off his suit and shirt, putting on a sports shirt from a bureau drawer and a pair of slacks from a closet. As he hangs up the suit, he pushes the other suits and jackets on the rack back to make room. Then, noticing that one of the other jackets is now hanging crookedly, half off its hanger, he takes the hanger off the rack to rehang the jacket properly, and the jacket falls to the floor.

The man bends down and picks up the jacket. Then, as he starts to put it back on the hanger, he hears a metallic jangle from the very bottom of the jacket. Something has slipped into the lining. The man's right hand locates the obstruction, while his left explores the interior of the pocket and finds the torn spot by which the lining was penetrated. Now carefully—for the jacket has been pressed since it was last worn—he works the obstruction up to the pocket and through the hole. When his left hand comes out of the pocket it holds two objects, stacked, just as they came from the jacket. The one on top is a silver dollar. He drops it into the pocket of his slacks. The other object engages his attention.

It is a disc, of the same diameter and thickness as the silver dollar, but lighter in weight, and darker in color, being basically a stamped piece of black plastic, into each side of which elaborate identical decals have been printed. Gray in background, the decals show a silver tower; above the tower are the words *$100;* below it: *Silver Hotel, Las Vegas* and the tiny imprint which signifies that the design is copyrighted.

The man puts the chip on the desk and glances for a moment at the woman's picture in the propped-up leather frame near it. Then he goes back to the main hallway, pausing to turn the air-conditioning down, for he is suddenly cold, then out into the front yard, where he looks for the afternoon paper, finds it under a bush, brings it back through the entryway and into the study.

The desk in the study faces a picture window; for a full minute, the man sits motionless, looking out the window, down the hill, over the sparkling swimming pools, down onto the flat, brown-gray floor of the valley, at the streets which wind down the hill and then, on reaching the bottom, straighten out and reach across the Valley, intersecting with roads running the length of the Valley, so that everything beyond the Boulevard resembles a warped checkerboard, bending monotonously away to be lost in the dust and low clouds which obscure the base of the Sierras fifty miles to the north.

Then he picks up the newspaper, discards the first section, which has a green front page, and begins leafing through the second section until he reaches the page at which the news ends and the classified advertising begins. The advertisement he is looking for is in the miscellaneous section, an area reserved for free-lance parapsychologists, massage parlors, tea-leaf readers, persons willing to listen to anyone's troubles for a fee, dispensers of internal baths, and package-travel deals. It is headed:

CHAMPAGNE FLITE—VEGAS.
$25 + Tax, No Adds

For his $25, the patron receives "rnd trip air trans," "champagne en route," "Vegas limo service," "free bingo," "two coktls @ show," "free golf," and "$5 starter-chips for casino." Departures are at 6 and 9 P.M.; returns are at 5 A.M. A phone number is given for reservations.

The man glances at his watch. It is 5:10. He reaches for the phone, starts to dial the number listed, then changes his mind. There is, he seems to be thinking, plenty of time.

Plenty of time.

There is plenty of time. I can get to Burbank in twenty to thirty minutes on the Freeway, twenty-five minutes if I avoid it. I can leave in twenty minutes and make the first flight; or in three hours and twenty minutes and make the second.

Or not at all. That is the point. That is what I must hang on to. Not that I must necessarily take the third choice, but that, until I have chosen among the three, I must not overlook its availability.

Gamblers, of course, lay less stress on the third choice than do non-gamblers. But even among gamblers, the degree of consideration given to *whether*—before *which* and *when* are decided—is an index to the quality of the gambler himself. The more attention paid to *whether*, the better the gambler; and I am not using better in the sense that casino operators and bookmakers use it. (To them, a good gambler is a persistent and enthusiastic loser with resources that defy his ever more strenuous efforts to exhaust them.) By good gambler, I mean one with a good chance to win. And such a gambler—and I was once one—does not back the bet closest at hand, nor the next bet to be resolved, nor even (necessarily) the best of the bets open to him at the moment, but considers first whether any of those presently open are sufficiently attractive as to obviate the possibility that, by waiting, by refusing to act, he might be increasing the likelihood of retaining a sufficient stake with which to back a more favorable proposition later on. If he considers seriously the possibility that no genuinely favorable opportunity to bet will ever arise, then he is moving on beyond the area of "good gambler" into the area of "non-gambler." I am, at this moment, a non-gambler.

But when I gambled I was, I think, a good gambler. I was not to be found, for instance, among those who, when in the seller's line at a racetrack, crane their heads toward the auxiliary tote board as they reach the window, a sure indication that they have decided to bet but do not know on what horse, which means they skipped over *whether* entirely and are now using every last second to consider *which*. But I, having a lifetime of races before me, was perfectly capable of refraining from betting for a race or two, or a day or two, or (in extreme cases) a week or two. And I, having that capacity, was able to consider not merely which horse in a race was most worth a bet, but also, having made such a determination, whether a bet on the horse so chosen was to be preferred to no bet at all.

On the other hand—that is to say, in favor of the proposition that, when I was a gambler, I was not always a good one—I have played roulette. In that game, the choice is between which of thirty-eight numbers (thirty-seven in Europe; thirty-nine in some remote parts of Nevada) to back. Only *systemiers* abstain from betting for an occasional turn or two of the wheel; and they do not have to consider the question—*whether*—for it is resolved for them by the little cards they hold in their hands with last night's number-order, or the phases of the moon, or whatever, scrawled on them. Whether to bet, in roulette, is never a valid question. There are no good bets, or bad bets, or good or bad times to bet. The chances against all the numbers are precisely and perpetually equal; each has, in gambling terms, the same negative expectancy; and each has it for all time.

But roulette, for me, was only something to pass the time; I rate my quality as a gambler from my conduct at the games I preferred. I was a horseplayer, crapshooter, poker-player, blackjack-player; these are games where *whether* matters, where *not-now* sometimes makes sense, and where I often gave myself that answer and acted upon it. If I go to Las Vegas tonight, it will not be to play roulette.

If. The silver dollar and the hundred-dollar chip make the trip possible; they do not make it compulsory. *If not.*

If not. If not, I can treat my silver dollar as a dollar, and spend it. And I can get my hundred dollars for the chip; I do not need to go to Las Vegas to redeem it; I need only, for instance, take it to work with me tomorrow. *If not.* The sensible, rational, safe course. Stay home tonight; watch television; read the papers. Go to work with the chip in my pocket. When Max Rosenberg (gentle, smiling Max, whom I first knew as a number at a poker table in the California Club, where he was an occasional customer and I was a house-player, and who thinks he redeemed me from a wasted life and may be right in his belief) comes into my office and asks, "How's my sales manager?" I can reply, as I always do, "Mustn't grumble," and, as I speak, I will slide the chip toward him across my desk. He will pick it up, and glance at it, and take five twenties from his money-clip, and give them to me, and never mention the matter again unless I were to bring it up, which I will not do.

And, in that case—*if not;* if I do not go—the chip will pass to Rosalind, Max's wife, who makes occasional trips to Vegas, or to someone else who is going there; in either case, the casino of the Silver Hotel will ultimately provide the hundred dollars, and the chip will have gone home.

And I will have a hundred dollars I didn't know, an hour ago, that I had; and tomorrow, when Kathy gets back from Seattle, I will tell her the whole story, and hand her the five twenties, and insist that she spend it on a service contract for the pool, and for the space of a summer neither one of us will have to stand in the backyard with the long metal vacuum wand and the bottles of chemicals and the long-handled net and the rest.

If not or *if. If.* If I go. If I take the "Champagne Flite—Vegas," I will take only the chip and the silver dollar and leave the rest of my money at home. The "$25 plus tax" can go on the Diner's Club. My betting capital will be $103.50: the chip, the silver dollar, and the "$5 starter-chips" which only count for $2.50 because they are replaced by real chips if you win with them, not matched by real chips, so that a man who wins a bet with a starter-chip has only transformed that chip into a real one and now has one real chip where he would have two had he bet a real chip in the first place.

5:25. I can still make the six o'clock "flite"; but it will be a tight fit. No time to change my clothes, which is of no importance since my destination will be Las Vegas where standards of dress are flexible, not to say nonexistent. No time to eat, which is of some importance. Hunger induces lightheadedness. Might I have played differently the last time I was in Las Vegas, the only time, in fact, if, sometime between lunch at Del Mar racetrack, where I paid my own check, and Andy's, and Lisa's, and Billie's, and did not stop for change, and the bowl of chicken soup in the snack bar near the bus station in downtown Las Vegas that Billie bought for me early the following morning, I had eaten? I don't know. And to say "I don't know" to a question that begins "Might I . . ." is to answer the question in the affirmative, since that is what "might" means.

And now, as the three hands of my watch come together midway between five and six, the question of "when" is decided by indecision, and only the question of "whether" remains. I can be in Vegas at 10:30, in action at 11, and home in time to have a nap, a shower, a shave, and still be in the office at the opening of business tomorrow, perhaps richer, but in any event no poorer than I was when I left the office this afternoon.

No poorer than I *thought* I was, that is. The distinction is an important one. Am I really asking myself to behave as if, because I did not know of the chip and the cartwheel until they clinked a few minutes ago, they did not exist prior to that time? Is money that is spent foolishly any less wasted if it is found on the street than if it is sweated out of an employer or extracted from a passerby at the point of a gun?

Is it, in fact, what I knew or know that counts? Or is it simply that I can go to Las Vegas tonight with the normal—which is to say strong—risk of losing, but without having to account for that loss to anyone else, which is to say Kathy? *Vis à vis* Kathy I cannot lose. For, if I go to Burbank airport tonight at nine, I will either be at International Airport tomorrow afternoon, when her plane gets in from Seattle, with a hired limousine and a basket of white tulips, and the story of a successful stand at blackjack or craps, or else I will be at work when she arrives, and, when I come home, everything will be exactly as it would have been had the clink in the jacket lining been caused by a dime jangling against a quarter.

If and if not and either and or; the questions without answers, and, above all, the question of the questions. Why must I debate this question and simultaneously wonder why I am debating it? I can go if I wish, and, given ordinary luck, not the luck of the casino or the luck of the game, but more prosaic luck relating to who else is on the plane, who sits second at the blackjack table when I play third base, who stands at the far end of the dice table when I throw the dice, barring the wildest of coincidences, no one—read *not Kathy*—will know unless I tell them (her); but if I do tell, or if the fact comes to (her) attention otherwise, there is nothing in the world she can do about it.

So why the debate? Why the questions? If I want to go, I will go; and if not, not; and it doesn't matter *why* I want, or if I really want.

Rocco, who was the box-man at the main game in the Americana Club in Steubenville, told me once, as we stood at the bar: "It isn't making wrong moves that means a gambler's cracking up. He can bet when he should check, call when he should raise, lay the odds when he should be taking them, and he's still getting action. But there comes a time when he can't make any move. Give him three of a kind and an off ace, and he knows a two-card draw gives him the best chance to improve his hand, but it shows the trips, and a one-card draw, holding the ace, looks like two pair and pulls in players. So drawing one builds the biggest pot, and drawing two gives him the most certain shot at it; and you can make a case for it either way. But when he can't decide, when he sits staring at his cards, giving away the hand by the length of time it takes him to decide, and then taps the table, not because he has a chance to convince anybody he has a legitimate pat hand but just because it's easier to take no cards than to choose between one and two, then he might as well face it. He's going to wind up playing solitaire with a greasy deck in the laughing academy."

Rocco was referring, of course, to something every gambler fears, maybe the only thing every gambler fears. Insanity. He will risk everything else; risk-taking is the gambler's business. But he will not—at least, I would not—risk the loss of his mind.

I faced that risk years ago, long before I came to California, faced it, and faced it down, in a horse room across the street from the Cattleman's Hotel in Elko, Nevada, at one in the afternoon, four o'clock in Florida, three o'clock in Hot Springs, Arkansas, when a horse I had liked and bet ran second at Hialeah, and one I had liked and not bet won the feature at

Oaklawn Park. The room employed two board men, and the results, by coincidence, went up almost simultaneously. And, as the winners' names were being circled, I was suddenly aware that this sort of thing had been going on all week, that every bet I had considered but abstained from had won, and every bet I had made had lost; and, for a moment, I began to see (and simultaneously not to see) a cause-and-effect relationship, to believe (and s.n.t.b.) that the winners had won *because* I stayed off them, and the losers had lost *because* of my bet. Non-belief quickly asserted itself, and I was rational before the running time and mutuels went up. But the moment was enough. I made no more bets that day; and, though I worked in gambling houses of one kind or another (mostly one kind) for eighteen months thereafter, I did not gamble, made no wagers on my account, accepted no risk for the sake of possible profit, not from that afternoon until the weekend of which this hundred-dollar chip and this silver dollar—and, in a sense, this house, this land, this life—are all souvenirs. Labor Day weekend, 1964. Which began on Friday, September 4th.

The day of the game dawned crisp and clear.

I heard the words as I awoke, as if they had been spoken in a dream I had been having, as if the words had survived the end of the dream and were running over into reality by some mechanical freak, in the same way that the sound on some old radios used to continue for a few seconds after the set was turned off.

The words had, however, a familiar ring, too familiar to be merely words I had encountered in a dream. The tilted beamed ceiling of the motel came into focus, and I tried to organize my memory, to identify just when and where I had described, or heard described, such a day and such a game. My memory had always been important to me. For as long as I could remem-

ber—a paradoxical qualifier if ever there was one—it had been
one of the tools by which I made my living or an essential skill
in the pursuit of my avocation.

I sat up, kicked back the bedclothes, and pushed my feet
into furry slippers that were, I decided again, much too warm
for California. I would replace them, I decided, with lighter
ones—terry cloth maybe; when they became sweaty I would
give them to Kathy, who would put them in her mother's
washing machine.

I looked at the sign on the coffee-maker ("another courtesy
of Gardena's Garden Motel") and felt some regret that the
machine didn't work. Now, en route to the bathroom, and
within it, part of my mind set out to identify the sentence that
had been in my mind when I wakened, while another part
admired the ease with which the unconscious part functioned;
my hands moved automatically, flushing, turning taps, laying
out razor, shaving soap, brush, after-shave lotion and, finally,
adjusting the shower water.

I was out of the shower, my face still warm and moist, the
rest of me drying into the towel or onto the bathmat now, and
the part of my mind reserved for self-admiration was pleased
that the shaving gear was preset. If memory was one of the
tools of my trade, anticipation was the other, and in that area I
have never doubted my own competence. The dim-distant past
might trouble me—it did at that moment, as a matter of
fact—but the future held no mystery. Today would be like
yesterday, and tomorrow like today, and only Wednesdays
would be different. The club was closed Wednesday; the law
required each club to be closed one day a week. There being
seven clubs, an interclub agreement gave each a different
closing day, insuring that, on every day of the year, there
would be exactly six clubs in operation, no more, no less.

There was lather on my face, and I was wondering what

would happen if an eighth club opened. The clubs, I decided, would probably try to put the State on an eight-day week, but since they no longer controlled the State Legislature, but only one house, they would probably have to settle for an amendment to the compulsory closing law to permit them to work seven days out of eight. Of course, an eight-day week was not entirely without precedent. The Russians installed a six-day week for a few years after the revolution. More in point, the U.S. Military Training Center operated during wartime on a seven-days-on, one-day-off plan, the irregular holiday being named for the commanding general. For an instant, I could not think of his name, or of the name given the holiday; then both popped into my mind. Banfield, the general; Ban-day, the octonary day of rest. Then, as if this irrelevant bit of memory work had removed an obstruction in the neck of my otherwise sound memory-bottle, I suddenly recognized the source of the phrase that had been rattling around in my skull since just before I woke.

Baseball Joe. There were dozens of books—I probably read them all—that traced his rise from high school, through college, across the sandlots. But whether the title was "Baseball Joe, Big Leaguer," or "Baseball Joe, Captain of the Team," or "Baseball Joe, League President," the common element was the Big Game that began around Chapter XXIV and ran nearly to the end of the book. The game could be a pitcher's battle, a slugging match, tightly or sloppily played, won at bat or in the field, an inspiring victory or an instructive defeat, but it was always played on a day that dawned crisp and clear.

The mnemonic feat gave me a sense of accomplishment that lasted through the shave and through the splashing of the aftershave lotion on my face and neck. Perhaps because the phrase was in my mind, I tipped back a slat of the Venetian blind and looked outside to discover that this day was dawning (for me, at least; it had dawned many hours before for most people) not crisp, but surely clear. This was par for the course. Los Angeles, in September, provides an assortment of days, but not even the local chamber of commerce would call any of them crisp.

This was, however—and I suddenly knew it at that instant—a special day that was dawning; dawning at noon, to be sure, as all of my days dawned at that time in my life, not because it was an indolent time of life but because my working night never ended before midnight, but special, just the same. Friday, of course, and therefore payday; but more than that. The day before a three-day weekend; but neither weekends nor holidays meant anything to the employees of the California Club. Frankie Pingo, the club's manager, told me that when he gave me the job, standing in his rather elegant office, holding the letter from the day pit-boss at the Bank Club in Reno testifying to my honesty and skill. "Twelve dollars a day," Frankie replied when I asked him about wages. Then, smiling: "And all you can steal. We pay weekly. Seventy-two dollars; six-day week. Closed Wednesdays."

"Only Wednesdays?" I asked. "What about Christmas?" I couldn't have cared less about getting Christmas off. Or any other day.

I took a swipe at my shoes with my dirty socks and dropped them into the laundry bag in my closet; and, just as the identity of the "Baseball Joe" quote came to me while shaving, the special nature of this day came to me while I was putting the laundry bag back in place.

On September 4, 1924, in Cleveland, Margery White had been delivered of a son. This day, this payday, this Friday preceding a long weekend was unmistakably my fortieth birthday.

Forty years old, I thought, looking in the mirror to tie my tie, and nobody to say happy birthday; looking now, not at the knot but at the face of Lewis Eldon White, forty, no fixed abode, no criminal record—you couldn't get a license to work in a club if you had a criminal record—no identifying marks or scars, no wife, no dog, no moustache, no per diem, no rice, no coconut oil.

And sorry for himself. I completed the description and stepped back a pace, the tie now tied. "You're sorry for yourself, Lewis Eldon White, forty," I told the reflection. (This habit—talking to yourself in the mirror—that I had at this time of my life is not at all rare. I've done some research.) "Your health is good; your taxes are paid; you have a hundred and some dollars in your wallet and a week's pay coming tomorrow; you are a free citizen of the world's greatest republic, residing in the garden spot thereof, where, except for a slight impurity of the air which occasionally causes your eyes to water, weather conditions are ideal; you come and go as you please, accountable to no one; and you are sorry for yourself. You should be ashamed." That should hold you, Lewis Eldon White, I thought as I turned and left the room; that should hold you, I thought as I patted my pocket to make sure I had my key and then let the door swing shut; that should hold you, you miserable, unfortunate, self-pitying son of a bitch.

Outside my room, on my way across the courtyard to the lobby and street entrance, I blinked in the glaring sunlight. This was the sort of day Yankel had in mind when, as he frequently did, he mumbled his long denunciation of Southern California, its people, its institutions, and, finally, its weather, which he always described as "just one god damn beautiful day after another." Yankel was a fat retired orange-rancher who came in once a week to play four-and-eight lo-ball. Yankel was also another of the self-pitying ones; all of us, I thought, crossing the patio toward the motel lobby, should be sentenced

to thirty days of Dr. George W. Crane, who would probably
tell us about the Chinaman who had no shoes, and wept, until
he saw a man who had no feet.

"Mr. White." I heard my name as I entered the lobby, and I
knew the speaker was Junius Alcott, owner, operator, room
clerk, and sometimes bellboy for the Gardena Garden. He
spoke diffidently; I knew he hated to raise his voice in his own
lobby and, adding this fact to my own unwillingness to speak
to him, in any tone, anywhere, I concentrated on Dr. Crane's
footless Chinaman, theorizing that a genuinely deep concentration might get me through the lobby unconversed-with. The
man with no feet, I decided, would be ashamed of his own self-
pity when he saw a man with no legs, and the man with no legs
when he saw a basket case, and the basket case when he saw a
blind basket case, and the *blind* basket case ("*Mister* White!")
when he saw a houseman in a Gardena poker club. Alcott was
out from behind his desk; there would be no avoiding him.
Turning to face him, I sensed the error in my train of thought:
the blind, whether limbless or otherwise, do not see.

". . . hope you understand," Alcott was saying.

"I'm sorry," I told him. "I didn't get that." The last part was
true.

Junius Alcott repeated what (presumably) he had just said,
the presumption strengthened by the impatience in his tone.
He, Junius Alcott was sorry. He hoped I understood. This was
not of his doing. Though he was its sole owner, the Garden
Motel was a member of a chain of owner-operated establish-
ments and had to be owner-operated in conformity to the
policies of the chain, as determined by the majority of such
owner-operators.

Having unburdened himself of these preliminaries, Alcott
suddenly stopped talking. I shifted my weight from foot to
foot, invited him to resume his discourse. On the fourth shift,
the invitation was accepted.

Junius's problem—on which he solicited my sympathetic understanding and cooperation—revolved around the forthcoming Labor Day weekend. I would realize, he hoped, that the demand for rooms on that Friday, Saturday, and Sunday night would far exceed the supply; it was, therefore, the policy of the chain to insist on payment in advance for that weekend.

"We've got a deal," I protested. I knew I was going to lose, and I didn't really care much, one way or the other, but the Junius Alcotts of this world expect resistance; if they don't meet resistance where they expect it, they increase their demand until they are resisted. My room ordinarily rented for $6 double nightly in summer and $10 double in winter. In return for my year-round occupancy, my rate was $90 single a month, payable by the fifth of the following month; one month's notice to vacate.

"Your rent concession's against the Association's rules," Alcott whined. "If I add to it, not collecting for Labor Day weekend in advance, they'll pull my sign."

It occurred to me that nearly every motel in California has a sign similar to the one Alcott was describing. APPROVED AND RECOMMENDED, his read. SOUTHLAND MOTEL ASSOCIATION. The signatures vary; if Alcott lost this imprimatur, presumably he could acquire one at least as attractive. Anyhow, how many people look for a sign?

"The sign doesn't matter," he said, exactly as if I had spoken what I had only thought. "I just want to stay out of trouble. Anyhow, it won't cost you anything."

And it wouldn't. It would be deducted from my $90 payment, either the one due September 5th, or, more likely, October 5th. There had to be an angle. If all Alcott was getting was the free use of my $9 for a week, or five, this was merely a senseless annoyance. I started to draw him out, hoping further conversation would reveal the angle; but I stopped without saying a word. That was the angle: just senseless annoyance.

Enough such senseless annoyances, and I might get out. I'd been a desirable tenant, even at my low rate, in May, with the slack summer season approaching. But with the coming of the busy season, I was going to be a liability.

Unfortunately for Junius's plan, my tolerance for senseless annoyances is almost infinite. I gave him $9. "Come over to the club," I suggested. "I'll take a piece of your action."

Junius pocketed the $9 and smiled. My irony, such as it was, had been wasted. It often was, in those days.

At three o'clock, on the afternoon of my fortieth birthday, I went through the front door of the Garden Motel, out onto Vermont Avenue, and walked north to the California Club, walked three blocks in the shimmering sunshine, to my place of employment.

2

The California Club, like the Gardena Club and the Rainbow Club, which flank it on the west side of Vermont Avenue, has the shape of two uneven circles overlapped to form a slightly irregular figure eight. Unlike the older clubs, which are housed in old-fashioned square buildings a few blocks south, these three are composed of various quantities of glass brick, redwood beams, and fieldstone, to produce a style of architecture and interior design that is sometimes called Las Vegas Modren, and sometimes called Swedish Casino.

Good food at moderate prices was available then—and I assume still is available—in the restaurant which, in the California Club, occupied all of the smaller ellipse. You did not have to be a player in order to eat, but, because all the entrances to the building were in the larger ellipse, you did have to go through the card room in order to reach the restaurant. (Las Vegas, of course, operates on the same principle. You don't have to shoot craps in order to hear Sinatra—or check your coat, or eat a meal, or go to the bathroom—but you do have to walk past the crap table.)

I went through the electric-eye-operated glass door at the main entrance and exchanged nods with Whitey, the uniformed guard who sat next to the stack of evening papers inside, his pistol gleaming ostentatiously at his hip. The pistol was unnecessary; Whitey himself was unnecessary; there was never a great deal of cash behind the cashier's cage; the real security of the club rested in the hands of the real guards, who held more potent weapons and lounged against the rails along the catwalks above the ceilings that looked like mirrors from below, where the players were, and like plain glass from above, where the guards were. Whitey was a tradition: a gambling house should have an armed guard visible just inside the entry. A smile accompanied Whitey's nod and mine. The smiles acknowledged that he was a guard who did not guard and that I was a poker-player who did not play poker.

The banner headline, two banks across the green front page of the evening paper, announced that the Dodgers, their game rained out, would spend the day resting in anticipation of the weekend set of three against the ever-dangerous Cubs, in Chicago. Less prominently located on the front page were stories relating to a speech President Johnson was to make in Los Angeles that evening, and to the verdict (guilty) in the case of a Covina mortician accused of causing his wife's demise and her divided interment in seven cemeteries. Yankel, moving his fat bulk along the rail toward a $40 lo-ball table, caught my eye and jerked his thumb at the stacked newspapers. I knew that if our paths crossed that day, the relative play given to the three stories would form the opening for another indictment of the mores of Southern California. But at the moment all that interested me was to note, with relief, that Yankel's arrival at the table filled that game to its eight-man capacity. I did not want to work until my shift started at four; nor did I have to work merely because I was in the club. But a short game, plus a request from Frankie Pingo, would have been hard to decline. I most particularly did not want to play lo-ball. Not on my fortieth birthday. Not before I had breakfast.

Chet Kelly was moving toward the p.a. mike as I came into the card room. I moved as inconspicuously as I could along the raised platform running along the edge of the playing area toward the entrance to the restaurant. "Starting a new three-and-six," Chet's amplified voice announced. I did not want to turn to look at the Board. The Board is a large slate on which initials or nicknames of prospective players are placed in columns arranged to indicate which games they wish to enter. A man's position on the Board is of vital interest to him; at the moment, my only vital interest was that the column headed "3–6 hi" should contain a great many initials. Without turning my head, I caught a glimpse of the Board. The "3–6" looked short, eight prospects at best, some of whom, I knew, would have given up, or taken open seats in other games. "J.B.," Chet went on. "Jockey, Don A., L.K., Sacramento, R.R., Tony, A.B. A new three-and-six. Table Ten."

Table Ten was just to the left of the restaurant entrance. I could see players moving through the gaps in the chromium rail, down the two steps to the playing area, headed for Ten. There seemed to be less than eight customers. Chet Kelly, now out on the floor near Ten, was looking around. Before he could look my way I was inside the restaurant.

"J.B." The loudspeaker system extends into the restaurant. "J.B. Table Ten." I moved to an empty booth in the rear and sat down. "Seat open." There was a p.a. outlet behind the counter. "Seat open in a new three-and-six. Last call."

Since only J.B.'s name was getting a second call, it followed that he was the only no-show. Chet would wait two minutes; then he would give J.B. his third and last call, accompanying it, as he had accompanied the second call, with an invitation to anyone not otherwise engaged to fill the empty seat. If J.B. failed to respond to the third call, and if no volunteer arrived to compensate for his vacancy, Chet would bring in a house-player to fill the empty seat. The three-and-six players bet three dollars before the draw and six dollars afterwards, but the key figure in the game was the 75¢ that the house collected from every player sitting at the table on the hour and half-hour. For that fee he received the use of the cards, the chips, and the table (all of which the player could probably duplicate at less expense and greater convenience in his home), the services of Chet Kelly or one of his deputies in settling disputes (not often needed), and the assurance that he would have seven opponents.

It was this last guarantee—the full table—that threatened to interfere with my breakfast. If J.B. continued to defect from the game to which his seniority on the Board entitled him, and if no other three-and-six player took his place, then those playing in the game would each have only six opponents and Chet would need a house-player. If he had seen me go into the restaurant, he would page me over the loudspeaker. "Lew, Table Ten." If he had not seen me, he would announce: "Player, Table Ten." In either case, it would be risky for me to continue eating. My primary responsibility as a house-player was to respond to such summonses; that was what Frankie Pingo was paying me for. And it was widely believed that many of Frankie's other employees—counter-girls, waitresses, chip girls, maintenance men, even the grinning Negro who tended the gent's room—received a little sweetener in their weekly checks for reporting the names of house-players who did not fully and promptly accept their responsibilities.

From my seat in the rear booth I could watch the entrance. If someone's going to talk to me while I'm eating, I like to know about it in advance. A waitress started over. I used the few seconds it took her to reach my booth to lay a silent curse on J.B. for putting his initials on the Board if he didn't intend to play and a slightly milder curse on those other customers who languished in easy chairs and sofas along the perimeter of the card room and failed to respond to Chet's call because three-and-six was not precisely what they had in mind.

"Scramble two with ham, toast, o.j., coffee now." Partly because her eyebrows went up at the breakfast order, partly because I didn't recall having seen her before, I decided this was her first day on the job. "What's the matter, SueEllen?" Her name was on a gaudy badge pinned to her uniform. "The ham-and-eggs throw you? This is breakfast time for a lot of us, you know."

"It's not that." She was flustered. "I was wondering if you'd have time to eat it." I smiled and said nothing. She had to go on. "All the house-players are working. And it sounds"—she gestured vaguely toward the silent p.a. outlet—"like they're going to be short. So . . ." A horrible possibility obviously occurred to her. "You are a house-player, aren't you?" she asked, blushing a little.

"Ahm in the oil business, honey," I drawled. "Oil 'n' cattle. Ah'd be mos' grefful if you'd fetch mah aigs."

She turned and took a quick step toward the counter. Then she stopped. I knew she was remembering that I had ordered without the Texas accent. She put it all together and grinned at me. I returned the grin. Suddenly J.B. was standing beside my booth.

J.B. was a Tennessean who used his skill at draw poker to provide himself with a moderate, but consistent, supplement to the sums regularly paid him by various governmental agencies on account of his advanced years. "Can I join you?" he asked.

"I'd be honored," I told him. "Only there's a seat for you in the three-and-six."

"I don't feel like it. Let me have one of those." The last was to SueEllen, who had arrived with my coffee. "I'll tell you what happened." He was leaving me very little choice. "I had Chet put me on the Board an hour back. While I was waiting, I took a seat in a dime-ante game. Damnedest thing I ever saw."

"The old bags took you to the cleaners?" Obviously the dime-ante game would have to be fully discussed before the question of the three-and-six could be raised again. I was trying to speed the process along.

"No. Oh, it's a tough game. Dime-ante." J.B. lit a cigarette and blew a ring toward the ceiling as a sort of salute to the toughness of the dime-ante. I nodded. I was in no mood to argue, and besides, he was quite right. In any poker club, the tightest play is in the games with the smallest limits; the players in such games can least afford to lose. No smaller game than "dime-ante, half-and-one" was played in Gardena, and, for some reason, the California Club's dime-ante was the toughest in town. It had been that way all the year I worked at the club. "Those old farts," Frankie Pingo once told me, referring to our dime-ante regulars, "stay with three of a kind, raise once with four, and need a straight flush for a reraise." He was exaggerating, but only slightly.

"Couldn't get a hand?" I guessed.

"Couldn't get nothing *but* hands," J.B. snapped. "I had three aces behind three queens; I drew one to a sixteen-way straight, and hit; another time I'm dealt, *dealt*, god damn it, four little fours right off the top, and old Mabel sitting with a pat kings full."

"They wouldn't raise?" *Something* must have convinced this old man that this was not his day.

"Raise?" J.B.'s hands began fishing chips from his pockets. They were mostly fives, with a few ones. He arranged them in stacks of ten on the table, moving the stacks to make room for my breakfast when SueEllen brought it. "A hundred seven," he announced, finishing his count. "I bought once. A hundred-two profit. Damn well told they raised. What's-her-name Ethel, loudmouth bitch, raised her nine-high straight into me three times. *I* wound up calling. Ace-high. The sixteen-way. I told you."

"What went wrong?"

"Ten-jack-queen-bug." J.B.'s card-by-card account rolled on. "Eight, nine, king or ace straightens me. I catch the ace. I know Ethel's straight, because Mabel threw a raise at her before the draw and she didn't raise back, but when Mabel hesitates on the draw—gives the idea that she just might be pat—then Ethel makes a little hand-move, and I know she's minded to break her straight and go flushing if Mabel's pat. But Mabel draws one. I figure her for three something and an off ace. She plays that way. So then Ethel's pat, and comes out betting, but real quick, like she hated it and wanted to get it over with. What can I give her but a small straight?"

"They'll give your three-and-six seat—"

"Suits me." J.B. was not going to be talked into that game. At least not until he'd finished his story. Probably, I reflected bitterly, not then either. "I raise. She raises back. Mabel folds. I raise back; now *she* raises back. I'm beginning to think Ethel's learned this game at last, and, old as I am, she's going to start with me, so I must just call, though I figure I'm beat. And I'm stuck with the pot. You play in that game. What goes with those dames?"

"Yankel's got a theory."

"I know." Yankel's theory is that the action in the dime-ante varies in response to variations in the female cycle of its players. From this, Yankel derives Yankel's Law of Dime-Ante: Don't Play Unless You Menstruate Regularly.

"Turn salty?" I asked.

"I don't wait to turn salty to quit," J.B. said. "Turn salty, run second a few hands, and you've blown back all you've won, maybe more. I just stopped getting hands. Way I figured, I'd had enough hands for one day. Sure enough, I went through a stack of antes—ten hands without openers or players."

"One dollar shot to hell." I tried to sound as if I approved his decision, but I bore down on the amount a little. I had to shake him out of his no-go decision before the p.a. crackled its summons.

"I had the hot hands. Christ, Lew!" His vehemence was a hopeful sign. After all, *I* hadn't been giving him an argument. "I had hot hands and cold hands. You know what's left?"

"I couldn't say." SueEllen, unbidden, had brought me hashed brown potatoes with my ham and eggs. The notion of finishing breakfast slowly, of having a second cup of coffee afterward, seemed to be becoming more and more attractive. And less and less possible. "I never figured cards to have a memory."

"That," J.B. said, "is why you wear a necktie."

The remark was an insult, and a bad one. In Gardena poker clubs, a house-player is required to wear a necktie, partly out of regard for the dignity of the establishment, but mainly as a means of identification. Special rules restrict him. Others may open on jacks or better; the house-player needs aces and *must* open if he has them. If, having jacks, kings, or queens, he passes, and another play subsequently opens, the house-player may not call. Others may check raise; the house-player may not; and only the house-player is restricted to a single raise on each round of betting. If the house-player opens and gets only one caller, the caller may, if he wishes, withdraw his bet, leaving only the antes for the house-player. The result of this last rule, of course, is that a player sitting behind a house-player will call the house-player's opener with a four flush or four straight, remaining if there are other callers, withdrawing if there are not. Since some players know the house-player on sight, it is essential that all players know his status. The requirement that the house-player, on entering the game, must declare "I am playing for the house" guarantees this information to those then playing. The compulsory necktie puts those who enter the game later on notice that the seat is probably being held by a house-player. (Neckties are not generally worn by customers of the clubs. In any event, a player entering a game may always ask if another player is playing for the house, and need ask only those opponents wearing ties.)

"Hell, man." J.B. was suddenly conciliatory. "I *know* you're really right. Cards don't know who's catching 'em. Just like a man's a fool to draw two to a flush, never mind he thinks he's got a hunch. That's science, and it ought to win, and you can prove it must win, and I got to admit you're right, only it god damn well *don't* win, and you got to admit I'm right!" It was beginning to look as if my time was going to run out before I even had a chance to try to talk J.B. into playing. "They run hot and cold," he went on. "A guy on a streak can draw three to ace-seven, and fill, and take the percentage player—you, me, anybody—right down to the table, because we've got sixes full, pat, and we just don't believe it. Right?"

"The story of my life." I tried not to make my agreement too hearty. "Doomed to play for the house because I don't play hunches."

"I play for the house, too," J.B. said. I braced myself to smile at the joke. "My house," he added. I smiled.

"I'd never argue a man out of his hunch," I said, starting, of course, to do just that. "You think you're cold, you want to sit around until something happens that makes you feel you're warm. O.K. Only . . ." I let the thought trail off.

"Only what?"

I had him. But I wasn't going to reel him in until I'd let him run with the line a little. "The three-and-six looks soft to me. But I'm talking percentage."

"So?"

"So if I tell you, and you get in the game, with half your mind on your hunch, and you blow all your potatoes, who are you sore at?"

"A soft game?"

"I better get out there." I pushed back my plate and started to get up. "I shouldn't wait for Chet to call me."

"Don't you want me in the game?"

I was on my feet. "Not if I have to steer you. I just fill up an empty seat. I'm not supposed to hustle the action. Anyhow," I sank the hook deeper, "it's a private fight."

"What is?"

I sat down. I knew I would have time for a second cup of coffee, perhaps even a third. "Jockey got into Sacramento pretty good last night?"

"How good?"

"I couldn't say. I got stuck in the lo-ball myself. But I hear they wound up butting heads in the five-and-ten. I was around the cage at close-up time. Jockey was cashing in at least twelve hundred. Sacramento was writing a check. And you know he took a thousand out of that game Wednesday night. Figure where it went."

"I saw him on the way in." J.B. was almost talking to himself. "Sacramento. He looked pretty sore."

"Greek told me Jockey had him running. Drew out on him like he had the deck trained. Raised back with nothing the last hand, and made Sacramento bust openers. Sacramento missed a flush, and Jockey won the hand with king-high. And made him call, too. At least," I added apologetically, "that's what Greek says."

"That could soften up a game," J.B. conceded.

"They'll be after each other," I chimed in. "Raising on nothing, checking openers, looking to set traps. If a man sat in, and just played his cards, and let them make the action—"

"Player, Table Ten," the loudspeaker said. Then, after a slight pause: "Lew."

"My master's voice." I put a dollar on the table and stood up again, this time waving to SueEllen to indicate the check was paid.

J.B. picked up the dollar and stuffed it into my jacket pocket. "I'll get it," he said, putting down some chips on top of the breakfast check. "And my seat."

"Tell Chet you told me. And play it tight." I had to speak the last loudly. J.B. was in full flight.

I signaled to SueEllen for another cup of coffee. A chime indicated 3:30; to the chip girls in the card room, that signified time to pick up their collections. To me, it meant half an hour before my shift began. Half an hour, barring further emergencies, before I would have to go to work. I lit a cigarette. As days went in those days, this one was starting painlessly enough. As, indeed, it should have. After all, this was my fortieth birthday.

3

I was finishing my second cup of coffee and giving some thought to a third when Kathy Barnett came through the door of the restaurant and started toward my table. Kathy was my girl. It even said so in *Cal Chatter*, the club's house organ: "Kathy Barnett, chip girl, and Lew White, night-side house-player, have found each other." Chip girls carry chips to tables and exchange them for cash, an essential service because the law forbids the use of actual cash in the games. They also pick up, twice an hour, a fee from each player, which is an even more essential service, since these fees are the club's basic source of income.

I knew the brown paper package under Kathy's arm was a birthday present, and this made me happy, angry, and sad. Everything Kathy did around that time—her very existence, in fact—made me happy, angry, and sad.

The happiness was because she was beautiful, and fairly bright, and completely decent and indisputably in love with me; the sadness was because Kathy was twenty-two, had slate-gray eyes, and an inconspicuously charming body, and wore her hair pulled back in what women called, that year, a tail, and was, for these and other reasons, exactly the sort of girl I could have loved. And the anger was because I was eighteen years older than she and, more important, I knew that love was one of many emotions of which I was then incapable, and to which I could not then aspire without the risk of destroying myself and the person I might love or attempt to love.

She sat down in the seat next to me. I could see how the pulled-back hair drew out the corners of her eyes, and smell the cologne-and-soap girl smell of her; and I knew, without turning my head to see, that other heads were turning, and that there were people in the restaurant, newcomers to the club, who were wondering why such a girl would sit at my table, and others, regulars, who knew of the relationship between the pretty girl and the one-time gambler, now reduced to the status of house-player, who were wondering how such a relationship could come about, even as I wondered. So I guess pride should be added to the happiness, sadness, and anger, previously listed.

"You look terrible." She put the package on the table. "Happy birthday."

"Thanks." I stripped the wrapping paper off the box and began opening the box itself. "I'm entering middle age. Why don't you say I look pretty good for a man in his early forties?" The box contained a briefcase, dark and rich-looking, unquestionably of genuine leather; no one would make such a case out of anything else. Before I had it out of the box I knew it was not bought in Gardena, nor bought cheaply, nor bought quickly. L.E.W. sparkled in silver above the lock. Individually, the letters were right for the case; together, they formed a rectangle perfectly proportioned to the rectangle of the case itself. "This is the only briefcase I'll ever carry," I said, meaning it. "I've never carried one before, you know."

"I know." Kathy was almost breathless. The pleasure of

giving is the purest of pleasures and, therefore, the most selfish. "You do like it." It was not a question, just a statement of fact.

"It's my best present since I was eleven and my father gave me O'Neil's Great Baseball Game. I could not be more delighted. Or more angry."

I spoke the last three words firmly, so Kathy would know I wasn't entirely joking. She ignored them. "Say: 'You shouldn't have done it.'"

"You damn well shouldn't have."

"Why not?"

"I can think of fifty-five reasons." I was guessing at the price.

"Sixty-four fifty," she bubbled. "Slightly higher west of the Sierras."

"And monogrammed." It was hard for me to stay angry with her.

"That's included in—"

"That's so I can't return it."

"Partly," she admitted. "I want you to keep it."

"And use it."

"And use it," she echoed. She put her hand on the case. I put my hand on hers. As long as I remained a house-player, I had no use for a briefcase. That was the fact that had, momentarily I now knew, come between us. I glanced at the wall clock. 3:57. "You don't have to go," Kathy said. "I told Chet it was your birthday. He said you could stay in here. He'll call you if he needs you. He was funny about it."

"No he wasn't," I said. "He just said he hoped he wasn't going to have to put up with this sort of thing every year."

"I thought it was funny." Kathy turned her wrist, so our hands were palm to palm. "He said every forty years."

"Not much funnier," I said. "How did he know? How did you know, for that matter?"

"The same way I know your middle initial. This place isn't terribly careful with its records. Lew?"

The spoken conversation ended, and a short, silent one began. It was like that a lot with us. There was a subject we didn't like to talk about. At least, I didn't. So we held hands and looked at each other instead.

"Say something, Lew." She managed to make her tone urgent, but not impatient. I knew it wasn't easy for her.

"You've been talking to Rosenberg." I tried not to make it sound accusatory. It wasn't easy.

Kathy nodded. "He was here last night. He's signed the papers. He wants to open the office right away. He needs a whole sales force organized—recruiting, training, the works. And fast. He needs *you*, Lew."

She was trying to help. It's very hard to convince people—women especially—that they can't help you because you don't want to be helped, particularly when you know you should want help, even though, oddly enough, if you wanted it, you wouldn't need it. "Nobody needs me," I said. "I'm the Miller of Dee. Remember?"

Now the soft gray eyes were on me, the eyes that demanded nothing, that only wished, wished I would be reasonable, wished I would listen, but were prepared to accept, without fuss, my decision not to listen, if I would just voice even that decision. I lowered my own glance and fiddled with the lock of the briefcase and wished I were somewhere else, or better yet, somebody else; and I sang, almost under my breath:

> "There was a jolly miller once
> Lived on the River Dee.
> And he sang this song,
> As he walked along.
> He sa-ang this song, did he.
> I care for nobody
> No, not I.
> And nobody cares for me."

"He could have tried." Kathy said. "You could try. No harm in trying."

No harm in trying. Someday I am going to make a list of those simple phrases that people—school teachers, mostly—are always repeating, and that sound true because they are said so often, though they are actually just plain nonsense. No harm in trying. Better late than never. It's just as easy to do it right. Where there's smoke, there's fire. Honesty is the best possibility.

Alicia, who had been my wife, had unloaded a great many such phrases at me in our last terrible hour together in the bedroom of the little frame house for which—as she did not neglect to mention—her father had provided the down payment. How often, she demanded of me, had I given her my word that I would not deceive her, humiliate her, cheat her? And she spread the evidence of my latest fall from grace in front of me: the checkbook stubs that did not match the bank statement; the checks made out to cash, unendorsed, but with Kentucky stamps on the back—*pay to any bank or banker— People's Bank of Newport, Ky.* What was she to think, she asked me, of a man who cashed checks in Newport and did not tell his wife, especially if I was the man? How many times, she asked plaintively, had I attended sales meetings at the Buick Agency (where, she added mechanically, I was employed only because her father, being a good and honest man, mistakenly attributed the same qualities to his son-in-law) that were actually poker games in the conference room of the Legion Hall? What about the time I had sold two cars to a horse trainer, but the sale had required three trips to Buelah Park where sums equaling 250 percent of the commissions on the deal had been stuffed into the machines, to be divided among the horse-park operators, the State, and the backers of faster horses? All this she had interspersed with banalities. No fool like an old fool. (Herself, for trusting me.) The leopard (me) doesn't change his spots.

And of course, honesty the best policy. "You didn't have to hide it from me." Her voice was heavy with outrage and damp with abnegation. "You could have told me you wanted to blow some money on the races. What the hell. You work hard. You could afford it."

I had been silent, that night in Cincinnati, and I was silent, there in the California Club, remembering. Would it have made a difference if I had spoken out, if I had told her that I had not "worked hard," that I could not afford to "blow some money on the races" and had no wish to do so. Shut up, Alicia, I could have said, but did not. Shut up, you, with your keening wail that begets more misery, and your intolerable resignation, and your insufferable toleration, and your insupportable suffering, and your (therefore) unacceptable support. The money is damn well gone; the checks have cleared the banks; the figures are all entered in red in eradicable ledgers, which cannot be altered even by the Great Posting Clerk Up Yonder. I am in trouble, Alicia,—I had thought and was thinking, but had not said and was not saying—and I don't want acceptance and understanding; those are appropriate for a skin blemish; but I need love, maybe a kind you're not capable of, not the kind that is put upon and forgives, or declares its belief when reason demands skepticism, not the love of the man in the story who said you-look-a-monkey-and-you're-covered-with-shit-but-you're-mine-god-dammit-and-I-love-you, but the love that helps when help is possible, and shuts up the rest of the time.

"Who are you talking to?" Kathy asked. "Alicia?" To this day, Kathy believes I am talking to Alicia whenever my mind wanders from whatever we are discussing.

"Sort of." This was almost as true, and considerably less

complicated, than telling her I had been thinking of things I had not said to Alicia and wondering what would have happened if I had said them. "She was like you, in a way. Only when you call me a dirty name, you're mad at me. She never got mad. Only disappointed. And hurt. And ashamed of herself for putting too much pressure on me. But I loved her." I was careful to sound the terminal *d*. "Does that bother you?"

"No more than a migraine." She took her hand from under mine and used it to prop up her chin. "I hate her for being good to you. If she ever comes in here, I'll scratch her bald."

"Snatch her bald," I corrected. "Scratch her eyes out."

"If you're so smart, why ain't you rich?"

"Don't change the subject. I loved her, and you got it wrong."

"So you did. And so I did. Satisfied?"

I was satisfied. The late afternoon sun slanted through the Venetian blinds and fell across Kathy's face. I stared at her; it was as if I were trying to memorize her. She had, I noticed—I had noticed this before—remarkable skin, firm and clear, but even looking at it you could tell it would be soft to the touch. Like the girl in the song, I thought. Then, not able, in the instant, to produce the line in the song I was thinking of, I hummed it, experimentally, matching the tune in my mind to half-remembered words until I came to the part I wanted.

"Me?" Kathy asked, childishly pleased. "I have breathless charm?"

"No." I sang softly. " 'With your smile so warm/ and your cheek so soft.' 'Keep that breathless charm' is in another verse."

"You can't tell from the tune. Did you really?"

She meant did I really love Alicia. The question was so surprising I answered it truthfully. "I thought I did. Most of the time we were married I thought I did. Then, later on, after we'd been separated a few months, but before she got the divorce, I began thinking so again. Only I found out I didn't. Maybe I found out I never had." I hadn't intended to say more, and she didn't ask me to explain, but I did. Maybe I explained *because* she didn't ask me to say more. "I found out in Steubenville, in the Americana Club."

"Another girl?" she asked. "Because that doesn't prove anything. A man can be in love more than once."

"Simpler than that," I said. "And better proof. I was at the crap table, with the dice coming at me. How long does it take for the dice to come out of a man's hand, bounce to the far end, hit the wall, and stop?" She didn't answer. I did. "Less than two seconds. But in that little bit of time, that one throw, I remember thinking, Four-trey, God. Seven now, God, and I don't care if I never see her again. And I meant it."

"I thought you didn't believe in God."

"I don't. That makes it worse. I was a right-bettor, caught betting against the dice, and an atheist, ready to trade a woman to a God that doesn't exist for a seven. I said four-trey, but any seven would have been all right."

"And did they seven out?"

"Did I love her?"

"Not that time."

"That's a good answer," I said. "It takes care of both questions. They didn't seven out that time, either."

"Did it matter?"

"It mattered that time," I said. "I had it all going. Three thousand to the shooter's five-hundred no hard six."

"He took six to one?" Kathy has an indisputable gift for cutting through to what she and I agree to be the heart of all matters. "He could have had nine to one from the house."

"He had a limit bet against the house—$4,500 to his five. He wanted more, and I took him on on the side. $1,600, which was all the cash in my pocket. And the box man loaned me $1,400 on the keys to my car. Rocco, his name was. A nice guy. He wrapped the car around a pole on U.S. 40 about a week later."

"Then it came hard?"

"The hardest possible six." I said it like a stickman. " 'Winner with the gag, front line and hardways to pay, and the comes are down.' And the stickman pushed my money over toward the shooter and flipped the car keys to Rocco."

"Man takes five to one, with one way to hit and ten to go wrong." Kathy was indignant. "You should have looked at the dice."

"They were the club's dice, the club's table, and the club lost $4,500 on the roll." I was impatient, and hated myself for sounding that way. She was right on her figures. There are six ways to make seven, and four easy sixes, and only one hard six, three-three. That the unfortunate, eleventh chance had materialized was just that—unfortunate. If it was anyone's fault, it was mine for putting myself in a position to be injured by an operation of chance, however unlikely. It was certainly not Kathy's fault. I squeezed her hand and apologized for my tone.

"That's all right." She squeezed back. She sensed that the exchange had given her a license to bring up the Rosenberg business again, and did so. "He'd start you at a hundred and fifty," she said, "plus commissions on your own sales."

I shrugged. I didn't want to talk about it. I knew the offer was legitimate and that it made sense, just as I knew that it was, in part, Max Rosenberg's way of squaring himself with his conscience. He had been a professor of economics for the first twenty years of his adult life. Then he had suddenly become impatient with the parade of graduates of his courses who would return to his small office, ten years after finishing his course, to tell him how much what they had learned from him had contributed to their success, and, he knew, to go back to their mink-swathed wives and their all-wool-carpeted drawing rooms to tell of the quaint, impractical professor who could teach the facts of economic life but could not put them to real application. "I gave myself ten years to make a million," he told me once. "I did it in less than two." He did it as a land developer, but, just as Professor Rosenberg and Developer Rosenberg had the same hobby—moderate-stakes poker—so they shared the same conscience. My rehabilitation would be something for him to throw into the balance on Judgment Day, against the despoiled acres and huddled cluster of residences that constituted a successful Rosenberg desert enterprise, against the forfeited deposits and foreclosed mortgages that marked those that failed.

"He'll be in tonight," Kathy said. "Talk to him. You can always turn him down. But talk to him. That's all I ask."

"All right. I will." I meant I would do both: talk to him, and turn him down. And she knew I meant both. But she could pretend I only meant to talk and would leave the question of acceptance or refusal for later, and, because she could pretend (and almost believe) that, she smiled. "Happy birthday," she said, getting up and heading back toward the card room. "I'll tell Chet you're ready to work."

"You do that. And thanks." SueEllen came by with her coffeepot, and I shook my head at her offer of a third cup. The bell chimed for the four-o'clock collection. I thought of myself as sales manager for Rosenberg's Desert Syndicators and Development Co., Inc. Up at seven-thirty, a big breakfast, with Kathy, in a housecoat, fussing over me; then out onto the Freeway in the inevitable Volkswagen. Into the parking lot—employees' cars only; all others will be towed away at owner's expense; city ordinance; then into the building—good morning, Mr. White; the morning mail—dear Madam, we regret that we are unable to refund your deposit on parcel #177/7; however

. . . territory to divide; a man to be fired—nothing personal, but things just aren't working out; another to be hired—

It was a fantasy, and too pleasant, and I brought myself out of it. Not that it was inherently impossible. But on that afternoon, I knew it was not going to happen, and that was that. No use telling me, as Kathy might have, as Max Rosenberg almost certainly would, that I had the ability, that it was simply a matter of deciding to do it and then doing it. I couldn't show you—or Kathy, or Max—what was wrong with your (or their) reasoning; you (or they) might remain convinced I was wrong. But it was my opinion that counted.

The four-thirty collection came and went. I sat at the booth, idle, but undismayed by my own inactivity, my conscience clear. I was paid to make myself available, and I was, indeed, available. Let my name come out of the loudspeaker, and I would shuffle to the appropriate table, identify myself as a houseman, and begin playing. Not playing, exactly. Holding cards. Until Chet chose to avail himself of my services, the onus for my non-use, if there was any, was his, not mine.

My mind passed from the future that was not to be and returned to the past that was. I was reliving again—which is not tautology; I had relived it before—the last night with Alicia, the final brutal exchange sounding again in an echo chamber somewhere in my inner ear. ALICIA (*bitterly*): I don't mind about the money. I'll get along without it. ME (*knowing she did mind*): But—. ALICIA (*picking up the monosyllable*): But I need a man. Not a whining little boy that gets caught dipping into Mommy's purse and spending the money for candy so the other little boys'll like him. And says I'm sorry; I won't do it again; I couldn't help myself. ME: What am I supposed to say? I'm glad? I'll do it again as soon as I get the chance? And the hell with you? ALICIA (*scornfully*): Oh, figure out what a man would say, and say that. Or don't you know? Don't you know any men? Don't they associate with your kind, the kind that preys on women for money? You're slimy, Lew. You're no better than a *pimp*.

Her hand fluttered to her mouth as if to grab back the word she had not meant to say. I stared at the ceiling, waiting for her retraction. I stared for quite a while, twenty-four and four-fifths seconds as a matter of fact. I know how long it was because, for all that time, I was rerunning, in my mind, the last quarter mile of the race on which the last thousand in the joint account had been lost, and for every tick of the 24 and 4, I was tempted to tell her what I was seeing and thinking. The horse's name was Red River (I could have said) and he was pounds the best, down in class, and 5–1 because 10,000 idiots didn't see there was so much early speed in the race the front runners had to cook each other and leave the race for those that could come on at the end, which could only mean Red River. And I was right; you could see it at the eighth pole, Red River fourth, down the middle of the track, coming on, third, then second, lapped on the tiring favorite a sixteenth out, moving, eating up the gap, so he had to win; but the boy on the favorite was tired too, and not strong enough to hold the horse straight, and the horse ducked out, into Red River, bumping him, making him break stride, carrying him wide, almost to the outside fence, which didn't matter, because it was a foul and the favorite's number had to come down. But the plodder, the miserable plug that Red River had put away between the eighth pole and the sixteenth pole, had clear sailing along the rail, and got his head in front of both of the others. Plodder, favorite, Red River, across the line like that, and the favorite's number did come down, but the plodder hadn't fouled. A fluke, a one-in-a-million chance, Alicia, I could have said. Six thousand dollars if the favorite hadn't drifted out, if the plodder hadn't been so close, if the race had been a foot longer or six inches shorter.

Bad luck; bad judgment; maybe I was reckless to take the risk; does that make me a pimp? God damn it, does it make me a pimp? I did not ask.

And because I did not ask, she did not reply, did not say No, not a pimp. Something else. Some other word. Something that bore some relationship to what I had done. Some word that did not require me to do what the word she had used required.

At the end of the twenty-fifth second, there was silence. Then Alicia said, "Well?" And I walked to the front door, walking slowly, waiting for her to call me back. And turned in the doorway, but the room behind me was empty.

Outside the house, as I backed the car out of the driveway, the motor sputtered and died. It usually did. In the sudden silence I could hear, from the bedroom window, Alicia's dry, racking sobs. . . .

"Lew White," the loudspeaker said. "Dime-ante. Table Four. Lew White, please."

4

The best you can say for the dime-ante game, from a house-player's point of view, is that you don't figure to get stuck in it for long. This is because, being the cheapest game in the house, it picks up players from the waiting lists for all other games. Sometimes they stay in the dime-ante when their names are called for the games they wanted in the first place; sometimes not. In either case, they tend to keep the game filled up.

This Friday, however, even this operation of the law of probability seemed to be suspended. I entered the game just before the five-o'clock collection. At six-thirty, I was still there. Players had come and gone, but the game had never attracted more than seven. Capacity is eight. The house-player does not leave a game in which his presence makes only seven hands without orders to do so, and he never receives such orders unless he is needed in another game where his presence makes six.

At that hour, the dime-ante in the California Club is a particularly bad game to get stuck in. It is always a tough, tight game. A player in danger of tapping out is never pleasant to play with, and in this, the lowest limit game, there is nearly always someone in that aggravating predicament. Moreover, because it is the lowest limit game, it produces the lowest fee: 25¢ per player per half hour. Accordingly the game is always placed at the oldest, least comfortable table which itself is placed in the least desirable spot on the floor, jammed in next to the rail, squarely below the window, so that the sunlight, in late afternoon, shines squarely into the eyes of the occupant of seat seven. When you consider that of those at the table all but one were paying for their time, and that one was, contrariwise, being paid for his, you will be able to guess who sat in seat seven and who was rapidly developing a considerable head-ache.

Madelyn, who could have been fifty, or seventy, or anything in between, and who was said, by some, to be the best player in Gardena, dealt. I picked up my hand and inspected it, spreading it narrowly, holding it close to my chest so as not to expose it to the bystanders behind the rail. Two kings, two unmatched small cards, and the joker. Since, in Gardena, the joker plays for an ace unless it can be used in a straight or flush, the hand read as a pair of kings, ace on the side. As a house-player, I needed aces to open. I tapped gently on the "7" stencilled in front of me. Mabel, a fat matron who licked her lips as she played and was rumored to have paid off her mortgage out of the dime-ante, shrugged as if confessing that even my tap would be more than her cards justified.

A pair of carhops, in seats one and two, were next. They played nearly every day, from just after four in the afternoon until five of seven in the evening. Their starting time sometimes resulted in their missing the four-o'clock collection; the girls were supposed to collect it from anyone who entered a game less than ten minutes after a collection, but this rule was not always rigidly observed. Their quitting time always exempted them from the seven-o'clock collection; in addition, it got them to Burgersville in time to begin their seven-to-midnight shift. I didn't know their names, but, because I needed some labels in my own mind in order to catalog their play, I had long ago given them the *noms de jeu* of Ying and Yang. There was no real resemblance between them, except that neither ever smiled or spoke any words not required by the game. Each passed by saying No; Yang, the redhead, sometimes hesitated an instant before speaking the word, and Ying sometimes spread her fingers on the table when she said No, but neither of these habits meant anything. I had decided long ago that they were consciously done in the hope, not always vain, that some stranger might attempt to draw a conclusion where none could validly be drawn. This time their No's came in rapid succession, without hesitation or finger gestures.

A young sailor at seat three was the only male in the game. I exclude myself; I was not really in the game. The sailor glanced toward Yang as if her No had upset him.

"Where we hung?" Madelyn demanded, looking up from her cards and capping the unused part of the deck with her ante. I nodded toward the sailor. "We're paying for our time," Madelyn pointed out, not unpleasantly.

The sailor fidgeted. I was sorry for him. That is one of the reasons I will never be—to use Chet Kelly's phrase—"one of your great house-players." Feeling sorry for people. Not that the sailor was losing an enormous sum. He had bought five times, and the buy was five dollars. He had nearly seven dollars in chips in front of him, which meant he was in the game about eighteen dollars. Bessie, another elderly regular who sat number five—four was the vacant seat—was probably twice that far back. But Bessie like Madelyn in seat six, and Mabel, was playing from a roll that could cover ten buys or a hundred if the need arose. All three were, thus, guaranteed to survive.

And, in the end—meaning 4 A.M. when the club closed—mere survival would usually mean all three would be winners, because they would have divided among them the losses of poorly capitalized players who would have tapped out along the way. (Don't misunderstand me; it isn't as simple as it sounds. A big bankroll helps, but only if you can play the game. A big bankroll in the hands of a poor player operates only to capitalize other players.)

The sailor had paid for each of his five buys with five-dollar bills, the first four from his wallet, the fifth from inside the top of his white blouse. I knew, of course, what that meant. The last bill had been pinned inside his blouse to distinguish it from those which were not his last and, not being his last, could be squandered with impunity. And having erected this barrier against disaster, he had run through it. When the seven dollars went, so would he. I knew somehow that he was beginning a long-weekend liberty. I told myself that saying I knew this *somehow* was the same as saying I didn't really know it at all, and that it didn't matter, and that it was none of my business. "Pass me," the sailor said unhappily.

Bessie allowed her head to settle back into her neck and passed. "Open," said Madelyn, who was dealing and therefore spoke last, throwing two quarter chips onto the area in front of her on the green baize. "You're not cold?" she asked. I did not realize I had shivered until I heard the question.

"Somebody walking over my grave," I said. I threw down my pair of kings in compliance with the rule forbidding house-players to back in, though I was sure they were high, that Madelyn was in with queens or jacks, playing position, trying to grab off the antes. I was starting to get mad. Mad because I was not free to win with the best hand. Mad because my shift was only beginning. Mad because the sailor had a dime in the antes and was going to lose it and the rest of his slim roll and would spend his weekend doing whatever the Red Cross or the USO provides for busted sailors on leave.

Mabel's cards followed mine to the table; the Misses Ying and Yang said No once more each. The sailor called too loudly, a sign of nervousness.

"Up." Bessie's dollar chip went in the instant the sailor took his hand off the two quarters that had been his.

"Back at you." Madelyn pushed four quarters into the pot and stared at the sailor.

The sailor's Adam's apple bobbed twice. I knew he was counting the chips in his stack, trying to balance the possibility of winning against that of throwing good money after bad. I also knew he was whipsawed, due to lose whichever way he moved. This was two-on-one. Not by prearrangement but merely because each of their interests would benefit from it, Madelyn and Bessie were engaged in the ancient exercise in which two poker-players undertake to take a third out of a game by breaking him. Unless the proposed victim is a poker genius, or the two substandard players, the two can never fail. In this case, obviously, neither saving exception was going to operate.

I began administering sedatives to my conscience. The worst player, with the least money, I told myself, must be knocked out sooner or later. Why should it bother me that his extinction from the dime-ante was going to come now, at a quarter of seven, because a couple of harpies have decided to crisscross him, or later because he doesn't play well enough to live with the game? "Call." The sailor threw another dollar in, raising his investment in this pot to $1.60.

"Up." Bessie's dollar chip fluttered in.

"Back." Four more quarter chips moved from Madelyn's stack to the middle of the table. The sailor worked his jaw. "Dollar to you," Madelyn said.

"God damn!" The sailor, now sweating, suddenly threw down his cards. "Looks like I picked the wrong time to get my feet wet."

The remark was addressed to Yang, who smiled but did not reply.

"Once more." Bessie put another dollar in.

This time Madelyn paused before replying. "You pat?" She studied Bessie's impassive face. "I believe you are pat," she said at last, spreading her hand, pushing the chips nearest her toward Bessie. "Next hand."

The rules called for jacks to open, and that was just what Madelyn's exposed hand contained. Two jacks, no help. I was not surprised.

The sailor seemed shocked. He pawed through the cards on the table as if he could not believe what he saw there. Then he looked, openmouthed, toward Bessie, as if he could not believe that because the pot had been won before the draw, he would never know what cards had inspired her to raise and reraise and drive him from a pot she had sucked him into by passing the first time around. I knew he was tempted to grab the cards from her hand, and I was ready to stop him if he tried it.

But Bessie dropped her cards, face down, into the discards. "Dead soldiers," I said, mixing all the cards together, then shuffling, then dealing quickly, counting a barely audible cadence as I went. "ONE-two-three-four, HIP-two-three-four, HUT-two-three-four," and, as the last cards came off: "HEE-HOE HAND-HALT."

"It's open," the sailor sang out, starting to throw two quarter chips in, then catching them before they could get out of his hand, turning red with the sudden realization that he was betting out of turn. There was a long silence. The other players stared at him as if challenging him to justify his breach of etiquette. I looked away and listened to Yankel, at a nearby lo–ball table, discussing the drainage of greater Los Angeles. "Must have been nearly a quarter inch of rain yesterday," he was saying. "Water only a foot deep at Sepulveda and Venice. Why don't they put in a storm drain?" He answered his own question. "Can't put it in when it's raining. And when the weather's nice, who needs it? Ah well, maybe it won't rain again. Whose deal?"

"I'm sorry," the sailor mumbled.

"You bet out of turn," Madelyn said affably. "Don't be sorry. Just drop your four bits in."

"That's not right," the sailor argued. "It's enough that they know I'm going to bet." "They" were Mabel, Ying and Yang, who were ahead of him in the betting order. "They can check now, and they know that I—"

"Houseman!" Madelyn called.

Sailor boy, you don't know what you did, I thought. Chet, in answer to Madelyn's summons, turned his board over to an underling and hurried over.

"He bet out of turn," Madelyn reported.

"I only started to," the sailor corrected. "I don't see why—"

Chet laid a restraining hand on the sailor's wrist.

I reminded myself that I had no choice and delivered my testimony: "He said, 'It's open.'"

"His money goes in," Chet ruled. "And he's barred from the betting." Not that it mattered, but Chet also had no choice. The rule was clear.

"Sorry, kid," I said, meaning it.

"Not your fault." The sailor put his chips in the pot and laid his cards down. "You were only doing your job."

My job, which was already getting onerous, suddenly became much more difficult. The women passed; I looked into my own hand, saw three aces, closed the hand, and was suddenly aware that Chet Kelly was standing behind me and had almost certainly seen them. I wanted to explain to the sailor that I was required to open with trips, even though I would have preferred to give him another chance at the pot which now stood at $1.20, half of which he had, thanks to his exuberance, contributed. Instead I said: "I'll open"; and I tried not to look at the dwindled stack in front of the sailor, but failed so badly that I not only looked at it, but counted it. Five one-dollar chips, one quarter chip. The collection bell rang, and I knew the quarter chip would go to the club as its fee.

With the sailor barred, there were no callers. I spread my hand and raked in the pot. The last thing I noticed before I succeeded in forcing myself to stop noticing was that the sailor's hand trembled as he pushed his cards to Mabel, who was the next dealer.

The game moved along. Ying and Yang left on schedule, and their seats were held by a series of two-stack players, each of whom had exactly ten dollars to lose, which each did, with varying degrees of speed, grace, and humor. Somewhere along the line, we lost the sailor, who called with his last chips and excused himself quietly when he saw the winning hand, as if apologetic that he had no more money to lose. His replacement was the tanned, blond wife of a tavern owner who was himself engaged in a nearby five-and-ten game, but the blond annoyed Bessie by constantly craning her neck to observe her husband's fortunes and misfortunes, and she left the game at Bessie's suggestion without quite having been involved in it. I was only vaguely aware of all this. My hands and reflexes adjusted to the movements of the cards and players, and the identities of each, but my mind was searching for the precise instant in my past at which everything had begun to go wrong; the precise wrong step, or extra step, or omitted step, that had brought me to this particular backwater of this particular world.

I don't mean that I was ransacking my subconscious for the moment or incident that had made me a gambler. No such existed. I had been a gambler for as long as I could remember; I had held other positions—honor student, salesman, husband —only temporarily, as a regular army sergeant may hold the wartime rank of major. I was searching for a more recent memory-nugget, one that postdated my breakup with Alicia, my abandonment of my temporary occupations, and my acceptance, full time, of the occupation of gambler.

It was not the moment of becoming an active gambler I was seeking; it was the moment in which I began to move from the status of active gambler, gambler on the long trail of the big chance, gambler looking for the killing, toward the status of broken gambler, unnerved gambler, gambler afraid to gamble, afraid to lose (and thus unable to win), therefore no gambler at all but merely condemned, as I was at that time, forever, as I thought I was at that time, to exist in the half-submerged shadow world of pseudo-gambling, with the stickmen, the wheelmen, the shills, dealers, sheetwriters, faro case-operators, cashiers, chip-stackers, and men who wore neckties and held cards for hourly wages in Gardena poker games.

What is worse, I was asking myself, than the true gambler, the man who can do nothing else, to whom nothing matters but the flying dice or the sliding cards or the bouncing ball at the rim of the turning wheel, or the running horses, or the chalked figures written on blackboards? I had no trouble answering that question. I *was* the answer. I, and those like me. Gamblers in one sense, for nothing else stirs us, But, in another sense, not gamblers at all, for having lost our nerve we have forfeited (forever, we think) the possibility of experiencing the only life that has meaning to us. Some, in this status, do not recognize it, or regard it as merely temporary. Those who do recognize it, as I did at that time, are far worse off than those who are able to delude themselves. They must gamble to live; they cannot gamble; and they know both these facts.

A gambler is, of course, a defective man; but all men are

defective, and there are worse defects than even the most compulsive gambling. The paralyzed gambler, however, is no man at all, but a vegetable; and I was, I knew, not merely a vegetable, but a thinking vegetable. Even a beet, after all, does not know he is a beet; much less does he reproach himself for not being something more exciting.

When and where had the degeneration begun? I had put those questions to myself before; the answers were always the same. Where: the Americana Club, just outside of Steubenville. When: a Friday night, about a year after I left Alicia. The Night of The Hard Six. The night I lost my car. The night I came, momentarily, not only to believe that there was such a thing as luck, but that luck was female, and a bitch with a wicked sense of humor, who derived satisfaction from tormenting me. That is a very bad thing to believe, even temporarily.

It had been going well. There was even a girl. Molly. Her name came back to me without any special effort. A redhead, young, not unattractive. I met her in the paddock at River Downs a few days after I broke up with Alicia; and I bought her a drink, and shared a bet on a horse with her, and took her into Cincinnati for dinner. Our relationship was as simple and as pleasant, as long as it lasted, as it had been the day we met. We spend our afternoons at racetracks and, at the beginning, our evenings in casinos in Newport or Covington. Later, when we shared an apartment, Molly gave up the evening trips across the river and waited for me to come home, waited with coffee and a smiling, interested face, and a warm body; still later, when the poker games began, she acted as hostess when it was my turn to provide the site for the game. She left about a month before Black Friday, left quietly, because whatever we had was ending quietly.

Neither Molly nor her absence mattered much. What mattered—what had been going well—was the gambling. At the racetracks—Maumee Downs, Ascot, Fort Miami, Cahokia, Ak Sar Ben, Fonner Park, Fairmount—I was free of the time pressure that had formerly jammed me in, that had required me to bet *now*, today, this race, because tomorrow I might not be at the track, might not be free to bet at all, and to bet this-or-that sum at such-and-such odds, because such a bet, if it won, would produce the payoff that I *needed* to cover the check, to replenish the savings account, to pay the past-due monthly installment on some item Alicia thought had been bought for cash. Without that pressure I became able to pass race after race, not betting, just watching, making notes in my scratch pad, waiting for a race in which one horse had substantially more (or less) chance than he was publicly assigned. It didn't matter whether it was more or less. In either case, the odds would be out of line, and somewhere in such a race there would be a horse worth backing. Betting only such horses in such races, I was backing measured opinions, not merely stabbing, not merely picking the best available investment from the dozen listed on a page of the program, but betting only when and if my own figures showed that the probable return, in the event of a win, exceeded the product of stake-times-risk. In the beginning, even without the pressure, this was not easy to do. The wish for a small bet to give myself a rooting interest led me to see overlays where none existed. My bankroll, which stood at just under $2,000 the night I left Alicia, melted more than 50 percent before I acquired enough self-discipline to restrict my play. Then it started back up.

My poker-playing required the same adjustment. Play for fun, look for huge profits, sudden coups, and important bluffs, and you may win from time to time. Play the game soundly— "tight" is the term—and you *will* win nearly all the time. I had never been a bad player; I became an excellent one by bringing myself to apply the rules and the percentages without regard for what might be fun or sporting or even gentlemanly, constantly aware that the good player plays with skill and dash, and the excellent one fights to stay alive or strikes to kill, depending on the situation.

The casino games—craps, roulette, and blackjack—were partly recreation, time-killers, something to do when there was nothing else to do, and partly a means of meeting poker-players under circumstances which offered an opportunity to assess their general intelligence, from which their skill at poker, and their approach to the game, could be assumed but not quite known.

Remembering how Black Friday evening began, I smiled with the recalled sense of well-being that I had felt just after sunset when, having left my car in the Americana's parking lot, I walked into the club with Andy Livoti. The beginning of twilight competed pleasantly with the Americana's ornate neon sign; the smell of approaching autumn was in the breeze that blew across the macadam; and the car—on which I had owed thirty-five payments the night I drove it away from the house on which I was four months behind in the mortgage payment— was mine, free and clear. The last twenty-five payments had been made in a single flourish of cash, paid on impulse. Andy and I had driven past the bank that afternoon, en route from Beulah Park to the Americana. "I believe I'll just stop and pay them off," I had said. And Andy laughed. "Long as they stay open late Fridays," he conceded, "you might as well give them some business." Then we both laughed. We were not laughing at anything in particular, unless it was at the people at Beulah Park who had thought Andy's horse, a short-coupled, bad-legged, much fired eight-year-old plater with a reputation as a quitter, could not go a mile and a half, and had backed their opinions with such enthusiasm that when Livoti's animal, favored by the sharp turns of the half-miler, and by the fact that there was nothing in the race to go with him on the front end, managed, as we had thought he would, to get home a winner. The mutuel payoff was $14 for $2, $700 for each of the ten $100 tickets we held, a $6,000 profit for us. I wondered what had become of Andy Livoti, and decided he was still out on the Ohio wheel, claiming gimpy ones, freshening them up, moving from track to track, looking for spots like the one we found for—the name came to me suddenly—Chrome Apple.

My $3,000 share of Chrome Apple's payoff, added to what I had squirreled away in case we turned out to be wrong about the absence of pace in the race, or in case someone else was hiding a horse in the same event, gave me a total of forty $100 bills when we left the track. Nineteen, and a part of a twentieth, went through the bank's wicket, to be exchanged for a copy of a conditional sales contract stamped PAID, and a bit more had been spent for gasoline, and tolls, and a sandwich somewhere between the track and the club. When I counted my money at the Americana bar, I had $2,080. And, I suddenly remembered, a fifty-cent piece.

The half-dollar went, at the bartender's suggestion, into a slot-machine which, according to the bartender, was "about ready." Two cherries on the first two wheels sent two half-dollars clattering out of the chute at the bottom. I reached for the coins, then stopped with them in my hand.

"Look what Bolton's got." Andy Livoti's voice was so filled with shock and admiration that I turned to look.

At first I saw only Bolton, a cheap, whiny fringe-gambler, leaning on the cashier's counter, beyond the machines, obviously waiting for the cashier to cash his check. I knew this would take some time. The cashier would have to check with the casino manager, who would have to check with his oppo-

site number in the nearby clubs to ascertain whether Bolton
had recently hung any paper locally. I could have saved the
cashier some trouble. Bolton's check was good. Two nights
before, in a Newport hotel room, I had seen Bolton needle,
whine, and cajole nearly five thousand out of a poker game.
The Boltons of this world are not separated from five-thousand-
dollar rolls in forty-eight hours. Then I saw the girl, leaning
against the wall beyond the cage, and stopped thinking about
Bolton's check, Bolton's roll, Bolton's anything else, or anybody's anything else.

She was more than a head-turner, though several heads
turned to look back at her in those few seconds. She had black
hair, fair skin, and was incredibly beautiful. She smiled my
way and I did not smile back, knowing—this girl, I somehow
sensed was not given to smiling at strangers—she was smiling
at someone beyond me at the bar. When she turned away I was
left with the impression, merely from the back of her head,
that her eyes would continue to smile when her face was in
repose.

I gave ground, allowing a newcomer access to the machine I
had played, and moved toward the cage for a better look at the
girl. The cashier appeared at his window and handed Bolton
the money he had been waiting for. I did not have to hear what
Bolton said to know that he was needling the cashier, half
kidding, half serious, all-annoying, for the delay. Bolton moved
toward the crap table; the girl went with him. In that moment,
I knew Bolton was going to lose at craps, knew it as surely as I
had known that Chrome Apple could go a mile and a half
against non-winners of two.

Of course to compare those two bits of knowledge is to use
"knowledge" in two different ways. I might have been wrong
about Chrome Apple, but I could, before the race, have made a

rational case to support my belief. The horse had, after all, a particular lung capacity and a specific metabolism, and his previous recorded efforts gave clues as to what these might be and whether they might suffice to do what he had to do in order to win. If I had been asked to make a similar case for the proposition that Bolton would lose at craps that night, I might have tried, but I could not have succeeded. This ugly man (I would have argued), this whining weasel, deserves nothing; it is unreasonable and unjust that he should have this girl's company; it follows that it is entirely impossible for him to succeed, simultaneously, in another endeavor. But I would have known that the operative words in that argument are "it follows that" and that they are (and were) untrue.

The slot machine I had abandoned coughed, clicked, and spat a cascade of half-dollars into its trough to the evident delight of its new patron. "You moved too soon," was Andy Livoti's triumph.

"It'll be there when we get back." I was moving toward the pit. "It's crapshooting time."

"You sure those little fellows are in season?"

"Got to thin them out," I said. "An act of simple humanity."

The crap game was uncrowded, as was to be expected at so early an hour. I waited to see where Bolton and the girl would stand. "Eight," the stickman sang out. "Big and red. Front-line winner. Comes on eight, and the back line down." The shooter was a large woman known as Gravel Gertie. I knew her as a shill; if I hadn't, the automatic, bored way she picked the silver dollar she had won off the line, leaving only her original stake, would have so identified her. A real bettor, removing his winnings from the table, leaving only his original bet standing, does so either hesitantly (adhering to a plan he begins to wish he had never made), or very quickly (afraid hesitation may lead to a change of mind). Gertie had no decision to make;

being a shill, she was required to "bet" a dollar on every come-out roll and was forbidden to make any other "bets."

"Seven," the stickman yelled. "Seven, a front-line winner, and the comes had action." The nearside dealer slid another cartwheel to Gertie, who added it to the silver dollars in the trough in front of her. Bolton and the girl moved to the open area to Gertie's left, just ahead of the dice. The stickman frowned and glanced at the box-man, who shrugged. Their gestures constituted a discussion of the rule that requires a new player to enter behind the shooter so that he will not get the dice ahead of others who have been waiting longer. The glance asked whether the rule was to be enforced in this instance. The shrug said no. I didn't blame the box-man. Play was slow; he wasn't going to do anything to keep fresh money out of the game.

"Itchy, isn't he?" Andy Livoti had also noticed the breach of protocol.

"Losers can't wait." Bolton and the girl were at the far end of the table. I went around the near end as far as I could go, until my right hip was against the rope that kept the customers from spilling into the inner pit-area reserved for management personnel. I will always take that spot at a crap table if I can get it. You can see the dice at both ends of the table there, and you can only be jostled from one side. With Andy Livoti at my left, even that was unlikely.

The dealers paid off. A few winners pulled back what they had won, or part of it. Between Gertie and me, a short elderly man I thought was a shill bet a dollar on the line. Bolton had not moved, and I wasn't going to move until he did. The stickman looked at Bolton, then at me. Then, evidently feeling that neither of us was quite ready to get into the game, he sticked the dice back to Gertie and yelled, "Coming out now!"

"Be natural," the old man muttered. He was not a shill; shills don't root. Gertie's arm crooked into the indolent, backhand motion with which shills throw dice.

"Ten the line." Bolton was attempting to bet with the dice, offering to bet ten dollars Gertie would win, but his words, blurted out as Gertie's hand started forward and accompanied by a hand-move of his own toward the dealer nearest him, caused Gertie to hesitate in midthrow. The dice popped out of her hand onto the table.

"That's nothing!" the stickman shouted, trying to sweep the dice aside with his stick. "No dice." He got the dice on his second try, by which time most of the players had been able to see they were resting four-trey.

"What the hell?" the old man demanded. "Why no dice?"

"Didn't hit the far end," the stickman explained.

"Haven't been hitting the end half the time," the old man growled. "Don't nobody holler 'no dice' when they miss out!"

The box-man raised his hands, and an angry murmur that had begun among the players died away. "Pay 'em off," the box-man said sadly. I knew him by name (Lefty), by home town (Detroit), and by reputation (good). "Please bet before the dice are thrown, sir," Lefty said icily to Bolton. "It avoids confusion." Bolton picked up two five-dollar chips as the dealer paid off and did not reply.

The girl was not smiling now. Maybe, I decided, she was ashamed to be with Bolton, ashamed of the ten dollars he had just won without risk by working an angle. Maybe not. I forced myself to consider that she had hooked up with him of her own free will.

Another protest developed as the dealer on my side tried to pick up a five-dollar chip which, resting on the kidney-shaped section marked *Don't Pass,* had represented a wager against the dice, a bet that the shooter would lose. The throw had been called a seven, the dealer was explaining to the swarthy bald man who had made the bet, a winner for the line, hence a loser for the "don't pass." But Baldy was having none of it. "Stickman said No dice!" Baldy turned to Lefty and pursued his appeal.

"I never seen that seven, Lefty," he deposed. "I never even looked. I hear 'no dice,' and I look away. It don't seem to me . . ."

"Stand off the don't side, Charlie," Lefty said wearily. "I figured," he told me quietly, "we weren't going to get the best of this." I nodded. I wasn't going to cry for Lefty and the house. Now and then, usually as the result of some angle-shooter like Bolton, the house finds itself forced to pay off the right-bettors while allowing the bets against the dice to stand as if no dice had been thrown. This is contrary, of course, to every principle of abstract justice, but a gambling house is hardly the place to look for justice, abstract or otherwise.

"Betting time!" the stickman proclaimed. I watched Bolton, not knowing whether he would go with the dice or against them—his first play, the angle shot, had to be with the dice, since most players are right-bettors, and the success of the angle depends on the support of most of the other players. I only knew that whichever way Bolton went, I was going against him.

He handed a hundred-dollar bill to a dealer and got a stack of five-dollar chips. I did the same. There was an exchange of words between him and the girl. Then he put two chips on the pass line. I put two on "don't pass." The stickman asked, "What else?" and, getting no reply, shoved the dice to Gertie. "Coming out!" he announced. Gertie lobbed them down the table. They skittered, bounced, and stopped. Six-deuce. Bolton put two five-dollar chips behind his bet on the pass line, meaning he was taking twelve dollars to ten that the pass line bet would win, that Gertie would throw another eight before he threw a seven. I staked twelve dollars back of my don't-pass bet, laying twelve of my dollars against ten of the house's that she would not.

That was how it began. Eight five-dollar chips and two cartwheels on the table, my bets the precise opposite of his, the house to win from one of us and pay the other, only the questions of from whom and to whom to be determined by the dice. With eight for a point, Bolton made a come-bet, which is, in effect, the same as a pass-bet except that it is made when the shooter already has a point, the point for the come-bet to be established by a new throw. I matched his come-bet on the don't-come space; and, when he took the odds against his come-bet, I laid the same odds and to the same amounts, just as I had when he took the odds on the pass line. He pyramided his action, letting his winnings ride whenever he hit; and I pyramided mine, matching his larger bets with larger ones of my own. The important difference was that because Gertie was not throwing any sevens, he was winning, so the additional chips he was staking were provided by the house, and mine were coming out of my bankroll. The ten-dollar basic bet became twenty, then forty, eighty, one-sixty, three-twenty; and suddenly I was hooked for a thousand and had another fifteen hundred spread around the board.

"Nine, a front-line winner, winner, winner!" the stickman yelled. Bolton had three-twenty on the pass line at even money, and would get three-to-two for the same amount for the odds-bet he had made after getting nine for a point. Three-twenty plus one-and-a-half times three-twenty was what he won for Gertie's six-trey. I didn't have to calculate it. $800. That was what I lost.

"Let it ride," Bolton sang out. He was grandstanding. He knew the house limit was five hundred, just as he knew the house would not remove that limit for a player who had started with a ten-dollar bet and an angle. I changed the rest of my cash into chips while Lefty, more politely than I would have wished, explained the limit. The stack of hundred-dollar chips I got was not high; it was lower after I matched Bolton's limit bet on the line with five black hundred-dollar chips on the don't-pass. But I still had seven hundred spread across the backside of the layout; these were don't-come bets; each was a wager that seven would show before the particular number stenciled into the come-box in front of it. A seven now would be a seven before any of them and would bring my seven hundred back with almost as much in profit. Of course, seven now, on the come-out roll, would cost me my five hundred, but the back line would more than make up for it. Better yet, Gertie could catch a point on this roll, and *then* seven out, and I would win both ways. Even better, craps this roll, then the point, then the seven. Without meaning to, I closed my eyes when she threw the dice. I never did anything like that before.

"Craps! Line away!" I heard the welcome words and looked down at my five hundred, waiting for the dealer to match it, perhaps with a single gold chip. The gold chips were five-hundreds. I had never had one. But the dealer passed me by, and, before I could protest, the curved stick tapping on the felt near my chips told me why.

"Bar ace-ace," I read.

"You want a drink?" Andy Livoti asked. He meant: "You poor *intelligent* bastard." I shook my head and smiled. I hope I smiled. The Americana was the only house in the area that barred the ace-ace; the others barred ace-deuce, which, since it shows up once every eighteen rolls, or twice as often as ace-ace, gave them twice as much advantage against a don't-pass bet. Which made the Americana the best house to play in. Which was why I was there, not as against all possible places I might have been, but as against all other clubs where the vigorish was larger. Vigorish is percentage, the built-in edge that gambling houses need in order to exist; and the intelligent player takes his trade where the vigorish is smallest, passing up the houses which take the advantage every eighteenth roll for the one that takes it every thirty-sixth roll. But this was the thirty-sixth roll. The dice down the table plainly read ace-ace, snake-eyes, craps-a-loser, as the stickman said, in the sense that Bolton's five hundred was lost, but a standoff, a tie for the don't-pass bettors, meaning me, Lew White, who needed a winner at the moment, hooked, down near the end of a big roll, with no desire to lose the rest.

Andy Livoti repeated his suggestion. This time he was really saying: *Come on, walk away before you have to walk away empty.* I gave it some thought. It would still be a winning day. I thought of that, and of a drink, a steak, later a motel room, perhaps alone, perhaps not.

But Bolton was ready to bet again, and the girl was smiling, her smile now unmistakably directed at me; and the moment when I might have quit had passed. "I got the back-line bets still," I told Andy, which was true enough. But Lefty would have handled them for me, if I'd asked him to, and brought me my winnings, if any, at the bar.

Bolton backed down to a hundred, and I gratefully did the same. Gertie threw the dice.

"Yo-leven!" the stickman yelled. "Pay it" (meaning Bolton's hundred-dollar bet) "and take it" (meaning mine).

The crap game had become the only action in the club. Even the slot-machine players, and the loafers who hung around the end of the bar waiting for the occasional free bingo abandoned their stations to crowd in six-deep around the table. Gertie continued to throw the dice, but the rest of the table personnel changed. Rocco's team took over from Lefty, Lefty identifying the bets and their holders to Rocco and the new stickman and dealers. The dice skipped up the table and were sticked back; and the chips continued to move out from my trough, onto the table, there to remain for a time, then into the rack, where they replaced the chips that went to pay Bolton. And the girl, cool, and smiling, said nothing. Melanie Sutton, her name was. Andy Livoti found it out somehow and told it to me because I wanted to know, though I had not asked him. From New Orleans, Andy told me. I hadn't asked that either.

The hundred-dollar bet marked the beginning of a new pattern in Bolton's play. He was trimming now, no longer parlaying, pulling back his winnings—and sometimes part of his stake—every time he hit. I was glad. The less he bet, the less I had to bet; this had to end; the run of winning numbers had to stop; seven had to turn up. The smaller the bets, the more likely I would be in action when this happened. But that was only part of it. Partly my pleasure stemmed from the revelation that Bolton lacked the guts to press, but why this pleased me is hard to say. Is it better to be defeated by one who reveals himself, in the act of destruction, to be a coward?

Slowly, mechanically, our back-line bets—Bolton's come-bets, my don't-come bets; his taking-full-odds bets, my laying-full-odds bets—disappeared as Gertie rolled the required numbers, as Bolton was paid for his winnings and did not restake, as my losing bets were collected and racked away.

Finally the back line was clean, and the point was six. Bolton had bet a hundred on the line and had taken the additional one-twenty to a hundred in back. He stood to win two-twenty if six preceded seven, to lose two hundred if it did not. I held the exact opposite position—one hundred don't-pass; one-twenty odds-laid; I had, in addition to my table equity, fourteen black chips remaining in my trough.

"Six-and-eight while you wait," the stickman chanted. "Bet come, bet craps, bet eleven. What about the propositions?" he asked suddenly, loudly. This was, like most of what a stickman says before the dice are thrown, just ritual. But the word "propositions" got through to Bolton. I saw him stiffen and look at the girl. I think I saw her nod.

"Hard six for a thousand," Bolton said, throwing two gold chips to the stickman. The stickman slid one of them on the square marked "3–3 nine to one" and, holding the other chip in his hand, glanced toward Rocco. The box-man shook his head once to each side, then stopped, eyes dead ahead, like a mechanical toy. The stickman returned the second chip to Bolton. "Five-hundred limit," he explained.

"Let's gamble a little," Bolton said loudly. He turned to Rocco. "Pretend it's two bets," he suggested.

Rocco gave him a sad smile. "I got orders not to lose the joint on one roll."

Bolton did not join in the nervous laughter. "Anybody lay it on the side?" It was a general dare, directed to anyone present, to bet that his luck would not hold. But he was looking at me.

I got my fourteen black chips out of the trough and held them in my hand. "Fourteen hundred to one-fifty-five," I proposed. "That's five dollars more than nine-to-one."

"God damn horseplayer," Bolton growled. "Can't do anything but multiply."

"You want it?" I stacked the chips on the table.

"I'm not looking for any bitty chicken-crap bet," he said. "Who'll lay the odds to five hundred?" And then, when no one replied, he said the words that compelled, from me, the reply that started me down the road from Steubenville to Gardena, twenty-two hundred miles as the crow flies, probably forty thousand by the route I took—but a trip that could, more meaningfully, be measured in fathoms: "I'll take six-to-one."

"You've got it," I said. To bet the hard six is to bet that

it—the hard six, two threes—will be thrown before seven and before any other six. There are, on two dice, six ways to make seven, and five to make six, of which only one is three-three. The chance of making it is, therefore, one in eleven; the natural odds against making it, thus, ten-to-one. Gambling houses in Macao, Estoril, Reno, Grand Bahamas, everywhere the game is played, lay nine-to-one, the spread between nine-to-one and ten-to-one being sufficient to finance the hard six's share of rent, salaries of employees, light, heat, two kinds of ice, depreciation, and profit. I could no more have refused to bet against the hard six at six-to-one than I could have kept my eyes from blinking if someone stuck his fingers at them.

"You ain't got but fourteen hundred there," Bolton pointed out.

I moved my fourteen chips into the corner, out of the way of the dice, and handed the keys and registration slip of my T-bird to Rocco. He glanced at the slip to make sure there were no liens against the car. Then he took three gold chips and one black one from the house's rack, capped the stack of gold chips with a small purple marker chip to indicate that this was a personal transaction to which the house was not a party, put the car keys down in front of him, and added the chips to my pile. "Three thousand to five hundred," he said. "You got action, mister."

Bolton slid his gold chip over next to my pile. The stickman, who had been caressing the dice back and forth during the negotiations, sticked them to Gertie.

In honor of the occasion, Gertie rattled the dice in her hand as if she were more than an employee of the house. "Be natural," she rasped, in violation of the rule that shills must take no interest in the points they throw and also of the underlying tradition that a shooter must be with the dice and not against them. If the dice were natural, Gertie, whose point was six, would lose "her" dollar on the line. "Natural," in this

context, means seven, and seven would have got me my fourteen hundred from the corner of the table, Bolton's gold chip,
my car keys and registration, my hundred from the don't-pass,
with a hundred as profit, my hundred-twenty odds-bet, with
another hundred as profit. An easy six—four-deuce, or five-
ace—would lose my don't-pass and odds-bets, but win my side
bet with Bolton. If the dice were something other than seven or
hard six or easy six, Gertie would throw them again, and again,
until a six or seven showed.

Probably because she was now throwing the dice after
fifteen minutes of lobbing them, Gertie's next toss was erratic.
One die flew true to the end of the table and flopped dead just
inside the lip, showing a four. The other veered toward the
house-side, struck a stack of chips, and bounced high in the air.
Rocco, the box-man, swiped at it, trying to keep it on the table,
meaning he hated Bolton more than he wanted my car; with
the four already showing, the two dice, if both of them
counted, could make seven, or easy six, but not hard six.
However, probably because he did not begin his lunge until he
saw the four, Rocco missed.

"Overboard," the stickman sang out. "That's nothing." He
sticked the remaining die into a wooden dish with half a dozen
others, and pushed the dish to Gertie, who selected a pair from
it. The missing die was retrieved and returned to Rocco, who
made a show of examining it, then dropped it into the dish as
Gertie continued to throw. "Yo-leven!" the stickman said.
"Right in the middle of the game." And then: "Eight, it's big
and red," "five, looking for six," "five right back, a good come;
nobody on it." The numbers were meaningless now, all of them
except seven and six; any of the six possible sevens, four out of
five of the sixes, these would keep me in action, and only hard
six, 3–3, would knock me out.

"*Another* five," the stickman said. "Where'd everybody go?"
Bolton was watching the dice, turning his head when they

were thrown, turning again when the stickman gave them back to Gertie. The girl gave me a narrow smile; I smiled back. It pleased me that she wasn't watching the dice; presumably the quality of her next meal might depend on what was thrown.

Gertie continued to throw the dice, throwing faster now because nobody was betting between throws; and the stickman continued to call the meaningless numbers. I kept my eyes on the girl. Then, just after the rattle and bounce of the dice, there was a quick, intense, too-quiet silence, and I knew, before the late call of the stickman, that this was the number that counted.

"Six-hard," he said. "Hardest possible six, two-threes, couple of sergeants, winner for the line and the don'ts are gone."

I turned away, not bothering to look at the dice, nor to watch what had been my chips being racked away, nor to see Bolton collect. "Tough one," Andy said, as we headed for the bar.

Halfway to the bar, I looked back at the crap game, at the people still crowded four-deep around it, those on the far side looking like half-people, their feet in darkness. Rocco, the box-man, came around the table and joined us at the bar.

"I should get out of this business," Rocco told me. He caught the bartender's eye and pointed toward the crap table, meaning the drinks were to be charged to the game. "I pick up a T-bird on the cheap, and I'm sick to my stomach."

I told him it wasn't his fault, and signed the registration blank and handed it to him, and told him where, in the parking lot, he could find the car, and where, in the car, he could find the insurance policy. Rocco continued to grumble about my catastrophe. "Never saw it to fail," he said. "A bastard like that gets hot, he can make nine the hard way." The joke, of course, is that, with two dice, there is no hard nine. I managed to smile. Rocco tucked something into my jacket pocket. "For the insurance."

"It comes due next month," I pointed out.

"Then it's a gift," Rocco conceded. "A yard for the road."

The pressure in the back of my neck was building into spasms. It always does that when I sit too long in a straight-back chair. I waggled my head.

"We're paying for our time," a player in a leather jacket said. I fanned my cards open, saw they were worthless, snapped them shut, and clicked them on the table. The collection bell rang. I turned to look at the clock and was pleased to see it read 11:30.

Kathy gave my neck a five-second massage as she went behind me to pick up the collections on the far side of the table. Leather-jacket opened. "Feel good?" Kathy asked.

"Feels good." The players behind leather-jacket threw their hands down in turn. I used mine to push the antes toward leather-jacket.

Kathy filled in her collection sheet. "Max is at Table One," she said.

"Big deal." I shuffled quickly, took the cut, and dealt carefully. I was angry at Kathy and ashamed of my anger. She meant well. Max Rosenberg meant well. That was the trouble: people who meant well. People who kept urging me—who, it seemed, had always been urging me—to stop wasting my life. My father (*meaning well*): I don't object to your gambling. I gamble myself. But it's something you do after the work is done. In your case, the work is going to school. . . . Alicia (*meaning well*): Gamble, if you must. But don't be sneaky. You hurt yourself when you're sneaky. . . . A casino manager in Wells, Nevada (*meaning well*): I don't want to lose you, but isn't there anything in this world you'd rather do than stack silver dollars? . . . Kathy (*meaning well*): Max is at Table One.

And later on, if I encountered Max, he would make a further contribution, I knew, to the benevolent babble. My father, and Alicia, and all the others who had attempted, in one way or another, to cajole, convince, or otherwise induce me to give up gambling had right on their side, of course. Every gambler would be better off if he were a non-gambler. They merely ignored the possibility that the implementation of their suggestions might—as it might if they advised a blindman to take up tennis—require something more than mere willpower. But the Wells casino manager, and Kathy, and Max, and all those who urged me to get out of Gardena, out of the California Club, did not understand that though I might be clean-shaven, clear of eye, express moderately intelligent thoughts in adequate grammatical form, I was nonetheless a gambler without the nerve to gamble, and, therefore, fortunate to have the job I had. It was doing me no favor to try to make me discontented with my lot.

The impatient leather-jacketed man opened, this time under the gun, got two callers, drew two cards to their one each, came out betting, got no callers, threw his full house down, face up, and raked in the small pot. I studied his face, hoping I would remember it when I met him again, even if he were dressed differently. His failure to check, with the second one-card draw then having an almost compulsory bet, was a piece of spectacular stupidity. Even though my winnings belonged to the house, I liked to win, and I did win most of the time. Knowing which players were capable of spectacular stupidity was part of the reason why.

"Skip him." Chet Kelly, behind me, was telling the next dealer to deal me out. "The twenty-forty's short," he explained.

"Table One?"

"You guessed it." It was an easy guess. Max Rosenberg was at Table One. Kathy wanted me to talk to him, or, more accurately, to listen to him. By reporting to the floor-man that the highest-limit game in the house was running short, she was, in a sense, doing well by doing good.

I pointed out to Chet that I was through at twelve. He pointed out to me that it wasn't twelve yet and shouted "Checks!" which brought Kathy back from the next table, where she had begun her collection, to cash me in. She would, of course, sell me another, larger stack of chips when I reached Table One, where the buy was a hundred, the ante a dollar, and the bet was twenty dollars before the draw and forty after, forty and eighty if the pot failed to open first time around.

"Another birthday present?" I asked her. Chet Kelly watched closely while I counted my chips into her hand; a false count at this stage of the proceedings was what Frankie Pingo had in mind when he stated the house-player's salary as "twelve dollars a shift and all you can steal."

"The table's short two," she said. "I had to tell him." Her grin was too bright; she was near tears.

"Of course you did." I squeezed her arm; the grin disappeared; I was forgiven. "Stow this over at the cage," I said, handing her the briefcase. I moved across the floor toward Table One. Behind me, I heard Kathy checking to make sure Chet had recorded my winnings properly.

Kathy was right, of course. Table One was two players short. Jockey and Sacramento, in seats one and six, were at the flanks of the occupied section. Max Rosenberg sat two; three was J.B.; four was a swarthy man with tattooed arms who was known as The Greek and would correct you if you referred to him merely as "Greek" by telling you his first name was "The" and his last name "Greek"; five was a prim, elderly man with steel-rimmed spectacles. I did not know him, which meant he was something of a rarity, a newcomer in the high-action game.

I said "good evening gentlemen" to the five players I knew, and sat down. "I'm Lew," I told the stranger while the hand in progress was being played down, he having already folded. "I play for the house."

"Monroe," he replied. I felt it was an appropriate name for him. I also felt he did not understand my special status.

"I can't open with less than aces," I explained. "Aces or better, I must open. I can only raise once. If I open and get only one player, I'll let him out before the draw if he asks. I must draw to my hand. I don't check-raise."

"You have got to be kidding," Monroe declared. Rosenberg assured him that I was serious, and The Greek began to explain the significance of the various restrictions on my play. I was glad. A poker game can support, at most, one conversation at a time. As long as this one went on, I would be spared Max Rosenberg's job offer, with its accompanying sales-talk.

It took ten minutes for The Greek to convince Monroe that I was just what I claimed to be. During that time, I saw enough to conclude that Sacramento and Jockey were still at war, that they had conducted their conflict, surprisingly, to their mutual advantage at the three-and-six and had moved their swollen bankrolls to the twenty-forty the better to destroy one another; that J.B. had played scavenger at the three-and-six, waiting for the carnage to develop, and had moved with them, and was still waiting; that The Greek was playing to kill time; that Max Rosenberg's mind was not on the game; and that Monroe's mind, even if fully directed toward the game, was insufficiently acute to allow him to survive without frequent infusions of fresh money.

The twelve-o'clock collection bell rang, signaling the end of my shift. I cut the cards for Jockey's deal, and picked my stack of chips off the table as an indication that, with the cut, my participation in the game ended. "Kathy tell you we're opening on Tuesday?" Max asked. "You interested?" he went on, not waiting for an answer.

I stood up. "Yes, I knew," I said. "No, I'm not interested. Thanks, though." The girls were going from table to table for their collections, moving quickly now; like me, their shifts were ending, and they were on their own time. I looked for Chet Kelly to check me out.

"I've had enough," Max Rosenberg announced, standing too, covering his chips with one hand as Kathy came by for her last collection. "How about coffee?" The question was for me. His arm on Kathy's shoulder included her in the invitation.

"One leaver," Kathy announced, as Chet arrived. "It'll take me a minute to change," she told Rosenberg.

I was tempted, which was why I had to resist. In the comfortable chairs of the coffee shop this man and this girl, who had only the best of intentions toward me, would press me to do what they wanted me to do; and, in those surroundings, what they would propose might sound so reasonable that I might forget the reasons that made it essential for me to refuse. "I'm sleepy," I said, which was the truth. Then, to Max Rosenberg: "Thanks again."

"We're pretty short here," Chet said, indicating the five remaining players. "Everybody else is working," he added, anticipating my reply.

"Here, gimme that." Jockey snatched his collection back from Kathy's hand. "I ain't going to play with five." Jockey, I noted without surprise, was still comfortably ahead.

"My neck—" I began.

"I gave you a break this afternoon," Chet argued. "You'll be on overtime, and you haven't even worked a full shift."

It was generally understood that house-players would work beyond their shifts in an emergency, and the threatened breakup of the twenty-forty certainly qualified as one. At capacity, the game brought in thirty-two dollars an hour, at two dollars per player per collection. Moreover, if the game broke up at this point, Sacramento, Jockey, and J.B., at least, and perhaps The Greek and Monroe, would wander down the street to the Monterey or up it to the Rainbow. If either of these, or the Normandie, or the Horseshoe, had a high-limit game in operation, the word that the action had left the California Club would be all over Gardena the following afternoon and would be true the following night. Among gambling houses, the action is where the word says it is. "Work an hour," Chet urged. "I'll take you out as soon as I can."

"*If* you can." I shrugged and sat down. I did not expect to be replaced; but the overtime wage was two dollars an hour. Besides, I had little choice. While Chet's prerogatives did not include forcing a house-player to work overtime, they did include firing an uncooperative one without specifications as to his uncooperativeness.

Sacramento returned his collection to Kathy. Max paid his collection and moved his chips to the vacant seat, his move setting off a chain of seat-changes, the losers moving "to change their luck," the winners to show that the fact that they were winning had nothing to do with luck. Chet Kelly, much relieved, went off to arbitrate a dispute at the five-and-ten. Kathy gave me a hard look, finished her collection, wrote her sheet, and moved off.

In the first hour of the new day, I began to catch hands. Despite the restrictions put on my play, I had built my hundred-dollar buy up to about $250 when Marguerite, the tough-looking brunette who was Kathy's late-night replacement, came by for the one-o'clock collection. "Eek," she said, as if she were surprised to see me. "Aren't we up late?"

"I love this game," I told her. "I simply cannot get enough of this game." I caught Chet Kelly's eye and saw him twist his palms in a gesture of helplessness that told me I was stuck in this game until closing time, which was 4 A.M. By this time, I no longer minded. The muscles in my neck no longer ached. They never did when I was winning, even if the winnings were not mine to keep.

"I am *not* being a good Samaritan," Max Rosenberg said. We had been discussing his job offer for fifteen minutes, getting nowhere. "I'm a businessman. I need you in my business. *Somebody's* got to organize my sales office."

"Somebody will," I said. "Play your cards."

"All right, all right." Max gave up. "Give me a monster," he requested J.B., who was dealing. "One monster makes me well."

I did not bother to tell him that, properly played, one monster should make any player well.

Since the near breakup of the game at midnight, Jockey and Sacramento had increased the savagery of their duel, as if the incident had called their attention to the possibility that they might not have an infinity of time in which to accomplish one another's downfall and had better, therefore, get on with the job. Since midnight, they had raised, false-carded, and bluffed with such frequency and on such poor hands that each had contributed approximately $500 to J.B., who had called when he had a calling hand and had let them fight it out when he did not. Monroe was gone, perhaps wiser, demonstrably $300 poorer. An owlish man called Professor, who, I suspected, really was a professor, had taken his place.

At one-fifteen, probably in recognition of my service beyond the strict call of duty, Marguerite visited us with coffee for the players and the news that the bill would go to the house. Five minutes later, on The Greek's deal, the pot failed to open. We anted again; with fourteen dollars instead of the usual seven as the starting stake, the bet became forty before the draw and eighty afterwards, instead of half those amounts.

"One thing about playing short-handed," The Greek said while the Professor dealt. "You get more passed pots."

"I'll go home, then," I proposed. "You'd be playing for doubles all the time."

"We could all quit," Max Rosenberg put in. "Leave one man to deal to himself, and share the collection."

"And save money," J.B. muttered.

"Too damn much conversation." Jockey picked up his hand, glanced at it, then folded it back together. "I pass."

Jockey did not usually say those words. Lacking openers, his habit was to rap his cards on the table and glance toward the next man. He might have substituted an oral pass for his usual gesture because he was in the act of speaking his complaint against the coffee-housing. Or he might have started to say "I open," and have changed his mind. While The Greek and J.B. were passing, I fanned my cards slightly, saw three queens, and closed the fan.

"It's open." Sacramento slid eight five-dollar chips toward the center of the table.

Max and I called. The Professor dropped his cards. Jockey answered the question that had been in my mind by raising. The Greek sighed, announced that he had been tempted to call before the raise, and folded. J.B., his eyes glued on Jockey's, slid $80 in, calling. Sacramento reraised. I decided my three queens were hardly worth another $80 even if it was the house's money, and dropped. Sensing the developing action, Chet Kelly took up a station at my elbow; because he did, players at nearby games began craning their necks toward

Table One. Max Rosenberg announced that his monster was late in arriving and folded.

"Once more." Jockey put in $80. J.B. called the $40 raise, still watching Jockey narrowly.

"My bet." Sacramento announced, pushing in another $80.

Jockey counted off sixteen five-dollar chips, started the stack forward, then stopped. "I just call," he said, dropping eight chips onto the table, returning the other eight to his won stack. "In that case," J.B. said triumphantly, "*I'll* bump." He turned toward Sacramento. "I ain't one bit scared of you."

"You better be pat," Sacramento growled, calling the $40 raise.

The Professor reached for the cards, tipped them so that the ante with which he had capped the deck fell back into the pot, and began to throw the top card aside as "the burn."

"Hold it." Jockey's hand went up in a traffic cop's gesture.

"One call coming, Professor," I explained.

"At least," Max Rosenberg said.

"At least," Jockey echoed, adding $80 to the pot. "When I hit," he proclaimed, "I want everybody pat."

"Time." J.B. looked unhappily from one stack to another, trying to estimate its present size, so that he could determine whether its eventual size would justify the additional $40 demanded of him by Jockey's last raise.

"Eight fifty-four," I told him.

"You city fellas are tough on a country boy," J.B. said. "Eight ninety-four, then."

"And I call," Sacramento said, putting in the final $40.

"The lid, Professor." Jockey's one-card discard beat the Professor's burn to the table. He slid his replacement card into his hand, leaving all five face-down on the table, not looking at the new card.

"I'd like to draw," J.B. said. "But I expect I already got the winning hand."

"Bet," Sacramento commanded.

"One one, and two pat?" the Professor asked. Getting no reply, he put the deck down.

Jockey slid his cards, still face-down, under his stacks of chips. "Eighty," he said, putting in a hundred-dollar chip, taking change.

"Blind?" J.B. asked.

"Eighty dollars," Jockey repeated.

I studied J.B. studying his hand. On the betting, I could credit him with no more than a small full house, more likely a high flush. In any case, he could win only if both Jockey and Sacramento were bluffing. Evidently he agreed with me that this combination of events would represent an unlikely possibility. "You maniacs have conned me right out of this pot," he announced, throwing down his cards.

Sacramento, now left with only Jockey as an adversary, proceeded to conduct an oral review of Jockey's play, either to aid himself in coming to a decision or to confuse Jockey as to his response. "You passed under the gun, raised like there was no tomorrow, drew one, and bet blind." He paused and announced his conclusion: "You got a sixteen-way straight flush, or three of a kind and crap in your bloodstream. Either way, you must call, because you know I'm just the son of a bitch to stay pat with two pair. I bump."

The moment Sacramento's $160 was in the pot, Jockey picked his cards up and turned them toward him, the cards still squared, not fanned, so that he could see only the card on the bottom. "Hello, stranger!" he said happily, and raised back. It was a strange play. The card he had seen was not his draw but one of the four he had held. I knew this because I had watched the draw-card when it went into his hand. Even if Sacramento had not watched as closely, he would know that it was four-to-one that Jockey was still blind, that he still did not know what card he had drawn.

"Again." Sacramento pushed two more hundred-dollar chips into the pot and took forty dollars' change.

"You want to go all the way?" Jockey asked.

"Suits me." Sacramento and Jockey looked my way, and I turned to Chet Kelly. As house-player and floor-man, we were responsible for enforcing the house limits. But with only two players, each convinced he had a winner, to insist that they continue betting in $160 segments until Sacramento, whose chip castle was somewhat smaller than Jockey's, ran dry, would be meaningless and time-consuming. At Chet's nod, I leaned across the table, counted Sacramento's chips, and announced, moving them into the pot, that they came to $910. Jockey added nine hundred-dollar chips and two fives to the mound of chips in mid-table. "And eighty for my last raise," Sacramento demanded.

Jockey threw an entire handful of mixed-denomination chips onto the table, laid his cards face-up under Sacramento's nose, and began raking in the pot. "I'm the one with the god damn two pair," he told the shocked Sacramento. "A pair of red nines, and a pair of black nines." Sacramento tried to grin and started to throw his hand into the discards. "Uh uh," Jockey said. "You opened. Remember?"

Sacramento nodded. Jockey exposed Sacramento's aces full and said, "Tough tiddy."

The mockery seemed to restore Sacramento's power of speech. "You passed out four nines?" he shrieked. Chet laid a restraining hand on Sacramento's elbow.

"Did I do wrong, teacher?" Jockey asked me.

"Cut it out," I said. Needling is as much a part of poker as

cutting the cards; but Sacramento was obviously finished for
the night.

"Suppose nobody opens?" Sacramento demanded.

"Then," Jockey conceded, "I have to wait to get you later
on."

"You shit!" Chet Kelly had Sacramento out of his seat and
moving before the *t* sounded, and propelled him away from
the table so rapidly that Jockey's "Yes, if I eat regular"—a
compulsory reply under the circumstances—had to be shouted.

The Professor, who had been shuffling the cards, set the
completed deck in front of Jockey. "Next hand," he said,
cutting.

Jockey reshuffled. "What about that play, Lew?" he asked.

"Any winning play is the right play." That was a truthful and
tactful reply. "You played it like a nut" would have been
merely truthful. A house-player is not expected to be ruthlessly
truthful in answering such a question from a customer who has
just raked in a three-thousand-three-hundred-and-fourteen-
dollar pot.

Play went on, quietly now; Sacramento's departure had
ended the feud and left the game with six players, myself
included. The Greek was about to deal a passed pot when Chet
Kelly returned to the table with a new contestant. "Colonel
Cole," Chet said, introducing the arrival, a leathery caricature
of a Texan, undersized, expensively dressed.

We studied the Colonel respectfully while Chet briefed him
on the house rules. When Kelly finished, Marguerite, in response to the floor-man's signal, came over and put $200 in chips
at his seat. Obviously he had already paid for them at the
cashier's cage.

Kelly moved away. "You gentlemen given to check-raising?"
the Colonel inquired.

"Some do," I told him. "Some don't."

"But you attach no onus to such a procedure?" Some of the richness of the Colonel's speech was merely a result of his being Southern; some, I decided, was alcohol-induced.

"Not at all." I pointed to The Greek, who was ready to deal. "Double pot, Colonel. You want in?"

The Colonel anted two dollars; The Greek started his deal. "One more question," the Colonel said, adding, as The Greek stopped dealing: "Nothing to do with the game." The Greek resumed. "I have a young lady with me. Are ladies barred from this table?"

"She can't play in the same game you're in, Colonel," I said. Jockey opened the pot; J.B. called; the others, including the Colonel and me, dropped in turn. "We can't prevent partnerships," I went on. "But we try to make it difficult."

"Perfectly understandable," the Colonel admitted. J.B. failed to call after the draw; Jockey pulled in the pot. "Still, as long as there's an empty seat—"

"Colonel—"

"I was wondering if she could sit with us and *not* play," the Colonel continued.

I was embarrassed at having assumed his failure to understand. "She'd have to leave if we got another player."

"Of course."

While Jockey dealt, Colonel Cole rose and waved to someone outside the guardrail, then sat down as the girl picked her way across the floor toward our table.

My first thought on seeing her was that she was not Melanie Sutton; my second was wonderment at my first. She did not resemble the girl who had stood next to Bolton on that long-before night in Steubenville. She was taller, blond, and blue-eyed, and, I decided, resembled Melanie Sutton only in that both were beautiful.

I tapped my worthless cards on the table. The Colonel put

his down, rose, crossed behind me, and pulled out the number
eight chair next to me. "Gentlemen, Miss Fortune," he said.
Miss Fortune slid into the seat. She had good legs.

"It's open." J.B. threw four chips in. "How's that?"

"Her name," the Colonel said. "I was not commenting on
your bet. The Professor having folded, the Colonel raised. The
others dropped; J.B. called, drew one to the Colonel's one, bet
$40 after the draw, called the Colonel's $40 raise, and was
shown the Colonel's three fours.

"Is that really your name?" I asked, as the Colonel dealt.

"Lisa Fortune," she said, smiling as if at some secret. I told
her my name and smiled as if I were party to it.

The Colonel, as Max Rosenberg put it more than once in the
next hour, came on strong. He played less than a third of the
pots, and won a third of those he played. His draws and his
bets were nearly always sound; he varied from strict percentage play only often enough to provide a protective confusion. In
the first hour he played, he won about five hundred dollars. I
picked up a much smaller sum in that time, about fifty dollars.
And I attributed even the fifty to the restrictions placed on me,
which made it impossible for me to be trapped, even as they
made it impossible for me to trap.

I sensed that Lisa was thoroughly aware of what she was seeing. She said nothing; but her eyes would sparkle at each new
instance of aggressive play by the Colonel. Once, when the
Colonel called Jockey's opening bet and then stood pat, causing
Jockey to break a perfectly good five-high straight to draw for
a double-ace flush, and then raised Jockey's after-draw bet,
causing Jockey to throw his cards on the table with such force
that they skittered on the floor, she laughed, not loudly, her
laugh more of a throaty chuckle really, so quiet I wondered if
I had really heard it.

In his second hour in the game, the Colonel's luck turned.

None of us was surprised. The distribution of hands in an honest game will, most of the time, give something like the same number of good hands to each player. Frequently, however, one player will undergo a hot streak, or a cold streak. Whether they come in streaks, or in a random distribution spread through an evening, a good player will extract the maximum advantage from good hands, invest as little as possible in poor ones, and measure his skill in his ability to distinguish one from the other. What was surprising was that the Colonel's skill apparently deserted him as his luck waned. He had played good cards superbly; now he played poor ones amateurishly, indulging in the primary sin of poor players which good players call "fighting the cards." He bluffed whenever his position in the game suggested it—as, for instance, when betting last after the draw, those ahead of him had checked—and was, as are all who bluff merely from position, called. He opened under the gum with the minimum hand, then betrayed his holding by drawing three, and compounded his betrayal by betting after the draw.

And each time he committed these, and other, sins, he was punished, as such sinners are nearly always punished, by a loss of money. Lisa's eyes no longer sparkled; she fidgeted in her seat but said nothing. I noticed that the Colonel had begun to take occasional nips from a flask he kept in his jacket pocket.

By 2:30, the Colonel's profits were gone, and he was halfway into his original $200 buy. I had about half of the $500; the others all had smaller parts. The Colonel was, since his entrance, the only loser. At 2:45, with only a few chips left from his starting stake, the Colonel announced—his speech now noticeably thick—that he was "playing $500 back" and sent Chet Kelly to the cage with a check for that amount. Five big pots consumed nearly all the proceeds of the check, the Colonel consuming a bit of whiskey after each. At 3:10, the check-cashing process was repeated, this time for a thousand dollars; this time, also, there was a delay at the table while Chet Kelly examined the check before deciding the signature was sufficiently legible to clear the bank.

The players now began to look on the Colonel's alcoholic intake as a mixed blessing, grateful that it exaggerated his tendency toward careless play, but aware that it would soon make it impossible for him to play at all.

At 3:30, that point was reached. The Colonel had raised, reraised, and reraised again; then, after drawing one against two who stood pat, he got into another raising match, finally forcing the others, who knew that even a drunk *can* improve on the draw, to call. The Colonel, predictably enough, turned out to have two small pair, third best to Max Rosenberg's flush. The Colonel shrugged, allowed he would rather have Max's luck than a license to steal, shuffled the cards, had them cut, and then held them in his hand, smiling happily. "On with the game," he commanded. "Deal, somebody."

Chet Kelly, who had, I knew, been avoiding Table One as much as possible, could not ignore the sight of the man with the deck in his hand smiling vaguely and calling for someone to deal. He took the cards from the Colonel. "You better get a little rest."

The Colonel was not disposed to argue. "Rest right here," he mumbled.

"I don't pay good money," Jockey said rising, "to play with four and a house-player." J.B. and Max Rosenberg also started to get up.

"How about five and the houseman?" For an instant, I did not know what Lisa meant. Then she reached across the table and pulled a hundred-dollar chip from the Colonel's untidy pile. "That's a hundred I owe him," she announced, tossing the chip toward The Greek. "Change, please."

Chet Kelly hesitated. "Can't bar her after he quits," I pointed out.

Chet Kelly looked at Marguerite, poised to make her collection, and at the five men and the woman ready to pay it, and decided. "O.k." he said. "If it's o.k. with him."

J.B. reached over and shook the Colonel. "O.k. for her to borrow a hundred?" he asked.

The Colonel made an affirmative noise, and Chet Kelly put a new deck into the game, handing it to Max to deal.

There was a half hour till closing time. I was watching Lisa closely, almost ignoring the others, as if there was something I had to find out about her, as if whatever it was would be revealed in the way she played her cards.

On the first four hands she was dealt, I learned only that she was able to refrain from playing unplayable cards. While this ability is by no means widespread, learning that Lisa had it was, I felt, learning nothing. I had the feeling that I had already known, somehow, that this girl would play as I did, as if there were no time limit, extracting from each hand only the values that were actually there, without regard to how many hands remained to be played. "You're a tight player, Miss Fortune," I told her, laughing a little at the sound of the name as I dealt.

"You can't call me that," she said, smiling. "Call me . . ." She hesitated, then looked down at the numbered circle in front of her. "Call me One. I'll call you Eight." She picked her cards from the table, opened the hand just enough to uncover the corners, and added, "I open."

Jockey and J.B. matched her twenty-dollar bet. "Two," she said firmly, discarding two cards from the still unarranged hand. I started to give her the top two cards. "The burn," she said hastily.

"I did that once before." I was angry with myself for the

mistake nearly made. "Back in Eisenhower's time." I discarded the top card, dealt the next two to Lisa, then one each to J.B. and Jockey.

"Forty," Lisa said.

"Call." This from J.B.

"Make it eighty." Jockey raised.

"Call for thirty-five," Lisa said. "I'm all in." She pushed her remaining chips into the pot.

J.B. raised back. I segregated fifty dollars in chips, and pulled them aside as the side pot. Any further betting would be on the side. Lisa, having called only $35 of Jockey's original raise, was eligible only for the main pot, which was closed at $292. I looked at her mobile but unrevealing face. As I did, I felt her knee touch mine, was suddenly aware of the warmth of her, and then that she was causing the contact deliberately, that the three steady thrusts of her knee against mine was in answer to my unspoken question.

J.B. called, bringing the side pot to $90. "Kings up," he announced, dropping his cards face-up on the table. Lisa spread her three queens and pulled in the main pot. J.B. reached for the side pot in front of me.

"I think not," Lisa said quietly, pointing to Jockey. "Three eights?" she asked.

"Sevens." Jockey grinned, showed his hand, and pulled in the $90.

"Nicely read," I said as Lisa dealt the next hand.

"Calls before the draw, draws one, and raises coming out?" She did not break the steady rhythm of her deal. "What else could *he* have?"

The slightly emphasized *he* made the question almost incredibly perceptive. Any player, qua player, could bet and draw and bet as Jockey had done, with two high pair, or with a four-flush or four-straight, whether made or missed, or, indeed, with nothing but a hunch. But Jockey, I realized, on thinking it over, would only have done what he did, sitting where he sat, with a moderate set of trips. "What happens," I asked, "if he fills?"

"I lose, but not much," she replied, firmly and truthfully. "Professor?" The Professor rapped with his cards, and the game went on.

When the four-o'clock closing chime struck, Lisa's record was still flawless; she had played only the three queens and was, therefore, about $180 ahead. I was winning about seven hundred. Thanks to the number of players they had broken during the evening and to the Colonel's generous contributions when his cards went salty, the others were also winning large sums. It was not surprising then that J.B., as he started to deal what would necessarily be the night's final pot, suggested: "No limit?"

I pushed my chair back and suggested that I be dealt out. No-limit poker would be a flagrant violation of the rules of the club, the laws of the State, and, I suspected, the Constitution of the United States and perhaps the Charter of the United Nations as well. But I was not a law enforcement agent; I could tolerate the breach so long as I did not participate in it. After all, the table had paid many good collections during the course of the night; and a no-limit hand would, when word, doubtless exaggerated in detail, spread through Gardena, confirm the California's reputation as the action club. "I'll get the deck," I told Chet Kelly as he came by to close down the table. I was proposing that he ignore what was going on and offering to assume responsibility for turning in the cards when play was done. He accepted my offer with a wink and moved on toward a two-and-four game where a dispute as to the division of a side pot was becoming noisy.

"If it's no-limit, I'll need more," Lisa said, leaving her cards untouched where J.B. had dealt them. She leaned across the table toward the sleeping Colonel. I found myself staring at her silk dress, her tan arms, her white chest. "May I?" the Colonel grunted in reply; the other players, to whom the question was actually directed, assented by silence. Lisa pulled four one-hundred-dollar chips from the Colonel's pile and added them to her own. "Five hundred I owe," she announced.

Max Rosenberg opened under the gun. "Fifty. Let's make it a family pot."

Lisa called quickly, without commenting. The Professor did the same.

"A hundred and fifty," Jockey said. "Let's make it a family that don't get along so good."

The Greek, J.B., and Max went along with the raise. Lisa hesitated; then, with a hundred needed to call, she put in a hundred-and-thirty, reraising Jockey's hundred, setting off a flurry of raises and reraises, so that, when J.B. uncapped the deck and asked "How many, if any?" the pot had gone past thirteen hundred dollars. All six were still in. Lisa had about three hundred dollars in front of her, noticeably less than any of the others. Also, for the first time, she seemed not entirely calm, her free hand flicking nervously at her cards as Max Rosenberg asked for two cards and got them.

"I'll . . ." she began. Then she stopped and looked from face to face, her eyes finally coming to rest on Jockey's. "You convinced me," she said, finally. "One." She pulled a card from the middle of her hand and slammed it down, moving quickly, forcefully. I could not tell if she was torn by indecision and did not want, therefore, to give herself a chance to change her mind, or whether she was merely playacting, trying to give exactly that impression. The Professor drew two; Jockey one; The Greek, to everyone's amazement, since he had not been involved in the pre-draw raising, was pat; J.B. drew one.

In view of Jockey's persistent raising and The Greek's failure to draw, Max Rosenberg's check was almost automatic. Lisa's request for "time" was not; she asked for the delay tentatively, stared at her cards, fingered her chips, and finally bet twenty dollars. This had to be a bad bet, no matter what she held: no bluff could possibly go through the raiser and the pat hand; if, contrariwise, she had caught something worthwhile, her bet would serve merely to alert the others to that possibility; worst of all, if her hand was neither very good nor very bad, her bet would be a middling bet on a middling hand in a game in which, whatever else there may be, there is no second prize, and, therefore, no room for compromise. I surmised that she had two pair; my estimate was that she had held three of a suit, to the ace, plus the joker, before drawing for the ace-high flush and pairing one of her smaller cards.

The bet was called around to Jockey, who glanced at The Greek and called, obviously anticipating The Greek's raise, all but sighing in relief when he got it. J.B. and Max Rosenberg called the hundred-dollar raise, which brought the bet back to Lisa. Her five-dollar raise brought groans from the others who were, like Lisa, victims of what seemed to be her poor play, giving The Greek another opportunity to raise, which he did, going up another hundred.

Twice more the bet went round, The Greek raising a hundred each time, Lisa raising her pointless five, the Professor, J.B., and Max Rosenberg dropping out along the way, the first two with visible and audible expressions of disgust. Then, as the bet came back to him, The Greek made one of his rare errors, switching from a hundred-dollar raise to an eighty-dollar one, eighty being all Lisa then had in front of her, obviously forgetting the implicit admission that he was doubtful of beating Jockey who was left with an opportunity to raise, and did, five hundred dollars' worth.

"I was pat, god damn it," The Greek snapped. "Back at you!"

Ten golden hundred-dollar chips came down beside Jockey's five, outside the main pot now, as Jockey and the Greek tried to stare each other down, Lisa and the main pot almost forgotten.

"And a thousand," Jockey said, duplicating his first stack of five golden chips four times, then knocking all five stacks over with a swipe of his hand.

"Call." The Greek matched the final thousand. Five thousand dollars was on the side now, to go either to Jockey or to The Greek, nearly twice as much as was in the main pot in which those two and Lisa were participants.

"You full going in?" Jockey demanded. "You better have been."

"Why?" The Greek asked.

"Were you?"

"I'm calling," The Greek said flatly.

"Three fives for openers." Max Rosenberg showed his now dead hand, picked up his remaining chips, and headed for the cashier's cage.

"Ten high straight," Jockey declared.

"Queen high," The Greek said happily, reaching for the side pot. "It's there," he added, as Jockey reached across the table to spread the cards apart.

"Double-ace flush for the main pot," Lisa said, putting her hand down, sliding the cards apart. The ace of diamonds and the joker were fully exposed, the diamond queen and eight somewhat less so, the five almost covered. She raked the main pot toward her, then turned her hand over and slid the cards to me. I started them toward the rest of the deck.

The Greek, whose attention had been centered on the side pot, shot out a hand. "I never saw it," he complained. His hand was too slow. I was already mixing them into the discards.

"They were on the table," I said.

"I should have had more of a look for two and a half thou," The Greek objected.

I handed him the deck, all but Max Rosenberg's openers, which were still face-up at Max's seat. "Look through the deck," I said. "You'll find the diamond ace, the bug, and three small diamonds. If you don't, it's your pot." I turned Rosenberg's cards over and squared them into a tight packet.

"Forget it!" The Greek slammed the deck onto the table, scooped his chips into his jacket pocket and stomped away. The other players were gone now. Only Lisa and the sleeping Colonel and I remained at Table One. The lights over the other tables were going out. From somewhere in the darkened part of the room, I could hear Chet Kelly's "Last call—cashier's closing."

Lisa touched my sleeve. "Thanks," she said. "That might have turned nasty."

I was stacking the Colonel's chips, giving the task my full attention, as if stacking them ten-deep was a matter of extreme importance. "It might," I said.

"Did I throw my hand away too fast?" she asked.

"Barely fast enough," I replied. She opened her mouth as if to speak but said nothing. A trace of a blush came and went from the tops of her cheeks. She had very high cheekbones.

"I didn't see your hand," I conceded. "But I saw this one." I made sure that, except for the somnolent Colonel, we were alone at the table; then I took Max Rosenberg's final hand, which I had not shuffled into the deck, and turned it over. It contained just what Max said it contained. Three fives, and two useless cards. Two of the fives were black; the red one was the five of diamonds.

I mixed Rosenberg's hand into the deck. Lisa picked five one-hundred-dollar chips out of her own pile. For a moment, I was afraid she was going to try to bribe me. Then she added the five hundred dollars to the Colonel's array of chips. "How come you didn't say anything?" she asked.

"I'm not here as a policeman." I restacked the Colonel's chips into stacks of equal value. "Anyhow, they were out to trim you. And they had an edge."

Lisa matched my pattern making, dividing her chips in similar fashion. "I don't think so."

"You had five strangers to figure out," I argued. "They only had one each."

"That goes both ways, doesn't it?"

"How?" Even before I asked, I knew what she meant and knew she was right.

"They knew each other's games. They didn't know mine."

"Suppose there hadn't been a side pot?" I asked.

"Suppose I'd made the fifth diamond?"

"I mean it."

"I might have got away with it anyhow. If not," she added thoughtfully, "all I would have lost was money."

"*His* money?" I glanced at the Colonel.

"Mine." Lisa made the correction firmly. Chet Kelly came by with Birdie, the cashier.

"The cage is closed," Kelly explained. "Anyhow, why drag the chips across the room?" He checked one of the Colonel's stacks, measured the others against it, and fingered the left-overs. "I make it seven-ninety for him."

Chet Kelly put the Colonel's chips into Birdie's cardboard box, got bills from Birdie, and stuffed them in the Colonel's breast pocket.

"Five and a quarter up," I said, holding my chips over the box, dropping them when Chet o.k.'d my count with a nod and handed me a twenty-dollar bill.

"Overtime, and a holiday bonus, Lucky," he explained. The overtime pay was eight dollars, which made the bonus twelve. I thanked him. I was grateful for all of the twenty, having forgotten I had worked four hours past the end of my shift.

"Twenty-seven twenty," Lisa said. Chet looked down at her chips, neatly stacked. For a moment, I thought he was going to count them. Then, in a single grand gesture, he grabbed a handful with each hand and began throwing them into the box. "You heard the lady," he said. Birdie obediently peeled bills from a roll, handed them to him, and noted the sum on a scratch pad. As he handed Lisa her winnings he said, "Always happy to serve you at the California Club, ma'am." Then, to my amazement, he brought his heels together and managed something of a bow.

"You brought out the knight-errant in him," I said. This was later; Chet and Birdie were gone.

"What about you?" she asked. Then, without waiting for my reply, she got an arm under one of the Colonel's and indicated that I was to get the other. "Upsie daisy, Randolph," she said as he came to his feet. Without much difficulty—the Colonel could stand erect and only needed to be steered—we maneuvered him among the tables, across the deserted club.

"Easy now." I boosted the Colonel up the three steps from the pit to the areaway that led to the exit door. "What *about* me?"

"Later. Here." Lisa leaned the Colonel against a wall while I opened the glass door. I held the door open with my foot and reached back. Between us, we eased the Colonel into the parking lot.

The cold night air blew in my face, waking me, making me aware, too, that for the last few hours I had not been fully awake. Apparently, the Colonel also found the breeze bracing. He straightened up, pushed us away, proclaimed himself "perfectly god all damn right," and walked gingerly away toward the only car in the lot, a white Cadillac, top down, silhouetted by the setting moon at the rear of the parking area.

"What *about* me?" I was holding her hand; I did not remember having taken it.

"You have a little knight-errant in you, too." She laughed. "I guess all gamblers do."

"I'm no gambler," I said.

"Not at the moment." She had an uncanny ability for anticipating my words. "Right now, you hold cards for hourly wages."

"Which is not knight-errantry."

"Covering up for me was, in a way, though." At the far end of the lot, a blast of the Cadillac's horn indicated the Colonel's safe arrival. I wondered if he was honking as a summons to Lisa; then, when the blast was not repeated, I decided it had been accidental.

"I explained—"

"You explained I was at a disadvantage, and you were letting me make things even. But there was no disadvantage. Remember?"

"Still—"

The sudden pressure of her hand on mine stopped me. "Tell me," she asked, "if the Colonel had tried to play four diamonds and a heart for a diamond flush, would you have held still for it?"

"I might not have seen it."

"You'd have seen it." She turned to face me, one hand still in mine, and put the other on my shoulder. I was aware of her perfume, and of the fact that the silk of her dress, which had seemed dull indoors, sparkled in the moonlight. "You'd have seen it more easily if he did it than you did when I did. You wouldn't have spent time looking down his shirt front, or energy not looking down his shirt front. Do I make myself clear?"

"You do."

"Then you would have seen. Would he have gotten away with it?"

She asked the question seriously. I gave it a moment's thought. "He's not as pretty," I said.

"Spoken like a true knight," she said, "one prejudiced in favor of pretty damsels."

"Always," I said. "Shouldn't you be joining him?" A faint light escaping from the distant Cadillac indicated that the Colonel had failed to close the door.

"Yes." She started toward the car, pulling me along with her. "You are chivalrous. Chivalry's obsolete and dangerous. But you can't help it, can you? It doesn't matter," she rattled on. "What did knights do for damsels?"

"Slept with them, as I remember it."

"No. I mean what they called rescuing them, retrieving lost gloves, breaking spells."

"Quests," I suggested. "They went on quests."

"Sir Knight, will you perform a quest?"

"Yea, verily."

"Drive Sir Sagamore the Bold to a hotel. Any hotel." She stopped next to the car. The Colonel, inexplicably, was in the rear seat. "Then drive me to mine."

"Agreed." I let her in from the driver's side, watching her legs as she slid under the wheel, revising my estimate of them upwards from good to perfect, then got in myself. "How do I get home?" I asked. But my hand was out to take the car key from her; I was only seeking information, not making an objection.

"Did Galahad ask the fair Elaine how he'd get back from Elsinore?" she asked. "And have I got my characters and my locations mixed?"

"And your centuries."

I drove out of the parking lot, turned down Vermont, and

stopped outside the Garden Motel. Five minutes later, the Colonel was asleep on top of my bed and I was back at the wheel of the Cadillac.

Lisa pointed, and I continued south on Vermont. "What about Sir Sagamore when morning comes?" Morning was, in fact, almost upon us. The sky, to my left, was perceptibly lightening.

"He'll figure it out."

"Will he know where to call you?" I had stopped at a grade crossing; three freight cars were being backed across.

"He'll know." Lisa had to shout to be heard over the clanging bell. "But he won't call."

I thought of the briefcase Kathy had given me, remembered that I had left it under my seat at the twenty-forty, and decided that, because it was initialed, George, the maintenance man, would know whose it was and would see that it was held for me.

The freight cars were gone. I drove over the track, still heading south, picking up speed now, beginning to wonder where Lisa's hotel was.

"That was ending anyhow," she was saying. "Me and the Texas Ranger."

I looked at the glowing dashboard of the car, at the elegant leather of the upholstery.

"The car's mine," Lisa said. "The pink slip's on the steering wheel. Mine. And all paid for." I whistled.

"You could say 'Goodness!'" Lisa pointed out. "Then I could say, 'Goodness had nothing to do with it.' That's a cheap joke," she said, her tone changing suddenly. "Forgive me?"

"Forgiven." There were no buildings in sight. The lightness in the sky was spreading as the road curved upward into the foothills. I could see oil wells and smell salt air.

I said nothing until, now in full daylight, we reached the

coast highway. Then I pulled to the shoulder. The coast highway was just below us; beyond it, beyond the strip of buildings seaward of it, the Pacific glinted in the morning sun. "What hotel are you staying at?" I asked.

"The El Cortez."

"I never heard of it."

"Sure you have." She put a finger to my lips. "Big. White. On a hill. With a glass elevator, running up the outside."

"That's in San Diego."

"So it is."

"Oh."

In the silence, I could hear the mounting roar of a trailer truck coming down the road we were on. By the time it had passed, I knew I would be in San Diego that morning. I did not know where I would be that night.

But I knew where I wanted to be.

5

There is no traffic on the winding road with the long name now. At seven-fifteen, the men are all home; those who are taking their families out to dinner have already left. Soon the earliest-eating families will begin to return, and the moviegoers and bowlers will begin to leave. Soon. Not yet. Not at seven-fifteen.

Seven-sixteen. Outside the house halfway down the switchbacks the sprinklers continue to throw water onto the green lawn. Now the man appears, wearing a bathrobe over his underwear and slippers, and turns them off.

This done, he stands for half a minute, breathing in the cool early evening air, its aroma faintly tinged with the scent of countless barbecues. Then he returns, through the back door, into the house, into the kitchen.

Seven-eighteen. An indicator-light on one side of the console on top of the electric stove indicates that one of the ovens is lit. The man squints at the wheel below the light, decides that the adjustment is correct, gets a frying-pan from a cabinet, opening two cabinet doors before finding it, and eggs and butter from the refrigerator, and a fork from a drawer, smiling when the fork turns out to be in the first drawer he opens.

He puts the pan on a front burner; then he pushes another button on the console to put heat under the pan, holding his hand close to the pan to be sure he has pushed the proper button. He cuts the butter with his fork, and uses the fork to drop the butter into the pan. When the butter begins to sizzle, he adds the eggs, dropping them carefully, as if trying not to break the yolks. When, despite his care, one of the yolks breaks, he shrugs and stirs the cooking eggs with the fork, scrambling them; when they seem about to stick to the pan, he uses the fork to push them to one side of the pan, then adds butter to the exposed surface, then pushes the eggs onto the freshly buttered area while he repeats the process on the other side.

When the eggs are done, he gropes frantically through the cabinets for a plate, finding one large enough to put the eggs on in such good time that only a small part of the eggs stick to the pan. Then, holding the egg-filled plate with one hand, he reaches down and opens the oven door.

Because he has not turned off the oven first, the escaping heat strikes his face, nearly causing him to drop the plate. Blinking, he shoves the oven door shut with his knee and puts the plate down on the stove, next to the burner, which he now notices is still on. He turns off the oven and the burner, opens the oven door cautiously, and, using pot-holders, removes from the oven a tinfoil tray of French-fried potatoes.

Seven twenty-one. He closes the oven door and takes plate, fork, and tray to the kitchen table. The smell of the potatoes fills the room.

It was the smell of frying potatoes, when a waitress, un-bidden, brought them with my ham and scrambled eggs that reminded me that I was about to eat my second consecutive breakfast, neither sleep nor another meal having intervened.

"I missed breakfast yesterday," Lisa said. The highway was behind her, and beyond it, the pink tile roofs of San Clemente; behind them, the beach; ultimately the Pacific. "We had lunch at the track. Club sandwiches. Iced tea. Fifteen hundred dollars."

I grinned. "I had an eight-hundred-dollar frankfurter once."

"It wasn't my fifteen hundred." She was finishing her toast, washing it down with coffee. "Randy Cole's. He was after the daily double. Took three horses in the first, tied them to five in the second, ten ten-dollar tickets on each combination. And didn't get a number on the board. That isn't easy."

"It is if you put your mind to it." As we finished our breakfast, she explained how the Colonel had finally managed to recoup by betting an even-money entry in a later race five thousand to place, the entry running one-two and paying more to place than to win, I, my memory still jogged by the slight coincidence of the potatoes, contrasting the blue and pink brightness of what I was seeing with the steel, glass, chrome, and cigarette smoke of my last previous breakfast; then, remembering that Kathy had joined me at the end of that meal, I had a twinge of conscience. Apart from everything else, Kathy would be worried when I failed to report to work. A double twinge, really: this was the first time I had admitted to myself that I was not going back to Gardena, not this day, at least, nor this night, the thought of which drove Kathy's square chin, gray eyes, pointed breasts, out of my reverie, ended the reverie, indeed. Suddenly the world was what I could see, Lisa smiling, her hair stirring in the breeze that blew across the terrace, the too-bright picture postcard behind her.

"I grew up around here," she said.

"You don't talk like a native." I considered that a compliment. Also, it was the truth.

"Meaning?"

"The natives say 'pinny' and 'Hairy.' "

"You're thinking of Tinnessee. They say pinny there. And what's the matter with hairy?"

"He's all right. I mean: they say 'Hairy Truman,' and 'Let's go down to the Pearamount and hear Hairy James.' "

"I'm not really a native. My family moved here when I was four. My father was a sheet metal worker at Consolidated."

That was bad news. Assuming that the elder Fortune was in the first tide of metal workers who came West to work for Consolidated and the other airplane manufacturers, which was the most favorable possible assumption, it followed that Lisa was born the year of my Senior Prom. I went with Alicia.

"I'm twenty-four. Stop figuring. We lived in San Diego for a while," she went on. "After the war, when you could get gas, we moved up near Del Mar. My father used to say we lived about a mile and seventy yards from the track. I found out later that was why we lived there."

"Your father's a horseplayer?"

"Was." A waitress refilled our coffee cups. "They're both dead now. My father was killed by a three-to-five shot in 1952, when I was twelve. You want to hear about it?"

"If you want to tell it."

"Shasta Something-or-other was the horse's name. A big colt that had been beating the best of the two-year-olds in allowance races, giving them weight. This was the Del Mar Futurity. At level weights, you had to figure he'd win it, didn't you?"

"You have to give him the best chance," I said, first waiting to make sure this was really a question. "I'm not sure he'd be worth a bet, though. You'd probably be laying the odds."

"Sure. But I was twelve years old. I couldn't say anything like that. So when my father, slightly stoned, came back from the betting windows and asked me if I thought the horse would win, I said 'I hope so.' Which was the answer he wanted, something a twelve-year-old girl could say, and the truth besides. At the start, another horse spooked and came out sideways, and almost knocked Shasta Whatisit into the rail. The boy got him straightened out, but he was twenty lengths out of it. I remember my father put down his field glasses and turned to me. 'Maybe it'll be like in the movies,' he said. But it wasn't. We left after the race, with two races still to go, so I knew he was busted." She paused.

"You don't have to . . ." I began.

"Our car was on the beach side," she went on, her voice quiet and level, "across the highway from the track. It was a long walk. When we got to the highway, we stood there, waiting for a break in the traffic. I remember he was holding my hand, and I looked up at him, and his face was white, and sad, and very tired. 'Are we in trouble, Dad?' I asked him. He said, 'Only if I live,' and let go of my hand and stepped in front of an eight-wheel Diesel semi-trailer."

"Jesus!" I started to reach across the table for her hand; then I knew this would be the wrong thing to do, so I grabbed the sugar container instead and shook some unwanted sugar into my coffee.

"I got over it," Lisa said. "I didn't think I would, but I did. Afterwards, I used to think I saw him at the track sometimes, and once I forgot and started toward him, but he turned out to be another middle-aged man, thin on top, in shiny black pants and a sweater. Excuse me."

I paid the check while she was in the ladies' room. When she returned, she said nothing; I did not ask the question that was in my mind, but rose and followed her to the car, and resumed the trip south, driving more slowly now in the early-morning traffic.

Four miles and six minutes later, the question was still unasked when she answered it. "Why not? I liked the excitement. It was all the excitement I had before he died; if I'd stopped going, what would I have had?"

It took me a moment to realize her question was not rhetorical. "I couldn't say," I said. "I was never a twelve-year-old girl."

"You didn't miss much." Lisa drew her feet up under her, bringing the top of her head almost level with the top of the low windshield, so that the wind swirled her hair over her face and she had to brush it back with her hand. "Watch the road," she said. "Female adolescence. That's what I mean. The awakening of the sex urge. The girl emerging into womanhood. I read about it, but it didn't interest me at the time. It happened to everybody. You know what I mean."

This was a statement of fact and no question. I kept my eyes on the road.

"Racing breaks people up into winners and losers. That was what I wanted. Even then."

"In spite of what happened?"

"Sure. My mother could never understand. He was a loser, always was, always had to be; but at least he had the guts to put it to the test."

For the first time, she had said something I did not begin to understand. I told her so.

"He had to lose, because he believed in magic and his faith controlled his play. He couldn't let his brain do the job. He had feelings—this was his day—this wasn't—and that was what made him bet, or not bet. Once he told me, 'The favorite is five-to-two, and I need five hundred. So, if I bet two hundred, I'll win, because this is my day.' You can't put it plainer than that. Or sillier."

"Did the horse win?"

"Wire to wire," Lisa said. "What does that have to do with it?"

The road curled down out of the hills, back toward the sea, bringing Del Mar racetrack into view on the landward side. A pretty track, I thought, seeing the brownish infield with the bright green turf course cutting across it, the white stucco grandstand, then, as we moved along, the parking lot between the grandstand and the highway, and finally, as I looked the other way, the auxiliary lot on the beach side of the road. "Where the turf meets the surf," Lisa said. "A thrill in every minute and a winner in each race." She was quoting from a song Bing Crosby had made popular when he had been a principal stockholder in the track's early days. "That's new," she said, lightly but somehow chillingly, as we passed under a blinker light that hung over a crosswalk connecting the auxiliary lot with trackside. "In the afternoons, it operates red and a green."

Beyond the crosswalk a billboard advertising the track came into view. "First post two o'clock," Lisa read. She did not have to say more.

At one o'clock that afternoon we were driving north, back from San Diego, the road now clogged with traffic. The top of the convertible was up. Lisa had changed into a green print dress. I wore a drip-dry shirt, a sport jacket that was almost appropriate to be worn with my gray suit-trousers, and a tie whose colors did not quite conflict with the jacket. I had bought all three in a store just off the lobby of the El Cortez.

Two pair of field glasses rested in their cases on the seat between us. Both had come from the closet in Lisa's hotel room. When I first saw them, I decided that the larger pair were probably the property of Colonel Cole, or of one of his predecessors; I also decided it didn't matter.

I had also acquired, before going upstairs with Lisa, two *Racing Forms* and a pencil that wrote blue on one end and red on the other. I was painfully aware that my purchases had left me with barely $130 in my wallet.

I had spent the time it had taken Lisa to shower and change (less, of course, the time it had taken me to change my shirt, jacket, and tie) in going over the past performances for the early races, marking, in each horse's record, favorable informa- tion—heavy weight in a previous race, a blistering early pace survived, a race against horses superior to those to be faced this afternoon, a good race under an incompetent jockey, and so on—in blue; and unfavorable indications—failure to display adequate speed under lighter weight, poor races to inferior horses, failure of a front runner to hold on after setting an uncontested pace, a series of dull races at progressively increas- ing odds, and many others—in red. This was supposed to give me something of a picture of the race: in theory, winners should be found among those animals having a preponderance of blue marks. But there was little to go on in the first two races; I had made few marks of either color there, and I was a little ashamed of the marks I had made. This was conspicu- ously true of the first race, which, being for California-bred two-year-old fillies, non-winners, and at a low claiming price, had attracted a field of such poor quality as to make any form, either good or bad, hard to find. The second race, a mile and a quarter event for cheap but older horses, was only a little better. The horses had run oftener, which justified a few more red marks. And it had attracted a smaller field, which increased slightly the chance of finding the winner by blind guess or incantation.

I followed the bulk of the traffic as it swung off and over the highway in response to a sign marked RACETRACK TRAFFIC KEEP LEFT, and continued to follow it down a narrow road that broadened into the parking area behind the grandstand.

"Over there," Lisa said. I swung the car out of line, pointing it toward a gate marked Turf Club Only. As we neared it, Lisa rummaged in the glove compartment and produced a six-inch square of glass on which a decal of a horse's head and the words *Member DMTC* were affixed, and held the glass against her corner of the windshield. The guard at the gate waved us on.

This saved me the dollar that was being collected at the plebe parking gate, but I was not happy with the saving. Obviously we were headed for the Turf Club. I tried to remember what Max Rosenberg had told me was the standard charge for admission to a California track's turf club, assuming a member supplied you with guest tickets; I could remember only that it was a rather high sum.

I parked head-on against a green wall that was part of the track enclosure, helped Lisa out, and followed her along the wall into an entrance plaza. People were queued up for Grandstand $1.75 and Clubhouse $3.50. There was no queue at the line Lisa led me to. It was marked Turf Club Will Call. No price.

"Ask for Colonel Cole's tickets," she murmured, stepping aside as I approached the window.

I did, and got a hard look and an envelope from the man behind the window. "Two guest tickets from Mr. Clay to Colonel Cole," he said. "Is this a charge?"

I was tempted, but I handed over a twenty-dollar bill.

I got eight dollars' change and followed Lisa to a turnstile where an attendant took the tickets and applied a rubber stamp to the back of my left hand and Lisa's, then to another turnstile where another man examined the stamp under an ultraviolet light which revealed that, though previously invisible, it was actually of an attractive four-leaf clover design and entitled us to admission to the Turf Club.

An entryway led into a huge room behind the grandstand.

The stucco walls, heavily interlaced with gold leaf, gave the room the appearance of an elegant Spanish dungeon. A stairway at the far end might have led to the torture chamber. I started toward it. Lisa touched my arm.

"Here." She handed me two bills. I began to enter a strictly *pro forma* protest. "No arguments," she said firmly. "No lady lets a gentleman pay for her gambling. That includes admission to the casino. I am a lady."

I conceded the point and pocketed the bills. "Would it compromise you if I bought the programs?" I asked.

The Turf Club turned out to be a sloping restaurant giving on the track. Ten minutes later, we were seated at a table in its last row. Below us, beyond the ranks of half-occupied tables, was a narrow cement lawn; beyond the lawn was an oblong saddling area, with numbered stalls for the horses; beyond that, was the track itself. A small tractor was pulling a harrow back and forth. The infield tote board lit up, with zeroes in all the slots in all the pools; the morning line flashed on across the top of the board; and the loudspeaker declared that daily double windows were now open, that they would close in forty minutes, and that in the daily double there were no overweights and no scratches.

That last caused me some distress. Somewhere along the line, without my really being aware of it, I had begun to consider the notion of wheeling the double. This would mean buying all the possible combinations, gambling that the payoff on the winning ticket would exceed the cost of the rack. Given the almost formless first race, and the generally poor form of the animals in the second, it seemed like a good gamble. There would be some return in any case; I would suffer a major loss only in the event, extremely unlikely, I felt, that well-backed horses won both races; and the possibility of enormous gain if both races went to outsiders was considerable. But I had only

$122 in my wallet; with ten horses in the first race and eight in the second, there were eighty possible combinations. At $2 a ticket, I could cover only three-fourths of them. Two scratches in the second race, or three in the two races combined, would have brought the wheel within my means; but there were no scratches.

The tote board blinked and began to reflect the early betting on the first race. What action there was seemed, in general, to follow the predictions of the anonymous author of the morning line. Lisa was reading the front part of her *Racing Form;* apparently she was engrossed in an article dealing with the bloodlines of classics-winners in Australia. I set about a restudy of the first race past performances in my own *Form.*

Even on reevaluation, it seemed a muddle. I could make a fairly plausible case against each of the ten entries. On the other hand, no one of them, if it won, would qualify as a genuine shocker. A re-survey of the second race was a bit more productive. The prospective winner was as hard to find as ever, but I was almost able to convince myself that I could spot two almost-certain losers. The two inside horses, it appeared, could not possibly get a mile and a quarter at anything like the speed that was needed to win unless one of the two was allowed to set a slow, unchallenged early pace. For each horse—and the One was the probable betting favorite—the existence of the other was a virtual guarantee that no such condition would prevail, since both would necessarily be fighting for the lead. It almost followed, then, that both could be eliminated as possible winners. This would leave six horses to be backed in the second race; they could be paired with all ten in the first to make up a hundred-and-twenty-dollar wheel.

But. There is always *but;* just as there is always *almost. But* one of the two might get left at the post, leaving the other to run unattended in front. *But* one of the trainers involved might—foolishly, in my opinion, but he might—deliberately elect to run his horse off the pace. He couldn't win a purse that way, but I had just demonstrated that he couldn't win it running his horse in accord with the beast's natural tendencies either. As between two ways of losing a race, could I safely assume—

"Here they come," Lisa said. The California-bred, claiming maiden fillies were brought to their stalls. Of the forty legs on display, twenty-two were bandaged.

"Was there ever a race without a winner?" I asked.

"Not according to the song," Lisa replied.

The favorite was taken from her stall and led back and forth in front of the others. Sweat formed a soapy band along her shoulders; her tail twitched nervously. If I threw the favorite out of the first race, and the two quitters from the second, the rest could be wheeled for $108. $120 was too much to risk; it would leave me with $2 and some change. Even $108 was probably too much: the table was set for lunch.

The more I thought about it, the better the full, eight-by-ten, impossible-because-it-cost-more-than-I-had, wheel looked. It would offer me action for my entire roll; the prospect of enormous gain was good; best of all, it offered its own built-in insurance against catastrophe. Lisa and I might make jokes to the contrary, but in each race, a horse would go past the wire first, and after each race a number would go up in the "1" slot on the board, and after the second race there would be some return to a man who held tickets on all possible combinations.

But. But. But-but-but. And also *or*. *Or* I could cover as much of the wheel as possible with my $122. *Or* part of it. The smaller the commitment, the greater the reserve against the possibility that the sheaf of tickets I would hold might not include the right one. *But* the smaller the commitment, the greater the likelihood of such a disaster became. And. And. And-and-and. And so forth.

"I'd be interested in fifty dollars' worth of a double wheel," Lisa announced. "That is, if you don't mind letting me in on the bonanza."

"No," I said, glad that my voice didn't crack. "I don't mind."

She handed me a fifty-dollar bill. "I have five-sixteenths of whatever the double pays," she said. "That should be ten dollars, or ten thousand, or something in between."

"I couldn't afford the full wheel by myself." Confession, they say, is good for the soul. My soul felt fine.

"You better go bet it," she pointed out. "I'll order lunch while you're gone. Chicken sandwich o.k. for you?" I tried to figure what the lowest possible daily double payoff might be. I was wondering whether 11/16th of that sum, plus the $12 I would have in my pocket after my trip to the windows, would cover the lunch. "This place," Lisa said, "is on the Diner's Club."

There is, I decided some forty minutes later, only one thing better than watching four long shots charging toward the finish line, any one of which will provide the start of a rich daily double, and that is watching the same horses heading for the same finish line with the double held in partnership with Lisa. "Come on anybody," I said quietly. The outside horse, as is the fashion of outside horses, drew clear inside the sixteenth pole. The win price was $39.60.

The possible daily-double prices were posted nearly half an hour later as the eight plodders entered in the second race went into the gate. I observed that the highest of the possible prices was in excess of $3,300, and that the lowest was $194, which would still provide us with a profit. Then the bell rang, and there was no more time for observation, even pleasant observation.

The favorite—which would produce the smallest daily-double return—broke on top. It was one of the two faint-hearted ones I had considered eliminating from my wheel before Lisa's offer made the full wheel possible. Passing the stands, the other speed horse came on to join him, the two heading into the turn together, fighting it out, drawing away from the field as they straightened into the backstretch.

"They'll need a taxi to get home," Lisa said. "Look at the three-quarter time."

I put down the field glasses and located the fractional time on a little board next to the tote board. 1:11 for the six furlongs, not spectacular time, but much too fast for this field. When I got my glasses back on the race, a small gray horse was cutting down the gap separating him from the leaders. He reached them as they headed into the final turn, slipped between them at the quarter pole; so that, when they were straightened away, there were, as the public address announcer proclaimed excitedly, "three of them 'cross the track!" The sprinters both shortened stride just inside the eighth pole; two others came on to chase the gray; seventy yards out, all three of the leaders were long shots; the question, as they flashed past the finish line together, was not whether we had made a killing, but merely how great a killing it might be.

"Three, five, six," I said. A moment later, 3 flashed on the board, and ten thousand voices read the number aloud. The bottom of the board lit up to signify a photo finish for second and third.

"A very convenient double," Lisa said.

I thought she had chosen rather an odd adjective until I glanced at the double-board and saw that 6–3 would pay 1,616, which is one of the few sums that can be split eleven parts to five without resorting to pencil and paper.

The numbers of the second, third, and fourth horses went

up; minutes later, OFFICIAL lit up across the top of the result section, and an attendant put a red frame around the 1,616; the chicken sandwiches arrived; I sorted through the eighty daily-double tickets for the live one, dropped the dead soldiers under the table, and excused myself.

Cashing the ticket took a few minutes; I had known it would. Not that there was a line at the window; there were fewer than fifty winning tickets all told, and, as far as I could tell, ours was the only winning one in the Turf Club. But I couldn't get the money until I had identified myself, until the clerk had satisfied himself that I was who my driver's license, social security card, and draft card said I was, and until he had filled out a W-1 Form for the Internal Revenue Service. They do this on all double payoffs that come to 299–1 or more. The following April, presumably, the government can quarrel with anyone who won a long double and failed to report it. I imagine this quarrel is one the taxpayer usually wins. Gambling losses are deductible from gambling winnings.

I went back to the table with the $1,616 in my fist, gave $505 to Lisa, added the $1,111 to the $12 in my wallet, sat down, and took a bite of my sandwich. It tasted good.

The pressure was off. I didn't have to find safe bets anymore, just good ones. I finished my sandwich and ordered sherbet and coffee. Then I reread the past performances for the remaining races. I made no more red or blue marks; I wasn't handicapping this time, just familiarizing myself with the outline of what was to come. The only question I had to answer at this point was whether there was anything in a late race that seemed likely to be such a good bet that reasonable bets in early races should be bypassed in its favor. There was not.

The sherbet arrived as the horses followed the outrider out of the ring and onto the track for the third race. "You like anything?" I asked.

"Maybe a vodka gimlet," she said. I signaled to a waiter. Then she answered the question in the sense in which I had asked it. "The Frenchman's a well-made colt."

The Frenchman was named Pair-Impair. He was making his first start in this country, which meant he had never previously raced on a dirt course. Worse, his breeding—he was a full brother to a British Derby winner—suggested that he might prefer a longer distance than the six furlongs these horses were to race. I pointed this out, also mentioning that Pair-Impair, whose last race had been at Cagnes-sur-Mer months before, might be short of condition.

Lisa admitted the validity of all this; but she pointed to a race Pair-Impair had won, a stakes race at a thousand meters at Deauville, this being a furlong shorter than three-quarters of a mile, as evidenced that, bred for distance or not, Pair-Impair was not a total loss as a sprinter; besides, he had worked three furlongs in 34⅕ two days before; besides, he was 25–1. That last convinced me. I did not point out that there was scarcely a horse on the grounds incapable of equaling the three-furlong work. Instead, I rose, took out my wallet, and raised two fingers of my free hand in her direction. When she shook her head, I added the other three fingers. Lisa grinned, raised both her hands, fingers extended, closed them into two fists, then opened them again.

"Twenty?" I asked.

"Oh," she replied. "Are we allowed to talk? Yes. Twenty. Five hundred if we win. We don't want to be pigs."

When I came back with the tickets, the horses were going into the gate. I gave Lisa her ticket and got a ten-dollar bill from her. Then the bell rang and, on the far side of the track, the starting gate opened and the field poured onto the backstretch. Shortly thereafter, Pair-Impair came out of his stall and set off after the others.

"You didn't mention that," Lisa said. The leaders were midway in the turn; Pair-Impair was a sixteenth of a mile behind
the next-to-last horse.

"What difference would it have made?"

"Not a bit."

The field came through the stretch, Pair-Impair so far in
back that the crowd had time to recover its breath after urging
the contenders on in plenty of time to jeer the forlorn foreigner
as he finished. It was, up to that time, the fourth best horse
race I had ever seen. The two that had made up the daily
double, and Chrome Apple's race on the Ohio wheel, were one,
two, and three.

I had taken a tiny flier on a horse that had been worth,
perhaps, a tiny flier. That the horse had not won, had not been
close, did not matter. What mattered was that I was back in
action. What mattered more was that I was in complete control
of my own action.

The rest of the afternoon went by in a hurry. Later, over
dinner, at a corner table in the top-floor restaurant of the El
Cortez, with the lights of San Diego winking on and off at the
foot of the hill outside, I slowed down the afternoon a little and
pieced it together, more or less. A lanky, extremely well-
dressed man, an old friend of Lisa's, or so I gathered, had
joined us briefly to relay a favorable opinion of his horse,
entered in the fourth race, and invited us to the paddock to see
the horse saddled. The fourth race itself we had watched from
the paddock, hardly able to see anything from our position at
ground level, not caring much—at least I hadn't cared much—
because the lanky man's horse was never in the hunt, which
vindicated Lisa's estimate of the lanky man's ability to take a
dispassionate view of his horse's chance, and because the 4–5
favorite, well placed at the top of the stretch, was an obvious
winner from the eighth-pole home, which vindicated my view

that the horse was unbeatable and the race, therefore, un-playable.

Somehow this had all seemed enormously funny to both of us; so that we fell, laughing, into each other's arms, disentangling ourselves only enough to make our way, laughing, to the patio bar, there to get slowly, laughingly, mildly, happily drunk; so that the fifth and sixth races were run without any awareness of them on our part. Mine, at least.

I cut into my steak and looked past Lisa. It was darker now than when we had begun dinner. I could see the harbor, outlined in lights, the amusement and fishing piers sticking out into the dark water, even an occasional light that was a plane, flying up or down the coast, far out to sea.

"One of my favorite sights. A harbor on a clear night. Sometimes," Lisa added, "it looks better than my horse's number on the board."

I nodded. "It depends." On how long it's been since you backed a winner. How much you've got going. How badly you need to win. We had had two winners that afternoon, not counting the daily double. And you could hardly count the double, since we'd bought all the combinations. But if the double was a cheap, not wholly legitimate, win—the stake being only partially committed—the other two, in the seventh and eighth races, were satisfyingly authentic.

In the seventh, the horse whose record drew a plurality of my blue marks was Khal Girl, the favorite. But a cheaper specimen named Mr. Dippy, with only one blue mark, had earned that one by running Khal Girl to a half length the week before when both had carried 115 pounds. Today's weights were 118 and 110 in Mr. Dippy's favor. Against the eight-pound weight shift, many arguments could be mustered to support Khal Girl's inherent superiority. Mr. Dippy had, demonstrably, no finishing kick; Mr. Dippy had won only two races in two years. Khal Girl could run all day. Khal Girl had won six of her last eight races. But Khal Girl was 6–5 and Mr. Dippy was 11–1; and, as I pointed this out to Lisa—we were back in the Turf Club, eating again—the board blinked, cutting Khal Girl to evens, and offering 12–1 against Mr. Dippy. "I think," Lisa had said, "that it's trying to tell us something."

The message, of course, was: better twelve-to-one that the weight shift would upset the form than even money it would not. Its validity was confirmed in the final twenty-four seconds of the race after the two horses came past the quarter pole, Mr. Dippy half a length to the good as they straightened away. "Mr. Dippy and, on the outside, Khal *Girl*." the loudspeaker declared as, approaching the eighth pole, Khal Girl came to Mr. Dippy's flank, both horses laboring now—Khal Girl because she was unfavorably weighted, Mr. Dippy because it was his nature to labor at the end of his races. Khal Girl continued to inch forward and was almost level with Mr. Dippy at the sixteenth pole. Then she hung, and the two went stride for stride to the wire, heads bobbing, the horse whose head was down trading the lead with the other as they went, Mr. Dippy's head down at the wire. There was a long delay, while the placing judges studied the photo; then, just as the more nervous patrons were beginning to shout "dead heat," the numbers went up:

1st	4
2nd	1
3rd	9
4th	8

Four was Mr. Dippy, and the straight price, when it went up, was $27, 12½–1, meaning a $625 profit for Lisa, who owned one of the $50 win tickets under the ashtray on our table, $1,875 and my $150 back for me.

The eighth race was a happy, sloppy parade, a parade because the nine horses entered slipped into single file in the run past the stands; a sloppy one because the intervals between them kept lengthening; and a happy one because I had taken 2–1 against the one that broke on top. The win price was $6.80, which is as much as a 2–1 shot can pay in California. The extra 80¢ on the $2 price meant an extra $160 to me, and gave me an unreasonable sense of accomplishment.

I took greater and more reasonable satisfaction from the fact that, as soon as the eighth race became official, I was the one to point out that by leaving immediately, without waiting for the ninth race, we would avoid most of the traffic congestion leaving the track. I was sure Lisa was about to make a similar suggestion. But I made it first, and when she smiled, agreeing to it, she was also, I thought, acknowledging some pleasure that I was, at that moment at least, aware that the event we would thereby miss would not be the last race but merely the ninth, that there would be other days, and other races.

"Dessert?" I asked, as the waiter removed the remains of the main course.

"Not for me." I asked for the check. "What now?"

"I should look for a hotel room." I was asking a question.

"Why?" Her question was, appropriately enough, an answer. "How about a hundred dollars' worth of jai alai?"

Twenty-five minutes later, we were on the Freeway, in heavy traffic, just north of the border. Lisa was explaining that jai alai, to the participant, is a dangerous combination of squash and handball. To the gambler, it is a sort of lottery in which form counts for nothing and the unknown, but obviously high, vigorish makes winning nearly impossible. "Exciting, though," she promised. I nodded. My own excitement came from the feel of her close to me on the car seat, from having left the California Club, and from the fact that, although I had left Gardena with less than $150, I now had $3,100 cached in Lisa's makeup case in the El Cortez and $60 in my pocket. She pointed out a parking lot on the American side of the border; I headed into it. $10 of the $60 was for expenses. I assumed that "$100 worth of jai alai" meant $50 each.

The jai alai was in progress when we arrived. Lisa was right. It is an exciting game. The structure is simple. A man uses a basket attached to his arm to throw a ball against a wall; his opponent tries to catch it in his basket, either on the fly or on the first bounce, and throw it back. The first to miss loses. The walls to the player's left and to his rear are also in play; the omitted wall to his right is replaced with a chicken-wire screen behind which are the spectators' seats. In doubles, the rules are the same, the server having a partner and two opponents.

For betting purposes, there are six or seven entries in each game, Number One playing Number Two, the winner receiving one point, then playing Number Three, and so on. Since the number of points needed to win is always set at one less than the number of entries, all have an equal opportunity to win. Whether all have an equal opportunity to be second or third is an abstruse mathematical problem. My feeling is that since no set number of points is needed to be second or third, they do not. It occurred to me that this was the sort of problem to which the Professor could probably give a quick, definitive, and correct answer. It was the first time in several hours that I had given a thought to anything in Gardena—Kathy included —except my financial status on leaving there.

"Five minutes to bet win, place, and show and the quiniela." The amplified announcement rattled the walls of the fronton. The announcer was a hustler; he was more like the stickman in the Americana Club ("Coming out now! Betting time!") than his racetrack counterpart who, except for a murmured "The horses are on the track and will be at the post in ten minutes," would never presume to remind the visitors of the purpose (presumed) of their visit. I turned to Lisa and found her conversing with a red-jacketed young Mexican.

"A runner," Lisa explained when the man was gone. "Buys tickets and cashes them for you. He likes the one-three quiniela."

I had encountered quiniela betting once before, when a coughing epidemic at a Midwest track had caused the commission to authorize it as a substitute for show betting in races with short fields. Quiniela bettors attempt to predict the first two finishers, not necessarily in order; the bets are, as usual, pooled and prorated among those who succeed.

I looked at my program. The fourth game of the evening, then pending, had six entries, which meant fifteen possible pairs for the quiniela, as opposed to six possible results in the win pool.

The game was doubles. Past performances were included in the program, but for some reason they revealed only how each team had fared in this particular event (that is, the fourth game) during the season, plus each player's weight (in kilos) and height (in meters). Next to each name, in parentheses, was the player's nationality—"Mexicano," "Vasco," and, in one case, "Americano." All four players on teams One and Three— which comprised the quiniela recommended by the runner— were "Vasco." Vasco, I decided, had to mean Basque. And, jai alai being a Basque game, I decided almost simultaneously, these should be the best players. Besides, since Basque is one of the most difficult languages to learn, the mixed teams would find it difficult to communicate. But even as these thoughts went through part of my mind, another part dismissed them as rationalization, an attempt to justify a bet I was going to make only because Lisa was making it. I got up, looked around, saw an arrow pointing the way to MEZZANINE MUTUELS and started to push past Lisa to the aisle.

"You're rocking the boat," she said. "Anyhow, Ramon's already getting yours. I told him 1–3, five times. Five two-dollar tickets." She held out her hand. I put a five-dollar bill in it and sat down.

Easier communications probably had nothing to do with it, but Team One beat Team Two in the first point when the game began some eight minutes later. (The announcer, it appeared, had been a little premature in his warning of the imminence of the game; and sometimes a stickman will hold the dice away from the shooter after shouting "Last call!") "We root for the Three this time," Lisa said, as the blue-uniformed Threes replaced the beaten red Twos on court.

I started to ask why and then was glad I had not. The answer was quite obvious. If Three won this point and ran out the match, our quiniela was good, since Three would be first and One—the only other team to have scored a point—would be second. But if One won the point and ran out the match, our quiniela would be only halfway home; One would be the winner, but Three would be one of five teams tied for second; for One and Three to finish first and second, which was what we needed to win our quiniela, Three would then have to win a five-team playoff for the place.

"Up!" Lisa shouted, as one of the Blues, returning the serve, slammed it, as if taking her advice, high against the side wall, so that it skipped against the very top of the corner of the front wall and bounced, high and deep, into the very rear of the playing area, where a white-shirted One could do nothing but lob it lazily back, an easy shot for the forward Blue to angle hard against the side wall, so that it caromed across the front wall, hit the edge of the wooden floor, and bounced into the wire screen. "Team Three," the announcer said, "has one point."

I began to get caught up in the developing play then, planning the attack for the Blues as they faced each succeeding team, yelling bits of advice to them, pleased that I was able to grasp that, in this game, position is everything, and that the measure of a team's chance to win is how far forward it can play its shots. The points themselves were long and beautifully played. Whether the play was entirely honest was totally immaterial. I told myself that the thirty players employed by the fronton would, if allowed to play honestly, necessarily develop the same sort of pecking order that a group of similar size would produce in a season of ping-pong. Perhaps the fact that this would have made betting impossible was why it did not occur; perhaps the game was crooked. It didn't matter. What mattered was the blue-shirted player, climbing high in the air as if on an invisible ladder, to catch the ball in the basket, and then loft it accurately forward to the precise point on the court at which no return was possible, or, if a return was possible, only a weak one that could easily be disposed of, by a smash that whistled past the opponent's basket, or a simple drop shot that barely cleared the low red foul line near the bottom of the front wall, and dropped at the foot of the wall, leaving the nearest opponent to run madly forward and then, unable to reach it, to stop and walk sadly off the court, head down, while the crowd booed and Lisa loudly demanded, "How do you say 'eat your heart out!' in Basque?"

The red Team Two came back on court. "This is it," Lisa said. It took me a moment to understand. Then I realized that this was the beginning of the second round, that Two, having been first to lose, was first to return. More important, since Three had beaten every team except Two, they needed only this point to end the match, to win, leaving Team One as second, making the 1–3 quiniela a winner.

I glanced at the scoreboard to see that this was true, that

Three had four of the five points needed to close out the game, One, one, and the rest nothing. A man behind me yelled, "*Avanti, Azur!*" I yelled the same, as the Blue front-court man served, the ball coming off the front wall hard, hitting the floor just forward of the rearward limit of the service area.

Red's return was defensive; Blue trapped it on the half-volley and slammed it on a line four feet off the floor, against the front wall, so that its trajectory carried it back deep, low, close to the side wall, an almost perfect shot that drew cheers. One Red made a pass at it on its way back, then withdrew his basket at the last instant, letting the ball go all the way to the rear wall. His partner took it coming off the wall and put it into a high arc that nearly hit a rafter but found the front wall. The taller Blue—the back-court player—caught the ball in mid-court; for a half a dozen exchanges he and his opposite number slammed the ball forward, each catching it on the fly, pure strength, no finesse in the play now, each trying by the force of his shot to drive the other back. Blue, to my distress, began to give ground, a stride, then two, until finally he was making only defensive shots, both Reds well forward now, nearing the point from which either could end the point with a kill, a three-cushion carom into the wire net, or a soft drop that would bounce twice before it could be retrieved.

I groaned as a passing shot came toward the back-court Blue, the ball so close to the side wall it seemed impossible to play, gasped in relief as he ran two steps up the wall, snared it, then, falling back to the cement floor, managed to launch it forward. "Uh oh," Lisa said, as a Red caught it coming off the front wall and wound up to slam it at killing speed toward the wall, barely twenty feet away, while both Blues, seeing what was happening, raced toward the rear wall in hopes of making the save.

"It's no kill." Lisa had to yell into my ear to be heard. "See?"

The Red, pausing in his motion like a baseball pitcher changing up, had released a soft, low floater toward the corner. Deep in back court, the Blues, alerted by the sudden wild moan of the crowd, reversed themselves and ran hopelessly toward the front wall, nearly two hundred feet away.

The ball slapped the side wall and flopped forward, toward the front wall, arcing downward as it went, heading down for the front wall, near the horizontal red stripe that was the foul line, dipping as it came to the wall, finally hitting the wall with a crazy metallic *klunk,* dropping straight to the floor, bouncing once, twice, three times.

Only when I saw the Red who had made the shot swing his basket in obvious disgust at the side wall, did I understand. The *klunk* meant that the ball had hit below the top of the red foul-line; the shot was no good; the point, match, and quiniela had gone our way.

The announcer confirmed the result and went on to explain the complicated rules for the four-way playoff for third. I wasn't listening. Lisa was in my arms, and I was feeling the wonderful warmth of her, and wondering how wonderful it would be later on. Behind her, over her shoulder, the prices went up on an electric board. The win and place prices didn't matter; the show prices could not be figured until after the playoff. The quiniela payoff mattered. It was $62.60 for $2, $313 for our ten-dollar investment.

Ramon, grinning, came down the steps into my line of vision. I kept one arm around Lisa's waist, reached out my free hand, and got three hundred-dollar bills from Ramon, who counted them into my hand, explaining that he was able to pay off so quickly because he had a friend among the *cajeros.* He fumbled in his pocket for the odd bills. I told him it was all right. He told me I was too kind, advised us to play the Two in the next event, and moved away.

"You *were* too kind," Lisa murmured. "He only expected the odd three dollars."

"The ten was a consolation prize," I said. "He'd have got a lot more from us if we stayed."

"We're not staying?"

I looked around. Below us, the *pelotaris* were warming up for the next event. The stands were emptying out as the customers moved toward the mutuel windows. "I may be the only man in the world who's ahead of the jai alai, lifetime. I have a sudden urge to keep it that way."

"Ten minutes to bet," the announcer said. I started to pull Lisa into the aisle.

"Do you only want to go because you're winning?" She pulled her hand free.

"Not only," I admitted. "To put it as elegantly as possible, I'm also in a hurry to get to bed with you."

"Too much of a hurry to buy a person a drink?" She grinned and followed me into the aisle.

The fronton's bar was quiet and strangely decorous. We drank tequila over chopped ice in glasses rimmed with coarse salt—Margaritas, the specialty not only of this bar, the barman assured us, but of all of Tijuana, of Rosarito, Ensenada, and, he supposed, the rest of Baja California as well.

"The game has something to do with it, doesn't it?" Lisa asked. She gestured toward a television screen set in the wall behind the bar, on which shots of the players warming up alternated with views of the odds board. "Your wanting to leave, I mean."

"Yes." She knew what I meant. Jai alai is pure chance; there is no form to point to the winner, no method to minimize losses or maximize gains. Had it been otherwise, it would have been both more and less than a game to bet at for the fun of it; then, between the fronton and Lisa's bed, there would have existed something of the business-pleasure relationship; I might still have left when I did, but there would have been a shade of guilt involved; and I might have wondered whether, in leaving, I had dodged an opportunity, almost shirked a duty. As it was, the choice—to stay or go—was a choice between pleasures. I had no doubt that I was opting for the greater pleasure.

"Ramon must have a lot of followers." Lisa pointed to the television screen on which the odds against Two suddenly dropped from 6–1 to 2–1. "You'd still be ahead," she argued. Then, the argument won, she added, "We can watch from here."

I got a twenty from my wallet and replaced it with a ten from Lisa. "The Señor will handle our case," she said, as the bartender came by to refill the glasses. "Number Two," she told the barman, taking my bill, handing it over the bar.

The bartender took the money to the far end of the bar, handed it to a customer, and watched as the customer left. "Tickets shortly," he promised, refilling the glasses, indicating by a glance that there was still enough salt on the edges to cut the sweetness of tequila. I decided after a sip that he was right; an instant later I realized that the stories I had heard of the insidious potency of tequila had some basis in truth.

"Getting to you?" Lisa laughed and climbed on a bar stool, spinning the stool so she faced me, and put her hands on my shoulders. My head bobbed as I reached for her, and the room's focus suddenly cleared. I was looking down the front of her dress again; when I tried to pull my head back, I lined up an equally interesting view of her legs as she crossed them, as her skirt rode up.

"I don't care," I said.

"You don't care what?"

It was, I thought, an unfair question. "Whether school keeps or not," I answered. I have always believed that any answer is better than none. A bell rang; the lights in the bar went even dimmer. "Fifth game," the voice from the screen said. "Player one, Lupo, plays Player two, Aguilar." Lisa spun her stool to face the television set. I shifted my feet and turned with her.

"Your tickets." The bartender handed them over. I stuck them in my shirt pocket and slid a half-dollar across the bar.

As play began, I could hear the crowd twice, first from the television set and, an instant later, directly, through the doorway at the far end of the bar that led to the grandstand. On the black-and-white set I could not distinguish Aguilar, on whom we were betting, from Lupo, his first-point opponent. Only Lisa's reactions—she grabbed my hand and squeezed it each time Aguilar got in trouble and relaxed her hold when he escaped—enabled me to keep track of the play. The double crowd noise began to roll in on me, as the long point went on, and the room, once again, was getting out of focus. "Now!" Lisa said. My head cleared; I saw one of the figures on the screen climb high on the rear wall, hang there for an instant, and then, reaching high over his head with his basket, and in a straight continuous motion, like that of a catcher throwing to second base, slam the ball horizontally forward so that it hit the front wall and bounced high and deep close to the side wall, too close to be played on the way back; but too close to be a winning shot, too, because the ball actually touched the side wall just before it reached the back wall, so that it ricocheted out of the corner, back into the middle of the fronton. Lisa groaned as the other player waited for it, moving his feet for better position, caught it easily, faked the soft low shot to the front wall, and threw it hard and deep against the side wall, so that it caromed well forward, struck the floor just in bounds, and flew high into the net where it could not be retrieved and was not retrieved.

"Quitting time," I said, as the television set showed the

scoreboard: one point for Lupo; none for Aguilar, whose number, on the firing order at the bottom of the board, was moved down to last place. I put a five-dollar bill on the bar.

"He could still win it, you know," the bartender said.

"So he could." I gestured for him to keep the change, helped Lisa down from the stool, and walked with her, leaning on her a little until we got outside, out of the bar, through the lobby, through the door marked SORTIE Y ENTRADA, straightening up as I hit the cold outside air. The bartender, of course, was right. It was unlikely that Lupo would go through the field without losing, and if he lost, Aguilar would play again. But five points would be on the board by then, and however they might be divided among the others, Aguilar would have none. Behind us, as we reached the exit, the crowd noise mounted again, and fell again. The announcer said something, but I did not hear it. I was not listening. Instead, I was trying to remember when, if ever, I had left a gambling house while holding an unresolved bet. Never, I decided.

People were still coming into the fronton. I led Lisa down the steps, past the spotlighted statue of a *pelotari* in action, up on one toe, reaching out into the night, the pose quite close to the one struck by Aguilar in making what might have been the winning shot against Lupo. Beyond the statue, a cab stopped; a sailor and a girl in tight slacks got out. I handed our box-seat stubs to the sailor and smiled until the sailor, evidently deciding there was no catch to the gift, thanked me. I handed Lisa into the cab and followed her in.

"One dollar each to the border," the driver announced, as if waiting for me to protest. When I did not, he swung the cab to the right, circled the fronton, and set out past a cluster of miserable shacks, downhill, until he reached the river bottom, then along it toward the border.

"Now we'll never know about Aguilar," Lisa said. She didn't seem particularly unhappy about it.

"Aguilar," the driver declared suddenly, "*es uno pollo.*"

The joke was a feeble one; but it was probably the only one the driver could have made that I, not speaking Spanish, but having eaten in Mexican restaurants and thus aware that *pollo* is chicken, and remembering somehow that *aguilar* meant eagle, could have understood. So I laughed. And suddenly all three of us were laughing, Lisa and I holding each other tight to keep from falling off the seat, laughing at that possibility, too, as the cab jounced along the river bottom; the driver laughing at his own joke and our response as well, fighting to hold the wheel steady through the potholes; all three of us still laughing, but more quietly, as he swung the cab left onto the smooth macadam main road and, not slackening speed until the last possible instant, jammed the brakes hard and brought us to a screeching stop next to the immigration station.

Outside, I searched through my wallet and found, in addition to some large bills, only two ones and a little change. "I have change," Lisa said, fumbling in her purse.

"No." I handed the driver the two bills, and the win ticket. "*Gracias, señor,*" he said, putting his cab into reverse, shooting back across the macadam, then forward, headed back toward the fronton, obviously curious about the value or worthlessness of the tip. I was going to look in the San Diego papers the next day to see how he (and Aguilar) made out, but I never got around to it.

The immigration agent took my word that I had been born in Cleveland, and Lisa's that she had been born in Terre Haute, and passed us along to the customs man, who was ready to believe that neither of us had bought anything in Mexico. Back on the American side, we picked our way through a maze of pedestrian crossings to the parking lot.

Five minutes later, as we were leaving the cluster of lights that marks the border, heading onto the unlighted Freeway toward San Diego, Lisa said, "Over here." I swung the car onto the service road which dipped down beside the Freeway, and under it, emerging at the entrance to the El Toreador Motel, which was identified by a tricolored neon sign somewhat higher than the building it served.

I wondered momentarily if, for some reason having to do with the relative respect given to convention in San Diego and National City, we would be spending the night at the El Toreador; but Lisa slipped quickly from her side of the car, not waiting for me. When she returned, three minutes later, she carried two newspapers which she tossed in the back seat. "Tomorrow's Caliente *Forms*," she explained.

I drove away from the El Toreador, back to the Freeway, back to San Diego, while Lisa explained that, since Caliente operated only on weekends, entries were taken early in the week, and *Racing Forms* for both Saturday and Sunday reached the dealers on Friday. The San Diego supply of Sunday *Forms*, it appeared, was nearly always exhausted by Saturday afternoon; but they were always available near the border. Whether this disparity was a result of some miscalculation by the paper's circulation department, or whether the San Diego players were better off and thus able to know on Saturday whether they would be able to visit Caliente on Sunday, she said, "deponent knoweth not."

"There'll be a fresh supply everywhere in the morning, though," I guessed.

"So we didn't have to stop?" Lisa was scornful. "There are fifteen races at Caliente tomorrow," she went on. "Fifteen, count 'em, fifteen. We'll have to do some sorting out tonight."

"I have other plans," I said.

"So have I," she admitted.

An hour later, I lay on top of the turned-down, extra-size bed. I had worn my undershorts from the shower to the bed, somehow unwilling to be naked while Lisa was still dressed. I am not usually so fussy. Now, while Lisa showered, I took the shorts off, threw them at a chair, missed, got off the bed, and put the shorts on a closet shelf.

In returning to bed, I took one of the two *Forms* from the bureau and sat on the edge of the bed to look at the front page, dividing my attention between what I was reading (BORDER 'CAP DRAWS ELEVEN) and the sound of the shower. Somehow I felt it would be a bad idea to be reading the *Form* when Lisa came out of the bathroom.

Forms are sold with uncut pages to guarantee that all those returned by the newsdealer for credit will be unread. I spread the *Form* wide, pulled it apart down the middle, then reassembled the halves. This method of cutting the pages would mark any man anywhere as a habitual horseplayer. I tried to remember whether I had ever used the other, one-page-at-a-time method, decided I had not, and took a look at the next day's past performances.

Lisa had not exaggerated. There were, indeed, fifteen races on the schedule. The feature, I was dismayed to see, had drawn eleven horses, nine of which had run against each other in their last two races with profoundly inconsistent results. Of the two strangers, one was a cheap sprinter from Arizona—this race was at a mile and seventy yards—and the other was an elderly mare who had run with better company at Del Mar but had not, in her last six tries, been within ten lengths of winning.

I decided that handicapping the feature was beyond my ability of the moment and glanced at the earlier races. The first two were for maidens, four years old and up; I had long since decided that if a horse could not win in his first two years of racing, it was a hopeless task to guess when he would win and that such horses should never be bet, even when entered against horses with similarly discouraging records. The third was for maiden two-year-olds, claiming price $2,000, with weight off for each $250 knocked off the claiming price down to $1,500. Of the ten entered, nine, running at Caliente, had accounted for two seconds and a fourth in over forty starts. The tenth, Pizza Pallor, had not run since finishing dead last in a three-furlong race at Santa Anita the previous January. He had, however, been the favorite in that race at 2.30 to 1.00 and he had taken the lead at the start. This sequence of events suggested that he had encountered trouble in the running; that he had been unraced since January suggested that he had gone lame; his return in this race reinforced that last suggestion.

The sound of the shower had stopped. I got out of bed, put the *Form* back on the bureau, and got back in bed, fixing Pizza Pallor's name in my mind, meanwhile, so that I would remember, sometime before the start of the third race, to examine the horse's recent works and inquire into the reputation of its trainer.

Then Lisa was in the bathroom doorway, her hair loose and tumbled over her shoulders, her nightgown, lemon-yellow, it seemed, covering her from neck to knees. It was thoroughly opaque, even when she stood full in the path of the bathroom light; and it was, I decided, infinitely more exciting than if it had been shorter, or tighter, or transparent. As she turned off the bathroom light and moved toward me, I realized that, as late as the minute before, I had not really thought this moment would come, just as, long ago, I had not really thought Chrome Apple would be drawing clear at the eighth pole; and I laughed, and remembered, with a sense of shock, that I had laughed then, too.

Suddenly Lisa was laughing too; and a moment later she was

in bed, still laughing, rolling against me, laughing before we
kissed, laughing afterwards, laughing after I stopped laughing,
until I had to kiss her a second time to stop her laughter; then,
when I took my lips away, she did not laugh but reached,
instead, for the lamp on the night table. In the dark, she took
off her nightgown so quickly that it was already over her head
when I reached for her; momentarily, our arms were tangled in
it, and then we were free of it and coming to each other
quickly, almost savagely; and I was not aware until it was over
that she had been murmuring "Now . . . now" since it began.

When Lisa turned the light on again, I estimated it was less
than a minute and a half since she turned it off. She settled
back into the bed and turned her face toward me, not laughing
now, just smiling, and kissed the tip of my nose. "That was a
good six furlongs," she said. "I think we could go a mile and a
half next time."

"At least," I said. She got out of bed. I started to ask where
she was going, then stopped short, guessing, having my guess
confirmed when she came back with the two *Forms* and, back in
bed, propped up her pillow, her head in a reading position, and
handed me the uncut copy.

"If I find any marks in here"—she was leafing through the
copy I had been reading—"the whole deal is off."

I spread, ripped, and refolded the second *Form* and told her
the feature was impossible.

"Maybe." She leaned across me and turned a page of my
Form back, bringing the past performances for the feature into
view again, and guided my forefinger to the column in which
the odds against the horses in their previous races were listed. I
scanned the column and compared it with the other columns,
finding nothing except that, among these horses who took turns
beating one another, the winner was never the favorite and

never an extreme outsider. This proved only that the bettors found this field as baffling as I did.

"But the winner," Lisa pointed out, "is always just a little shorter price than he should be. Look." She stabbed a finger at the Number One horse. It had won the week before at 6–1, I saw, which was surprising, since it had been 8–1 in its next-to-last, a race in which it had quit cold and finished seventh, nine lengths off the winner, which, I now noticed, had paid only 5–1 after trailing all the way round in his previous try at 7–1.

"Somebody's playing games," I said, checking the betting pattern in the other past performances, finding evidence to support my statement everywhere I looked.

"I don't think these are boat races," Lisa said. "But somebody knows something and acts on it. Not enough to start a panic; enough to show up."

While she was talking, I suddenly saw how this discovery could be made to work for us. "We've got to forget the betting entirely."

"Forget it?" Lisa's voice was edgy. "You said yourself the race is impossible on form."

It was the first time I had ever been a step ahead of her. I enjoyed the sensation for a moment; then I explained. "We make our own price-line, as tight as we can, just on what's on paper, as if—"

Lisa caught up quickly. "As if he didn't exist. Mr. X. The Man Who Knows. Something."

"That," I said, "will be a legitimate line. Any large difference between our line and the actual line—"

"I get the idea. Don't spell it out for me." Lisa switched off the light.

Two hours later, the light on the night table went off for the last time. In those hours, I had made a price-line on the feature, with a theoretical price against each horse, all prices conditioned only on what form had been publicly displayed, weighted to reflect what use I thought a racetrack crowd would make of the information, and adjusted to provide for the 22 percent that Lisa thought the Caliente management customarily deducted from its win pools before dividing the balance among the backers of the winner. And we had reached some tentative conclusion about horses entered in other races. Pizza Pallor would have to be looked at and looked into when the field came out for the third race, looked at for indications as to his condition, looked into as to his jockey—R. Chavez, the meet's leading apprentice was listed overnight, but he was listed on two other horses in the same race—and what betting action he attracted. (30–1 would mean his connections were giving him no support at all and would be an indication that whatever caused his withdrawal from racing had not been ameliorated; a very short price would not justify the risks inherent in backing him; 7–1, we agreed, would be almost irresistibly attractive.) I contributed a distance horse who, away from the races six months, had returned two weeks before to run a creditable fifth in a seven-furlong sprint; reading the sprint for a speed tune-up, he figured to improve at the mile-and-an-eighth at which he was entered. Lisa made a powerful case for a horse who, having quit in three successive sprints, might, paradoxically, be expected to do better in a distance race in which, in Lisa's opinion, there was no real early speed.

And during those same two hours, following what Lisa had called our "good six furlongs," we had run distance events of our own, the last and longest of which had consumed half an hour and left me agonized, ecstatic, and exhausted, my face dripping wet when the light went on to show Lisa's invariable smile that (I hoped) expressed (at least) contentment.

I knew the light had gone off for the last time because Lisa, before turning it off, had returned both *Racing Forms* to the bureau. In the dark I reached for her again, determined, for reasons of pride and passion, that she would be the one to quit, but she kissed me lightly and edged away. "Whatever it was, you proved it." I was about to add that I hadn't been proving anything, when she added, "you can prove it again tomorrow night," and took my outstretched hand as she turned over, and tucked it under her chin. "Maybe tomorrow morning."

6

Leaving the border, the cab swung onto a wooden overpass over a dried-up river and was instantly engulfed in traffic; I was glad, as we came off the overpass and jounced through downtown Tijuana, that, by private treaty calling for a $3 payment in addition to the regular $1-per-person, I had arranged for Lisa and me to travel without companions. Even at 11:30 in the morning, the heat was oppressive.

"We'll miss the third race," I said.

"Nonsense." Lisa looked up from her *Form.* "The paper says eleven. That means they go at eleven-fifteen."

"*Sí,*" the cabdriver put in. "It is always so."

I started to point out that even if the first race was late going off we would have, at the rate we were going, very little time to consider whether to bet Pizza Pallor in the third.

"The third won't go till twelve-forty," Lisa said.

"Forty minutes between races?" The usual interval is thirty or less. And, with fifteen races on the card—

"They'll make up for it in the afternoon," Lisa said. "When there's a good crowd, and they want to keep them busy so the women won't convince the men it's time to go over to the bullfights."

"*Sí,*" the cabdriver said. "Bullfights."

We were out of Tijuana now, heading up a dusty hill, past a decorative archway. "Welcome to the casino," Lisa explained. "Over there."

I looked where she pointed and saw only a ramshackle, half-collapsed building with a pile of blue tiles in front of it.

"Thirty years ago," Lisa went on, "that was the gambling capital of this hemisphere. Las Vegas twenty times over. It had to be. Hollywood a hundred miles away, and this was the nearest place you could gamble or drink without breaking the law. The blue tiles were imported from Spain for the chimney of the bathhouse. It was supposed to cost two hundred thousand, just the chimney. Discount it ninety percent; it still must have been a hell of a bathhouse."

"What happened?"

"Repeal happened. Hard times. The income tax. Horse racing in California. Finally the Mexican Government closed the place down and used it for a sort of CCC camp. Under Cardenas, I think."

"Sí," the driver said. "Cardenas."

"You talk as if you were alive at the time," I said, realizing she couldn't have been.

"My father told me," Lisa explained. "He made it sound like a gambler's heaven."

"I thought he moved out here during the war."

"I know. I used to think he'd seen it. But of course he was only telling what he'd heard about. I guess that's part of heaven, too. Only knowing it from hearsay, I mean. There," she said, "is the track."

The cab had come to a stop, under the eye of a Mexican policeman, across the street from the racetrack's parking lot. Behind the lot, the track was half stucco-and-red-brick, half steel-cement-block-and-glass, an oddly appealing architectural mismatch, as if a California motel-builder had decided to finish an incomplete mission. The policeman turned and raised his hand and the cab gunned across the road, under a wooden archway (Bienvenidos Amigos), across the lot, past the grandstand, and pulled to a stop near the clubhouse entrance.

I paid the driver. "You want passes?" he asked.

I started to say we did, but Lisa, rummaging in her purse, had come up with a pad, from which she tore the first two pages. "I keep a pad of them," she said. "It's only a dollar to get into the grandstand, but you'd be ruined socially if you paid it."

Apparently all the other racegoers were also concerned about their social status; none of them bought tickets before lining up outside the turnstile. "There are passes," Lisa explained, "at all the better motels, gas stations, and barbershops." I took my place behind her at the end of the line.

Inside, I bought programs, then hurried on after Lisa, catching her as she headed through the tunnel leading to the clubhouse. As we reached the point where the tunnel widened into the mutuel area, public address horns blared: "Two minutes to post. Two minutes. Hurry along, please." An odds board on a side wall showed prices against ten horses but gave no indication of which race was forthcoming. There were, I saw from my program, ten betting interests in each of the first three races. Pizza Pallor was Number Eight in the Third; if the third race was next, Pizza Pallor was being quoted at 6–1.

"Come on." Lisa had moved on beyond the mutuel area to the back of the clubhouse restaurant. I fought off an urge to bet the Eight immediately, just in case, and joined her. She pointed across the tier of tables, out over the lawn, toward the track itself. "The horses," the announcer said, "have reached the starting gate." It took me a moment to figure out why she was pointing. Then I noticed that the starting gate was set just back of the six-furlong pole, at the very end of the backstretch, not midway between the five- and six-furlong poles as it would be for the third race. The infield board made the Two the 4–5 favorite. Now the numbers blinked, and the Two dipped to 3–5. "Well backed, for a four-year-old maiden," I pointed out.

"The crowd follows the money here," Lisa said as the horses came to the gate. (The announcer's previous declaration that they had "reached the gate" was a form of hyperbole customary at most tracks, designed to speed laggard bettors into timely action.) "Everybody figures somebody knows something and wants the bet the insiders are taking. But the pools are so thin, you never know. A drunk can bet a hundred on an outsider and start a panic."

"All in the gate," the announcer said. Ninety seconds later the last two horses were led in, and the flag went up; and, moments later, the bell rang and the race was on. The people at the tables promptly stood up, blocking each other's view as well as mine, and I led Lisa to a better vantage point in the aisle. So doing, I bumped against a fat red-faced man who had his hands at his sides and a pair of field glasses around his neck. I murmured an apology and wondered why he did not use the glasses to watch the race.

The Two, in flaming red silks, was easy to pick out as she took the lead down the backstretch and drew out to four good lengths at the quarter pole. I began to think the idiots who had taken 3–5 against her were right; then she began to shorten stride and I knew they were not.

At the eighth pole, the four-length lead had dwindled to one; two hundred yards out, the filly all but stopped as three horses swept by, then a fourth. The middle horse of the first three was the strongest of that group, but the fourth horse to pass the favorite was going fastest of all on the extreme outside. Like most clubhouses, Caliente's is situated beyond the finish line, from which point it is almost impossible to call the winner of a close race, especially where one horse is extremely wide at the end.

"Inside horse?" Lisa guessed.

Beyond her, the fat man was backing up the aisle, moving slowly. He was using the glasses now, but they were pointed, not toward the track, but toward the grandstand area to our left. "Lord, I hope so, dear," he said loudly. Max Rosenberg, who is a student of such matters, could have identified his speech-pattern as between Cockney and Australian. I could only say it was one of the two. "I backed him, you see?" he went on, now turning to face us. "It was a short-head either way; no saying from here. You want to hedge out?" he suggested hopefully. "Assuming you backed the outside one, the Ten. And, forgive me, the way you said 'inside' made me think you *had* backed the outside."

Lisa did not reply; the fat man, evidently assuming she lacked the capacity to understand him or the authority to conclude the bargain he was proposing, turned to me. "You see what I mean, don't you, Governor? If the inside wins—the Four—I give the lady ten out of my winnings; if it loses, then she wins with the other, and she gives me ten out of hers. That way, each of us knows 'e'll have a bit to go on with, come what may, eh?"

I was beginning to understand and said nothing, wondering what his next move would be. "Look here," he said, "they'll be putting the numbers up any second, and I don't mind admitting I *need* to hedge out. Suppose I lay two-to-one? Twenty for you if my horse gets it; ten for me if it don't." Lisa, I noticed with pleasure, was digging into her purse for money.

"No." I pulled Lisa's hand away from her purse and held it, gently but firmly.

"I'll give you the dead heat!" The man was almost pleading now. "Twenty-to-ten, and you get the draw. What could be fairer? Come on. Have a go."

"No hard feelings," I said, in a tone that indicated there might be a few. "But I've been to the track before." I grabbed

Lisa's arm and propelled her up the aisle before the man could reply.

"That was a good bet," she complained as we reached the flat area behind the tables. "Who gave you . . ."

She stopped short as the sudden hush around us told us that the "photo" sign was down and the numbers were going up. Then a shout of "Ten!" told us which order they went up in. I said nothing.

"He couldn't have known," Lisa said. "Not standing where he was."

"Where do we go to get seats?" I asked, lengthening my moment of triumph.

"Here." Lisa led me along the back of the restaurant and under the stands. "You couldn't call it either? Could you?"

I admitted neither Fat Stuff nor I could have known anything more about that finish than that it involved the Four and the Ten. "We had the same view of the finish. As if they were coming straight at us."

"Well, then."

"But Fat Stuff didn't look at the finish," I said, trying not to sound triumphant. "He looked at his partner on the finish line. The partner knew. And flashed it. Maybe one hand for the inside, the other hand for outside, leaving two hands for a three-horse finish that goes to the one in the middle. An old hustle. Maybe as old as racing."

Lisa had her eyes on my mouth, as if this explanation of a minor racetrack racket was of vital importance to her, as if I were the only man who could unravel this bit of mystery. I decided she had probably looked at many men this way, but not many lately; there seemed too few gaps in her knowledge of racing remaining to be filled in. "It's a public service, really," I explained. "A track special might catch you in the act; but the customers never complain."

"I see." Lisa nodded. "They want to lose."

"Exactly. Suppose he'd been right, about your having a bet on the outside horse? In effect, he gives you a bet on the inside horse. Now you can't lose. Either you cash your ticket, or you beat Fat Stuff out of a small side bet."

"But—"

"But unless the man on the finish line makes a mistake, forget about the 'or.' And he never makes mistakes. If he isn't sure, he doesn't flash a signal. Fats is selling peace of mind, but only to people who don't need it. By the end of the day, he's won every bet he's made and made a friend each time."

Lisa smiled. She was storing away what she had just learned against a day when it might possibly be useful. We had arrived at the foot of a stairway leading up toward the rear of the stand. Two young Mexicans in gaudy uniforms stood guard under a sign that read: TURF CLUB—MEMBERS ONLY.

"The one on the far side," she whispered, "is named José."

I put a five-dollar bill between my fingertips and approached José. "José," I said, "you won't believe this, but I've forgotten my tickets again."

José harvested my offering. "Perhaps you will not believe me, *señor*," he said, "but there are no tickets. Just a plastic membership card." He drew the velvet rope aside. "There are others in your party?" he asked, as Lisa and I went through.

"Maybe." Lisa spoke before I could reply. "They might meet us downstairs later on."

"Five dollars is enough to admit a regiment," she explained, as we went up the stairs and into the entryway to the Turf Club. "Who knows? We might meet somebody."

The tables in the Turf Club were more steeply banked than those in the clubhouse. Even from where we stood, next to the maître d'hôtel's stand, I could see that the first row of tables would provide a better view of the racing than I had ever enjoyed. But they, like all the vacant tables, bore small RE-

SERVED signs. The maître d'hôtel was consulting a seating diagram while he talked with a customer. "His name is Don," Lisa prompted in an undertone. "His cousin Louis works at Perino's in L.A."

I watched while Don shrugged and snapped his fingers for an underling who led the customer and his girl to a table in the rear rank. "Reservation, sir?" Don asked.

"Your cousin Louis said you'd take good care of us," I said. "How about something down front?"

"I'm sorry, *señor*," Don said. "But those are all tables for four."

"We're expecting friends." I dropped my hand into my pants pocket and left it there. Don thought the matter through. A waiter joined the group. "Table four," Don said, at last. "A very nice front-row table."

Figuring that if five dollars was an excessive bribe it would be an outrageous tip, I passed three ones to Don and was thanked so effusively I regretted at least one of the three. "Take good care of the Señor," Don told the waiter. "He is a friend of Louis."

The table was an excellent one, next to the glass panel which could be opened, giving us an entirely unobstructed view of the track some seventy feet below. Although, being squarely above the clubhouse, the Turf Club was also beyond the finish line, the added height would make it possible to call any but the closest finishes. The horses for the third race were in the paddock fronting the track. The tote board indicated 28 minutes to post time; the morning line offered 10–1 against Pizza Pallor, but with $400 in the win pool, $52 was in the #8 slot on the money board. Allowing for a 22 percent takeout, he was then not much more than 5–1.

"That's not just twenty-six hunches at two dollars a hunch," Lisa pointed out. "Look at the show pool." Fifty dollars had already been bet on Pizza Pallor to show, more than half the pool.

The board blinked. Post time was now twenty-seven minutes away. There was nearly a hundred dollars on Pizza Pallor, but the win pool had gone past eleven hundred, and, as the actual current odds replaced the morning line, Pizza Pallor was eight-to-one.

I handed Lisa the smaller of the two pair of binoculars and aimed mine at the paddock. Pizza Pallor, a big black colt with a touch of silver-gray along his flanks, was being led around the ring by an attendant. He walked briskly, with his head held high.

"Four legs and a tail." Lisa's words expressed, as they often did that afternoon, my thought. I turned toward her. "What else can you tell by looking?" she asked.

"You can see if he's walking on three legs."

"So can the track vet."

She was right, of course. If a horse is so lame that his infirmity is apparent to the spectators, he will not be allowed to run. "You can see if he's sweating," I argued.

"And if he is?"

"Then he's nervous."

"And can't win?"

I was not going to fall into that trap. Most horses do not sweat when they are feeling right. Most. Not all. "You could record how each horse looked in the paddock and then how he ran," I said. "I knew a fellow that did that."

"Did he win?"

"Sometimes."

"So do I." Lisa began to study her *Form*.

I glanced at the board again. Pizza Pallor was down to 7–1. The 9–5 favorite was something named Royal Zoo, Post One according to the program, a quitter according to the *Form*. He had been second his last out, having blown a clear lead in the stretch after galloping a slow half-mile on the head end. Still, I reminded myself, this was a race for maiden two-year-olds and we were well along in the season.

"Wait for one more change," Lisa suggested. I checked out Pizza Pallor's trainer and jockey in the standings in the back of the program. The ten leaders in each category were listed; Pizza Pallor's trainer's name did not appear. R. Chavez was indeed to ride Pizza Pallor; one of his other mounts had been scratched; the third had found another rider, waiving the apprentice allowance in the process. Chavez, who was entitled to the five pounds, had had 140 mounts at the meeting, of which 31 had won. He had also, I discovered by turning the program back to the second race, been on the favorite in that event. I reran the race in my mind, saw the favorite far in front down the backstretch, saw him hang inside the quarter pole and die in the stretch, and wondered if he could have been better ridden. A check of the past performances indicated he could not. The horse was a one-run sprinter, the kind that has to be hustled into the lead and pressed to keep going. So far, with or without Chavez's services, he had not kept going far enough; but in the three times Chavez had ridden him, he had succeeded in getting the lead. Other riders had not done even this well.

The board blinked again. The favorite was 8–5; Pizza Pallor held at seven. Lisa reached across the table and put her finger on Pizza Pallor's name in my program. "I think so."

I nodded. The horse, away for a long time, was obviously receiving some support from his connection; with a rider of at least moderate competence, against horses necessarily cheaper than those he had opposed the winter before in Florida, Pizza Pallor was obviously worth a bet. "Five hundred?" I suggested.

Lisa laughed. "You'd start a panic," she said. "Bet that kind of money, and when the crowd gets through, you'll be laying the odds. Here." She handed me a bill. "I put up fifty. You put up two-fifty. Bet it in a little at a time. When the price starts down, stop. However much you get down, I've got one-sixth of it."

"All right."

I went back up between the tables, past Don's station, and looked at the bank of sellers' windows. There weren't many of them; and there were no lines at any. But this group of windows served only the Turf Club where admission was, nominally at least, restricted to members. And there were still fifteen minutes to post time. Probably there were lines at the windows below, in the clubhouse and grandstand areas; presumably there would be lines here later on.

At the ten-dollar-win window, I asked for the Eight, five times. The clerk's eyebrows went up in surprise. Mine did not, but I was surprised too. A fifty-dollar bet at a ten-dollar window should be as common as a ten-dollar bet at a two-dollar window. I moved back to the edge of the betting area and looked at the board. Pizza Pallor was 6–1. A full minute later, the money changes flashed; a new line went up—7–1. I doubled the dose, this time taking my trade to the five-dollar window, buying twenty tickets. This time the odds went to 6–1 and did not bounce back. Two flashes later, Pizza Pallor was still 6–1. With eight minutes to post, the tempo of the betting had increased. I decided the machine could digest another hundred without developing the sort of gastritis Lisa feared and, ignoring her advice, bought two fifty-dollar tickets this time. The man ahead of me in line gave me great pleasure by buying four tickets on the One.

With four minutes remaining, Pizza Pallor was still 6–1. Then the six blinked to five, but, figuring quickly from the money line that it was a long five, nearly 11–2, I bet the last fifty and went back to the table.

"Two minutes to post," the announcer said. "Two minutes." The horses were in the backstretch, walking away from the gate. I told Lisa I had got the entire $300 down and was about to point out that, even at a flat 5–1, this would mean a $1,500 profit—$1,250 for me, $250 for her—when the money line changed. Seven hundred had been bet on Pizza Pallor in the previous minute. Before I could determine whether this was proportionately more than had gone on the others, the odds-line indicated that it was. Pizza Pallor shortened to 4–1, and a murmur from the crowd indicated that many people had noticed, as I did, that the price had skipped past 9–2.

The 4–1 became 7–2, then 3–1. It was a minute past post time, but the betting continued. "It stops when they're off," Lisa said. "They try not to shut anybody out."

"All in the gate," the announcer said. The last three horses were led in. I put my glasses on the starting gate as the backup doors were closed and the flag went up.

"Five to two," Lisa said sadly. "The favorite's gone out to two. One more flash—" The flag dropped, and the doors opened, and I could not hear Lisa, could not hear anything but the clanging of the alarm bell as the mutuels were locked and the yelling of the crowd as the field skittered along the backstretch.

Royal Zoo, easily discernible in scarlet silks, came out fastest, opened a length in the first hundred yards, and continued to draw clear as the field headed for the turn. I could not see Pizza Pallor and suspected he had been left at the gate. Then I picked him up on the outside of a group of four, running strongly, three lengths back of the favorite. The field swung into the turn. At the table an old man began to croak, almost prayerfully, "Royal Zoo, Royal Zoo, Zoo-Zoo-Zoo."

"Here we go," Lisa said.

Pizza Pallor had detached himself from the second group and set out after Royal Zoo. Midway round the turn, passing the black-and-white quarter pole, Royal Zoo led by only a length, a half length, a neck, until, as they started to straighten away, heading for an instant straight into my glasses, they seemed side by side, and the gray along Pizza Pallor's neck seemed forward of Royal Zoo's neck. In the stretch, with three hundred yards to go, I could see they were neck and neck, running like a single eight-legged horse.

"Get into him, Chavez," I said, not shouting, because it was unreasonable to think the boy could hear me, speaking only because keeping quiet was impossible. "Zoo-Zoo-Zoo," the old man croaked. "The five pounds should help," Lisa said.

Passing the eighth pole, either the five pounds helped, or the fact that Royal Zoo was in slightly deeper going along the rail helped, or some inherent superiority in Pizza Pallor's musculature helped. Pizza Pallor took a slight lead, a neck, then half a length.

A sixteenth out, Royal Zoo was beaten, but the long brush had, as I feared, taken a lot from Pizza Pallor. Past Royal Zoo, on the outside, a huge fresh animal charged up, his green-jacketed rider whipping hard as his horse closed in on Pizza Pallor. "Hand ride, hand ride," I mumbled, hoping that Chavez had somehow acquired the experience that would tell him his horse was doing his best, that a crack with the stick could not produce more speed but would cause the horse to swerve or to break stride. The green jacket was at Pizza Pallor's rump, then his flank. The finish post loomed up in my glasses and was passed, with Pizza Pallor, his head down, in front—so it seemed—until a stride past the finish.

"Got it," I said. "By George, he's got it."

A man standing behind me said clearly, to no one in particular, "Eight, I think. I'll bet the Eight. Who wants to hedge out?"

The voice was a familiar one. I turned. The man had his back to me. He was walking to a woman in the second row of tables. "You got the Eight, lady? Bet the outside horse with me, and neither one of us can lose." Recognizing him, I stood up and shouted over his shoulder: "I'll lay three-to-one the Eight got it."

The woman shrugged and returned to reading a tip sheet. "What are you, some kind of wise guy?" Until he whirled around me, I had a moment's doubt. Then, seeing his face, I knew this was indeed Andy Livoti, somewhat the worse for wear, but Andy, nevertheless. He recognized me an instant later, and stopped his tirade at "You—"

Then we were pounding each other's arms and shouting each other's names. "I figured you were still on the Ohio wheel, claiming horses. How come you're down here?"

"Just lucky, I guess."

Something in Andy's expression made me sorry I had asked. "Sit down." I gestured toward a vacant seat at the table. He hesitated and began looking at the people at nearby tables. "Forget it," I told him. "Nobody's going to bet against the Eight up here."

"That was a close finish," he argued.

"But it didn't look close."

"That's because we're way past the finish line."

"You're right," I admitted. "But the people up here come in two kinds. Too stupid to know that; or too smart to bet with you."

"I guess so." Andy was still standing next to the table. He shaded his eyes and looked down and to the left, toward the grandstand. "My guy makes it the Eight by a half length," he said.

"A fat Englishman?" Lisa asked.

Andy was obviously stopped cold by the question. "We met him," Lisa explained, before he could speak.

Andy grinned and shook Lisa's outstretched hand. "I'm Andy

Livoti," he said. "Don't I know you from somewhere?" From his quick glance at me, I knew he too had been momentarily struck by the not-quite-physical resemblance to Melanie Sutton.

"No, you don't," I said. "This lady's name is Lisa Fortune." Andy sat down. "You remind him," I told Lisa, "of someone we knew back in Ohio. Right?" The "Right?" was for Andy.

"Right."

"Should I be pleased?" Lisa asked.

We both nodded. Andy picked up the stack of mutuel tickets from under the ashtray and riffled through them. "You folks are doing all right," he remarked. The tote board flashed the official and the payoffs. The Eight was $7 straight. "A thousand-fifty."

"He was seven-to-one when we started to bet him," I said. "If the price held up, those tickets would be worth $2,400."

"And if Royal Zoo had brushed with him two more strides, they'd be wastepaper," Lisa said.

Andy told us he shared both our joy and our sorrow, and showed me a five-dollar win ticket on the horse. "That one shrunk from $40 to $17.50."

"If we'd known the closing price, we wouldn't have bet the horse at all," Lisa put in happily. "Look at it this way: we're stuck with the money."

I asked Andy if the horse had been a tip.

Andy was indignant. "I got him the same way you did. The layoff; the big drop in class; the fair works; the hot rider; the price, the way it was."

I asked why, given such powerful arguments, Andy had made only a five-dollar bet.

"You taught me yourself," Andy said, not quite defensively, "to stay away from maiden races. 'If a horse is worth a bet,' you used to say, 'he's won a race *some* time, *some* where.'" I was beginning to get the idea. There was in Andy's eyes, I suddenly realized, the same casual acceptance of inevitable defeat that, I suddenly realized, I had seen in my own eyes, in my mirror, the morning before. "I'm lying to you," Andy blurted out. "Five at a time is a big bet for me. Mostly I bet a dollar."

I started to say I didn't know the track accepted dollar bets. "They book it," Lisa said. "They pay the tote price. That's all that's left of their handbook. And you'd be surprised how much business they do. Right here in the Turf Club, for instance."

She was, of course, trying to turn the conversation away from Andy Livoti's poverty. But Andy wouldn't cooperate. "I was around Ohio a few years after you left," he went on. "Win a few, lose a few, you know how it is. I had the favorite for the Ohio Derby one year. $15,000 that would have been. But he blew a fuse getting the lead a hundred yards out. Finished fourth on three legs. $1,500, but they had to destroy the horse."

"Insured?"

Andy ignored the question, which was answer enough. I knew that he was only partly with us, that the rest of him was at Thistle Downs, watching his three-year-old rush to the leader, rush past him, then bobble and falter. "After that," he went on, finally, "everything seemed to turn salty. A two-year-old I was high on got to coughing and I never did get him back to the races. That was at Cahokia. I had two platers ready to win at Fort Miami, but there was an epidemic of coughing sickness, and they closed the track and quarantined the stable area, and I couldn't get my horses out. The feed man was going to take them on a lien. So I took Chrome Apple—you remember Chrome Apple?" I nodded; I remembered Chrome Apple better than I remembered Pizza Pallor on whom I still held three hundred dollars' worth of uncashed tickets. "I had her at Ak-Sar-Ben and dropped her into a fifteen-hundred-dollar claimer."

I could see what was coming. "Pretty cheap for that mare," I said.

"Damn cheap. But I needed the purse to stand off the feed man. Anyhow, would you have claimed her at that price?"

I shook my head. A horse entered at a claiming price far below its apparent value is considered a dangerous claim. The theory is that its owner is trying to lose it, which raises the presumption that the horse is unfit.

"Of course not," Andy went on. "Only a sucker'd claim a $4,500 horse entered for $1,500. A sucker. Or a wise guy who knew the owner was desperate for a purse, any purse. So the feed man claimed him."

"The son of a bitch." It was all that could be said, and Lisa and I said it simultaneously. The claim was a plain violation of the unwritten, unenforceable, but almost universally respected rule of ethics dealing with claiming races.

"I took a swing at the bastard right in the unsaddling enclosure when the horses came back," Andy went on. "The stewards clipped me for a hundred for it, but it was worth it. The purse and the claim money squared off the feed bill, but by the time the quarantine was lifted, my two platers had the coughing sickness and died of it. I lost my last horse in a stable fire at Centennial Park. Near Denver. It figured. Did you know they have stone stables here?" Andy's recital of woe was causing him to lose contact, to drift into a sort of pointless reverie. "All kinds of things can happen here, but not that. No stable fire."

"What did you do after the fire?" I was trying to get Andy back to the present, back to reality.

"What didn't I do?" His eyes brightened. "I set up as a public trainer, but nobody'd give me a horse. Then I hired on as a stable hand, walking hots, mucking stalls. I guess I cleaned stalls in ten states. Let me tell you, horseshit smells the same all over. I beg your pardon, lady."

Lisa admitted she had heard worse. "After Denver . . ." I prompted.

"I'm telling you. I even turned exercise boy for a while. Me. Forty-five years old. Up at five, pushing lousy horses around beatup tracks for a fiver a trip, sometimes only a deuce. Not bad work, really, but tough on the kidneys. Like whoring, in a way."

"That's tough on the kidneys?" Lisa asked. "I hadn't heard that."

"No. I meant the other. If you can't get five, take two. You get it?" Lisa nodded. "Salty? I scrunched up a hundred once and got into a poker game with a real fish. May I drop dead if I didn't trap him into staying with a pair of deuces against my three queens, and I fill and come out betting, only he catches the other two deuces on the draw. Well, I figured it couldn't run that way forever, and it didn't. Last year, out at Raton, I ran into a dame from the old days. Martha Dickens. You didn't know her, Lew. Used to run horses in Maryland mostly. Anyhow, she was on the skids, like me, only not as far down the chute. She wasn't going to last long, hooked up with some phony cowpoke trainer that pitched her horses too high and gave her a story after every race. 'Shucks, ma'am, the ground broke from under the critter's feet.' 'Crazy dude couldn't rate him.' You know the type. She was about ready to split with Joe Cactus. I guess I helped things along, telling her he was robbing her blind, that she didn't have a horse that could win at that track, especially with that butcher training for her. So she ditched him, and gave me the horses."

"And a problem," I said. "If they were over their heads at Raton . . ."

Andy smiled. "I remembered you used to agree with that New York trainer—what's his name, the pigeon man—that said for every horse there is a race somewhere. So I talked her into shipping down here. Not that the horses here are so bad. They just don't have any really good ones. You can get a $1,250 claimer into a race every week. They pay purse money all the way back to sixth. First two months we were here, I got a piece of five purses for her, won three of them, bought me a horse of my own, nice little four-year-old, not about to go a distance, but nice."

"Along toward morning . . ." Lisa said.

Andy stared at her. "You're right. Along toward morning, the farmer got lucky." He stopped and cleared his throat. "You ready for the finish?" he asked.

I realized we still had the saddest part of the story to hear. "You're not going to believe this," Andy said, when his question went unanswered. "Remember about the fireproof stables. Like I said, they're stone. But the motels around here are made of wood. A month ago one of them—the Sunshine Rancho in San Ysidro—burned to the ground. Martha Dickens was asleep in her room." He spread his hands in an umpire's "safe" gesture. "That was that. Lawyer came down from L.A. to represent the estate. Paid me off for the odd half-week—Martha died on a Wednesday—and had her horses auctioned off."

"And your horse?"

"His name's Jesse's Hand. I want you to see him." Andy started to get up. I pretended to develop a sudden interest in the program. "There's an hour before the afternoon program starts," Andy argued. "And you don't want to see the first race. Whoever said 'there's a winner in every race' never looked at that field."

I looked toward Lisa, leaving the decision to her.

"I take it," she said, smiling, "that we're not just going to have a look at the brute's conformation. I've seen horses. But I have the impression there's what you might call an angle involved."

"What you might call a hell of an angle," Andy Livoti declared.

7

It was a hell of a *complicated* angle, I decided, fifteen minutes later, as I sat beside Lisa on the edge of a tack-trunk, our backs against a stable wall (stone; Andy was right) our feet stuck out in front of us. There was the horse, Jesse's Hand, roughly made, not thoroughly filled out, without a touch of class in his looks, the sort of horse racetrack people call a tool, meaning that he is consistent ("honest" is the anthropomorphic term more often used) and will always do his best unless he is sick. There was also a girl named Billie, who looked about fourteen when she appeared in tight blue jeans and a man's shirt to lead Jesse's Hand out of his stall, and turn him around for our inspection, and lead him back in. But I could see she was much older when she returned without the horse, and more conventionally dressed (culottes and cardigan) to participate in the conference that followed. It did not need to be said that Billie was Andy Livoti's girl.

She apparently had no last name. As if to make up for that deficiency, Fat Stuff, who was waiting for us when we reached the barn, turned out to have three—John Barrie Barnes. And he used them all in introducing himself. He was English and had trained there as well as in France and Italy. Somehow I got the impression that he was no longer licensed to train on the Continent or in the United States. He was, it appeared, an equal partner with Andy in their "bet-the-photo-finish" operation, and a minority stockholder in Jesse's Hand.

"I couldn't say which part of him's mine," he admitted. "But he's four-fifth's Eyetalian and the remainder British." He looked to Andy who nodded. "Well, Mr. White," John Barrie Barnes went on, "do you know what's meant by 'trying a horse'?"

"Working him?" I should have known, but I didn't. Failing that, I should not have guessed, but I did. It was obviously the wrong answer.

"Care to have a go?" he asked Lisa.

"I'd rather hear you explain it," she replied.

"Right-o." Barnes stepped to the center of our little group and assumed a professorial manner. "Now the United States is the only country in the world that times workouts. You can blow a horse out, three eighths in 35, say; and you've proved he's not deathly ill. You can test him three quarters in 1:12; you've proved he has some speed. But neither tells you what you really want to know; and, in both cases, whatever you do know, the world knows too; for there are always clockers hanging about that earn their keep because they can tell one horse from another, and whatever shows on your watch probably shows on theirs, and if there's a difference, you're probably wrong, because timing is their business, not yours, am I right?"

The last words were just punctuation, not a question to be answered; he knew he was right. "I don't object to your system as a method of *conditioning* horses, though I think your stock would show more stamina if you galloped them a few miles a day as we do abroad. But as a source of exclusive information about your own horse, it's a total bust. Anyone with the price of a *Racing Form* knows as much about the horse as his trainer. Now *we* never work a horse a set distance on a racecourse. We gallop them for condition, and we *try* them, one against another, to find out how good they are. Say you've got a stakes horse, a proven quantity in your string. And another that you picked up somewhere. No form at all, or form you can't trust. Understand?" This time he didn't even give me time to nod. "What could be simpler than to take them both—the known quantity and the unknown—out on the moors and run them, horse to horse, over a distance of ground until you *see* how they compare? I ask you."

This time he paused as if inviting a reply. I obliged. "It works if your unknown is a stakes horse. Otherwise, all you'll find out is that stakes horses beat platers. To get a line on your whole stable, you'd need as many trial horses—"

"You need one," John Barrie Barnes snapped. "If you've got one, you've got an infinite number. Follow?"

"No."

"Weight, sir. If I use my handicap horse to measure my plater, I put plenty of lead in the good one's saddlebag. A little experimenting—different weights, different distances—and I get answers. *This* one is so-and-so-many pounds better than *that* one. And I can compare a third horse with the second, without ever running them against each other, on the basis of how each compared with the first."

He had me. "Still," I argued, trying to save a little face, "what you see, other people can see."

"No."

"Do you close the track to outsiders while your experiments are in progress?"

"Wait a minute," Lisa said. "This is interesting."

"Thank you." Barnes made a small bow in Lisa's direction. "Like many of your countrymen, sir," he said, making a small insult out of "sir," "you have reached maturity without coming to know that you can't learn anything by talking." He widened his discourse to include the others. "We're not interested in time, so we don't need a measured piece of ground; we don't need to use the racecourse. We can run trials in private. And even if someone should see a trial being run, what would he have to show for his spying? He'd have seen X and Y run together for a while; he'd have seen one draw off from the other. But he wouldn't know the weights. Don't you see? For all he knew, the winner might be getting a stone, or giving a stone, or running level. You," he challenged, "were saying?"

"I was wrong." I should have let it drop. "If everything you say is true," I asked, "why isn't your method used all over the country?"

"For the same reason you people race your horses on dirt, which breaks down their feet, instead of grass, which doesn't; and on flat tracks without hills to test their stamina; and mostly dashes, a mile or less, so your stock has to be constantly replenished with foreign studs and mares or you'd be breeding individuals too fainthearted to race at all. For the same reason you race two-year-olds for purses in January, and you positively *demand* that your trainers break down their best prospects by putting up purses he daren't pass up for horses in their third summer, which is to say horses whose bones are just beginning to set. For the same reason you won't let men gamble against men but insist that men gamble only against a machine."

I could only lob the ball back for the kill. "Which is?"

John Barrie Barnes put the ball away. "You're a backward nation."

I knew it was an effort for Andy, Lisa, and Billie to refrain from laughing, and I was grateful to each of them for making it. John Barrie Barnes handed me a *Form,* folded to show the past performances for the third race. "Last Saturday's," he said. "You'll find Jesse's Hand down among the also-eligibles. As it turned out, he didn't get in."

I read quickly through Jesse's Hand's history. His sire was Aces Paired, whom I remembered for an undistinguished record both on the track and as a sire. Jesse's Hand's name derived from that of his sire. Jesse James, when gunned down, had, according to legend, been holding aces and eights.

The form told me little. Four years old, Jesse's Hand had been unraced since his three-year-old year. At three, he had run eight times, four times at Portland Meadows, Oregon, where he had won twice, breaking his maiden in his second out at 4–1, later winning again at Longacres, where he had been twice second, then once third, and finally, in his eighth and last effort as a three-year-old, failing to finish. ("Pulled up," the past performance line read.) His workout line had a single entry: "Aug 24 AC fst 3f 37b" meaning that, more than a week before, at Caliente, over a fast track, he had breezed three eighths in 37 seconds, a meaningless bit of data since any thoroughbred on the grounds could have duplicated it, even one that was, as Jesse's Hand's record implied he *had* been, lame. I started to hand the *Form* to Lisa when I saw that Barnes had already provided her with one.

"If you're wondering who killed Jesse James," Lisa said, "it was the dirty little coward who shot Mr. Howard. In the movie, it was an ugly little man with a moustache who kept offering people 'cigareets.' "

"His name was Ford," Billie said. Except for whatever she had said when we were introduced, it was the first time I had heard her speak. Andy Livoti kissed her happily. Jesse's Hand, inside his stall, nickered and kicked the bangboard. Far off, recorded bugle notes summoned the horses for the first race of the afternoon program. It was a good and pleasant moment.

"If you're all done." John Barrie Barnes waited for the laughter to subside. "He went lame a year ago, as you might suppose from his record. His legs have been fired, but that didn't do him any good. Man that owned him in the States couldn't give him away, so he used him for a stable pony. How he got down here I don't know or care. Fact is, here he was, sound of wind, nice head, as you saw, but what he couldn't do was race. I suppose you've heard of aqua-therapy?"

"I've read about it," I said. "Running them in the surf. There's a fellow does it up around La Jolla."

"And another in Mexico. Your servant, John Barrie Barnes, E-S-Q. Well sir, chap that owned this horse had another that wasn't quite sound. Flaky hoofs, tendons that went into spasms, and he knew I did this work. So he asked me to take his horse—the other one, mind you, not Jesse's Hand—to my place, little beach near Rosarito, and see what a little sea-bathing might do. A hundred fifty for the week, says I, feed and transportation to and from the Cove included. Done, says he, but I must take the stable pony along, Jesse's Hand, because the other one's nervous and more than likely'll sulk without the pony. Righto, I say, and I did it. Took his horse—name of Bailey Bridge—and the pony down to the Cove and left them there for a week with Diego, my spick assistant, very reliable fellow, he under orders to see Bailey Bridge got his fill of swimming and splashing about in the surf."

A klaxon sounded in the stable area. This, I figured, was to warn stable employees with an interest in the first race that the start was at hand. "Anyone for the race?" Barnes asked. No one moved. "Congratulations. There's twelve of 'em in it. If I was making the book, they'd be nine-to-one each, a hundred-to-forty any three, and, with any luck, no payout afterwards. You can probably guess what Diego told me when I went back at the end of the week to get the horses. And I'd've told the owner, but I hadn't been paid, and I gave myself marks for decency just for giving him back his horses. Two weeks later, I still haven't seen a copper, and Mr. Owner isn't being half evasive about when our transaction might be liquidated, and Bailey Bridge goes into a $2,500 claiming race, and wasn't there a lovely row when your obedient servant shows up with a halter and blanket, having claimed the winner, who went in 1:51 with his ears pricked back, all but running out from under the boy, the last eighth in 12 seconds flat. I can't do this to him, and I'm an unethical this and a dishonest that, using a personal relationship to pay $2,500 for a horse I knew to be worth more. $2,350, I said, for I'd had the foresight to file my bill for the week at the seashore with the racing secretary. When I said this, it touched off a hue and cry that made the other seem tame. It turned out he wasn't the real owner, just the nominee, and he hadn't bothered telling his principal that Bailey Bridge'd been swimming, and with the brute paying 10–1, his principal might get the idea something was being put over on him, which it was, of course, my man having got down for a hundred with a bookmaker, but the thousand wasn't his either because he was in the back of that fellow's own book for five times that. In short, he stood a chance of being knocked about and maybe even killed—though frankly I thought that last a bit much. So, not wishing to cause suffering to my fellow man, I told the racing secretary I'd made a mistake: the bill had been paid; but I got a little something in return."

Far away, the starting bell rang and the crowd began to rumble. "Jesse's Hand," I said.

"Not quite. I told him I'd need the pony for a day or two to keep Bailey Bridge calm until he got used to his new barn, and maybe I'd want to buy him outright, so I wanted a free option at five hundred dollars. He agreed; what choice did he have? The next morning, before it was quite light, I took an exercise boy name of Esteban, good rider, but not bright enough to understand what he might see, and that's the most reliable kind, believe me, and the two horses, Bailey Bridge and Jesse's Hand. We trotted them down the dirt road out back of the track to the Wash, which is a great sandy place that's part of a river for three days in the spring and bone dry the rest of the year. We went down that wash a couple of thousand yards and raced back. The horses were cooled off and back in the barn by six that morning. I doubt we or they were missed. It didn't matter. You could have full-color movies of the run through the Wash, but you couldn't make anything of it. I rode Jesse's Hand, you see, and I weigh eleven stone, one fifty-four, you barbarians say, stripped; and I was far from stripped; and Esteban, dripping wet, wouldn't go nine stone with saddle and tack, so Bailey Bridge was getting thirty pounds, not to mention that Esteban has the seat and hands and I don't. Esteban made the running, by about three lengths, all the way. And Jesse's Hand hung on, just breezing, mind you. Twice I asked him for something, and both times he moved toward the other, and both times I took back, and it wasn't easy. I had the feeling I could have taken him, weight, better rider, and all, but of course I can't be sure, can I? But I can be sure of this: Jesse's Hand can give Bailey Bridge thirty pounds, and run a distance of ground with him, and come back bone-dry and with a breath that wouldn't blow out a candle. And Bailey Bridge, you'll remember, had just won against a pretty fair lot, in good time, like breaking sticks. Now, sir, if you're me, what's your next move?"

He fell silent. I knew this question was not rhetorical. "Buy Jesse's Hand, and find him a race." It was an obvious answer. I had the feeling it was not quite the right answer.

Barnes frowned. "What sort of race?"

"Allowance race. Non-winners of two this year."

"Half marks for that," John Barrie Barnes intoned. "It accepts that we know Jesse's Hand's a good one; but it makes no allowance for our not knowing whether he's a very good one. Granted his breeding's not much, but his second sire was Case Ace. You've heard the name."

I had heard the name. Case Ace had sired Alsab; Alsab, once a plater, had improved at three and eventually won nearly a million. Barnes explained all that as I recalled it. "It might be," he said, "that this distant cousin, though of less than full blood, has some of what made Alsab what he was. In which case, taking a fair price and picking up a small purse against moderate opposition—and believe me, they've nothing better than that down here—that would be a waste, well, wouldn't it?"

I agreed that it would.

"Furthermore, it turned out that your friend here—curse his sharp dark Latin eyes—" (Barnes clouted Andy good-naturedly on the arm) "had once had the notion that this stable pony might amount to something, had owned him briefly, in fact, until circumstances dictated otherwise; and, as luck would have it, he'd been down near the paddock where he'd overheard some of the discussion relative to my taking title to Bailey Bridge from the man who, at that moment, also owned Jesse's Hand. Well, something in his Mediterranean soul was stirred, some bit of that suspicious curiosity that made Rome great. He asked himself what could have been unethical about that claim, and what the hundred and fifty had been about. And the more he asked himself these questions, the more he did not get any answers. And, being a straightforward lad, more Nero than Borgia you might say, didn't he come to me straightaway and ask me. And what did I do, Andy?"

"You told me."

"I bloody well did. Better to have you know than asking questions, arousing wonder and puzzlement which are the sire and dam of rumor. Rumor was what I wanted none of. To prevent it, I let my option drop on Jesse's Hand, who was still just a stable pony, mind. A week later, Andy went round and bought him of his owner, who was ready to sell anything he had, no questions, never mind the price, which, in this case, was one hundred dollars cash, plus the cancellation of a small poker debt—"

"Seven hundred dollars," Andy corrected.

"Multiplied by your chance of collecting it, it was a small debt," Barnes argued. "I left the horse in Andy's name," he went on, "but I'm supposed to get twenty percent of any purse money. Frankly, purse money has never interested me. I sent Esteban to Andy with orders to work the horse the slowest three eighths of all time, which he wasn't quite able to do, that being more a reflection of the horse's strength than the lad's skill. Andy entered him last Saturday; fortunately, he didn't draw into the race. If he had, we'd've scratched out. Yesterday morning, I called a friend up at Del Mar, and he entered the horse in tomorrow's seventh race there, the secondary feature, a mile and a sixteenth, seventy-five hundred dollar, three-year-olds 110, four-year-olds 116; we're bottom weight of the older horses, tied for low weight in the field. This morning, we had our two horses out on the Wash again, Livoti on Jesse's Hand, Esteban on Bailey Bridge, even start, level weights."

"He never seen which way I went," Andy declared proudly.

"I saw it," Billie said. "It looked like Bailey Bridge was tied to a plow."

"Maybe he's lost his edge," Lisa suggested.

"He was moving right along." This from Andy Livoti.

"You can't tell by looking at a horse if he's going a mile in 1:40 or 1:50. And," I added, icily, to John Barrie Barnes, "of course you couldn't get a time for the work."

"Not work." He matched my tone. "Trial. Fortunately, however, we will be able to get an objective measurement of Bailey Bridge's current condition this afternoon." While Barnes spoke, Livoti, like the vendor in a burlesque house passing out samples at the end of the talker's spiel, distributed programs to me and to Lisa. "Directing your attention to the eleventh race of the afternoon," Barnes proclaimed. "Have the kindness to note that Bailey Bridge will break from Post 11, with a good sprinter inside of him to guarantee him the worst of the start. The race is at a mile and seventy yards; he will doubtless have a rough trip all way round the bend. Observe also that this race is for $5,000 claimers, or twice the price for which I acquired Bailey Bridge, with weight off for non-winners and for horses entered for $4,500 or $4,000, and that Bailey Bridge, being a recent winner entered for the top price, is not eligible for either concession. And I have secured the services of one Lopez, who is perhaps the worst rider on the grounds, which is saying a great deal."

Barnes paused as if to let the full effect of his words sink in. "I believe Bailey Bridge will win; I will be surprised if he is not placed. I will not insult your intelligence by asking you what a good—or even a fair—race by this horse, under these conditions, would tell us about the one who ran away and hid from him at level weights. Instead of asking that question, I will answer the one I am sure is in your mind."

The question (why are we telling you all this?) and the answer (because we need some cash money to do what we have in mind) were both in my mind. I looked at Lisa, who nodded. "The moment of truth," she murmured.

"The moment of truth indeed," John Barrie Barnes declared in a truthful moment. "At this time, bad luck, which so often manifests itself at the precise instant of opportunity, has descended upon me and upon this friendly son of Italy. You know that his patroness was recently deceased under the most distressing circumstances. I can only tell you that fate has been equally unkind to me. The details do not matter. Suffice it to say that my horse van is presently in the hands of a Tijuana auto-repair shop as security for a $400 repair bill and that the management of this racecourse will not permit Jesse's Hand to depart until certain jockey fees, amounting to nearly $100, paid by the track on Signor Livoti's behalf, are repaid. We will also need, say, $50 to engage, at Del Mar, a jockey of somewhat greater skill than Mr. Lopez whose ineptitude renders him so marvelously fit for this afternoon's assignment. Another $100 for such items as gasoline, and incidentals, would make our total minimal requirement—front money, as you say—about $700. Against this total, Mr. Livoti and I have approximately $40. Mr. Livoti's notion that we might make up the difference by betting photo finishes has proved a failure. We both did a fine job of spotting, but neither of us apparently has the touch to induce trade among the punters. However, every cloud has a silver lining. It is our distress that creates your opportunity."

"You might get a purse with Bailey Bridge," I pointed out.

"Regrettably, there is a lien against it. A sordid matter involving a purse one of my owners claims I failed to remit to him." Barnes shook his head as if in sadness at such intransigence. "Two thousand dollars," he said at last. When he said nothing more, I began to understand that this was the sum he was asking me to put up.

"If you only need $700—"

"Please, sir." John Barrie Barnes obviously found this sort of haggling distasteful. "Seven hundred will only provide for our expenses. The winner's end of the Del Mar purse will be on the order of $5,000. My twenty percent would be only a thousand. I don't think it's unreasonable of me to expect more, especially since I propose that most of the excess be amassed from the Del Mar mutuels, where I expect to bet every dime I can lay hands on and advise you to do the same. Very well. Fifteen hundred."

Billie nudged Andy Livoti. "It's a good deal," he said. Obviously some, but not all, of this had been rehearsed.

"Are we supposed to decide *now?*" Lisa asked.

"Certainly not," Barnes snapped. "After the eleventh race." In the distance, the bugle sounded again. "Nine races and ten minutes from now. If Bailey Bridge shows us enough to make us want to do it, and if he shows you enough to make you want to back us, then you advance $1,500 to Mr. Livoti, to be repaid off the top of Jesse's Hand's purse at Del Mar tomorrow. What do you say, Mr. White?"

"It depends," I said.

"Of course it depends. It depends on Bailey Bridge."

"That's right," I said. "It depends on Bailey Bridge."

8

The field for the fourth race of the afternoon—the seventh of that day—was going to the post when Lisa, Billie, and I joined Andy Livoti and John Barrie Barnes at the table in the Turf Club. We five had left the stable area together an hour before; but we had split up when José turned Billie away from the velvet rope at the entrance to the Turf Club, refusing to regard the bright blue culottes she had put on in Jesse's Hand's stall as anything but slacks. He had yielded neither to Billie's promise to keep her knees under the table most of the time and close together when exposed to view, nor to my straightforward attempt at bribery. Lisa had suggested a tour of the track's souvenir stands to find one that sold serapes, and I had volunteered to accompany her and Billie in their quest for attire that would pass José's inspection.

Now, seeing the second and third race winners in Andy Livoti's program, I was pleased I had not been at the table for the previous hour. Both races had gone to short-priced favorites. I could say what horses I would have backed, had I backed any—Lisa and I had passed these races over in our preliminary sorting-out the night before—but I would never have bet form to stand up among horses of such poor quality,

176

and the $4,050 in my wallet—which included the $750 I had won on Pizza Pallor—would have been a smaller sum.

I put my glasses on the horses as they came out of the turn. "Anybody have any ideas?"

"Esteban's on the Three," Andy said. "You can't count the horse out, and I know the boy'll be trying."

I put the glasses down and glanced at the board, then at my program, then at my *Form*. Three was Dos Frijoles; the race was for $1,500 claimers at six furlongs. Dos Frijoles, a ten-year-old mare, was running her eleventh race in twelve weeks. In the preceding ten, she had demonstrated an ability to run creditably with $1,250 claimers and a total incapacity to keep up with those valued at $1,750. 10–1 seemed an attractive price against the proposition that she would find the $1,500 field more like the $1,250 ones than the $1,750 ones.

Seven minutes later, the field was in the gate; Dos Frijoles was 14–1; and my $20 ticket on her would be worth either $300 or nothing a minute and eleven seconds after the bell rang.

Lisa had declined any part of the bet. "I can only concentrate on one thing at a time," she explained. At that time, the one thing was the luncheon menu.

"I'll have a dollar's worth," Billie said, producing three quarters, two dimes, and five pennies from her purse and sliding them across the table to me, "if it's all right."

I stacked the coins to indicate it was. The bell rang and, at the top of the chute, the horses came out of the gate, one showing a little in advance of the others. "Dos Frijoles gets the lead" the announcer said, and I could see the number, and the green-and-white silks Esteban wore as the horse went down the backstretch a length in the lead. The half-mile pole flashed through my glasses; Esteban's arm rose and fell; he was keeping the horse clear so he could move toward the rail and save ground. But Dos Frijoles failed to respond, and a horse slipped up along the inside, cutting the lead to half a length. $4,030, I thought, ashamed of the sudden realization that I already figured that my bankroll would stand at $4,330 if Dos Frijoles won.

Dos Frijoles held the pole horse even around the turn; another joined them on the outside as they straightened away; the three were head and head at the eighth pole and beyond it, and I felt a quick surge of hope as, coming to the sixteenth pole, Esteban switched his whip to his left hand and the mare responded to the unfamiliar flailing on her left hip with an extra burst of speed. But, even as the horse along the rail, exhausted by the long drive, gave up the chase and fell back, the outside horse, still fresh, got his head in front, and still another horse, on the far outside, joined them, the newcomer strongest of all, moving quickly past the other two, then hanging, so that in the last hundred yards he remained just a half length in front, just out of reach of his two pursuers, shortening stride only as he hit the wire, going under it a long neck ahead of the horse in the middle, with Dos Frijoles another head back, third.

"The pace did him in," Lisa said quietly and accurately. The infield board showed very fast fractions; I reproached myself for not having even considered determining whether the pace would be too fast for Dos Frijoles, and told myself, in mitigation, that there wasn't time, which was an excuse, not an explanation, because it presupposed a time limit within which a bet had to be made and left out the qualifier "or not made at all." The fact that I had bet only twenty dollars—nineteen, subtracting Billie's share—cheered me up, but not much.

"Mexican plates all around," Lisa proposed. I agreed and began what I promised myself would be an exhaustive analysis of the fifth race, in which Lisa had, the night before, made a strong case for a sprinter, Miss Tut, despite Miss Tut's demonstrated tendency to quit in sprints, or, more exactly, because of that tendency. Quitters in sprints will frequently hang on at longer distances. They are not required to expend their energy in taking the lead from other sprinters, but are frequently allowed to go along in front on sufferance, which leaves them with enough strength to stand off the late closers at the end. I could find nothing in the *Form* to contravene Lisa's arguments.

A bus boy appeared at the table with a stack of yellow forms and put them on my service plate. "Five-and-ten slip," John Barrie Barnes explained, picking up the stack, giving one form to each of us, putting the others aside.

"A handicapping contest, isn't it?" I asked.

"Bloody damn lottery," Barnes replied. "You pick a horse in each race, Fifth through Tenth. Ticket or tickets with the most winners gets three-fourths of the pool. Ties for second split the other quarter. Lottery or not, it appeals to everybody. Limeys especially, because we're used to perms and bankers from the penny pools. Everybody because, if there are no ties for first, somebody wins about eighty thousand dollars for a two-dollar bet."

The "perms and bankers" method, it turned out, involved picking one horse in some of the races (bankers) and several each in the others (perms). If your bankers all won, and your perms stayed within the limits you had set for them—that is, if one of the horses you picked won in each race in which you had picked more than one—you had one all-correct line, a line being a series of selections running through all six races. The cost of the ticket, of course, would be the cost of the total number of lines it encompassed, times the $2-a-line that was the basic wager. The number of lines would be determined by multiplying the number of selections in the first race with the number in the second, multiplying that product by the number in the third, and so on until all six races had been figured in.

"And you don't," I guessed, "have to write every line on a separate ticket."

"Lord no," Barnes agreed. "Just write the numbers of the horses you want in each race. Do your multiplication, give the clerk your ticket and your money, and the track does the rest. It is my suggestion," he concluded, "that we perform this ritual as a sort of corporate entity."

"Everybody names a horse in a different race?"

"Not much action that way," he argued. "We'd have five bankers. However many horses we went for in the other race, we'd have just that many lines. I'd rather see if we can't get a consensus as to three bankers. Pick a few in the other three races. Figure the cost and divide it out as we wish, sharing the proceeds, if any, each member to receive a share equivalent to his share in the stake."

The horses for the fifth race were being led into the saddling area. The public address announcer promised they would be on the track in ten minutes.

"Liar," Billie muttered. "Dirty liar."

"He's only doing his job," I pointed out.

"That's the worst kind." The Mexican plates had arrived. Billie speared part of a tortilla and stuck it in her mouth. "Dirty hired liar," she gasped, reaching for a glass of water, draining it in a gulp. "Watch out for the tortilla," she warned.

Lisa laughed. "I endorse her suggestion," she said, "and those of the member from Epsom."

"Hear hear," Barnes sang out. "Hearing no objection, I call this meeting of Blue Sky Enterprises, Ltd., to order. Fifth race?"

"No speed in here," Lisa said. My study of the *Form* had

convinced me she was right. "Miss Tut ought to be able to gallop in front for a half. She'll be fresh when they come to her. Maybe they'll catch her; maybe not. But they'll have her to catch."

"Amendments or corrections?" Barnes asked. When no one spoke, he passed the pencil to Lisa, and she wrote the number "3" in the space reserved for the fifth race.

"In the sixth race," Billie said, speaking tentatively, as if she were afraid of being interrupted, "there's something called Dark Plot. It doesn't show in the *Form*, but he came on again last out. I remember because I bet on the winner, and he put Dark Plot away at the quarter pole, I thought, but then I got scared half to death when Dark Plot made another run at him."

I looked quickly through the past performances for the sixth race, one mile, $2,000 claiming. There was nothing as impressive as what Billie had said. I moved the pencil and the blank from Lisa's place to Billie's; Billie, after a nervous glance around the table, wrote Dark Plot's "7" into the sixth-race selection area.

"Those'll be good prices," Barnes said. "We can afford a short-odds banker. I say Presto can walk the Eighth. All right?"

Presto had won his last three, all sprints as was the Eighth. He was carrying more weight; and his opposition was a shade better. Obviously he would be no better than even money. I would have preferred not to bet him, but this would involve determining which of the others might get the job done, and there was, in their records, no real indication that one was any better than the others.

I wrote Presto's number on the blank and announced that I liked Scrim's Queen in the Ninth. I had pointed this one out to Lisa the night before. The four-year-old mare, unraced for a year, had run a creditable fourth at seven furlongs a week back and was almost a mandatory bet according to the rule that states that between-race improvement in horses is most marked following the first and second races, either the first and second of the horse's career, or the first two following a layoff.

"Four's enough bankers," Barnes declared, picking up the partially completed blank. "We needs perms in the Seventh and Tenth."

The Tenth was the "Mister X" Handicap, the one in which Lisa and I had decided that the sensible procedure was to back the horse whose odds were significantly less, but not too much less, than those on the tentative line we had prepared. "I'll take care of the Tenth," I said, suddenly seeing the only way our plan could be applied to a bet which had to be made now before betting on the race had begun. "You people do the Seventh."

Lisa, Andy, and Barnes quickly named a horse each for the Seventh. Billie declined to name one, announcing that she wished to be recorded as seconding Andy's nomination. I took the pencil and form and wrote the numbers they had named into the seventh-race slot. Then, while the others watched, I wrote "1-2-3-4-5-6-7-8-9-10" as our selections for the Tenth.

Barnes whistled. "It makes sense," Lisa said. "Any one of them can win it."

"Most of them," Andy Livoti said, looking up from his *Form,* "already have."

"One more addition," I proposed. Barnes shrugged. The others did nothing. Still unhappy about Presto, the even-money shot Barnes had named for the eighth race, I glanced quickly at my program, saw that Esteban was on the third choice and that the horse was 6–1 in the morning line, and added his number "6" next to the "2" Barnes had put down.

"All right," Barnes said. "Now figure the cost."

I studied the ticket.

RACE	11071109 SELECTIONS	ALTERNATE (in event of scratch)
5th	3	
6th	7	
7th	2 5 6	
8th	2 6	
9th	6	
10th	1 2 3 4 5 6 7 8 9 10	

NUMBER OF COMBINATIONS: ....
$\times$ $2.00 = STAKE: ....
VOID IF ERASED OR ALTERED
VOID UNLESS VALIDATED

Lisa picked up the pencil I had just put down and returned it to me. I knew she wanted me to fill in the blanks at the bottom of the entry quickly and without asking help from Barnes who was beginning to get under her skin as well as mine. One horse in each of the first two races; one times one. One. Times three in the next, I reasoned, making three. Times two in the next. Six. Times one again in the next to last, still six. Times ten in the tenth and last race. Sixty. Sixty lines. $120 stake.

I wrote the figures in and passed the ticket to Barnes, who

was satisfactorily disappointed. Quickly, Barnes filled in the "Alternate" column, using a "1" in every race but the tenth, leaving that space blank. "They don't allow scratches in the five-and-ten unless your horse is demonstrably dead," he explained. "Still, if a horse were withdrawn, and you hadn't named an alternate, you'd be paying for bets you weren't getting."

"What about the Tenth?" I asked.

"I don't know," he confessed. "No good naming a substitute; you've already named all the horses. I suppose," he added thoughtfully, "they'd have to refund two dollars."

In the paddock, a bell rang, and the jockeys were boosted onto their mounts. The horses began to circle the ring before going onto the track.

"Twelve dollars," Lisa said abruptly. I looked at the ticket and, suddenly seeing her meaning, grinned in delight.

"For one scratch?" Barnes challenged.

"Ten times three times two is sixty," Lisa said sweetly. "A scratch in the tenth race leaves us with nine runners. *Nine* times three times two is fifty-four. The difference—"

"Six then," Barnes conceded. "You said twelve."

"Six *lines*," Lisa cooed. "Twelve dollars. Now," she went on, proceeding to another matter, the debate ended, "what about shares in this bubble?"

"Handle it like the ownership of a casino," I suggested. "Points. One point, one percent of the stake, one percent of the return, if any. A dollar-twenty a point."

"I'll have five points then." John Barrie Barnes, somewhat chastened, handed me a five-dollar bill and a one.

A word from Andy sent Billie rabbiting through her purse. A moment later, Andy said, "We'll have the same," and handed me four crumpled ones and two dollars in silver.

"Thirty points for me." Lisa passed over two twenties and a

one and took John Barrie Barnes's five in change. "You're left with sixty points. Seventy-two dollars." I picked up the blank. "Won't cost you a dime if you get shut out," she said. "And you will if you stop to check my arithmetic."

"I wouldn't dream of it." I was in the aisle.

"Just a second, though." I turned to face Lisa, who held out her hand. "You want anything on Miss Tut separately?" Miss Tut was 4–1 on the board. I put a hundred-dollar bill in Lisa's hand, and she rose and went with me up the steps to the betting room; then she pointed out the five-and-ten desk and headed for the $10 win line.

At the desk, a clerk checked my arithmetic in a single glance, took my $120, validated the blank with a time stamp, and returned the underneath half of it—I hadn't even noticed that it was a double-thickness—which turned out to be a carbon copy of what had been printed and written on the top half.

Lisa was waiting for me at the table when I got back a few minutes before post time. The board made Miss Tut a 3–1 co-favorite, the other 3–1 shot being Tenubob, a horse that had been gaining at the end of its sprint races and that was being bet here, I knew, by horseplayers who made the usual assumption—usually false—that horses with such a record will benefit from racing a longer distance. Fifty feet below us, and a hundred and fifty yards up the track, the horses were going into the gate. The board blinked again; Miss Tut held at 3–1, but became the undisputed favorite when Tenubob went out a half point to be 7–2.

The bell rang. A minute and thirteen seconds later, Miss Tut was passing the quarter pole, straightening for the stretch run, four lengths ahead of Tenubob, eight lengths ahead of the others, having gone easily the entire trip except for a brush for position going to the first turn. "Tenubob coming on," the announcer rattled. In my glasses, I could see Tenubob's rider flashing his whip, putting his mount to a drive, while Miss Tut's rider sat still. At the eighth pole, I put down the glasses and picked up the sheaf of win tickets Lisa had put under my ashtray. $4,050. Less $20 lost on Dos Frijoles. Less $72 invested in the five-and-ten. $3,958. Plus at least three-hundred profit on Miss Tut. $4,258. The crowd began to yell; inside the sixteenth pole, Tenubob was getting closer, but this was plainly because Miss Tut's rider, with the race won, was easing his mount. At the wire, Miss Tut was a clear half length to the good. A fat woman, standing in the aisle beside us, announced to no one in particular that Tenubob would have won in another stride, and Lisa, speaking to me, but loudly enough so the woman could hear, expressed the view that the horses could have gone twice more around the track with Tenubob getting no closer to the lead than Miss Tut's rider cared to permit.

The woman moved off; the waiter cleared the table. The *Official* sign and the prices went up. Miss Tut paid $8.40 straight, twenty dollars more than the minimum, running my bankroll to $4,278.

"One banker home," John Barrie Barnes pointed out. "All sixty lines are still alive."

Lisa drew a circle around the number "3" on the carbon copy of the blank.

"I'm sorry I opened my mouth," Billie said nervously. "All I said was Dark Plot came again last time, and now I could be responsible for killing sixty lines."

"Wouldn't kill 'em dead," Andy said reassuringly.

"Make 'em pretty sick then," Billie amended. "Me too."

Dark Plot, however, took Billie off the hook nicely, going off at 6–1, laying back of the first flight until the field straightened away, then bounding quickly to the leaders, catching them at the eighth pole, a length clear at the sixteenth pole, two and a half at the finish. Andy and Billie embraced; Lisa circled another number; John Barrie Barnes, a note of excitement now apparent in his voice, announced the safe arrival of another banker. Dark Plot paid $15 straight. I had what I was beginning to think of as my customary hundred-dollar bet on him. Profit: $650. Roll: $4,928.

"I'm going down to the receiving barn to check Bailey Bridge," John Barrie Barnes announced. It took me a moment to place the name; then I remembered and, momentarily, regretted my commitment to finance Jesse's Hand's trip to Del Mar if Bailey Bridge's performance later that afternoon, coupled with what I had been told about the relative quality of the two horses, seemed to justify such an investment. Barnes left the table; Billie, in response to his gesture, followed him out. I took Lisa's hand, kissed her fingertips for no special reason, put her hand back on the table, and began a study of the seventh race.

"She's a good kid," Andy Livoti said suddenly.

I looked up from the *Form*, realized that Andy was soliciting my opinion of Billie, and gave it. "Good-looking, amiable, nice ankles, and a good judge of pace. What more could a man ask?" Andy and Lisa exchanged smiles. I pointed to Lisa's *Form*, which lay folded on the table. "You've already figured this one?"

"In a way," she said. "I figure with the first two winners in the five-and-ten, and with three five-and-ten picks in this one—"

I was, for the first time, disappointed in her. "The horses don't know how we're doing in the five-and-ten," I said. "If we can get an edge—"

"We'd just be hedging."

"Yes. If we bet another horse. But—"

Lisa read the numbers off the *Form*. "Two, five, six. Bet something else, and we're betting against ourselves. Bet on one or all of these, and we're only protecting ourselves against the possibility that the horse—or horses—we back will win, but we won't have enough winners in the next three to make our ticket pay off. 'Protecting yourself' is just another word for hedging. Tell me," she added too sweetly before I could reply, "do you take insurance?" I shook my head. "Not even when you have blackjack?"

It was, as between us, an ugly question. In blackjack, the object of the game is to get closer to twenty-one than the dealer gets without going over twenty-one. "Insurance" is offered by the dealer when he has an ace face-up. In effect, he is offering to lay two-to-one that his face-down card is not a ten or a picture. Notwithstanding the fact that the proper odds against that possibility are considerably more than two-to-one, inexperienced gamblers—or experienced ones who lack the intellect or capacity to learn from experience—will sometimes take insurance if they themselves already have blackjack; that is, if their own two cards are ace-ten. The reasoning is that since a player's two-card twenty-one earns him three-to-two for his bet unless the dealer ties him (in which case the hand is a standoff and he neither wins nor loses), by taking insurance for half the amount of his bet—which is all the rules allow—he guarantees himself a profit. If the dealer has a ten, jack, queen, or king in the hole, the dealer has twenty-one, the hand is a tie, and the player wins the insurance bet. If the dealer has any other card in the hole, the insurance is lost, but the bet on the hand wins at three-to-two.

The fatal flaw in the reasoning is that the player, holding blackjack, can do no worse than tie in any case. Under those circumstances, for him to bet that he *will* tie, at lower odds than chance would justify, is simply to take a certain small profit rather than an uncertain larger one by making a smaller bet against himself at unfavorable odds.

The question, though blithely asked, invited a rude reply. Only the memory of the night before and the anticipation of the night to come pushed me in the direction of good humor and evasion, but they were enough.

"Three subjects the wise man disputeth not," I declaimed. "The beauty of a woman, the name of the Almighty, and the theory of a gamble. An old Kurdish proverb I just made up."

In the silence that followed, I resumed my study of the race, concentrating on the three horses we had in the five-and-ten. Lisa, Andy, and Barnes had, I remembered, supplied one each. "Which was yours?" I asked Lisa.

"The Six. Tico T. Not much of a sprinter, but there's a lot of speed in the race." She leaned across the table and kissed the end of my nose. "Go ahead. Any bet's a good one if it wins. That rule overrides all the rest."

The past performances made that a tempting view. On the face of it, it seemed that no fewer than six horses would have to fight it out for the early lead, since six had demonstrated they could not win from behind. There were two plodders, steady-going animals who could run at an even pace but who lacked the ability to put on the sort of burst of speed that could carry them into contention. There was a horse who had shown the ability to run at the end of his races, but he was stepping up in class, dropping down in distance, and picking up weight, a complex of factors that only rarely precedes a win. And there was Tico T. His recent form indicated that he needed only to be held off the fast pace that would surely develop, but not so far off as to make his task impossible when he was put to running. He was dropping ten pounds off his last, a good second to Titania, one of the sprinters; and in that race, Titania had been allowed to run in front unattended.

I watched the horses leave the walking ring for the track, then looked over to the odds board. Titania, one of our three selections in the five-and-ten, was the 2–1 favorite; another, Tico T. was 6–1. The other was 40–1, heavily bandaged fore and aft, and seemed barely able to walk onto the track.

I fingered the uncashed tickets from the sixth race, ten bits of pasteboard, exchangeable now for $750, but which could as easily have been worthless. I could bet $300 out of the $750 and lose it, and still be $400 ahead of where—I broke the thought off sharply, reminding myself that I was not a simpleton who distinguished between "my" money, which had to be bet cautiously, and "theirs," which was to be stuffed back into the machines promiscuously as if my title to it were questionable.

Across the top of the tote board, an arrangement of light-bulbs suddenly lit up. *5–10 Pool: $141,360.* The track would take 10 percent, which would leave approximately $127,000, three-quarters of which would go to the holder (or holders) of the ticket (or tickets) picking the most winners, and a fourth to those picking the second most winners. Below the message, the odds changed again, Titania shortening to 8–5, Tico T. holding at 6–1. "I think it's time to send it in," I said, rising.

"The horse figures," Lisa admitted. "But you can't be sure about speed."

"With six of them to fight it out?"

"That's what the *Form* says. It doesn't always show up on the track."

It would show up, I decided, pausing on my way to the cashier's window to bet $100 on Tico T. Form whose message was so obvious that all Lisa had to say was "the horse figures" without mentioning a name or number, knowing I would understand which horse she had in mind, was form that could be relied on.

Six horses had to get the lead to have a chance. I was at the cashier's window now, watching the teller count out the seven hundreds, the twenties, the ten. If even three of them fought for the lead, the race would be made to order for Tico T.

The small auxiliary board in the betting room still showed 6–1. I went to the ten-dollar window and bought the six twenty more times.

When I got back to the table, the horses were in the gate at the top of the six-furlong chute; the flag was up. I checked Tico T.'s colors in the program—silver, scarlet hoops, scarlet cap, noted that he was still 6–1, and put my binoculars on the starting gate.

A moment later, the doors opened and the field was on its way. I got a glimpse of the silver and scarlet, well back, noting with satisfaction that the boy was easing Tico T. toward the rail, and moved my glasses to watch the speed jam on the front end. The four inside horses were driving hard for the lead, with the Eight and Seven just behind; Tico T., now on the rail, came next; the plodders were already far back, the shape of the race, in the first quarter-mile precisely what my reading of the *Form* had indicated it had to be.

The quarter-time—twenty-three and one—indicated a well-contested pace, but the horses seemed to slow slightly in the backstretch. No sooner was I aware of this than I saw Esteban, on the favored Titania, begin to move his mount out of the group of four and into the lead. "Titania a length, a length and a half, look at 'im go," the announcer chanted, as the red silks drew clear as the field came to the turn. "Come on," I muttered. "Don't give that pig a breather."

"The idiots," Lisa said quietly, "are letting him steal it." Midway round the turn, the Eight, moving powerfully from sixth place, drove past the Seven, on which he had been lapped, past the Four, the Three, the One, and set out after Titania. Tico T.'s rider, now having no choice, compelled by the lack of pace to move early, followed the Eight past the others; so that, as the field straightened away, Titania had only two lengths on the Eight, and Tico T. was at the second horse's throatlatch. But, at the eighth pole, I knew it was hopeless. Failing to press Titania for the lead, the other speed horses had given her an advantage she ought not to have had; in so doing, they had cost themselves a theoretical chance to win, and they had cost Tico T. (and me) a real one. Inside the sixteenth pole, Tico T. put the Eight away; but the unextended Titania was untouchable, drawing off at the very end, winning by three.

"Damn!" I said. "God *damn!*"

"You were right," Lisa said. "You knew those five parking-lot attendants couldn't win backing off that way. Only they didn't know. It could have been worse, though." She picked up the pencil and circled the "2" in the seventh race on the five-and-ten slip.

"Sorry, Lew." Andy Livoti was rubbing his hands together. "Three for three. Two more winners, and I start figuring five percent of seventy-five percent of ninty percent of $147,000."

"Fifty-five hundred," Lisa said. "Give or take fifty dollars."

"Damn good shot, if I say so myself, as shouldn't," John Barrie Barnes boomed, returning to the table with Billie. "You will recall," he said, with an elaborate bow, "who picked that one for the syndicate."

"I wouldn't bet that horse," I said, "if they ran the movies of the race."

"Hard lines, lad." The Englishman assumed a wounded expression. "Had the second horse, I daresay. Never suppose that a pack of jockeys have enough sense to see what their own interests require."

I got the thirty tickets from my breast pocket and dropped them under the table. "How's Bailey Bridge?" I didn't know what answer I was hoping for; but I knew I wanted to change the subject.

"Tip-top," Barnes replied. "You agree, Billie?"

Billie agreed. "That's what the guinea said," Barnes rambled on. "No offense, Signor Livoti." There was no one at the table, of course, who was unaware that a racetrack guinea is a groom; Andy's expression indicated that he knew this and that he was getting tired of Barnes.

"This blackamoor," Barnes was saying, "told me the horse will win for sure. 'He got a light in his eyes, boss,' he said. Maybe he does. I must say I put more store by his coat than his weight, but I'd be alarmed if his eyes were dull."

Billie picked up the five-and-ten ticket. "Three for three!"

"Only the beginning, lassie," Barnes said. "Only the beginning. I marked the favorite in the Eighth. And, just among us, mind you, he'll walk it. Just walk it." He looked at the ticket and wrinkled his nose. "You've added one," he said accusingly.

"You saw the ticket," I snapped. "And you saw me figure it."

"I must have forgotten." Barnes shrugged. "I'd have warned you against it. The favorite'll be two-to-one on, but in this thing, a winner's a winner, hang the odds."

I made a show of lowering my head to reread my *Form*. Barnes had selected Presto, who was looking for his third consecutive win over similar fields, his last two having been won wire-to-wire, eased up, carrying only three pounds less than today's weight. I had added Borneo, who had been second to Presto last out. I wondered why I had done that; then I noticed that Esteban was listed on Borneo. On the board, Presto was 1–2, as Barnes had said. Borneo, at 5–2, was equally unplayable. "A dollar, horse against horse," I proposed.

"Done and done." We shook hands.

Twenty-three minutes later, as the field came down the

backstretch, it appeared that Barnes, along with those bettors who had backed Presto with such enthusiasm that he went off at 1–3, had been right. Midway round the turn, Presto was four lengths in front and, as Lisa pointed out, winging. At that point, however, he unaccountably began to drift wide, going almost to the fence, the others sweeping by him on the inside as he lost ground. In midstretch, I could see Borneo, third, on the outside, closing, but not closing fast enough, then flattening out in the drive to finish fifth, behind four outsiders but ahead of Presto, who staggered in last as the crowd booed.

I held out my hand for my dollar. But Barnes refused to pay, arguing that a horse-for-horse bet was void unless one or both got his number on the board. A Texan at the next table volunteered that this was certainly true of Texas quarter-horse racing, where, in the absence of any legal betting system, head-to-head, horse-for-horse betting was "practically all they *is*, for Chrissakes."

It was a foolish argument, and I felt guilty at my elation at Presto's poor performance, aware that it had dealt a blow, perhaps a mortal one, to a previously live five-and-ten ticket in which I held a 60 percent interest. When the crowd whooped, I looked at the result board for the first time and saw that the winner had paid $200.40 for $2.

"That's a help," Andy said.

It was, of course. The five-and-ten is a contest; prizes go to those who make the best score. Since we did not have the winner, it was obviously to our advantage that as few people as possible have it, and the long odds against the winner made it extremely unlikely that anyone now had four-for-four, in which case our three-for-four would still have us tied for the lead.

In any event, Lisa pointed out, our chances were still excellent. With three winners already marked, and only two races remaining, and all ten entries in the last race marked, our ticket would necessarily show a minimum of four winners when, with the running of the tenth race, the contest ended. Unless someone had six, which would involve having the 99–1 eighth-race winner on the same line with the winners of all the other races, an almost incredibly remote possibility, five winners would be enough for a share in first money and tickets naming four would split among them the consolation prize. If Scrim's Queen, my selection for the ninth race, won, we would have five winners; if it lost, we would have four.

I restudied Scrim's Queen's record and became more convinced that, if form meant anything, she would win. She had been away from racing for nearly a year, but had returned a week earlier in a seven-furlong race in which she had run with the best, held on well, and finished fourth. Now, going back into her races before the layoff, I saw again that in seven races she had been first twice and three times third, a good record made more impressive by her having closed ground in all seven stretch-runs, once having closed six lengths in the final quarter of a five-furlong race.

I was sure that her failure to finish more strongly the week before had been the result of lack of condition, induced by the year's idleness. I turned, for the first time, to the handicapper's selections in the front of the *Form*. He had Scrim's Queen on top. "Needed last." The probable odds, according to the *Form*, were 3–2.

I put my glasses on the paddock as Scrim's Queen was saddled. A clean-legged bay mare, with a white off-front hoof, she stood quietly, nuzzling the hand of the man who stood at her head talking to her jockey. The trainer stopped his discourse with the rider, threw a blanket and saddle over Scrim's Queen, and reached under her belly for the girth, planting his head hard against the mare's rib-cage as he tightened the cinch.

"Good-looking mare," Lisa said. "How much are you betting?"

I put down my glasses and was about to reply that I had no intention of betting Scrim's Queen individually, that the five-ten ticket, with its certain second prize and possible first prize, represented a sufficient investment in her chances, when I saw the smile that flickered around Lisa's mouth and realized that, except in degree, the problem of whether to bet was no different than it had been when the race in question was the seventh and the horse was Tico T. If I didn't bet Scrim's Queen, I would be admitting that my bet on Tico T. was, in part at least, a hedge.

I looked for a way out. "Three-to-two's not much of a price," I began.

"No," Lisa agreed. "But she's six-to-one and going out."

I looked at the odds board. Lisa was right. "She'll be seven or eight next flash," Lisa was saying, as the money board blinked, and then the odds board, and Scrim's Queen was 7–1, and the even-money favorite, Kee Bird, had shortened to 4–5.

Kee Bird was the first horse I had thrown out in my preliminary sorting partly because the price would be short; partly because, though it had won three straight, it had been winning by narrower margins; partly because it was picking up a lot of weight.

My bankroll was down from its high of nearly $5,000 to just over $4,600; but this was irrelevant. Even if the question were whether or not to stake my entire roll, that fact would have no valid bearing on the question which would have to be resolved entirely on considerations involving risk and return. The horses were out of the paddock. I had not heard the bugle.

"Nine-to-one," Lisa said.

The horses were walking, single file, toward the clubhouse turn. Now they wheeled, the late afternoon sun glinting off the riders' safety helmets, and began their parade, the wrong way of the track, below us, past us, toward the eighth pole. Chavez, on Scrim's Queen, sat loosely, relaxing, saving himself and his horse, I thought, for the race. I remembered the ride he had given Pizza Pallor.

"All right." I stood up. "Who else?"

"Not me," Barnes declared. "I don't like to bet against a favorite that's being backed that way." Kee Bird had shortened again and was now 3–5.

"You really like this one?" Andy Livoti asked.

"No. I just hate carrying money around."

Andy and Billie held a whispered conference. Then Billie put a hand in her shirt pocket, produced a crumpled ten-dollar bill, and handed it to me. Lisa passed me a fifty. I moved toward the windows.

A minute after what the board declared to be post time, the horses still milled behind the starting gate. I stood at the front edge of the betting room, looking down over the tables in the Turf Club, across the paved lawn, as the assistant starters began putting horses into the gate. My shirt pocket held fifty tickets, all bearing the number six, the denomination of $10, and the challenging legend: CASH IF FIRST ONLY. The announcer declared, "They're in the gate," and, indeed, three of them were. Kee Bird had dropped to 2–5; Scrim's Queen was 7–1. I considered buying an additional six tickets to replace the six I was holding for Andy and Lisa, then decided that the time I had spent considering the question had rendered it moot.

I had taken a step toward the aisle leading down to our table when, along the backstretch, a horse broke through the gate, and the loading process was halted until the runaway—not Scrim's Queen, I noticed with relief—was recaptured. I walked back to the ten-dollar window, waited for the half dozen in front of me in line to make their transactions, bought six more tickets, and was back in the aisle, almost at the table, when the bell rang and the spectators informed one another that the horses were running.

Out of the gate, Kee Bird showed in front; the outside horse, easing down the slope, moved out to engage him and as Kee Bird's rider struck his horse with his whip, the horse—perhaps, I thought, astounded at being so treated so early in the race—ducked out, opening a hole along the rail into which the Two slipped; and all three of them flashed along the backstretch side by the side, driving for the lead as if the finish line were at hand. As the half-mile pole was reached, I picked out Scrim's Queen, going steadily in fourth place, five lengths off the torrid pace, Chavez sitting still, waiting for the others to come back. I put the glasses down and looked at the quarter-mile time as it flashed on the fractional time indicator. 22 flat; none of the horses in the first flight could possibly have anything left for the stretch-run. I offered to lay two-to-one against the favorite; when John Barrie Barnes did not reply, I raised the offer to four-to-one.

The field was turning for home when I picked them up in my glasses again, the same three still contesting for the lead, all three now shortening stride, Scrim's Queen only two lengths back now, easing up on their heels under Chavez's steady hand-ride.

"Any time at all," Lisa said happily. "Here comes the Nine." The Nine, silvery gray with a white tail, was fifth, closing steadily without apparent urging.

"Outside, boy," I murmured. Orthodoxy commands that a jockey should go outside of a single horse but inside when passing two or more who are going side by side. I was hoping Chavez would ignore the rule. Scrim's Queen was the strong horse, much stronger than the three in front. She could concede the loss of ground involved in going three wide and still get the lead. If she remained snugged on the rail, there was always the possibility that no hole would open, that Chavez would find himself, in midstretch, behind a phalanx of quitting front runners, locked in as the Nine came on.

"There he goes," Lisa said. Chavez eased Scrim's Queen off the rail and angled forward at the leaders. "Move now!"

"You may take three giant steps!" Billie shouted.

Past the quarter pole Scrim's Queen continued to move; she was obviously strongest as all four turned into the stretch, continuing to gain despite the enormous advantage Chavez wisely conceded the others by going wide. They were straight now, Scrim's Queen within a half length of the leaders and gaining, the four of them almost abreast. The Nine, whose rider lost all possible choices when Chavez moved—he could scarcely go outside of *four*—scampered along the rail, a length and half farther back, with no running room, locked in as Scrim's Queen would have been had Chavez attempted to save ground.

We were all shouting now, excited by the race Scrim's Queen was making and by what it would mean to us if she continued to gain, good bets cashed for Lisa, Andy and me, a lock on the five-and-ten for all of us.

"Uh oh." For a fraction of a second, I did not relate Lisa's expression of distress to what was happening on the track. I took my eyes from the race to see whether she had spilled a drink or touched a live cigarette. Then, as Andy Livoti moaned, I looked back at the track.

Kee Bird, second from the rail, probably exhausted from a five-furlong all-out drive between horses, had begun to bear out, making contact with the horse outside of him. As if it were all occurring in slow motion, I saw the third horse shy away from Kee Bird, saw Kee Bird, stumbling now, almost falling, hit the third horse, saw the third horse flinch and start to bolt as his rider tried frantically to snatch him up, saw the black mass cut erratically wide, squarely in front of Scrim's Queen.

Chavez used the only move left to him, pulling Scrim's Queen's head up sharply, causing her to rear, throwing her front feet down again when the other was clear, his acrobatics resembling those of a bicycle rider who hauls his front wheel up to miss an obstruction and then puts it down in the proper direction.

My first thought was that this maneuver, which I had never seen executed on a racetrack, which I had never even heard of, had reduced the break in Scrim's Queen's momentum to the minimum. Then I saw that even the minimum was too much. In bearing out, Kee Bird had left an opening through which the Nine's rider had driven his gray mount, so that he was nearly a length clear when Scrim's Queen found her stride again. Chavez went to the whip for the first time, and the horse responded, cutting the gap to a half length, a neck, a head, barely failing to catch the now tiring Nine at the wire.

"Sheeyit!" Andy Livoti growled. "Shee-yit!"

The photo sign was on the board; an instant later there was a yell as the word "inquiry" was illuminated. But I knew, as did Lisa and the others, that the Nine had won the photo, and that the inquiry could only affect the placing of Kee Bird, whose bobble in midstretch had caused the near collision.

Two minutes later, the photo sign came down, and the order of finish went up, showing the Nine, followed by Scrim's Queen, Kee Bird, and an outsider. After another five minutes, the inquiry sign blinked out, and the numbers of the third and fourth horse were reversed, Kee Bird being moved back from third to fourth for its antics inside the sixteenth pole, and the stamp of finality was placed on the race with the lighting of OFFICIAL and the posting of the prices, $10.60 straight on the winner, $9.40 on Scrim's Queen to place.

In the silence that still enveloped the table, Lisa produced the sheet of paper on which she and I had, the night before, made what we considered a proper price line on the tenth race, from which we had agreed to consider any deviation as the work of Mr. X, the man, or combination of men, whose betting on previous races involving these same horses seemed to have been based on information more valid than the publicly displayed and publicly recorded form of the horses. I took the sheet from her and made quick arithmetical adjustments in the odds to reflect the fact that our line had been based on a field of twelve, of which only ten were listed to start.

I explained our theory to Andy; he agreed it was sound. "Not," he added, "that it matters to me. That ten-spot was case money."

Billie put her arm around Andy's shoulder. "Don't feel bad," she said. "We got a hell of a run for our money."

John Barrie Barnes excused himself to attend to last-minute preparations relating to Bailey Bridge, who was in the eleventh race.

I could hear the conversations at nearby tables. For the most part, they consisted of declarations of the number of winners each person would have in his best five-and-ten line, assuming that his tenth-race pick won, and speculations about whether that number (usually three) would be enough for a share in the second-prize money. If there was anyone within earshot who had a serious hope of participating in the major end of the five-and-ten pool, he was not giving voice to his hope. It was the general opinion that five winners would win first money, and that four, therefore, would be good for a share of the quarter of the pool set aside for consolation prizes. Estimates of the possible value of such a consolation prize ran from a low of fifty dollars to a high of a thousand. I took a pencil and began, on the back of an unused five-and-ten entry, to calculate how many holders of tickets with four winners might be expected, but I gave it up when my first calculation revealed that, with ten horses to a race, there are fifteen hundred different combinations containing four winners in six races. The question was, of course, far from academic. With the first three winners, followed by Tico T.'s failure and the tragedy that had befallen Scrim's Queen, and with all ten horses listed on our entry for the tenth and last race, our ticket, of which I held sixty percent, Lisa thirty, John Barrie Barnes five, and the partnership of Andy and Billie five, would have exactly four winners, could only produce four winners, and could not produce less.

"You know what we need?" Andy Livoti's face brightened.

"We need a drink," Lisa said.

I signaled for a waiter. "We need a dead heat," Livoti said. He read from the back page of the program on which the five-and-ten rules appeared: *In the event of a dead heat, both horses will be considered winners for the purposes of the five-and-ten pool.*

I told him I didn't read the same meaning into the rule he did. Whatever its literal wording, it did not mean that if two of our horses in the tenth race ran a dead heat, we would receive credit for both on the same line.

"Just let it happen," Andy said. "I'll read them the rule, and they can explain to me why I don't get paid for five."

"The lines run from race to race," I said. "Not from horse to horse in the same race."

Andy couldn't see it, and insisted on explaining why he couldn't. I wasn't listening. I was disturbed that my bankroll was only slightly bigger than it had been at the beginning of the afternoon program. I hadn't bet favorites; two winners in six races should have produced a handy profit. I had the feeling I should be doing something; I didn't know what it might be, but, whatever it was, it would involve thought—which was hardly possible while Andy blathered about an incorrect interpretation of an event which was not at all likely to occur.

"Hon," Billie put in gently, "suppose you had the first five winners, and you picked two horses in the last race, and they ran a dead heat. Would that give you seven?"

Andy subsided.

"There." Lisa pointed to the tote board. Comparing the price line there with the one I had recently corrected, I saw a substantial discrepancy. The horse we had selected as second choice, our tentative price being 3–1, had opened at 2½–1 and had now gone out to 4–1. This had not been the result of a rush of money to the favorite, which had opened at even money (we had predicted 6–5) and held at that price. But Chop House, against which our line quoted a probable starting price of 12–1, had opened at 10, an insignificant variation, but was now barely 6–1, that last switch being anything but insignificant.

The horse's past performances, as I reviewed them, revealed no reason for this action. Chop House had won once in its last seven starts; it had run fifth last out, behind four of those entered today, having been sent off then at 7–1.

I put my glasses on Chop House as the horses and riders made their preliminary turn of the ring. As I studied the horse, I had the dizzy sensation that I was looking for nothing as, indeed, I was. If there was anything in the horse's appearance, or indeed in the manner or appearance of any horse in the ring, to justify what was going on at the betting windows, then there was no Mr. X, and we would be reduced to handicapping a race we had already declared unfigurable.

Chop House was small and lean, a little too lean, I thought, noticing the play of his bones and muscle beneath the thin layer of flesh, the fleshless rib-cage, the ribs displayed washboard-fashion. His forefeet were heavily bandaged, which might indicate a tendency to soreness, unless they were there to protect Chop House from rapping himself when running; in either case, the bandages were an adverse factor in evaluating the horse's chance to win. Sore-legged horses are only slightly more likely to win than those whose stride is so choppy that rear hoofs have struck front fetlocks and are likely, in the trainer's judgment, to do so again.

The favorite and the second choice were clear-limbed. "They've got it all over ours on conformation," Lisa said as the horses went onto the track. "But of course the less we see, the more we know."

I smiled. Chop House seemed to have steadied at 5–1; but even to maintain that price, in the face of the rapidly developing support for the favorite and second choice, he had to be getting a far bigger play than could be justified by his record or his appearance.

"We went to a lot of trouble to find out which way Mr. X is betting," I said. "I guess we have to bet he's right."

"We do indeed." Lisa produced another fifty-dollar bill. I added two-fifty of my own and bet the whole three hundred at the fifty-dollar window in one trip. There was no reason now to avoid touts or to slide the money in by dribs and drabs. Chop House had already been established as the hot horse. Bettors who were accustomed to follow the hot money would back him regardless of anything we did or did not do.

It was immediately apparent, when the race went off, that there was a Mr. X, and that he did know something not generally known. Chop House went to the front at the start, charging forward through the middle of the pack as the horses came past the stands the first time in the mile-and-an-eighth race, the boy easing him to the rail as he drew clear, going past the Turf Club into the turn with a good hold on his horse, skimming the rail two lengths ahead of his field, going easily. There was nothing in his record to suggest that Chop House was a speed horse of this sort.

"He's not being pressed," Lisa said happily.

The field moved along the backstretch; I looked as the half-mile time—48:1—went up on the indicator. This was slow time, indicating a pace that could only benefit the horse in front. As Chop House made his way down the backstretch and into the turn, I moved my glasses back to his closest pursuers, who seemed to be dropping farther off the pace, past them. I was looking for a horse who might be beginning a move; and I found one, a brown horse, a jockey in brown silks, brown cap, the horse dead last when I picked him up, but moving, lapped on the next to last horse, then past him in a jump, moving on the rail now, past three others who labored along, side by side, then outside to go past another. "Bingo Bingo closing ground from far back," the announcer said. I moved my glasses back to Chop House and was unpleasantly surprised at how small a move that was. But Chop House was going easily, his jockey sitting still with a double-handful of reins.

Midway in the turn, Chop House's rider let out a notch on the reins, and the animal responded. Bingo Bingo had disposed of the others. For an instant, the two appeared to be almost side by side, but this was an optical illusion, I knew. The effect of the angle, however, did not diminish as sharply as it should have as the horse straightened out. I knew Bingo Bingo was coming on.

Inside the eighth pole, with Bingo Bingo only a length and a half back, Chop House's rider began to use his whip. For a few strides, Chop House seemed to be coming away as he had the first time through the stretch, but at the sixteenth pole he hung again. This time there was no holding Bingo Bingo who came level with him, got his head in front, then his neck, then, as Chop House's rider saw further punishment was useless and put his whip away, drawing off quickly to win by a clear length.

"Not a bad one for us," Andy Livoti said as the numbers went up. "The winner was never shorter than twelve-to-one."

I nodded. Bingo Bingo was "not a bad one" because, as an outsider, he would be named on very few five-and-ten tickets, which would diminish the possibility of a six-winner line and reduce the number of four- and five-winner lines. As holders of a four-winner ticket, we would receive no payoff at all if there were a six-winner line, and the size of our payoff, if any, would be inversely proportional to the number of other four-winner tickets.

"When will they announce the five-and-ten results?" I asked.

"As soon as they can figure them," Andy Livoti replied. "It's a hand-operation, though. Probably just after the eleventh race."

The horses for the eleventh race were coming into the paddock. Bailey Bridge, as Number Twelve, was in the nearest stall. I picked out John Barrie Barnes standing at the horse's head, talking quietly to a Negro groom, the same one, I assumed, who favored Bailey Bridge's chances because of the horse's brightness of eye. Bailey Bridge seemed to have a shinier coat than he had had in the stable. I put my glasses on him and decided this was the result of a quick brushing, probably by the groom, not an indication that the horse was sweating.

A waiter came by and removed the drinks. I did not remember when he had brought them, and I had no recollection of having drunk mine, but the empty glass taken from my place was evidence that I had. The tenth race was declared official; betting on the eleventh race began. Though Bailey Bridge was 5–1 on the morning line, $600 of the first $1,100 in the win pool was bet on him.

"Hoo hah!" Lisa said.

Apparently this turn of events was called to Barnes' attention; I saw him turn and walk back a bit, so that he could see the board over the stall, look at the board, shade his eyes, and look again. When he resumed his conversation with the groom, he was obviously angry, pounding his fist into his palm as he spoke, turning his back when the groom started to reply, staring out into the crowd as if he did not trust himself to keep his temper in check if he continued the conversation.

"Somebody blew the whistle," Andy said, understating the case. $2,200 went into the win pool, $1,200 of it on Bailey Bridge. The morning line odds blinked out and were replaced by the actual momentary odds. Bailey Bridge was 1–2.

The pattern held. With twelve minues to the advertised post time, Bailey Bridge was quoted at 1–3. Now the surprising betting on the eleventh race began to replace speculation about the possible five-and-ten payoffs as a subject of conversation in the Turf Club. Probably this was because everyone was at least potentially involved in the eleventh, while only those having a minimum of four winners could have any personal stake in the distribution of the five-and-ten pool. The Texan at the next table returned from a scouting expedition and reported, on the authority of a motion picture producer whose sources of information were considered reliable, that Bailey Bridge had broken the track record for a mile in a moonlight workout the previous Wednesday night, news of which had leaked to the outer world because of the chance presence in the infield of a local farmer who had cut across the track on his way home from a Tijuana gin mill.

"Farmers," Lisa said, "are the same the world over. Forever staggering home at midnight, barely sober enough to operate their stopwatches."

Billie laughed. Bailey Bridge's rider reported to John Barrie Barnes in the paddock. I could see Barnes gesturing frantically as he tried to get his riding instructions across a language barrier. Then he hoisted the boy—tall and thin, a very bad build for a jockey since it implies a constant need to diet with probable loss of strength—into the saddle. A moment later, the bugle blew and the horses started onto the track.

9

The horses for the eleventh race were milling around behind the starting gate, waiting for the assistant starters to come out and lead them into their stalls, when I came out of the elegant Turf Club gents' room, which I had visited partly for the usual reason and partly because I needed a quiet place and a moment to count my money and think.

The money came to $3,600, $450 less than I had had at the beginning of the afternoon program. But I had just bet $150 on my own (and $50 of Lisa's) on a horse named B-Hive, the form horse, Lisa and I agreed, in the race; the rush of money that had sent Bailey Bridge down to 1–3 had run the odds against B-Hive out from 8–5 to 3–1. In addition to the live $150 worth of tickets on B-Hive, the $450 deficit had bought me a 60-percent equity in an almost certain five-and-ten payoff. Not bad, I decided; not good enough, but not bad.

John Barrie Barnes had returned to the table, and was in full cry when I got back there. "You'll see plenty," he promised, moving to let me get to my seat. "I told the boy to take him right to the front, and, of course, the horse is totally unaccustomed to making the running. And then he's to go all out in the straight, no matter how far back he is. Lord, I hope he understood."

I gave Lisa her ticket and put my three under a water glass. "Congratulations, Mr. Barnes," Lisa said. "That was quite a performance."

"My show of wrath when the first figures went up?" Barnes asked. "My Mum always said I was meant for an actor. Still," he conceded, "you saw through me."

"It was a little broad," I said. Actually, I had been fooled completely, but I was beginning to see what Lisa was driving at and was prepared to claim, by implication, that I had always seen it.

"As you've both guessed, there's another horse in the race," Barnes said. "A very well-meant horse, Marimba. And mine being quite the reverse, and me being a good friend of the avaricious owner of Marimba, we contrived to start a bit of a rumor, our hope being to start a bit of a betting boom for Bailey Bridge. We had a better success than we'd dared hope. The populace today seems particularly disposed to accept rumors. I heard talk about Bailey Bridge that nearly tempted me to back him myself."

"You backed the other?"

"A tiny flier," Barnes said. The last horse was in the gate; the flag went up. I aimed my glasses at the front of Bailey Bridge's stall. "I hope that boy understood what I was telling him," Barnes muttered. "Sometimes I think I may have to learn their blasted heathen tongue."

With the ringing of the bell and the start of the race came the answer to Barnes's doubts. R. Lopez, aboard Bailey Bridge, might be faulted as a jockey, but he understood orders and he carried them out. His mount, under severe punishment, went forward, the outside horse in a five-horse spread, and, incredibly, stayed even with the four inside of him; halfway round the turn, despite the fantastic disadvantage imposed on him by his outside position—I estimated he had already run seventy feet farther than the horse on the rail—Bailey Bridge put his head in front and inched away from his company. As the field straightened for the run down the backstretch, his lead was sufficient so that Lopez was able to ease him to the rail.

B-Hive was going easily in sixth place under a tight hold. "Please remember," John Barrie Barnes was saying, "that Jesse's Hand is a full stone better than this one."

A minute later, I had to admit—with some inner reluctance—that Bailey Bridge had shown that Jesse's Hand was indeed worth the investment required to get him to Del Mar. Bailey Bridge, of course, had not been able to maintain his lead around the final turn; his extreme exertions in the first five eights had made that unthinkable. But he had held on well; and when Lopez, as ordered, went to work on him again at the quarter pole, he had responded with a run as incredible, in its way, as the one with which he had begun the race, catching two of the four horses who had passed him on the turn—he was giving weight to both of them, and neither had been involved in the early speed-jam—finishing a respectable third, three lengths back of the first two, that pair having run head and head the last eighth, B-Hive on the inside, Marimba outside of him, Marimba getting up in the last jump to win narrowly but perceptibly.

I pulled my tickets out from under the water glass and dropped them under the table. John Barrie Barnes took a mutuel ticket from his pocket and held it in front of me, so close to my nose I had to pull my head back to read it. Like the three I had discarded, it was a $50 win ticket. Unlike them, it was on the winner.

"A tiny flier?" I asked. I tried to keep myself from getting angry, reminding myself that even if Barnes had shared his confidences with me before the race, I would not have backed a horse on his say-so, which was all true, but insufficient to quiet my temper. Barnes could not have known I would have ignored his advice; he must have thought I would have acted on it. Why else would he have withheld it?

"The ticket's not entirely mine," Barnes said. "I'm holding most of it for a friend."

It was a ridiculous answer, of course. When betting partnerships are capitalized at more than $4, no one holds another man's bets; individual tickets are easily had. The Official and the prices went up—12 on the winner; Barnes and his "partner" had won $250; and the public address system clicked. A sudden quiet enveloped the Turf Club in anticipation of an announcement concerning the division of the five-and-ten-pool.

There were some preliminaries. Post time for the twelfth and last race was announced; patrons were reminded that this would be the quiniela race. Patrons were invited to remain, after the twelfth race, for the dog races which would follow. Then, as the five-ten results went up on the infield board, the announcer read them off.

The gross pool and net pool figures—$130,254 and $117,228 —had been on the board for some time. Now they were read off with dignity and received respectful cheers.

"No tickets with six winners." The cheering began with the word No: the regulars knew what the rest of the sentence had to be; the occasional visitors took their cue from the regulars. At our table, Billie shrieked with delight. The rest of us smiled; with no perfect lines out, our ticket had to be good for a consolation prize.

"Three tickets with five winners," the announcer continued. "Each ticket worth $29,307." Away off in the grandstand, a woman screamed with joy, and there was laughter from those near her. "Eighteen tickets with four winners," the announcer went on. "Each ticket pays $1,622.60."

Billie clapped her hands in glee. Andy Livoti breathed a deep sigh of relief. My 60 percent share of the consolation prize would put me comfortably ahead; so would the 5 percent Andy and Billie shared; probably the win was more important to them than mine to me; I doubted if either owned anything in the world other than the clothes on his back and his equity in the ticket. Lisa, obviously, was the big winner in our group. In one sense, she was the only one who had won anything of importance; Andy, Billie and Barnes had lacked sufficient capital to play seriously. I had, during the time that the five-and-ten ticket matured, backed other horses on which I had a net loss. Thus, whether or not I had actually hedged, I had achieved the effect of a hedge, which is to say I had evened out the result. In the case of a winning bet, a hedge vitiates a part of the winnings as the price of diminishing or eliminating the risk of loss.

"About Jesse's Hand," Barnes said. He did not finish the sentence.

"We'll ship," I said. I decided that in reckoning my own position as against Lisa's, in evaluating the changes in her position and mine, I would also have to include that I, and not she, had acquired John Barrie Barnes for a partner.

Barnes picked up the five-and-ten ticket. "I'll collect our dividend," he proposed. "We can straighten our accounts and get cracking when I get back."

As soon as he left, I used a pencil on the tablecloth to figure the division of the $1,622.60. I took pleasure in carrying it out to the second decimal, and pride in the swiftness with which I did the job and in the fact that I got it right on the first try. I wrote down the amounts payable to each shareholder—$81.13 to Barnes; the same, jointly, to Andy and Billie; $486.78 for Lisa; $973.56 for me—proved my figures by adding them up and getting $1,622.60, and looked up to see Lisa writing something on a blank five-and-ten form.

I asked if she were checking up on me. She shook her head

and handed me the paper on which she had been working. I passed mine to her. Hers turned out to be a hastily written duplicate of the five-and-ten ticket Barnes had taken to the cashier, with the four winning numbers circled, and two lines drawn through the layout.

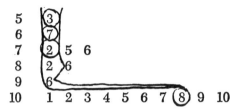

I studied her work, unable to see its significance, but aware that something was wrong. Then John Barrie Barnes was back, grinning and piling bills on the table, and asking if I had finished my calculations since he, John Barrie Barnes, wanted only what was coming to him, neither more nor less, which was only right and proper, what? Lisa handed him my figures.

Barnes was still talking, complimenting me on the exactitude of my distribution, offering, however, to forego the odd pennies due him if it would help make things easier, even offering to contribute some pennies from his own pocket when Lisa's knee found mine under the table and nudged it sharply, once, twice, and I understood.

"You son of a bitch," I said, getting to my feet. "You crummy, angle-shooting, cheating son of a bitch." I wasn't shouting, but I wasn't making any effort to keep my voice low either.

"For God's sake, Lew—" Andy Livoti tried to push between Barnes and me; Barnes was protesting that he hadn't a clue what I was talking about, not the foggiest, so help him; but I could tell from his eyes that he had more than a clue.

I banged my hand on the table, and the glasses and ashtrays

jumped, and there was silence, not only at our table but at
nearby tables too. "Two lines," I said in the hush. "*Two
winnings lines.*" I read them quickly from the paper Lisa had
done. "Three-seven-two-*two*-six-eight, three-seven-two-*six*-six-
eight."

"What?" Barnes's astonishment was now painfully false.

"You played penny pools all your life," I said. "Perms and
bankers. You know a multiple ticket can have more than one
winning line. You knew this one had two. Let's have it."

"I give you my word . . ." Barnes was edging out into the
aisle.

"Grab him, Andy." Andy, who still obviously didn't understand, used Barnes's arm as a lever to bring him back to the
table. "I don't want your word," I told him. "Just the other
$1,600."

"If I told you the clark only paid me for one . . ."

"Don't be coy. I'd want to know which clerk it was, and I'd
go straight to the mutuel manager. Come on!"

Slowly, Barnes put his hand in his shirt pocket and withdrew
some bills. "You found me out," he said, trying to smile. "No
harm done." Nobody said anything as he counted out the bills,
sixteen hundreds, a twenty, two ones.

"And sixty cents," I said. He added six dimes to the pile.

"A share of it's mine," he said. "A share of both. You've no
right to do me—"

"We don't *do* people," I told him. "We leave that to you." I
sorted out $162.30 from the money on the table and pushed it
toward him. "There's your share. You can keep the odd four
cents."

"I'm terribly sorry," Barnes began. "I don't know why—"

"Shut up!" He subsided. "Now, as to Jesse's Hand," I went
on, "I'm going to *give* you a hundred dollars—"

"A *hundred*—"

"Give you a hundred," I went on, knowing he had no choice but to accept, "for any interest you may claim in Jesse's Hand. Take it or leave it." I picked up a hundred-dollar bill and held it in the air just over the $162.30.

"I've got debts . . ." Barnes began.

"You'll manage," I said. "And," I added, "if I see you at Del Mar tomorrow, I'll have you arrested."

"On what charge?"

"I'll make one up. And when your prints get sent to Washington, I'm sure they won't come back marked unknown." Barnes's eyes narrowed, and I knew I had struck pay dirt. "How about it, Mr. Barnes?"

Barnes hesitated and looked around the Turf Club as if hoping to find an ally at one of the nearby silent tables. Finally he shrugged. I dropped the bill onto the pile, and he picked up his money and moved away up the aisle. The Texan at the next table applauded; someone else took it up, until finally there was a wave of applause, which I acknowledged with a half-salute before I sat down.

"Let's get this pot divided up," I said when the applause was replaced with the sounds of conversation. "And if we're going to bet the last race, let's do it now, and then watch from downstairs. We've got a lot of work to do."

"You sure stopped his clock," Andy Livoti said admiringly.

"She figured it out." I pointed at Lisa. "Good thing for you, too. You get an extra eighty-one from the five-and-ten, and you get all but a hundred of the fifteen hundred I was going to have to give the two of you."

"You don't have to do that," Andy pointed out.

"If I don't," I said, aware that this was not going to be a hard argument to win, "then I make a profit out of dealing him out, and that wouldn't be right because it was too much fun." I turned to Lisa, who was studying the *Form.* "You see anything in the last race?"

"I see twelve platers that can't raise a gallop," she said.

"We can wheel the quiniela," I pointed out. "Sixty-six two-horse combinations—$132. Can't lose it all, and we might catch a big one." I had the feeling I was rolling now. Logic told me there was a good chance these cheapest-of-all horses would not run to form. The feeling told me they *wouldn't.* "Who wants shares?"

10

The things that had to be done both before and after the running of the twelfth race at Caliente on Sunday had been done; and now it was two o'clock Monday morning. Labor Day. I had begun the weekend holding cards, at a dollar-and-a-half an hour, in the California Club. I had been unable, prior to first post Saturday, to wheel a daily double; tonight I had paid one-fourth the cost of such a wheel for a room in the Luna Del Mar Hotel, a half mile south of the Del Mar race-track. I relaxed in a canvas chair on the dimly lit balcony attached to that room, and thought about these and other matters, and smoked a cigarette, and watched the ocean below me as it lapped at the beach, and could decide only that the tide was coming in.

Lisa came out and sat in the chair next to mine. For a moment, I thought I could see two moons. Then I realized that the second was merely the emblem on the motel sign, visible in reflection because Lisa had not quite closed the glass door to the room. In the half dark, I saw Lisa get a cigarette from her robe pocket, found a pack of matches in my own, struck one, and started to light her cigarette. In the match-glow, I saw a laugh start in her eyes; the sound of it died in her throat, but the laugh went on, silently, both of us laughing so noiselessly we could hear the whir of rubber as the traffic went past on the highway behind us, and the lapping of the surf on the beach below.

"A nice quiniela," she said, somehow getting the words out without interrupting the silent laughter. I touched her arm in agreement, the laughter building up inside me, remembering that twelfth race, the favorite coming away riderless at the start, the two outsiders galloping unchallenged in front, the riderless favorite three lengths back as a hazard to be dealt with by any possible challengers, the desperate run by the third choice, who wound up herded next to the rail by the unguided favorite, the two outsiders continuing to alternate in the lead inside the sixteenth pole, it making not the slightest difference in the world which was first and which second, the only important fact—that one would be first and the other second—long since demonstrated.

"Which one did win it?" I asked.

"Does it matter?"

I shook my head. We had watched the race from an impossible angle on the lawn in front of the grandstand. I had handed all 66 two-dollar tickets to Lisa as the two long shots came to the finish line, leaving it to her to sort out the winning combination while I moved with Andy and Billie toward the stable area.

A veterinarian's certificate had to be obtained in order to clear Jesse's Hand through the border and a horse-van engaged to transport him to Del Mar. When Jesse's Hand first refused to enter the van, and then, after having been intimidated into doing so, attempted to destroy it and himself in a display of temper, it had been necessary to bring from the animal's stall a certain white rooster which, the horse's guinea said, was Jesse's Hand's stable pet. When it was seen that this did, indeed, quiet the horse, an inquiry had to be made as to the admissibility of roosters into the United States. I was unable to obtain a reliable opinion on this point; so I put a box and an extra horse blanket inside the van and told the driver to place the rooster in the box and cover the box with the blanket on approaching the border, advised him to pray that the cock would not crow, and gave him a small bribe to compensate him for the risk and for the damage to be done to his conscience.

Stable space at Del Mar had to be arranged; when a phone call by Andy Livoti to the racing secretary produced only regrets that what did not exist could not be supplied, I found Lisa and referred the problem to her; and she passed it on, by phone, to a public trainer who was shipping part of his string to Golden Gate Fields, who solved it.

We needed a rider for Jesse's Hand. Andy Livoti argued in favor of waiting until morning when, being at Del Mar, he could hang around the jockeys' rooms and chat with the agents and find out what was available. I favored an immediate move. With twelve horses entered overnight, the contract riders and the first-rate free lances would already have mounts; Andy would be shopping among the culls and rejects.

"We're better off with the twelfth best rider at Del Mar," Andy argued, "than the cream of what they got riding horses here."

"I don't know," I answered. "One of them showed me something today."

"Chavez?"

"Esteban."

Andy's surprise was evident. "What did Esteban show us?" he asked. "The one time we bet on him . . ."

Andy stopped in midsentence and turned beet red, and I knew he would have given anything he had or hoped to get to call back those last seven words. I could have covered up for him with a quick reply, but I had been surprised to the point of hesitation and could now only regret his distress. Lisa, who was sitting on a stack of blanket rolls in the stable, turned her head away. Billie, who had been brushing Jesse's Hand, dropped her brush and called attention to her clumsiness in words that, because they were too strong and too loudly said for the situation, made it obvious that she was trying to direct attention away from Andy, which only made Andy's predicament worse. Only Jesse's Hand, who pawed aimlessly at the fallen brush, seemed unaware of the gaffe.

When I spoke up, much too late, I forebore to point out that only a pleasure-player limits his surveillance to horses and riders he has backed. Instead, I explained that while Chavez's ride on the beaten Scrim's Queen had included a splendid piece of horsemanship in the stretch, Chavez was, nonetheless, an apprentice, lacking judgment and experience; Esteban's winning ride on Titania, on the other hand, though made possible by the poor judgment of the other riders (Chavez included) who permitted Titania an uncontested early run on the front end, could not have been accomplished had Esteban, on Titania, been anything less than a highly skilled judge of pace, and that the ability to judge pace was far more likely to be required of Jesse's Hand's rider than a facility at eluding a bolting horse.

"Maybe." I knew Andy might have argued further if he had not, momentarily at least, forfeited his right to debate.

The decision made, Esteban had to be found and notified that he had been tapped for the honor of riding, at Del Mar, a horse whose record contained nothing to indicate that he was capable of winning at Caliente.

When we found him, in front of the jockeys' room, dressed to leave the track in over-sharply cut sports clothes, and wearing enormous dark glasses, Esteban's appearance was hardly reassuring. Furthermore, John Barrie Barnes had told the truth about Esteban's English, which was slight to the point of near invisibility. Surprisingly, it was Billie who solved the linguistic tangle, using—for the first time, she said—the two years of Spanish she had completed at Commerce High School in New York City.

Now the arrangements were made and the machinery was in operation. Jesse's Hand was safely bedded down in his stall at Del Mar; Andy and Billie were bedded in the tack room next to the stall. Alejandro Esteban was asleep in a motel between Caliente and the border but would, according to Billie's understanding of his remarks, arrive at Del Mar before noon. The seventh race would go at about five. I glanced at my watch.

"Three-fifteen," I announced. "Less than fourteen hours to go."

Lisa sat up. I noticed there was only one moon visible. For a moment, I thought the real one had set; then I realized that the operators of the Luna Del Mar had turned off their sign. "It's only a horse race," she said. "Don't make it sound like a wedding. Or an execution."

"It's a big race for me. A sort of moment of truth." I hoped that last didn't sound pompous. It was, in any case, true. "If the horse looks sound, I may go for broke. That makes it a big race."

"And a moment of truth?"

"I have five thousand dollars. I was just about empty night before last."

"So?"

"So, if I send it all in, that's something special. For me."

"Something special." Lisa relit her cigarette. "But no moment of truth."

"If I lose . . ." I left the thought unfinished.

"In that sense it's a moment of truth," she conceded, her tone

telling me there was another sense in which it was not. "Lose
and you maybe change your whole life."

"Or prevent it from changing."

"You mean 'back to Gardena'?"

"Yes."

"And if you win?"

"What's that got to do with it?"

"Everything." She turned in her chair, put her legs across my
ankles, and eased her head back on her hands. Suddenly her
face and hair were silver and white in the moonlight, and only
the fact that this conversation had to end soon made it possible
for me to go on with it at all. "A moment of truth has to cut
both ways," she said. "Understand?" I had barely heard the
words and didn't understand at all; but I said nothing. "The
bull can kill the matador. But the bull can also die. What
happens if Jesse's Hand wins?"

"I don't know."

"I do. You cash your tickets, and you take a long look at the
eighth race. If you don't find another rendezvous with destiny
there, you look for it in the ninth race. Then there are no more
races, so you look for it somewhere else. You have more money,
which makes finding it more difficult, but not impossible. You'll
find it. And if you win again, you go on looking, on a different
level now, but looking until you find it again. And, if necessary,
again. Gamblers don't have a moment of truth, because what
they're fighting can't be killed. They play a game that never
ends. Remember the carnival stands, with the signs 'Pitch Till
You Win'? That kind of game." She laughed and sat upright
again. "Only with the gambler, it's 'Pitch Till You Lose.'" She
rose and stood over me and bent down to kiss my forehead as if
unaware of what this did to her robe or of what was done to
her robe did to me. "It's a shame."

"And you?" I was determined to ignore, for the moment, what I was looking at. "If you understand it so well . . ."

Lisa straightened up again. Now we were only conversing. "That's why I'm not a gambler."

"What were you doing?"

"Gambling," she admitted. "But drinking doesn't make me a drinker, and I . . ."

"A matter," I suggested, "of degree."

"Of kind," she said firmly. "A difference in kind."

"What . . ."

"I just explained it to you." She stood at the edge of the balcony and looked down at the ocean. "How about a swim?" she suggested.

"I haven't got a suit."

She smiled; I felt some of what Andy had felt in Jesse's Hand's stall. "Neither have I," Lisa said. "So we better not wait until morning."

11

At lunch, in the patio back of the Del Mar club-house, I felt a sense of well-being stronger than any I could recall, quite unlike any other really, the air fresh and sweet-smelling and somehow conveying in its scent the notion that it would always be the same, and the colors so fiercely vivid they would have hurt my eyes except that, at that moment, I knew no part of me could be hurt.

Jesse's Hand was part of the reason I felt the way I did; and so was Lisa; and so was having won on Saturday and Sunday; and so was the certainty that Jesse's Hand would win today and so would I. But there was more to the feeling, I knew, than merely the sum of these parts. The horse could lose, though I doubted that it would. I could lose; that was less unlikely. Lisa could desert me as readily as she had departed from her association with Colonel Cole; that ranked, in probability, midway between the other two. But I accepted as a possibility that all three might occur, that I might end this weekend as I had begun it; that is, moneyless and alone. But even if all this happened, I felt I would not be what I had been, because I was sure some of the feeling would remain. I was, I decided, alive again; and on second thought I substituted *at last* for *again*.

Because I was alive, Lisa mattered; but, also because I was alive, she didn't matter all *that* much, whatever *that* might mean. The world, I suddenly came to understand, was full of girls; most were not Lisa's equal in beauty or charm, but I told myself that some perhaps exceeded her in both. There would be other horses, too, if this one failed; other days if this one turned sour; other games if this one ended badly; but the feeling would always be in me. It would diminish when I was tired, when I was losing, when I made mistakes, when I was unlucky; but from this it followed that sleep, skill, caution, or a change in luck, would bring it back. I decided I had come a long way and still had a long way to go, and perhaps would never get wherever I was going, but it didn't matter; I was moving; I would keep on moving.

"What are you thinking?" Lisa asked.

I considered a truthful reply; but the sort of truths I was contemplating could not be appropriately discussed over a table on a racetrack patio. "That dress is your second nicest costume," I said, which was also true, but not the truth. The dress was green; and so, at the moment, were Lisa's eyes.

"Second nicest?"

"Next to your bathing suit," I explained.

Lisa grinned. "You ever do that before?"

"In Ohio. With three guys in my high school class. Not exactly the same thing."

"I should say not," Lisa said. "Ohio. That would be fresh-water swimming."

"Last night was better."

"Salt water always is. Well, aren't we the dude?" The last was directed toward Andy Livoti, who arrived with Billie. Andy was wearing a new blue linen duster and, I noticed, the same slacks and shoes he had worn at Caliente.

"Billie's idea," Andy explained.

"A good one, too," she said. "Only there's not much of a selection on a Labor Day morning, even in La Jolla, which is supposed to be a resort. I got this in the same place." *This* was a large straw hat, the kind my father used to call "a madam's Easter bonnet." "Makes me feel I should be selling seconds of Jap pottery," Billie admitted.

Andy and Billie sat down. Lisa and I paused in our eating to let them order and catch up. Meanwhile, Andy reported on Jesse's Hand's night (quiet), his apparent condition (excellent), and the appearance, on his arrival, of Alejandro Esteban (nervous).

"He says he appreciates being asked to ride this horse and he will do his best," Billie said. "Or his worst," she added thoughtfully. "I really don't know. I must have cut class the day they covered adverbial nouns."

"I could get him a ride in an early race," Livoti proposed. "One turn of the track before he goes for the money."

"He hasn't ridden here before?"

"Not for a year, and then only a sprint," Andy said. "He's never been in a race around both turns." I started to look through my program to see what horses lacked riders. "One boy turned up sick, and took off about four horses. Quite a scramble over by the jockeys' room. I saw Charlie Ferrell—you remember him from the Ohio wheel—looking for a boy for a horse in the sixth."

It sounded harmless enough. "You offer him Esteban?"

"I didn't know how much to tell him."

"You mean about why Esteban's here? Jesse's Hand?"

Andy nodded. "He must know we brought the boy up."

"Admit it. Tell him you think Jesse's Hand's got a hell of a chance, and you're going for the house and lot and advise him to do the same."

"All right." Andy sounded doubtful. "It's going to kick the bejesus out of the price."

"Not as much as leaving him wondering why we shipped here in the first place. And maybe finding out."

"How—"

"When he sees the betting, he'll know somebody's taken the rubber band off."

"If you say so." Andy was still unconvinced.

"I say so."

"I'll go look for Charlie." Andy rose as the waiter arrived.

"Eat first," I suggested.

"You sound like my mother," Billie said. "If a guy was bleeding in the street, and you said you wanted to go down and put a tourniquet on him, she'd tell you to eat first."

"He'll get another boy," Andy pointed out.

"Then go."

"I'll go with him," Billie said. "Somebody's going to have to translate the good news for Señor Esteban."

Billie followed Andy out of the restaurant. A waiter, seeing them leave, covered their sandwiches with glass bells and brought coffee for Lisa and me. "Aren't you afraid of confusing people?" Lisa asked. "Telling the truth about your horse."

"A small dose of the truth never hurts, even on a racetrack," I said. "Charlie Ferrell's a small-bore angle shooter. Here's a horse that shipped in, and nobody knows why. When the betting starts, Charlie and a hundred like him are going to watch to see if he gets a play. When he does, they'll look for a reason. If they'll settle for Andy Livoti backing his own horse, they won't follow along. Not heavily, anyway. They'll figure if Andy knew which end of the horse bit and which gave milk he wouldn't be down at Caliente with one bad-legged plater, so why go along with a tip when he ships in?"

Lisa sipped at her coffee. "You're betting the horse, then."

It was not a question, but I answered it. "Yes, I'm betting him." I knew why I was betting him, too, having acquired that knowledge in the same instant that I knew that I was betting him, but I kept the reason to myself, partly because it was hard to express, but partly, more importantly, because Lisa would have ridiculed it. She could not ridicule it unless I said it, even though she knew what it was, because her method of acquiring that knowledge was as contrary to reason and as susceptible to ridicule as the reason itself. Lisa might or might not be a gambler, but she had a gambler's point of view. Could she say: "I've got a hunch you're playing a hunch, and that's a stupid thing to do. Something tells me something tells you I'm a lucky charm, and the quicker you forget that idea the better."

She could not, I decided, deciding in the same moment that whether she could say it or not, it was true, and it had better not be true, and resolving to find other, better reasons for betting Jesse's Hand or to abandon the notion.

Lisa finished her coffee and excused herself to go to the paddock; a two-year-old, much fancied on conformation and breeding by Colonel Cole, was entered in the first race. While she was gone, and before Billie and Andy returned, I continued to examine the question of betting on Jesse's Hand, not *whether*—for I knew I would—nor *how much*—for the answer to that was fast resolving itself into a choice between *all* and *nearly all*—but *why*. Not because of Lisa, nor because of the way I felt, for these did not relate to the race, the horse, the odds, the chances of success, and the penalties for failure, and these were the factors that had to govern my play. If they did not, I was a hunch-player, a sucker, one of the many who say "I expect to lose when I go to the track; I figure I'm paying for an afternoon's entertainment; whatever I come home with, that's what I figure I won." I had never been such a fish and did not propose to become one at forty.

Why then? I examined the other possible reasons. I had committed myself to bringing the horse from Caliente to Del Mar; in fulfilling this commitment, I had incurred considerable expense. In order to protect that investment—I broke the argument in mid-thought. The bet was sound, or not, on its merits, not because of any other action I had, or had not, taken. To believe otherwise would be to believe that there were good bets for one person which were, at the same time, bad bets for another, which is absurd.

Absurd? one part of me asked.

Absurd, the rest of me replied. A bet is a bet is a bet; cards do not know who is holding them; and a pari-mutuel ticket does not know for whom it is punched out. If a horse has one chance in five of winning and odds of seven to one are available against that possibility, to back him is to make a good bet, good for the man who understands, the man who does not understand, the hunch-player, and the drunk who buys the ticket by mistake. But if the horse has a chance in seven, and the odds are five-to-one, the bet is a bad one for all the world, including, but not limited to, the above-mentioned.

Not always. Suppose a man has ten dollars, but he owes a hundred to a bookmaker who means to break his arm if the debt is still outstanding at four o'clock, and it is now 3:50, and someone offers the man ten-to-one he cannot cut an ace from an honest deck, well shuffled, one cut, a hundred-to-ten—

Hoo hah.

Which is ten-to-one against a twelve-to-one shot, but a good bet just the same, because the ten-spot will not save him from a broken arm, and is, from that point of view, useless. So, in a sense, if he cuts the deck he has a chance in thirteen of avoiding a broken arm, but if he passes up the bet because the percentage against him is intolerably high, he has no chance whatsover of avoiding a broken arm. Is not any chance better than no chance?

Isn't that a little extreme? Twelve times out of thirteen, the card-cutter will end up broke *and* crippled. Observe how readily the man who wishes to play a hunch ignores what has to be ignored to conceal—

Unfair!

To conceal the fact that he is betting on a horse because the sky is blue, the sea is green, a girl is blond, and he feels great.

No, no. Not because of those. But because Bailey Bridge outclassed his field yesterday at Caliente, and Jesse's Hand gave weight and a beating to Bailey Bridge—

According to John Barrie Barnes.

Yes.

Who is a liar and a cheat.

A cheat.

But not a liar?

An important distinction.

An impossible distinction.

I know what took place on the Wash.

What he said took place.

And I feel.

Aha. Now you've said it.

Feel?

That's it.

I feel—

There you go again!

The two parts of me, having concluded their debate, with-drew and permitted my entirety to re-form itself and to finish its coffee. There are some problems, I thought—all of me, now—as to which the solutions depend properly, in part, on feelings. And one of them is whether a man like John Barrie Barnes has told the truth. On or off the racecourse, there are the facts, hard, finite, susceptible of reductions to columns of type in the *Form,* or of reduction to reasonable words; and there are soft, indefinite interpretations, opinions, and judgments; and in forming these, feeling plays a part, as it does again in determining how to weigh the facts against the interpretations.

"Daily-double windows will close in five minutes." Hearing the announcement, I realized that there must have been others, one when the windows opened, one when the horses came on the track, at least; but I had missed them all. It was as if I had forgotten that the program included a daily double. In fact, since I had made no marks whatsoever in my *Form,* it was as if neither the first six races nor the last two had any reality, and as if I knew all I had to know about the seventh.

Lisa came back then with the word that the two-year-old in which Colonel Cole had indicated an interest had looked washy in the ring and was not striding out in the post parade. I didn't care. This was going to be a one-race, one-horse program for me; the race would be the seventh and the horse would be Jesse's Hand; and when the horse had run his race I would be much richer or much poorer, which mattered, but what mattered more was that either way I would be "right" as I used the word. And now, as the traffic quickened in and out of the patio restaurant, I knew that the reasons for all this had nothing to do with blue skies, or green water, or a blond girl, but derived from the fact that I knew something about that horse in that race. (To have added, even in my thought, the words "not generally known" after the words "knew something" would have been tautology. On or around the track, the expression "to know something" connotes exclusivity of knowledge.) What I knew, what I would be acting on, was the following information. One: Jesse's Hand *had* run and hid from Bailey Bridge. (Barnes's testimony might be written off as part

of a con too subtle for me to comprehend; but Andy's corrobo-
ration had to be valid; Andy was many things; he was not
subtle.) Two: Jesse's Hand was well meant, not out for exercise, not being reserved by her connections for a later effort at
better odds; Lisa, Billie, Andy and I were Jesse's Hand's connections.

Lisa and I moved, hand in hand, through the tunnel under
the Turf Club and stood on the cement lawn, looking out onto
the track. In the backstretch, the two-year-olds were being
loaded into the gate.

"Lew!" Without letting go of Lisa's hand, I turned. Max
Rosenberg was standing next to me. His presence was surprising; his costume (chartreuse Hawaiian shirt, green tie, blue
blazer) was astounding.

I grinned, genuinely glad to see him. Through him, Kathy
would learn, with less pain than if I called her and told her,
assuming I had the moral fiber to do it which I doubted, that I
was not, as she had probably feared, in the hands of the
police, nor in another Gardena, but back in action. "We got the
Seven," Max said, moving a little so that I could see the woman
next to him. "My wife," he said, answering my unspoken question. The woman was much younger than Max, an extremely
attractive brunette.

"Hello, Mrs. Rosenberg."

"Rosalind." She had a pleasant voice.

"Hold the chitchat," Max commanded. "They're in the gate."

He put his field glasses on the race; I did the same. The
Seven turned out to be a small black filly who broke second,
chased the leader into the turn, ran the leader down at the
head of the stretch, but, despite Max Rosenberg's harsh "Stay
there, baby! All the way!" proved unable to hang on, finishing
fourth, beaten two lengths.

"What did you have?" Max asked, throwing a half dozen pari-mutuel tickets of various colors on the ground.

"Not a thing." And I was proud of it.

"You're kidding!"

"Not everyone bets, Max," his wife put in.

"At the track?" Max snorted. "Her first time at the races," he explained.

"And how many times for you?" Before he could answer, she went on: "Mr. Expert didn't know he'd need a tie and a jacket."

"How's that?" I was looking at Max, who was wearing both.

"The management supplied these gems," he said. "The sport shirt's o.k. where I usually sit."

"With the gamblers and loafers," Rosalind Rosenberg added, Max chiming in on the last three words.

"You think you're going to like racing?" I was just making conversation.

Mrs Rosenberg gave the question some thought. "It's outdoors, at least," she said. "On our honeymoon, he took me to a casino in Havana." She held her nose, to dramatize the principal advantage of outdoor gambling.

Andy joined us, and I made the introductions, pausing momentarily after saying "You know Miss Fortune," remembering suddenly that I might be using material that would be new to Rosalind Rosenberg.

She sensed my discomfort. "Max has no secrets from me," she said. "We have an arrangement. He's allowed to gamble, and I'm allowed to not gamble. We agreed on our wedding day."

"Was that the whole ceremony?" Lisa asked.

"And we broke a glass," Mrs. Rosenberg said.

The official sign was lit and the prices went up. Andy gave a whoop of delight and flashed a ten-dollar ticket on the winner, then worth $240.

It was the beginning of a most enjoyable three hours. I spent most of the time at the table, leaving it only to watch the running of the races, enjoying most of the time at the table, relishing the look of respect—almost of awe—Max Rosenberg gave me when he saw that the program listed "L. E. White" and "A. Livoti" as owner and trainer of Number Eleven in the seventh race. My satisfaction was in no way diminished by my awareness that Max would not have had as high a regard for the owner of a $20,000 house or a $200,000 lot, though these items were worth, respectively, four and forty times the value of Jesse's Hand. And I took unashamed pride in the fact that Rosalind Rosenberg accepted my opinions on the relative merits of the horses entered in the early events as holy writ, eventually going so far as to risk two of her own dollars on my opinion of the probable outcome of the fourth race, for which act of faith she was rewarded by the return of her deuce and a profit of $4.40.

Andy and Billie were in transit during most of these three hours, going to and from the stable, and later the receiving barn, to observe Jesse's Hand and report on his apparent state of health. In addition, Andy made a number of trips to the sellers' windows, to back opinions arrived at in conferences with me, and an only slightly smaller number of trips to the cashiers' windows to complete the transactions thus begun.

Lisa left the table only to accompany me on my trips to trackside. The rest of the time, she sat with the Rosenbergs and me, and the three of them listened while I delivered horse-by-horse analyses of the races and told, to perfection, jokes I had not known I knew.

"What about the Fifth?" Max asked as Rosalind returned with her $6.40 from the Fourth.

I marshaled the revaluations of the *Racing Form* into argument, pro and contra, as to each of the seven entered, making up my mind as I talked, eventually indicating a preference for the pole horse, a three-year-old filly who, because of her age and sex, would have a considerable weight advantage. The filly was demonstrably fainthearted, but there didn't seem to me much speed in the race, and I thought she might last out six furlongs.

"I'm sold," Max announced, rising. "Can I help anyone?"

Lisa asked what window Max proposed to visit; learning that he planned to buy a ten-dollar win ticket, she handed over a twenty-dollar bill and asked for "the one, twice."

"Lew?"

"I'm waiting for Jesse's Hand," I said.

"I admire you," Max admitted. "You sure you don't want ten dollars' worth for a rooting interest?"

"I'll root for you people," I promised. "I need all the ten-spots I've got for Jesse's Hand."

"Did you mean that?" Lisa asked when Max was gone. I nodded. "How far are you planning to go?"

"As far as I can without wrecking the price." The qualifying phrase was a lie, pure and simple. Or simple, at least. From that moment on, while I hoped the pool would be large enough and my timing sufficiently adroit for the odds to remain respectable I knew I was going to bet it all, all I had on me, which is to say all I had, on my own horse, Jesse's Hand, in the seventh race, then an hour and a half off.

Billie and Andy came back to report a late scratch in the seventh, which would reduce the field to eleven. Andy considered the scratch good news; after restudying the record of the withdrawn horse, I agreed. The horse was cheap; his absence would hardly affect the odds against mine, for he was not, on form, a contender; and the few players who would have backed him would be long-shot players of the sort who do not demand that the horse they bet on have a chance but merely the illusory possibility of an enormous return on a small investment. Their money would go on other horses of comparable status, not on Jesse's Hand, who was not going to be the favorite, in my opinion, but was surely not going to go at big enough odds to be called a long shot.

"You people!" Rosalind Rosenberg said with a careful tolerance. "The way you go at this! If you put the same effort into some legitimate business—"

"We know, lady," Andy Livoti said gently.

Max Rosenberg returned with a wide grin and a fistful of tickets, from which he dealt two to Lisa. Then, still grinning, he announced that this was one bet he could not lose. "These," he said, gesturing with the tickets, "these I paid for with the track's money."

Lisa's "oh" was noncommittal; Billie, who was sipping from a water glass, coughed violently, nearly spilling the water into Mrs. Rosenberg's lap. The group moved onto the lawn to watch the race. It took two minutes to get the horses loaded and off, and another minute for the field to reach the eighth pole. The filly I had recommended was then three lengths clear; having attained and held the lead without being pressed, she was also still a fresh horse and required only eleven seconds to cover the last two hundred and twenty yards, so fresh that, though hard held, she was drawing off from her field at the end, her final margin being a half dozen lengths.

Max was effusive in his thanks. I took pleasure in his pleasure; as far as I could remember it was the first time my joy at someone else's win was not tinged with some portion of envy. This was particularly astounding because Max had just demonstrated that, as a horseplayer, he was not the sound gambler he was at the poker table but an unsophisticated bettor whose action was determined by how he stood for the day and who admitted that, for him, the track retained at least a partial title to the money he had already won.

Charlie Ferrell, a straw-hatted Midwesterner who was giving Alejandro Esteban his only opportunity to go round the track before he did so astride Jesse's Hand, appeared to invite us to accompany him to the walking ring. The Rosenbergs tagged along without any specific invitation. The entire party was admitted to the saddling area, the women and Max Rosenberg delayed at the entrance only until Lisa could catch the eye of a trainer, inside the ring, who apparently swung more weight with the management than did Charlie Ferrell.

"Can this boy ride at all?" Ferrell asked me when we were all inside.

"Some," I said. "He had a lot of winners at Caliente."

Ferrell spat into the peat moss and shavings that made up the floor of the ring. "Will he follow orders?"

"If he understands them."

"Who don't understand 'bring him out easy'?"

"He doesn't speak English," I said quietly.

"Keerist!" Ferrell was outraged. "I do you guys a favor, and you stick me with some dizzy Mex that I can't even tell him what to do so when he don't do it I can't even get mad at him."

"I'll translate for you," Billie volunteered.

"Who are you?" Ferrell demanded.

"My girl," Andy Livoti said.

Ferrell looked about wildly as if this were the last, most incredible blow visited on him by an unreasonable providence. Then he shrugged, said "Serves me right," and walked toward his horse who stood in a nearby stall, a groom at his head, Alejandro Esteban standing nearby.

With Billie's help, Ferrell informed Esteban that his mount's name was Guide Line, that Guide Line was a piece of pig meat and unlikely to win, but that he, Charlie Ferrell, was in dire need of even a fourth-place share of the purse, that

Guide Line would shy away from the whip with equal consistency when the whip was applied with the right or left hand, but that, if eased out of the gate, if treated gently in the first half-mile, if ridden carefully throughout so as not to lose ground, he might then respond to an enthusiastic hand-ride sufficiently to pick up some tiring horses in the stretch, which might or might not put him in the money. Esteban made an affirmative noise; a bell rang; Ferrell gave the boy a leg up, and Guide Line followed the others onto the track.

Charlie Ferrell announced he was going in back of the stands to vomit, and departed. Max Rosenberg went back to the Turf Club to bet the race, first asking me for advice, getting none. Andy went to the receiving barn to be ready to bring Jesse's Hand to the walking ring when the sixth race was over. Billie, Lisa, Rosalind Rosenberg, and I remained in the walking ring, which, being at track level and two hundred yards from the start, gave us a good view of Esteban easing Guide Line out of the gate as Ferrell had requested, and a worse view of Esteban saving ground on the turn, well back in the pack but down on the rail. As the horses went along the backstretch, they passed entirely out of sight behind the tote board. Guide Line, the public address system told us, was now eighth, now seventh. I picked up Guide Line in my glasses as the field came back into view, followed him into the final turn, then lost him in the glare off the Pacific as the quarter pole was reached, then picked him up again as the field swung into the stretch, saw Esteban slip him inside a horse and then come wide for the drive, well back but moving nicely, Esteban hunched on the horse's neck, pumping, scrubbing, pushing, refraining from using his whip, following all of Ferrell's instructions to the letter. At the sixteenth pole, Guide Line had caught all but two of the field; he caught the trailer of that pair a hundred yards out, but failed to reach the other, finishing second.

Charlie Ferrell suddenly reappeared looking as if he might well have done what he had announced he would do. "Nice ride," he said. "Thanks."

"Any time," I told him.

"What about yours?" he asked.

"Andy's high on the horse," I said truthfully. "I'm going to send it in. Don't say I didn't give you the word."

Ferrell said he would think it over and went out on the track to pick up his horse. A few minutes later, Andy brought Jesse's Hand into the ring, led him into Stall Eleven, and threw a blanket over him. Max Rosenberg returned, lamenting the fact that, without my advice, he had made a poor selection. "Ten horse's behinds he was looking at in the stretch," he said, tearing a small stack of tickets in half and depositing them in an ornamental trash can, "but he wasn't looking at the biggest horse's ass of all because I was up in the Turf Club."

I smiled and backed into the angle caused by the intersection of the last stall and the fence at the edge of the walking ring; I turned away from the others, so that the walls served to discourage interruptions, and took my final look at the past performances of Jesse's Hand and the ten horses he was about to run against. On my understanding of that form, my riding orders would be based; and it was now apparent that riding orders were, potentially, of considerable importance. Esteban's ride on Guide Line had proved not only that he could follow orders, but also that Billie was sufficiently bilingual to serve as a transmission belt. When Esteban arrived, wearing silks of an intricate orange-and-white pattern—the former silks, I decided, of Livoti's late patroness, more recently his own, now those of my one-horse stable—I was ready.

I spoke slowly, pausing frequently so Billie could do her translations in short takes, watching Esteban carefully for any evidence that any part of the instructions was unclear to him.

"This is a good horse," I told him. "He can get in trouble and still win this, so don't give up if things don't go the way we plan. The contention is Lindo-Mar, over there." I pointed across the ring to the Seven, a big black colt. "Number Seven. White bandages, red silks, red blinker." I realized I had forgotten something. While Billie did her translation, hesitating a little over (I assumed) "blinker," I slipped a hundred-dollar bill into Max's hand and gestured narrowly toward the Turf Club. Max, understanding, hurried off in the indicated direction.

"Lindo-Mar is probably a natural speed horse," I went on. "But lately they've been taking him back off the pace. If Lindo-Mar goes to the front, don't fight him. But don't let him loaf on the lead. Make him use his speed. Lay a length or two off, and force the pace. Keep the pressure on; he'll come back to you. If you can, wait till you get to the quarter pole to make your move. But don't take a chance on getting trapped. If you have to move early, do it." I paused. "If Lindo-Mar doesn't go to the front, then you go out there and make the pace. Get on the head end and stay there. Try to give the horse a breather down the back-side, but only if you're clear. You got that?"

Esteban waited for Billie to complete her translation. Then he nodded vigorously. "We've got a minute," I said. "Ask him to tell me."

A short conversation in Spanish ensued. Then Billie reported: "He says: 'The Seven goes to the front, I lay off, a length or two back, force the pace, move when Seven tires. Seven doesn't go to the front, *I* go for the lead and try to go all the way. The horse should have a breather around the half-mile pole.'"

"That's it." Max, puffing but grinning, arrived and handed me a mutuel ticket. I checked to make sure it was correct as to denomination, sort and number, and tucked it into Esteban's shirt pocket. "Tell him that's a hundred-dollar-win ticket." Billie told him; Esteban grinned in appreciative understanding. I looked toward the tote board, saw the horse was 3½–1, and looked back in time to see Esteban look toward the board.

"Watch my smoke," Alejandro Esteban said. He added a few words in Spanish, which Billie translated. "He says that is all the English he knows. He says he is very grateful. He says he will win the race if he has to pick the horse up and carry him."

Six minutes later, I stood with Lisa inside an areaway leading into a salon which, because its floor was carpeted, and because only tickets of $50 denomination and up were handled by its wickets, was called the Gold Room.

"You going for the house and lot?" she asked.

"And my watch and gold ring," I said.

She fumbled in her purse. "I'm not a high roller like you," she said, handing me three hundred-dollar bills. "Still, if you say so . . ."

"I have to. It's the red dog principle."

"You're the boss." Lisa kissed my cheek and was gone.

I was glad that Lisa knew the red dog principle and more glad that she did not choose to debate whether or not it was applicable. The principle derives from a card game called red dog, in which the players ante to form a bank and bet against it in turn, the minimum bet being the smallest chip in the game, the maximum being whatever is in the bank when the bet is made. The bet turns on whether or not the player, who holds four cards in his hand, holds a card which can "top" the top card in the deck; that is, whether he holds a higher card of the same suit. If he does, he wins the amount of his bet, withdrawing that sum from the bank. If he does not, his bet goes into the bank, which continues to expand and shrink as bets are won or lost until it either disappears completely or grows to a prearranged point at which it is divided evenly among the contestants. Gamblers quite correctly call the game "pure arithmetic," by which they mean that the favorable and adverse chances of a single play can be determined by simple counting. A player holding four aces cannot lose and must bet the maximum. A man holding four deuces cannot win and must bet the minimum. A holding of four eights creates an even chance to win; the hand can "top" all deuces, treys, fours, fives, sixes, or sevens, but loses to all nines, tens, jacks, queens, kings, and aces. The casual gambler will usually choose among a variety of sums for his bets, reserving the maximum ("pot") bet for a perfect, or near perfect, hand, betting the minimum when he has only a slight chance, increasing his bets when his chances increase. In so doing, he defies the red dog principle which states that there are only two possible situations and that two bets cover them all: with less than an even chance to win, only the minimum may be bet; with better than a fifty-fifty chance to win, the "pot" bet *must* be made, as readily when the unknown cards are distributed 25–23 in favor of the player as when they break 40–8, or even (when the player holds four aces) 48–0.

Students of the science of probabilities agree with the gamblers on this point, since they classify all bets as having a positive expectancy (meaning that, given an average distribution of the chance-factors, the bettor will, over a period of time, win more money than he will lose), or a negative expectancy (given the same distribution, losses will exceed gains). There is also something called neutral expectancy, which describes the position of the man whose red dog hand contains four eights. Students say that neutral expectancy produces equipartition. Gamblers say the man who holds four eights figures to break even. Neither students nor gamblers can offer a rational program for dealing with situations of neutral expectancy. But each will assert, though each will put it differently, that the basis of sound gambling is the reduction of negative expectancy and the enhancement of positive expectancy; from which it follows that a player with an opportunity to make a bet with a positive expectancy must make as large a bet as the rules of the game permit, limited only by his own ability to make good his loss in the event that chance produces a negative outcome.

"Eleven, ten times." I got my tickets from the hundred-dollar-win window and stepped back to the far wall of the Gold Room to let some time pass before going back for more. The possibility of starting a big rush of money to the horse was less here, where pools were larger than at Caliente, but, of course, it still existed and was to be avoided.

The trouble with applying the red dog principle to this bet, and the reason I was glad Lisa had not chosen to debate its application in this instance, is self-evident. Racing, unlike red dog, is not a game of "simple arithmetic"; I could not prove that my bets on Jesse's Hand possessed a positive expectancy; I could not prove what his chances of winning the race were, and I could only estimate what odds the tote might finally offer against him. I was multiplying a *sensed* probability by judged odds and claiming that my product was as accurate as my multiplication.

I continued to examine my motive and to be dissatisfied with what I found as I went from line to line, buying ten tickets at a time, an investment of $500 or $1,000 each time, depending on which line I was in. When I left the Gold Room, I had $5,500 in win tickets—including Lisa's $300 worth—and $40 in cash; and the knowledge that, in invoking the red-dog principle, I had mixed logic and feeling into a homogenous blend, forced felt premises through a valid syllogism, and staked all but $40 of my worldly portion on the answer thus attained.

I moved from the Gold Room into the patio, and the sunlight seemed to drive the confusion from my mind. I was suddenly sure that it didn't matter how much was known, how much felt, and how much was an intermingling of the two; what mattered was that I had acted, acted as everyone must, on what he *feels* he knows and what he *knows* he feels, in various unmeasurable proportions; and whether I was right in acting as I had would be resolved, not in my mind, which, because it was a mind, was a place where confusion crossed doubt, but on the racetrack where doubts are resolved into certainties expressed in fifths of a second, and niceties are resolved by the study of photographs, and all answers are certified by the flashing of the word *Official* in yellow lights across the top of the green board.

Max Rosenberg touched my arm. "You do it?"

I nodded. I could see Lisa at the table, her head close to Billie's. "I figured you would. Lew?"

Lisa had not looked up from her conversation. I turned back toward Max.

"I filled the sales manager's job," he said.

"Good."

The odds board at the open end of the patio showed Post Time: 5:12, Time O'Day: 5:06 and made Lindo-Mar and Jesse's Hand co-favorites at 5–2. Time O'Day moved to 5:07; the odds against all the horses blinked off and on in turn, the prices against Lindo-Mar and Jesse's Hand remaining unchanged.

"I gave the job to Ros's brother," Max went on. "But I'd rather have him in my own office. In case you're interested."

"No."

"Why, Lew? Just tell me why? I used to think you had something to prove. But haven't you proved it?" I caught Lisa's eye and made a come-here gesture and received an in-a-minute response. "What do I tell Kathy?" For the first time, his questioning tone held a note of irritation and another of urgency.

Lisa and Billie picked up their purses and started toward us; then, as they left the table, Billie went back for my field glasses. "You owe her something," Max was saying.

"I do," I agreed. "But what I owe I can't pay. I can only give her advice."

"I'll carry the message."

"Tell her to marry some square with a steady job and a future," I said quietly. "Tell her to stop looking for a husband in a Gardena poker club."

"And tell her you said so?"

"Yes. And give her my love." I meant every word of it, including the last.

Four minutes later, our band had reassembled at its vantage point overlooking the lawn. One of my hands held one of Lisa's. The other swung my glasses down and focused them on Jesse's Hand as an assistant starter grabbed his bridle and started to tug him toward Stall Eleven in the gate, just beyond the sixteenth pole, a hundred and fifty yards to my left. I smiled, seeing Esteban wave his whip at the assistant, who dropped the bridle and smiled more broadly when Jesse's Hand went into the stall on his own. "It is now post time," the announcer declared. I put down the glasses and looked toward the odds-board; Jesse's Hand was down to 2–1, Lindo-Mar the 5–2 second choice; but the money board showed less than $1,000 difference in money bet on the two; Lindo-Mar had to be a flat 5–2; Jesse's Hand was a long 2–1 and would probably pay $6.80 if it won. $6,800 for two thousand, twice, would be $13,600 for four, plus $3,400 for another thousand, would be $18,000, plus $680 for the odd $200. $18,680.

The announcer said: "There they go!" in the fashion of

California race-callers, and the crowd shouted "They're off!" in
the fashion of racetrack crowds everywhere. A chill went
through me; the field glasses shook, and I took my free hand
from Lisa's and used both hands to steady them; and now the
horses were level with me, and Jesse's Hand, orange-and-white,
white cap, was driving for the lead, had the lead, was trying to
come clear enough to get down to the rail, was clear, and the
field was into the clubhouse turn, Jesse's Hand in front by
"three-four lengths," the announcer said. The chill passed.
Midway round the turn, I spotted Lindo-Mar, bandages, red-
and-white, white cap, caught on the outside of a three-horse
spread in the middle of the field. The pace seemed slow, which
was to the advantage of Jesse's Hand since Esteban, in the
absence of Lindo-Mar as a pacemaker, was now committed to a
wire-to-wire effort. The boy on Lindo-Mar must have reached
the same conclusion at about the same time; he swung his whip
once, twice, and Lindo-Mar lunged forward, leaving the other
two quickly, flying now, catching and passing the fourth horse,
continuing forward to be lapped on a pair running together
three lengths back of Jesse's Hand, the other two picking up
speed to match hers, the three moving together, so that, as the
field turned into the backstretch, Jesse's Hand's lead was only
two lengths and contracting rapidly as the three pursuers
closed in.

Down the backstretch, past the five-eighths pole, I saw
Esteban sneak a backward glance and, in response to what he
saw, let out a notch on the reins; and now the gap was a length
and still diminishing, but diminishing slowly. Esteban was
doing the only thing he could do, and not many jockeys would
have had the sense to attempt it: he was trying to time the
advance of the other three so that they would come abreast of
Jesse's Hand just as the turn was reached, hoping that, as the
four went round that last turn, the shorter distance Jesse's

Hand would run would leave her the fresher horse for the run to the wire. But Esteban's hope, and mine, died almost in the instant in which I identified it. Lindo-Mar's jockey flashed his whip again, and the filly, full of run, dashed forward, drawing clear of the pair she had been lapped on so quickly that the rider was able to angle her down toward Jesse's Hand before being quite lapped on, so that she was running downhill, favored by the bank in the track, in her brush for the lead; and a moment later Lindo-Mar was pressed tight on Jesse's Hand's flank, so tight I thought the two jockeys' legs must scrape; and the next moment Lindo-Mar was clear and on the rail, a length in front, a length and a half, two, three, still three at the quarter pole, midway in the final turn.

The usual optical illusion caused an apparent lessening of the gap just before they straightened away, but it was still three lengths, maybe a bit more, as the horses hit the stretch. Esteban flailed at Jesse's Hand with his whip, switching the bat to his left hand at the eighth pole, changing hands deftly, but without effect. Lindo-Mar was going easily, four lengths clear at the sixteenth pole, five at the wire, winning unchallenged, unextended, a sharp contrast to Jesse's Hand, who had a wreath of foam at his neck as he came, exhausted, to the finish line, a half length clear of the third horse.

"Sorry," Andy said. "But you were right about the boy. That was a hell of a ride." I did not reply. With the air of a man revealing a shameful secret, Andy produced a stack of tickets and showed it to me. "I wish I had your guts," he said. "But cowards last longer." The top ticket, at least, was a $50 place ticket; I assumed the others were too and felt an unreasonable rage mount in my throat. The crowd murmured as the numbers went up on the board.

"At least he saved the place," Lisa said.

I glanced at my program and confirmed my recollection that

second money was $1,100. It would, of course, have to be divided with Andy. I looked at the result board and told myself that things were not so bad. I had started the weekend, I argued with myself, with $140. When the purse was paid, I would have nearly $600 and a half interest in a horse that, while it was not good enough to win a Del Mar co-feature, was not by any means valueless. And Lisa.

Lisa was saying something. I looked away from the board, toward her, and in that instant, before I could understand what she was saying, the crowd shrieked with mingled fear and delight. I looked back to the board as the *Inquiry* sign lit up; the crowd shouted "inquiry" in response; a moment later, to signify that the inquiry involved the apparent winner, Lindo-Mar's "7" in the winner's slot began blinking on and off.

I had no hope that Lindo-Mar's number would come down and said so. Andy claimed to have seen interference at the half-mile pole, the point at which Lindo-Mar had taken the lead; but even if he were right, even if, as Lindo-Mar moved to the rail while passing Jesse's Hand, the two had bumped, or if Lindo-Mar had crossed too sharply in front of Jesse's Hand, causing Esteban to check, this could only be grounds for a $25 fine against Lindo-Mar's jockey for "careless riding," or, more likely, the basis for a stern lecture by the senior patrol judge to as many jockeys as could be coerced into attending a screening of the patrol films of this race. No such incident could be the basis for a disqualification, because the rules require that, in order to justify a disqualification, the infraction of the rules complained of must have affected not merely the running of the race but the order of finish. And it was perfectly plain that, whatever occurred or did not occur at the half-mile pole, Lindo-Mar would have beaten Jesse's Hand without its occurrence or non-occurrence.

Eight minutes later, I sat at the table and tried to keep from looking at the result board but failed often enough so that I knew it still showed 7-11-2 as the order of finish, that *Inquiry* was still lit, and that "7" was still blinking. Max Rosenberg stood up. "I'm going to turn in this tie and jacket," he announced. "Bet the eighth and beat the traffic back to L.A." He started to unknot his tie. "You want a lift, Lew?"

I knew he was offering not only a lift but reoffering the job as well, and, in a single instant, reconsidered the offer and rejected it, deciding, still in the same instant, that I did not know what I would do or where I would go when the racing for the day was done and assigning to that ignorance no importance whatsoever. In the succeeding instant, the people at the surrounding tables oohed. I looked back to the board and saw that the *Inquiry* light was off and that the "7" had ceased to blink. With only the flashing of *Official* remaining before the race would pass into history, I was holding Lisa's hand, squeezing it, and she was squeezing back; and as I looked at her and managed to grin, the *ooh* changed tone and became an angry *boo;* and now, when I looked back at the board, the 7-11-2 was out. Even before I realized that the impossible had happened, the result section lit up again, 11-7-2 this time, and then the *Official* sign was lit, and the prices went up—including $6.80 straight on Jesse's Hand, the winner on a foul—and the announcer was explaining, his words barely audible over the crowd's manifested anger, that Lindo-Mar had been disqualified and placed second for interfering with Jesse's Hand at the half-mile pole, that the result was official, that the winner was Jesse's Hand, a brown four-year-old, bred in Washington, owned by L. E. White and trained by A. Livoti, that post time for the eighth race would be 5:52, and that, in the eighth race, there were no scratches and no overweights.

Suddenly it was hard for me to breathe and impossible for me to let go of Lisa's hand. Something like fear churned my stomach into a knot, and, suddenly looking at Lisa, I knew that neither the red dog principle nor anything like it had determined the nature and amount of the bet I had made, and I knew what had; and I knew that that Other Thing had caused the incredible act of the stewards to happen. Then, as my hold on Lisa's hand relaxed, I knew that none of this was true, that the explanation for what I had done lay inside of me somewhere, and that the rationale for what the stewards had done lay similarly with them, that men have overbet before and would again, that this was not the first horse wrongly disqualified and would not be the last, but my head ached, and my next few breaths came short and with difficulty because of what I had, if only momentarily, thought.

12

Outside the airplane window, far below, the orange groves gave way to brown sandy hills, meaning that the plane was leaving the coast; I tried to remember which one of us had suggested Las Vegas and decided none of us had. Going had been a common decision, not discussed and agreed on among Lisa, Andy, Billie, and myself, but simply arrived at, accepted without ever having been proposed. At some point in time, between the flashing of the official result of the seventh race, and the moment when the crowd ceased its mutinous murmurs and settled down to a consideration of the eighth race, we all knew, without an exchange of views on the question, that the eighth and ninth races were not for us, that the thing for us to do was go, that the place to go was Las Vegas, and that the time to go was at hand.

There followed the tumult in the winner's circle, the taking of the ceremonial photograph of Andy and me holding Jesse's Hand by the lead, with Alejandro Esteban in the saddle, grinning, while the outraged white-haired admiral who owned Lindo-Mar fumed and vowed to all who would listen (and some who would not) that he would sue the track, the stewards, the racing commission, and the Governor who appointed them.

"Nothing personal, young man," he would say to me, pausing in his diatribe, "but they got no right to take that horse down when he won it by six panels of fence."

But even then the decision had been made, for Billie, at that moment, was looking up the man who ran the air taxi service to Los Angeles, to arrange for the charter-flight to Las Vegas, while Charlie Ferrell, who showed up full of smiles at the horseman's gate (he had bet Jesse's Hand on the theory that I knew which end was up even if Andy didn't) was spreading the word that Jesse's Hand was for sale, spot cash, no reasonable offer refused, unreasonable ones considered.

The high bidder was another of Lisa's friends, this one a tall, soft-spoken man who was called Frenchy because he had once lived in New Orleans. He was one of three who bid $5,000, and I resolved the informal auction in his favor because he was willing to advance the purse, giving me his check for $9,800, $4,800 to be recouped from the track's Racing Secretary on the strength of a slip I signed transferring the winner's end of the $7,500 purse from my account to his. He sweetened the deal by initialing the face of the check in addition to signing it. The initials, he (and Lisa) assured me, would, when shown to the casino manager of the Shamrock Club, cause the manager to put his own initials on the back of the check and the casino cashier to cash it. As a final lagniappe, Frenchy undertook to return Lisa's car to the garage of the El Cortez and the two pair of binoculars to the hotel's bellman. None of this was essential. It would have been easy to find a driver for the white Cadillac; and my wallet already held $18,720, all but forty dollars having come to me through the cashiers' windows in exchange for my win tickets on Jesse's Hand. But I was, at that time, in a hurry to wind things up, to get going, to move along, and anxious to leave no loose strings behind, and I sensed that the others felt the same way.

Darkness fell; the plane passed over another belt of green—
San Bernardino, I figured—and began gaining altitude as the
mountains approached. When we leveled off, I signaled to
Andy who stood beside me in the aisle while I counted $4,900
into his hand, this representing one-half of the purse and one-
half of the sales price of Jesse's Hand. "Good thing we met,"
Andy said, looking at the wad of money I had left—it actually
amounted to just under $14,000; there was also the $9,800
check, still uncashed, now wholly mine—and Billie, across the
aisle, let her eyes roll up in her head in embarrassment. Andy's
remark implied that the money was, at least in part, a result of
what he had arranged; and Billie's gesture told me that she
shared my view that this was nonsense, that my handicapping
had provided the capital necessary to bring Jesse's Hand north,
and that that same handicapping would have made me a
winner, and a big one, whether or not Andy Livoti or Jesse's
Hand existed. I knew that was true, just as I knew that my long
dry spell was over, that, for the present and the foreseeable
future, I would be able to take risks without flinching and
losses without panicking; and, because of this, and because I
was a sound gambler with a good basic knowledge of the
games, I would continue to win.

I must have slept. Suddenly it was quite dark outside, and
the door to the pilot's compartment was open, and the pilot
was calling our attention to the "string of lights on our left"
which was, he explained, Highway 91, the faint lights marking
billboards, the thick clusters the Strip hotels, the expanse of
colored lights well ahead being Las Vegas itself. "Fasten your
seat belts," he shouted. "McCarren Field next; nice to have
flown with you; and come back loaded."

The pilot's door slammed, and the plane went into its 180°
turn, slanting onto the lighted runway, gunning its motors as it
came to a stop; and Andy was on his feet, opening the door,

then jumping down and holding his arms to catch Billie. I performed the same service for Lisa, marveling at her litheness as she seemed barely to touch me in descending. Then we were into the terminal and out of it, down a walkway toward the cabstand, past a wall lined with posters, each depicting the entertainment at a Strip hotel or calling attention to the advantages of gambling at a particular downtown club. Two of the clubs boasted "the most liberal slots in town"; most offered free parking and/or free souvenirs. The Shamrock Club made a less specific appeal, describing itself as "where the action is."

The action, the manager of the Shamrock admitted, had not yet developed. This was, he pointed out, early in the last evening of a long weekend. Many gamblers had already departed, having reached their self-imposed limits, or, in other cases, their actual limits based on the credit the hotels and casinos were willing to extend them. Others were eating or, as the manager put it, almost apologetically, spending a little time with their wives. "Come back any time from ten to three," he invited, "and I'll guarantee you'll have to wait for a seat at the twenty-one, and it'll be a fight to get close enough to the craps to get a bet down."

So saying, he took Frenchy's check into the cage, made a squiggle below Frenchy's squiggle, handed the check to the cashier, and watched as she got a packet of hundred-dollar bills from her drawer, removed two, sliding them out of the paper wrapper, and handed the remainder, still banded, to me. "Nine thousand eight hundred," the manager said. "Count it if you want. We never made a mistake yet, but there's got to be a first time."

"I'll count it," Billie said. "I got no class." She took the packet from my hand, sat down in a corner of the office, and began to count the bills onto a coffee table. I thanked the manager for cashing the check and hoped we hadn't come at a bad time, what with the banks closed and the action about to begin.

"Nothing like that," the manager said. "In the first place, there's never a time in Las Vegas when there isn't at least one bank open. Maybe you couldn't get the loan committee to meet at midnight on Christmas Eve, but you could sure as hell get a hundred thousand dollars for a good check. Though why you'd want to bother with a bank, I wouldn't know; you could always get it from the joint down the street, and it wouldn't matter what street you were on." In the second place, he explained, while Billie divided the bills into piles of ten, facing each pile in an alternate direction as she stacked the piles, Las Vegas has a cumbersome surplus of hundred-dollar bills, the town being the natural home of such notes, the one point in the circulatory system of the Federal Reserve where, if artificial steps were not taken to break the jam, all or nearly all such would come permanently to rest. "They come into town in pockets," the manager declared, "and they come across the crap table, and down the slot into the box, and back to the cage when we empty the boxes. And the high rollers come to the cage with checks and markers and we deal the bills out, and they put them on the tables and into the slot and the whole thing keeps going round and round. Now and then, a player makes a good score, but you'd be surprised how often he'll take a check, especially if he's leaving town; and if he takes bills, he probably won't take them far. Just to another joint, most likely. One place may run short of them, but the town, taken as a whole, is constantly accumulating hundred-dollar bills. The casino operators take them to the bank, and sometimes take them out of the bank if the joint runs cold or takes in a lot of paper, but mostly they stack up at the banks, too. So help me," he swore, "every couple of weeks the banks have to bail them up and ship them out of the state because they're needed someplace else, I don't know what for, and the clearinghouse make the adjustment. Don't apologize for taking bills; big bills are a storage problem around here. If you wanted a thousand fifty-cent pieces, you'd be making trouble. The half-dollar is in very short supply here; the four-bit slots are starting to pull trade, who knows why? But hundred-dollar bills? Any time. How," the manager asked, "is Frenchy?"

I told him I had met Frenchy for the first time that afternoon at Del Mar, but that he seemed in good health. "That's Frenchy," the manager said. "Five minutes after he meets you, he's writing you a big check and worried you might not be able to cash it right away. He used to come in here a lot."

"It's all here," Billie announced.

"Good." The manager smiled. "I'd hate to fire one of the girls. We never see guys like Frenchy anymore," he said sadly, returning to his discourse. "We don't give their kind of action." By "we," he made it clear, he referred to his own club and to most of the downtown gambling houses which had adopted what he called the supermarket approach to gambling, amassing steady and impressive profits by putting small dents into thousands of casual gamblers whose bets were small and scattered, rather than taking the risks implicit in catering to men like Frenchy. "He came in once," the manager reminisced, "with a hundred thousand in cash and wanted to roll high dice for it. Two rolls. Fifty thousand a roll. High roll wins."

"And ties?" I asked.

"Ties wouldn't count. Except if we both rolled seven. Then the house would keep half the bet."

"Did you take the proposition?" Billie asked.

"Of course. We were here to gamble back in those days, and Frenchy was welcome because he was a gambler. Now nobody wants gamblers. They want customers. Guys that sell reapers all week long and come up here Saturday night to lose a few bucks, win a few bucks, not guys that worked and gambled and angled to make a stake and come up here to break somebody, you or them, it doesn't much matter. When Frenchy came in with his proposition, I owned the place outright. All I had to do was figure the risk, figure the percentage, figure if it was worth it. I had a thirty-five-to-one possibility of winning half his bet, which comes out to one point four percent, the same vig as the line in craps only a hell of a lot faster. So I took the action. Today I got rugs on the floor, a band in the lounge, free bingo every hour on the hour; I also got partners, banks, loans, and guarantees. I tell my pit men five-hundred-dollar limit, and that means five hundred dollars. And five hundred is what we stand to lose, not what the player bets. So you can have five hundred dollars on the line at craps, but only fifty dollars the hardways, five hundred dollars red or black against the wheel but only twenty dollars one number, straight up; and the money comes in nice and steady and goes out nice and steady, only it comes *in* a little faster."

"How did Frenchy do?" I asked.

"He split. Won the first roll and lost the second. We didn't make a dime on the deal. But we filled up the casino with people that wanted to watch."

"And beat them out of a lot before they left," I suggested.

"As I remember it," the manager said, "the dice got hot when Frenchy left, and we lost forty thousand dollars in two hours to two hundred bums that couldn't have lost forty thousand if we hung 'em up by the heels. But we had action."

The manager walked with us out of his office toward the front door. The strip hotels, he told us along the way, now offered the best action, none having a limit below $500, most quoting $1,000 routinely against every bet in the house, hardways and roulette single-shots, which paid 35–1, included. Most of them, he thought, would raise their limits on request, if the request was made before beginning play, and if the proposed relationship between the player's minimum and maximum bets bore a relationship comparable to that between the regular limits. "A guy starts with a dollar and doubles up every time he loses," he explained. "Eventually, he must catch a winner, so he must wind up with a profit. But the five-hundred-dollar limit cuts him off. Nine losses in a row, and he won't be allowed to bet enough to recoup. If he wants to start with a hundred-dollar bet, and go against a fifty-thousand limit, he's running the same risk. So the strip places let him do it. We don't down here, because he might hit us with a fifty-thousand-dollar bet right off the reel, win, and go out the door."

"How likely is that to happen?" I asked.

"I only run this place," the manager said. "If I owned it, I'd take the limit off entirely, and if a guy had a system he thought would beat us I'd send a cab for him. System players!" He paused in the entryway to the club and looked back at the activity within. "The only advantage a system player has over a pleasure player," he said, "is that when the pleasure player is finished he has nothing, but when the system player taps out he's never entirely broke because he still has his system." He waved to a cab parked up the street, and it started toward us. "Higher limits on the strip," he admitted as the cab arrived, "but the games are easier downtown."

"How can the games be easier downtown?" I asked. I was in the front seat of the cab; Andy, Lisa, and Billie were in back. The cab was en route from the Shamrock to the strip hotel Lisa had named as the "nicest."

"The rules," Lisa said. "On the strip, you get Danny Kaye. Downtown, they pay triple for ace-ace in the field at craps, and the blackjack dealers hit the soft seventeen."

The field bet at craps is a one-roll proposition. If the roll is two, three, four, five, ten, eleven, or twelve, you win; if not, you lose; two and twelve usually pay double. If two paid triple, the field became less of a sucker bet but still not enough less to interest me. Not enough to give up the higher limits available on the strip.

The difference in regard to soft seventeen was, it seemed to me, more important. The basic rule in gambling-house blackjack is that the dealer must stand on all seventeens and hit all sixteens. Soft seventeen is a seventeen arrived at by counting an ace as eleven. Ace-six is soft seventeen; so are ace-four-deuce, ace-trey-trey, and so on. Since "hard" (i.e., intelligent) play is based on giving the dealer maximum opportunity to bust (i.e., to go over twenty-one), every rule that requires the dealer to hit is advantageous to the hard player (e.g., me). I thought about this for the rest of the cab ride and on the way into the hotel, finally deciding that, limit be damned, I could play blackjack only downtown. Accordingly, I took a position at the left-hand edge of the most active crap table in the hotel—the hotel had a desert motif in its décor and dressed its dealers as sheikhs and its barmaids as houris. Lisa was on my right; Andy and Billie were beyond her. I peeled fifty bills from my roll and handed them to the dealer who shouted "Change," counted them so quickly it occurred to me that anyone who pushes queer hundreds anywhere but at Las Vegas crap tables is running needless risks, and shoved fifty sand-colored $100 chips my way. I put five of the chips on the line. When the shooter threw eight for a point, I put five more chips back of them, taking six-to-five for my second five hundred, and filled up the back line with place bets, putting five more chips each on the four, five, nine, and ten, and six chips on the six. The extra chip on the six was for my convenience and the hotel's; the odds paid for a winning place-bet on the six are seven-to-six. "Be right, dice!" Billie shouted. Looking down the table I could see she had followed my play, using one-dollar chips instead of hundreds. The next throw was seven. "Two rolls, no coffee, sor*ree*," the stickman sang out, and the dealer raked in $3,700 worth of my chips and $37 worth of Billie's.

Lisa offered no objection when I suggested moving on. The next place we visited was done in steel, chrome, and glass brick, and outfitted its barmaids in abbreviated Martian costumes with huge antennae in their hairdos. It was also a luckier place for me. I remained at the dice table for nearly an hour, never able to get up what I considered a decent head of steam, but winning, though slowly, just the same. When I retired to the bar, I had recouped nearly all of the $3,700 previously lost.

There were other places then, one after another. A pseudo-riverboat, complete with ragtime pianist in sleeve garters, a plush Western saloon that equipped its barmaids with gigantic six-shooters and not much else; a Parisian *boîte;* a rathskeller; a deeply carpeted swish joint featuring dripping chandeliers; an extended and multiplied pueblo—

"The Big Chief would like to buy you firewater," an Indian maiden suggested in tones of purest Glendale. I ordered a horse's neck.

"Seven, nine *was,*" the stickman proclaimed. I turned my attention back to the crap table in time to see a large number of my chips being racked from the line and the come into the towers that house the management's ready reserve. "A tough game," I said. "Sometimes I almost wish we didn't have to play."

Surprisingly, it was Billie who laughed, Billie standing next to me at the crap table. I looked around for Lisa and saw her standing behind a chair at a nearby blackjack table. When she moved a little, I could see it was Andy's chair.

"All the hardways, a hundred each." I handed the dealer four chips and watched him put them on the layout.

"Easy," Billie cautioned.

"Just relax, honey." I took the dice from the end of the curved stick, rattled them in my hand, and pushed a silver dollar onto the line in case the house rules required a shooter to have a bet "with" the dice. "You are about to see inanimate ivory cubes responding to their master's every command."

I believed it; I knew it; I felt it. When I threw the dice I didn't have to look at them when they came to rest, to know they were hard-something.

"Eight, two fours, mark eight, eight the point, and he made it hard," the stickman sang out. He rapped on the table in front of me with his crook. "Nine hundred for the gentleman," he told the dealer.

"Parlay it," I said.

The dealer changed directions in mid-action and added the nine chips to my original one on the square marked "4–4–9–1."

My next hard eight, which I threw on my second roll, which I knew I would throw, felt I would throw, had not the slightest doubt I would throw, was worth $9,000. The box man snapped his fingers, and a hand rack of blue-and-gold $500 chips was brought to the table. Eighteen of them were put down in front of me.

"Eleven," I said, throwing one of them to the stickman. As an afterthought, I fished a $100 chip from my trough and lagged it after the $500 chip. "For the boys," I explained.

I slammed the dice, low, into the far corner of the table and watched them ricochet, but did not look at them when they hit. Joyful yells from the table's staff a moment before the stickman yelled, " 'Leven! 'Leven! We got us a *gunner!*" told me I had won another $7,500 for myself and $1,500 for the boys.

Ten minutes later, the dollar I had put on the line because I thought the rules might require it had become a stack of chips and silver totaling $128, meaning I had made eight consecutive passes; my hardways had grown to $10,000 each, and I had (nearly) $60,000 in (mostly) $500 chips in my trough.

"Five, front-line winner," the stickman yelled; I had forgotten my point, but was gratified to see my $128 suddenly doubled.

There were appreciative murmurs around the table from those who were also winning on my roll and muttered imprecations from those who were not winning as much as some of the others. As far as I could see, no one was betting against the dice.

I let my bets stand and threw the dice. I had no feeling one way or the other about them now. "Seven," the stickman said. "Front-line winner, and the hardways are down." The dealer matched my $256 on the line, making $512, and put what had been my $40,000 in hardway bets back in the house's portable $500 chip rack.

"Pass the dice," I said. I took my chips from the table and the trough, jammed them into my jacket pocket, and turned away from the table.

"The right move," Billie said. She had not said a word during my ten-minute stand at the table, but judging from the stack of chips she was jamming into her purse, she had not been idle. "You ought to get a room and go to sleep for a while."

I did not reply.

Andy and Lisa were still at the blackjack table. Andy slid from his stool as I approached, and, playing the hand standing up, stood pat against the dealer's face-up six and frowned when the dealer turned up an ace in the hole, for soft seventeen, turned Andy's cards up, and removed Andy's bet—rather a large one, I noticed with surprise: several $25 chips, and at least one $100—from the stenciled square in front of Andy's cards and put them in the house's horizontal rack.

"You should have been here," Andy said, removing a stack of chips from the table and putting them in his pocket. "This guy's been busting like he was on my team. I'm nearly $1,500 ahead."

"I did all right at the craps," I said.

"About $55,000 worth of all right," Billie squealed.

Lisa smiled and squeezed my arm. Neither the smile nor the squeeze was quite right, but I gave little thought to either one. "You might have won that hand downtown," I pointed out. "That was soft seventeen."

Andy thought this over then, comprehending, grinned. "Try a little blackjack downtown?" he proposed.

Billie pulled the flap of my jacket pocket back with her thumb and, peeking inside, pantomimed an excessive degree of awe. "I'd be afraid," she said slowly, "to play that kind of game with that kind of money."

I knew what she meant, and I agreed with her. Blackjack has always been one of my favorite games because in it, the player is required to make judgments and act on them, the result of the game depending to so great a degree on the player's skill that, of all casino games, this is the only one for which no fixed "house-percentage" has been determined. How much a roulette table will produce for its proprietors, on average, over a period of time, is a function of how much is bet; at craps, the equivalent figure varies not only according to how much is bet but as to where, as among the various propositions, it is staked. But in blackjack, the figure depends, at least in part, on who is playing, on whether the play is sound or unsound, or, as housemen put it, whether the dealer is going against hard-players or soft-players. My liking for the game stems from the fact that since the player makes the action, the player's fate is largely in his own hands. My fear of the game, which is equally meaningful, derives from the fact—accepted as such by anyone with even a moderate knowledge of gambling—that a dealer of reasonable skill can give the player more or less any card he wishes to give him. In a well-run gambling house, there is rarely any reason for a dealer to cheat; indeed, in Las Vegas, where the dealers are permitted to accept tips and are likely to get them only from winners, the dealer is, if anything, more likely to cheat in the player's favor than against him. But the possibility that a dealer might, given the proper circumstances, bust a player out is always there.

"At the Silver Hotel, they deal from a box," Lisa said.

I no longer marveled at Lisa's ability to answer questions that, until they were answered, had existed only in my mind. The game dealt from a box would be the same game; as a player, the decisions that would make or break me would me mine. But, with the deck surrounded on three sides with strips of wood, a dealer would have to be fantastically adept if he wanted to bring the cards out in any order other than the order that existed inside the box.

The Silver Hotel, though it looked like a strip hotel, and though its limits were as large as those used on the strip, was in downtown Las Vegas. Accordingly, the dealers were required to hit soft seventeen, and the place was noisy. I have often wondered why the downtown places are noisier than the strip hotels. Perhaps it is because there are more slot machines; perhaps it is because the carpets are not so deep. Probably it is a combination of these and other factors.

In any case, there was noise from the beginning of my stand in the Silver Hotel until just before the end of it, nearly three hours later. It was noisy when I asked for a ten-thousand limit at the blackjack, with a minimum bet of a thousand, noisy when the pit-boss nodded his consent, noisy when I covered the square in front of my seat and the squares at each side with thousand-dollar bets. I was dealt three hands out of the box; they totaled thirteen, fourteen, and twelve. The dealer had a six up. I made an umpire's "safe" gesture, meaning I wanted no cards on any of my hands, and watched as the dealer turned up his hole card, a ten, and hit sixteen with a king, making twenty-six, busted, five points over the limit, and matched each of my bets with chips from his rack.

It was noisy at the crap table; I spent half an hour there the first time without really getting started, returning to the blackjack with the same $63,000 with which I had left it, that being about $5,000 more than I had entered the Silver Hotel with. It was noisy at the blackjack table as, still betting $1,000 or $2,000 at a time, I built my roll up to nearly $80,000, then saw it dwindle again so that there was only about $60,000 left when I returned to craps.

"Three, craps, line away," the stickman shouted. I had been at the table for nearly an hour now, an hour and a half counting my first visit. I looked down at my chips in my trough, taking a quick count before making my next bet. They were mostly $500 chips, and I had arranged them in a long cylinder, with silver dollars inserted, one every ten chips. There were eleven silver dollars, meaning eleven sets of ten $500 chips, meaning $55,000, plus eight hundreds, plus, of course, the eleven silver dollars. $55,811.

"You want to sit down?" I asked.

"I'm getting a little tired," Lisa admitted.

I put the odd $811 on the line and watched the shooter throw boxcars. At the far end of the pit, Andy and Billie were the only players at a blackjack table. I steered Lisa toward them.

"Still ten-thousand limit?" the pit-boss asked as I sat down. The question reminded me that I had yet to make use of the full limit agreed on.

Somehow that mere fact seemed reason enough. I put twenty $500 chips in the box at my place, was dealt a ten and a four, stood—I have never hit fourteen in my life, and never will—and saw the dealer's twenty as my $10,000 was racked away. $45,000. I made the same bet again, caught a queen and a deuce, noticed that the dealer had a ten up, wagged my cards for a hit, and saw the box disgorge another queen. $35,000.

"Oops," I said, sadly. I cut my bet to $5,000, resolving to stay at that level until my roll either shrank to $20,000, at which point I would quit for the night, or rose to $50,000, at which point I would try $10,000 worth of craps, and *then* quit for the night.

"Anybody else?" the dealer asked. My three companions shook their heads. I was the only player at the table.

The dealer's hands went to the box and dealt me my two cards, face-down, and his own pair, one down, one up. His up-card was a six. I had a pair of eights.

In this situation, the rules permit a player to double his bet and split his hand, and common sense demands that he do so. Since there are sixteen tens in the deck, and only four each of everything else, the dealer's most likely hand is sixteen, and his most likely count after his compulsory hit is twenty-six. Similarly, the player who splits is not only increasing his bet when the likelihood of winning is strong but is actually increasing that likelihood also, since he is exchanging a valueless sixteen for two hands, neither of which can be worse than sixteen (there are no worse hands than sixteen; all hands below seventeen lose equally if the dealer does not break and win if he does) which may be better than sixteen and probably will be. I put ten more $500 chips on the table, separated my eights, face-up, so that they constituted two hands, and was dealt an eight on one and a three on the other.

The argument in favor of splitting the eights was as valid at this point as it had been the moment before. I put another $5,000 in chips up, turned my third eight face-up, and was dealt two more cards, a seven and a deuce.

This gave me $5,000 on 8–7, $5,000 on 8-deuce and $5,000 on 8–trey. With the dealer at an obvious disadvantage, going down for double on the two hands that totaled ten and eleven was as automatic as my splits had been. I put $5,000 more on each of them and received the single permissible card, face-down, on each. My hands, I noticed with some pride as I restacked the twenty $500 chips I had left, were pleasingly steady.

Quickly, the dealer turned up his hole card, an ace to go with his six. Before I had time to congratulate myself that because I was playing downtown, he could not stand on the soft seventeen, he hit it with a ten, making hard seventeen, making the point academic, and winning my $5,000 bet on my first hand, which totaled only fifteen. The disposition of the two $10,000 bets, however, still depended on the value of the unseen cards. To tie, I needed a seven-or-better with my eight-deuce, a six-or-better with my eight-trey—a higher card, in either case, would win. My hole cards both turned out to be fours.

"No," Andy said; but I knew what I had to do. The deck was now almost devoid of small cards, and in casino blackjack, small cards are dealer's cards.

I looked toward Andy and saw Lisa beyond him and was puzzled. Lisa should have been between us. Somehow, the terrible frightening sensation I had experienced that afternoon at the moment Lindo-Mar was disqualified came into me, and now I knew my hands were shaking, and I felt that I was about to say something foolish, that I would have except that Billie, who sat beyond Lisa, who stood beyond Andy, grinned as if, whatever it was I was going to say, she already knew it, so I didn't have to say it; and somehow all this made sense and did not make sense, all at the same instant.

"It all goes," I said, pushing my twenty $500 chips into my square.

Now, suddenly, and for the first time since I had come into the Silver Hotel, there was a stillness, a dead quiet in the casino, broken only by the whirring of a few slot machines. I looked around, surprised by the hush, and saw I was the cause of it, that the other games had stopped because there were no players, that all the players were ranged behind me at the blackjack table, all of them apparently having sensed, without knowing how they sensed it, that something worth seeing was about to happen.

I turned my cards face-up as they were dealt to me. There was no need to conceal them; the dealer's play is automatic, and, by turning my cards up, I was making the game more interesting to the audience which had become for me, at that time, *my* audience. My first card was the jack of hearts; my second was the ace of spades. Together they totaled twenty-one, blackjack, the name of the game, an unbeatable hand, a hand that entitled the bettor to three-to-two for his bet instead of the usual even money; so that, unless the dealer also had blackjack, my $10,000 would become $25,000. "You may have *in*surance," the dealer rasped, and I saw that his up-card was an ace.

I was, of course, tempted. Insurance, if I took it, would have guaranteed me a $10,000 profit on the hand: 2–1 for the permissible $5,000 "premium" if the dealer had blackjack, the main bet, in that case, a standoff; $15,000 profit on the main bet if he did not have blackjack, the $5,000 premium, in that case, lost. But it was a bad bet, just the same, a bet at odds that were adjusted to give the house a ridiculous edge, a bad bet if you were betting a dollar from a million-dollar roll, or if you had everything you owned on the table, as I did. A bad bet. A bad bet.

"I'll loan you the five thousand," Andy said.

"Screw you," I said, speaking angrily, intensely, partly because Andy was the voice of temptation, partly because Andy had no right to be sitting between Lisa and me, mostly because Andy had no right to have $5,000—much less $5,000 to loan— at that time.

"Lew's right," Billie said. She was standing at my shoulder now.

"Take a look," I told the dealer.

"No *in*surance?"

"I'd like to." The words came easily now. "But they might hear about it at home and cut off my credit at the bank."

The dealer thumbed up the corner of his hole card, squinted at it, then turned the card over. It was the ten of spades. The hand was tied. The spectators buzzed; I could hear several men explaining to their women that I had just passed up "the best bet in a gambling house."

The dealer scooped up the dead cards, put them face up in the discard box, and waited a moment. He was giving me an opportunity to decrease my bet or to remove it entirely. When I did not move, he dealt again. Again I turned my cards up. I had a pair of nines; his up-card was also a nine. "Good," I said. He turned up his hole card, a seven, giving him sixteen against my eighteen, then hit the sixteen with a three, making nineteen. The spectators groaned as he removed my bet. "Come back and see us," the dealer said as I got up.

"Let's go back to the Strip," Lisa suggested.

"Not me, thanks." I had my hand in my pocket. I could feel two coins there. Since they constituted my total capital, I began to wonder what they were.

"You need money?" Andy asked.

"I always need money," I replied.

"I'll pay you my share of the plane trip," Andy suggested. "A hundred. You could get started again with a hundred."

Behind me, the quality of the room sound changed as the spectators became players again. The whir of the slot machines increased. Near me, a stickman was heating up his players. "What goes, men? You cannot win if you do not bet, and whatever happens, it only hurts a minute. Come out time, betting time. Are you all done?"

"Lew . . ." Lisa began, and now I noticed that she and Andy were holding hands.

"Forget it, Andy," I said. "Next time, you can pay for the plane. I'll walk out with you and make sure you get a cab."

An occasional car goes up the winding street that leads from the Valley to the crest of the foothill now, or down from one or another of the houses on the twisted street into the Valley itself. The cars coming up contain families coming home from dinner, or, in rare cases, visitors for families who have stayed at home. Those going down contain families in search of entertainment. It is five minutes after eight.

In the small master bathroom off the bedroom in the house halfway up the hill, the man is showering, luxuriating in the foam, letting the steam from the hot water swirl around him, watching it spill out of the shower into the bathroom itself, clouding the mirrors. Eight-oh-six.

Now he comes out, wraps a towel around his middle, notices with satisfaction that his shaving gear is properly laid out, each article just where it should be for easiest use. He wipes the mirror with a hand towel, clearing away the steam enough so that he can see his face. Then, without any special reason, he moves to the window and wipes that, too.

Even when the fog has been wiped away from the glass he cannot see through it; because this is a bathroom the glass is, of course, frosted.

Eight-oh-seven. He opens the window a crack at the top and peers out, watching the taillight of a car as it goes past his house, up the hill, turning in the darkness, disappearing as it heads into one particularly wide turn, reappearing a moment later, then disappearing for good over the crest of the hill.

Eight-oh-nine.

13

The cab's taillights grew smaller as the cab pulled away. Then they stopped growing smaller, and I knew the cab had stopped. I was, at that moment, unable to keep myself from hoping that the lights would increase in size next, that the cab would back up, that, when it came next to me, the near door would open and Lisa's hand would reach out and pull me in. She would smile at me as the force of the cab starting forward again would tumble me onto the seat and laugh and say— But before I could think what she might say (more accurately, before I knew I could never think of the words she might say because there were no words that would have made things right) the lights resumed shrinking and the cab, in pulling away, revealed the traffic light that had caused it to stop in the first place. I watched the cab, saw it continue to the end of Fremont Street and turn left toward the city line, toward the Strip. I gave no thought to the possibility that it might—or they might—return for me, either then or later; there was no need to consider such a possibility; I had already played that fantasy out while the cab waited for the light to change, and I knew where it led, which was nowhere.

12:41. An electric sign, strangely conspicuous in a welter of neon on the far side of the street, blinked the time at me. I shivered and regretted that I had not included among my clothing purchases during the long weekend now ending, a topcoat. And I wondered, not altogether idly, if among the many signs I could see, there might be one that gave the temperature. If the night was warm, I was experiencing a chill. HOME OF MORE JACKPOTS a neon sign declared. PLAY RACE-HORSE KENO its neighbor invited. Farther up the street, a seventy-foot neon cowboy winked a five-foot neon eye at me and saluted me with a wave of a twenty-foot neon sombrero. I let my gaze rise and fall with the hat, then continue downward and outward, past FREE SOUVENIRS, past CRAPS—25¢–$500, past an electric 68 which blinked and became 69 and proved, on examination, to be not the temperature but the number of jackpots won since midnight in SLOTSVILLE, down toward street level, past the WALK and WAIT signs on the corner. A news-stand offered the Los Angeles *Times,* the Las Vegas *Sun,* the Detroit *Free Press,* and the Cleveland *Plain Dealer.* I smiled, wondering, idly now, if this was the only place west of the Rockies where Cleveland and Detroit papers were available and New York papers were not. I decided that it was, and that the reason for this discrimination was that Las Vegas casino opera-tors were the assigns of combines based in the Midwest and not in the East. I wasn't looking at the newsstand anymore, but at the sidewalk directly in front of it. It seemed to glitter; and I suddenly saw that this was no illusion. Pyrites were inter-mingled in the cement of the pavement; so the city rises, in this sense at least, quite literally out of fool's gold, a profound thought, I decided, profound at least for a man who had not eaten in nine active hours and who had made $45,000 and lost $60,000 in those same hours and had 35¢ in his pocket and—my hand went to my chin—needed a shave. Suddenly a single speck of pyrite began to grow larger, as if it were moving toward me. Something jostled my elbow; a flat surface banged at my chin and there was pain there; now the pyrite was two enormous glowing specks, mirror images of each other; and I rolled away from the pain in my jaw. The twin glows vanished and were replaced with a jumble of neon and electric signs. I concentrated on one pale yellow light, unable, momentarily, to identify its shape. Suddenly I knew it was the crescent moon. I tried hard to remember when I had seen two crescent moons side by side, but, as I was about to succeed, the moon itself blinked off.

There were voices in the darkness, confused voices, jumbled up together, overlapping, so that I couldn't always hear what they were saying and sometimes wasn't sure they were saying anything. My father asked me to pass judgment on myself. "I'm serious, Lew. What should I do about you?" Alicia keened her martyr's lament, but only an occasional "untrustworthy" "disgust" and "liar liar" were audible. "Please hold all tickets," a man said crisply. "This result is not official." Lisa laughed and said she was sorry, but I did not know what she was sorry for and could not ask. "He's got a four in the hole," Rocco said, and I knew he was right because the dealer, who had a ten up, had taken a second look at his hole card and only a four, viewed from a corner, looks enough like an ace to require a second peek; and I held the nine of clubs and trey of diamonds, and putting the dealer on fourteen meant that I should stand or draw but I didn't know which. "It only hurts a minute," Lisa said, and her laugh was warm and I knew it didn't matter what the top card was or whether I got it or the dealer got it, that the result was foreordained, but would not be revealed until I had decided, hit or stand, red or black, call, raise, or fold, they do or they don't, and you may bet eleven at any time. Now Billie was saying something, and it was important that I hear her, but I could not, because another voice was louder, a man's voice, that sounded like Andy's but wasn't. "Nine, centerfield, comes on nine," the man said. "Lew," Billie said, but the man's voice overrode hers again. "Eight, big and red, wasn't hard at all. On and off eight." "Lew?" Billie said. "Five, winner-winner, five." The man was shouting now. "Coming out now; betting time. Pick up the don'ts; odds are off on the come-out; here we go."

I felt a hand at my shoulder. "Open your eyes, Lew," Billie's voice commanded, clearly now.

"Six, caught it easy, bet it hard," the man said. I was aware of the lower murmur of many voices and the hum of a battery of slot machines. A breath of warm air filled my nostrils, the air flavored, unmistakably, incredibly, by the aroma of chicken soup. "Open your eyes, Lew," Billie repeated. I opened my eyes.

I was seated on a couch at the rear of a casino, midway between the main pit and the Keno desk. Billie sat beside me, a bowl of soup on her lap. "One for mama," she said, thrusting a spoonful at my mouth. I sipped at it and, finding it not too hot, drained it. "That's my boy," Billie said. "Chicken soup with matzoh balls cures everything. Israeli penicillin."

"I'm all right," I said, moving the bowl of soup to my own lap and taking the spoon from Billie's hand. I gulped down another spoonful. "Thanks."

"Don't thank me." Billie bobbed her head toward a young man who stood between me and the crap table. "Thank Rabbit. Rabbit Burns, Lew White."

I started to get up, changed my mind, and put out my hand instead. "Thanks," I said. "I guess I forgot to eat."

"That's all right," Rabbit replied. "If it had happened to me the way it happened to you, I'd be on the deck, no matter if I ate or not."

"Rabbit saw the whole thing at the Silver Hotel," Billie

explained. "He and I were the only people in the place that said you were right to pass up the insurance."

"Insurance pays the light bill in these joints," Rabbit said. I spooned up more of the soup and followed it with a matzoh ball; the warmth spread through my body and into my feet. I had not realized before that my feet were particularly cold. "I don't know if I can afford this," I said, fingering the coins in my pocket.

"That's all right," Rabbit said. "The pit-boss got it. Charged it to the roulette."

"Who brought me in here?"

Rabbit and Billie exchanged glances. "We did." They spoke at once and giggled nervously afterwards.

"I take it you found out in the course of defending my play," I said, pausing in midspeech for more soup, "that you had something in common."

Billie got off the couch and stood next to Rabbit. "We got to talking," she said. "Now we're partners."

"In anything special? Or just partners?"

"My uncle manages a place in Winnemucca," Rabbit said. "I'm going to deal craps for him. Billie's going to be a change girl."

"That's for a start," Billie said. "With both of us working, we can save our money and buy into something of our own. Rabbit's got his eye on a place in . . . You tell him, Rabbit," she urged.

"Where U.S. 40 comes in from the east," Rabbit said. "There's nothing much there now. A couple of gas stations, one crap table, one blackjack table, maybe a dozen slots in the bus depot. But there's an air base on the Utah side of the line, and Salt Lake City a hundred miles down the road. You could run buses."

I stood up; the room started to tip, and I leaned with it.

Billie reached for my arm, but I drew it back and the room steadied. "I hope it works out," I said. "When do you start?"

"There's a four-fifteen bus," Rabbit said. "We'll be in Winnemucca about eleven."

"Check if it's going out on time," Billie said. "And get me a ticket."

"It starts in Vegas," Rabbit pointed out. "So it always goes on time. And we can buy your ticket when we go to get on it. Winnemucca's not exactly a hot ticket."

"Please."

Rabbit looked at Billie and shrugged. "Talk to a woman," he said, not quite under his breath. "I'll be right back."

When Rabbit was gone, Billie steered me past the Keno desk, past a deserted faro layout and an idle Wheel of Fortune, to the club's lunch counter.

"Bacon and egg on rye and two coffees," she told the attendant. "And I'm not listening to any arguments," she told me before I had decided whether to make any. "I'm going to put some groceries in you. You've been feeding me long enough." She put a five-dollar chip on the counter and stared at me as if daring me to object. I heard the sizzle of the eggs as they hit the griddle, thought of the two coins in my pocket, and said nothing.

The counterman brought coffee. "Why don't you come with us?" Billie suggested.

I sipped my coffee. "Winnemucca?"

"It's not much," Billie admitted. "Rabbit says the population is about five hundred including livestock. But the ranchers come in on the weekends, and the tourists stop between Salt Lake City and Reno. Rabbit'll buy your bus ticket. You can pay him back."

I shook my head.

"Rabbit's uncle'll give you a job," she argued. "You can deal blackjack. They only pay twenty-a-shift up there, but they say it doesn't cost so much to live."

The sandwich arrived. I offered half of it to Billie and, when she refused it, salted it and began to eat. "You've already got a partner," I pointed out, between mouthfuls.

"So I'll have two partners."

"Forget it," I said. "It won't work."

"It's forgotten," Billie conceded. "How's the sandwich?"

"I've never tasted better," I replied. Behind us, over the Keno desk, the winning numbers went up, and a fat lady shrieked with delight. "There goes $3.75," I said. "You going to have Keno in your place?"

"My place?"

"You and Rabbit. U.S. 40, at the Utah line."

"Sure we will," Billie said. "Keno, craps, roulette, baccarat, chemin de fer, Lena Horne in the lounge and Tommy Dorsey in the main room." Billie was becoming a little shrill. "I'm not drunk," she said, a little defensively. "I haven't even had a drink."

"Tommy Dorsey," I pointed out, "is dead."

"What difference does that make?" she demanded. "In fact, now that I think about it, I'm canceling Lena Horne out and putting Marilyn Monroe in the lounge. If you're going to dream, dream big. Dig?" I dug, and nodded, so indicating, but she went on. "Don't go putting pins in my balloon. I hate guys that do that. I went with a fellow once, a high school teacher in Forest Hills. We used to sit around on the sofa in his place and talk about how, some day, we were going to run off to Tahiti and lie around on the beach drinking the milk out of coconuts. Me in a sarong, him in a loincloth. We even got a map of Tahiti and picked out the beach, just far enough from Papeete so nobody'd bother us, but close enough so United Parcel would deliver whiskey. Then, one night, his roommate came in out of

the kitchen and told us the beach we were talking about had a
jet strip in back of it and a Hilton Hotel down the road. He was
a son of a bitch, the roommate. Don't you be a son of a bitch."

"You're pretty intelligent, for a nut," I said, meaning every
word of it.

"Why not?" she replied. "I'm a college graduate. Hunter.
1960. Maybe I should put something in the *Alumnae News.*
'Billie GOLD, '60, is now the lobster-trick slot-machine change
girl in the Depot Club, Winnemucca, Nevada. Jackpots to you,
Billie.' You just damn well bet I'm intelligent," she went on. "I
could even answer your question?"

"I haven't asked one."

"I didn't say you'd asked it."

"Which—"

"You've only got one question." Billie was getting shrill
again. She gulped her coffee and went on, pitching her voice
lower as if with an effort. "It has to do with her. The ice-water
blonde. You want to know why she picked you up when she
did, but that's not quite The Question. And whether she loved
you at all, but you know the answer to that, which is 'no,' so
that can't be it. And why she dropped you when she did, but
that's not it, not The Question, not quite. Not *how* or *when,* but
what and *who?* Am I right?"

Her way of saying the last three words reminded me of
something; by the time I dredged it up and realized it was the
little man in *The 39 Steps,* Mr. Memory, I knew she didn't
mean the question to be answered any more than he did;
that, like Mr. Memory, Billie knew she was right.

"What is she, and who is she, and what is she not?" Billie
went on. "It's all one question; and you've got to answer it; only
you can't even ask it. That's why you passed out."

"I forgot to eat."

"You've done that before." It wasn't a question. "You've won and lost; you've been wiped out; you've missed meals. Did you pass out?"

"No."

The counterman refilled the coffee cups. "Shall I ask it straight out?" Billie demanded. "You can't, because you don't know the answer, and it's not the kind of question you can ask until you know the answer. But I do know, so I can ask it. Shall I?" I could not answer. "Is Lisa—"

"No!" The word came out automatically. "Go on," I said lamely. "I'm just tired."

"Not *just* tired," Billie said. "But all right." She asked The Question slowly, without emphasizing any one word: "Is Lisa Fortune Lady Luck?"

"There's no such thing as Lady Luck," I snapped.

"Don't get excited." To conceal the fact that I was excited, I tried to take a sip of my coffee and, in so doing, knocked the spoon out of the saucer and onto the counter and grinned to cover my shame. "Of course there isn't," Billie went on. "No Lady Luck, no Easter Bunny, no Santa Claus, no God on high, no fairy godmother."

"But we got an uncle we're not so sure of." The punch line of the old joke only made the tension worse.

"Just listen," Billie said. "Don't make jokes, and don't pretend this doesn't hit you where you live. I'm about to exorcize the evil spirit that inhabits your body. This is a medical procedure, and it may hurt a little. But it's easier if you don't wiggle. So stop wiggling."

"All right." I made myself stop drumming with my fingers on the counter top.

"Now the reason it gets you when I even *ask:* is Lisa—"

"It's a stupid question."

"Interrupting is wiggling. It is a stupid question, but that's not the reason. Most questions are stupid, and most people get mad if they're asked a stupid question, which is why the average person is mad from seventeen to ninety-one percent of the time, according to independent laboratory tests which I just made up. But you're not that kind. You could be standing under an arrow marked MEN, and if some farmer asked you the way to the head, you'd just point to the sign. So it's not just stupid questions. It's *this* stupid question. Why?"

"You tell me."

"You already told me part of it," Billie said. "You said there's no such thing as Lady Luck. That's because there's no such thing as luck; and *that's* the proposition you've built your life on. Right?"

"Not quite," I said flatly. "Two guys toss a coin . . ."

"And the winner is determined by chance, which some people call luck. The lucky one wins; the unlucky one loses. But suppose one guy wins all the time?"

"He's cheating."

"Not just lucky?"

"Of course not."

"Of course not," Billie echoed. "Because luck is what doesn't exist. Luck as in Lady Luck. Luck as in lucky star, lucky day, lucky streak. That mysterious extrasensory something that divides The Winners from The Losers. That's what doesn't exist. That's what there's no such thing as. Anybody can win a hand of poker; nearly everybody can win over an evening's poker; but the consistent winner is a good player."

"Or a cheater," I amended.

"Or a cheater," Billie agreed. "You've believed that as long as you've been a gambler, and that means as long as you can remember. Whatever it is, it isn't luck. A guy can beg the dice to be natural, and they may come back six-ace, but not because he begged. The trainer rubbed the hunchback's hump, and the horse won, but not because the trainer rubbed. Put your dollar on five because you met on the fifth; and the ball will drop in the five-slot once every thirty-eight times in Vegas and once every thirty-seven in Reno. You've believed that, whether you were living it up on the beach at Del Mar or eating off a hot plate in half a room over a candy store in Collinsville, Illinois."

"Grand Island, Nebraska," I corrected.

"It's all the same." I smiled because, in a very real way, it is. "When you were in good shape, you were with it," Billie went on. "Nerve, skill, knowledge, concentration, timing, patience, you name it. They made you a winner; and when you lost them, you became a loser. Oh, chance—not luck—was part of it, but not a big part. Not the deciding factor. Everybody gets his share of horses that win because the favorite falls down, pat hands, hardway bets that win and win back when you forget to take them down. His share, and no more. You became a loser when you lost the touch, which meant you'd be a winner when you found it again, not when you wore your lucky tie. And that was important to you."

"Maybe," I admitted. "So what?"

"So Lisa. Along came Lisa, and you started to win, and you figured this was because she gave you confidence, settled you down; hell, some horses can't run unless their buddy, the lead pony, goes out on the track with them, so what's so unreasonable about a guy coming out of a fog because of a girl?"

"Which," I pointed out, "has nothing to do with luck. Or Lady Luck."

"I'm coming to that. I don't know when it first occurred to you that Lisa had more to do with your winning than just waking you up. Probably at Del Mar, when they took down that number and made you a winner."

"I never thought—"

"I only said it *occurred* to you. You were holding her hand when the *Inquiry* sign went out, and you knew the *Official* had to light up next, only you hoped it didn't; you wanted the numbers on the result panel to go out, and you were holding her hand, and they did go out, and they lit up the way you wanted them, the way you had to have them. But there wasn't any reason for it. Nothing that happened on the racetrack—"

"They were wrong!" I blurted. Then, because there was no reason for anger, I steadied myself. "The stewards blew it. They're paid to be right, and they have the movies to help them; and nine times out of ten they get it right, but this time they blew it. That's what happened."

"Exactly. And you acted on what happened. You went down and had your picture taken, and got a chit from the racing secretary, and a check from an idiot that wanted to buy the horse."

"But I didn't fool you. You knew I was out of my head."

"Not at all. You were rational. You're rational now."

"Don't be so sure." I wasn't entirely sure myself.

"It's just that it had occurred to you—"

"Occurred—"

"That there might have been a connection," she went on relentlessly, "between what you were doing and what happened. You were holding her hand when they disqualified the winner. Maybe they disqualified the winner because—"

"And the day before?" I cut in. "I had my arm around her when a sure winner got cut off in the stretch at Caliente. Where was her fairy dust when that happened?"

"Maybe you didn't want that one as much," Billie said. "And, let me point out, you just admitted it did occur to you."

"The hell I did."

"You've thought about that Caliente race before." Billie was talking quickly now. She glanced toward the passage that led from the snack bar to the Keno lounge. I knew she wanted to finish whatever she had to say before Rabbit got back with the bus ticket. "You've used that race the same way you just used it, to refute the idea that Lisa has the power you don't want her to have. And you don't refute a proposition that hasn't occurred to you."

"A lot of things occur to me. Ideas. Possibilities. Rob a gas station, become a history teacher, or an alcoholic. I've considered them all, one time or another." I was talking too much. "All right," I conceded. "It occurred to me."

"Like a pearl *occurs* to an oyster." Billie bore down on "occurs" so hard it jangled in the phrase like an untuned note in a glissando. "You took that grain of sand in, and you're growing a shell around it, and now it's an extra piece of bone stuck down in your flesh, and it's got a nerve pinched off, and you're paralyzed."

I smiled. "Come on. One semester of college psychology doesn't entitle you to set up your couch in a gambling house."

"I had three years of it. I was a psych major. But what I'm telling you I didn't learn in any classroom. I learned it in bars and bookie joints and high-class resort hotels. I could give you a road map. Jersey City, Kearney, Cicero, Miami Beach, Hot Springs . . ."

"I made the same trip," I told her. "Only some of the places had different names. What did you learn that I missed?" How long, I wondered, had Billie been holding an unlit cigarette between her lips? I reached along the counter for a deck of matches, struck one, and lit the cigarette.

Billie took a long puff and let the smoke drift out of her mouth past her face. "I learned about Lisa," she said, talking through a murky gray cloud. "What she is. What she is not. I don't know why I should tell you."

"But you're going to."

"That's right." Billie took her coffee cup out of its saucer and used the saucer for an ashtray. "Stop me if I'm wrong," she instructed. "But I won't be wrong. I've known her too long to be wrong."

"I didn't know—"

"Don't be so literal. Not Lisa. Her twin sisters. Mostly they were white, but sometimes brown, and one was an Indian girl. I haven't known many; there aren't many. And we don't move in the same circles exactly, the Lisas and I. Still, if I'm at the bar, or in the lounge, and she's inside with the tablecloths and the long dresses and the white dinner jackets, we still use the same powder room. I can spot them there. There's a smell about them, a special good smell, that doesn't come so much from the good perfume they're wearing as it does from the fact that they've always worn good perfume. And they look good, but it's a funny thing about that. It isn't so much that the clothes are right and expensive, or even that they're used to that kind. I think the way they wear clothes reflects the future, more than the past. It's the security they get knowing that, whatever they wore last year, the clothes they're wearing now are right, and they always will be. Does that make sense?"

"If you're saying she smelled good, and she looked good, yes, that makes sense."

"That's not what I'm saying, but forget it. When you met her, she was with another guy—remember, you're going to stop me if I'm wrong—and he was winning, the other guy, and you were losing. Boy, were you ever losing! You'd been sour so long you'd almost forgotten what it felt like to win. Almost. And then, when she showed up, you remembered, and all of a sudden you were winning, and the other guy was nowhere, and you were off to the races." Billie bit her lip. "Literally, I guess."

"We should have ordered tea," I said. "I bet you could do something spectacular with tea leaves."

Billie ignored the interruption. "You went on winning. Not all the time, but consistently. You were making money, but you weren't making it fast enough, only you didn't know what it wasn't fast enough *for*. And the two of you were good in the sack, but you got the feeling that wasn't quite good enough, but you didn't know what that wasn't good enough for either."

"*I'm* beginning to sound a little squirrelly." I said it the way Durocher is supposed to have said: "Oh, was that a strike? *I* must be going blind!"

"You were scared," Billie went on. "And you didn't know what you were scared of, which is bad; but you found out what it was after the thing you were scared of already happened. And that's worse."

She paused, as if expecting me to speak, and I cleared my throat but could not talk. The word *Peanuts* on a wall sign behind the counter came into alarmingly clear focus; and half of my mind quickly determined that the letters making up the word could be rearranged to spell "untapes," while the other half recalled the swirl of neon signs that spun as I went down to the sidewalk and the feel of the pavement against the point of my chin. I shook my head violently to bring the two halves back together. The first try failed. The half that had been at work on the anagram began to listen, but the other half was filled with distaste for the things being said and the girl saying them. The second try brought me back to normal, or to what I hoped was normal.

"I'm sorry," Billie was saying. "I've got to go close to the nerve here. When she left you for Andy—who was winning—you knew what you were afraid of, and, if you were right to be afraid, it was too late. If she was Lady Luck, the Golden Goddess who smiles briefly on one man and then leaves and gives her favors to another, you'd muffed your chance to lay by treasure for a lifetime, blown it sky high; and, of course, you'd never have another. You'd been through the green door into the room with the winners, but you hadn't stayed, and now you'd be on the outside with the rest of the losers, the tired ones, with the hot eyes and the horse that got beat a nose to wreck the round-robin and the dice on Thirty-Fourth Street with all the comes working. But you'd be worse off than they were, worse than any of them, because they'd never found what they were looking for, but you had, you found it, you had it, and you lost it, without knowing how or why. Had you been too greedy, like the man with the goose that laid golden eggs? Or too indifferent? Or not indifferent enough? Remember the Goddess who had to be loved for herself alone, and woe betide the wretch who loved her for the goodies she dispensed? Was that it?"

"No, it wasn't!" My voice was much too loud, and even before Billie's mocking "It wasn't *what?*" I knew that, in answering the question, I had admitted the truth of everything Billie was saying. For Billie was only charging that I had considered the possibility that Lisa was, indeed, not just a girl I had met in a poker club and with whom I had spent a weekend and from whom I had parted in a casino, but something else, Lady Luck herself; and on this tenuous premise (that I might have considered the possibility) she had built an entire structure (that I feared I had met and won Lady Luck only to lose her) and on top of the structure she had built an ornamental superstructure, like the dirigible mast on the Empire State Building (that I did not know why I had lost Lady Luck) and the various reasons that she said I might have assigned to this loss were like rooms in the superstructure. And "no, it wasn't" was an objection to a suggested arrangement of furniture in one of the rooms; such an objection conceded the existence of the room, the superstructure, the structure, the foundation, admitted that I had not merely entertained the irrational possibility but had, indeed, accepted it, at least to the degree that I now no longer asked myself *whether* but, instead, *why*. And so I did not reply to "It wasn't what?"

Billie shifted her weight on the stool and caught the counter-man's eye. "You still hungry?" she asked, as the man approached. I shook my head and watched as she slid the five-dollar chip across the counter, got three one-dollar chips and some change in return, demanded paper dollars for the chips and, after a brief delay, got them, the counterman producing them from his own pocket and accepting the chips himself. "I'm going over to the bus station to see what's holding Rabbit back," she announced. "You o.k.?"

"I'm o.k." I was pleased that the words sounded all right. "Thanks for the sandwich. And thanks for talking to me."

Billie slid off her chair and stood next to me. "That's all right. I'm sorry it was no good."

"It was fine."

"I didn't mean the food. The conversation. You were in no shape to understand. Now you'll have to find out for yourself." Suddenly, quickly, she leaned toward me and kissed me. I responded to the pressure of her lips with my own, and when she finally pulled her head away, I could see she was near tears. "You wouldn't come to Winnemucca," she said. "No, you said you wouldn't."

Then she was gone. I turned in my seat to watch her as she made her way through the Keno room, where the loudspeaker was, once again, calling off numbers, and around the corner into the casino itself, out of sight.

"Some dame," the counterman said. "No business of mine, but god damn if I'd let a broad like that get away." When I did not reply, he added "No offense" and moved away. Carefully, I eased myself off my stool, keeping a hand on the counter in case the dizziness returned. When it did not, I let go of the counter and walked, as Billie had walked, through the Keno

room and into the casino, not following her, because I knew
she was surely gone by now, and not because I particularly
wanted to go into the casino, but only because I knew I did not
want to remain at the counter.

The casino was crowded, a double semicircle of players
around each of four crap tables, all the seats in all the blackjack games occupied, other customers standing behind the
seats, watching the play, hoping, a little guiltily, I knew, for
the dealer to make his hand and break the players so that a seat
might open up. I moved past the fringe of the pit toward the
front door. An exultant chorus of shouts from a crap table told
me the dice were, for the instant, or had been, for the instant,
hot. "They were hot at the Silver Hotel," I heard a man drawl.
"Hot and then cold. I saw a guy win $100,000, blow most of it
back, and wind up giving the blackjack table a $25,000
marker." I knew this was an account, vastly altered by imper-
fect observation and inaccurate repetitions, of my own mis-
adventure; I wondered how big the win and the ultimate
marker would grow before another spectacular passage at dice,
cards, or wheel would drive my legend out of circulation. The
crowd was thicker as I moved on, clotted where the slot
machine banks abutted on the pit; the machines themselves
were almost deserted as I moved between two files of them
toward the air curtain that divided the club from the street.

I slowed down near the entryway and studied the machines.
They displayed the customary variety of appetites, nickel to
dollar. Assuming no adjustments had been made in their in-
sides to give one denomination an advantage over another,
they offered the same odds, two coins for a cherry, four for two
cherries, on up to sixteen coins for three plums, and 125 times
the stake for a three-bar jackpot. To notice this was to accept
that I intended to risk my last 35¢ in one or more of them.
Thirty-five cents, my supporting, ex post facto reasoning ran,

was worthless; I would not be appreciably worse off for having lost it; contrariwise, a hundred and twenty-five dimes . . . A ten-cent machine came into my line of vision. I stopped, fished the coins from my pocket, fed the dime down the slot and pulled the handle. The left-hand wheel showed a cherry when it stopped, and two dimes clattered out. But the next two insertions produced nothing. I considered changing the quarter into nickels, decided against it, moved on to a quarter machine, dropped, pulled, smiled when the first two wheels stopped with cherries showing, banged vigorously on the face of the machine when no coins emerged, looked around for the change girl, then stopped banging, noticing a metal tab slanted sidewise across the area where the winning combinations should have been displayed: JACKPOT OR NOTHING.

I moved past and stepped between the pair of silver-dollar machines that flanked the exit to the street. Behind me, a girl's voice crackled through an amplifier: "Jackpot, machine eleven, sixty-two-fifty jackpot"; farther away a stickman shouted: "Five, six the point, make six and win"; and then I was out on the sidewalk. The neon signs still blinked and winked and cascaded, but I had no time to look at them. "Paper, mister?" the newsstand man asked. I shook my head and asked the way to the bus station. The man gestured with his thumb. "Three blocks down," he said, adding, to my departing back: "Just beyond the Lucky Club."

It was 2:40 A.M., according to the enormous clock over the ticket counter, when I entered the Las Vegas bus depot. I could not remember having seen a clock since my arrival, which was not surprising. Clocks are not usually displayed in gambling casinos. They might remind a potential player of an obligation to be elsewhere when, unreminded of that fact, he might make a further contribution to the casino's action and thus (in the sense that casino-profit is a function of casino-action) to its profit. Moreover, time being real, and being the same in Las Vegas as in California (though one hour removed from the time in the rest of Nevada), and the time in other zones being determinable from it, a clock might remind a viewer that there was a real world outside the casino, where the money was green and bore the signature of the Treasurer of the United States rather than plastic with the imprint of a gambling house, and that it could be spent for objects, finite or intangible; a clock would thus intrude an element of reality into a world deliberately made unreal for the benefit of its makers, and was thus to be eschewed.

WINNEMUCCA-RENO 4:15. I read the line on the departure board and remembered that Rabbit had already given me this information and wondered why I had forgotten it and whether my memory was failing. Then I stopped wondering about that, about anything except the one question to which I now had to know the answer, my chance of finding that answer depending only on finding Billie.

I spotted her quickly, asleep on a wooden bench near the back of the waiting room, her head on the sleeping Rabbit's shoulder, both of them covered by Rabbit's overcoat. She stirred when I sat down beside her, and opened her eyes, and smiled at me. I held the coat up and steady while she eased away, then tucked it gently around Rabbit's shoulder, and went with her to the next bench back so we could talk while she kept an eye on Rabbit.

We spoke quietly, so as not to awaken Rabbit; and our voices reverberated oddly, partly because the big waiting room was sparsely populated, and partly because my ears had become attuned to a background of slot-machine noises intermingled with the chants of stickmen, the announcements of jackpots, and the muttered imprecations and pagan prayers of the players.

Quietly, aware of the echo then, I admitted to Billie that she had been right, that she had named my fear only moments after I had named it myself; and I told her of the bigger fear that derived from the one she had named, the fear that was in the second half of me, the observing half that watched the acting, thinking half and commented on its acts and thoughts: that I was afraid even to allow myself (my use of *I*, subject, and *myself*, object, a plain admission of the bifurcation) to consider the possibility that Lisa Fortune was Lady Luck, or that she might be, or that such a person as Lady Luck existed. Because if I did, even that consideration might damn my thinking half, stripping from me, from both halves, my (our) claim to being a reasoning mechanism; and turn my thinking half into a superstitious half; and condemn me, thinking/superstitious half and observing half alike, to the circle of hell on earth reserved for that subspecies of gambler epitomized by the crapshooter who spits on the dice before throwing them and the horseplayer who crosses his fingers when the photo sign lights and keeps them crossed until the numbers go up.

"Considering something doesn't mean you accept it," Billie said. "You said you considered sticking up a gas station. That doesn't make you a holdup man."

"Superstition—"

"You have to consider *whether* it's bad luck to walk under a ladder. Considering it doesn't make a man a fool. Or superstitious. A man can even be of two minds," Billie went on, smiling, "be in doubt, yet not be superstitious. Three on a match is bad luck. Don't eat pig meat. These are superstitions today, but probably they once had some basis, and maybe they will again."

"But gambling superstitions—"

"You're working awfully hard to convict yourself," Billie said. "But even gambling superstitions may have rational aspects. 'Dice on the floor; seven's at the door,' " she quoted. "But maybe the house used to ring in bad dice when the shooter threw away the ones he started with. 'Six and eight, they alternate.' If a man turned the dice over just once every time he threw them, they would. The more we learn," she concluded, so earnestly I was slow to realize she was not entirely serious, "the more we understand that science and religion are not opposed, but complementary."

"And Lady Luck?" I tried not to sound bitter and did not quite succeed. "Does she have a scientific basis too?"

"There is no Lady Luck," Billie said firmly. "Lisa is Mr. and Mrs. Fortune's little girl Lisa. The earth did not tremble at her birth; when she walks in front of a mirror, she casts a pretty reflection; she can shed tears even as you and I, though she probably does so less often."

"You're saying what happened was coincidence?" I asked.

"You're saying it wasn't? We seem to have changed sides. It was not coincidence," she went on, before I could interrupt. "You won when she was with you; you lost before; you lost afterwards. And I'm sure that Andy Livoti, who's been a champion loser since his hands got big enough to hold cards, is winning right now, with Lisa at his elbow helping him stack chips. When she's gone, he'll be back with the losers. None of this is coincidental. But that doesn't mean it's supernatural, occult, or even spooky."

"What then?" I was suddenly doubtful that she had the answer, and was angry at her for not having it, and angrier at myself for having thought she might.

"I'm trying to tell you," Billie said levelly. "It isn't easy, and it doesn't help when you fight me; and I'd have flunked you out of the course a long time ago, but you were kind to me when you were up and I was down, which entitles you to special consideration now that I'm down and you're way down. But pay attention," she commanded. "Were you in the Army?"

The sudden irrelevancy startled me, but I nodded. "You shot craps in the Army." It was not a question, but I nodded again anyhow. "What did they lay against the six?"

Suddenly I could see where this was heading. What I did not see was how it related to Lisa, to me, or to the question. "Even money," I said. "And that was wrong." I didn't wait for further questions. "The right price is six-to-five. So I laid the odds every time I could. Even-money against six; even-money against eight. I figured I had the game by the tail."

"But—"

"But I didn't," I conceded. "I lost my paycheck, month after month, laying evens against six and eight. Then I figured what the hell, logic be damned, it may not make sense, but I must believe what I see, and if I'm losing my duff laying the bet, the guys who are taking it must be getting rich, and, since I can't beat 'em, I'll join 'em. Which I did."

"And did you get rich?"

"I made money. I'd have made more, but it was hard to get faded."

"Everybody saw what you saw. Forget the book, forget the fact that there are six ways to make seven and only five to make six or eight; six and eight win more often than they lose, so bet it. But there were always new guys who believed in the book, so you took them, just the way you'd been taken, until they caught on. Then you had to fight them off to get action from the newer new guys until they got the idea. But why? Why did the five-way chance show up more often than the six-way? Did you ever figure that out?"

"Yes."

"Tell Mama."

"Partly it was cheating. Guys not giving the dice a real roll.

Operators shaking the dice in their hands so you'd swear they were mixing them, but not letting them turn over. Greek rollers."

"And the rest of it?"

"Most Army games were on a G.I. blanket. No more than a seven-foot roll, on a soft surface. Sometimes there wasn't even a wall for the dice to hit. If there was, it was flat, and perpendicular to the roll. You couldn't help exercising some control."

"But you don't call that cheating."

"Of course not. If a man's looking for eight and throws nine he doesn't throw his next toss with the same shake and motion he'd use if he'd thrown ace-ace. He knows he's got to change one spot on one die, and knowing it has an effect on his fingers."

"A pretty big effect," Billie suggested. I shrugged. "If money could be made taking evens on a natural six-to-five shot, whatever was happening was wiping out a ten-percent edge."

"I guess so."

"You know so."

"I know so."

"And some guys were better at it than others. Right?" I hesitated. "Some guys made three-quarters of their sixes and eights. Right?"

"I don't know about three-quarters . . ."

"They made more of them than other guys did."

"All right."

"They were good crapshooters?"

"Yes."

"We're not talking about cheaters or angle-players now," Billie pointed out. "Just good crapshooters. What made them good?"

"I don't know."

"You said it before. Their fingers tended to make the dice do what their brains wanted the dice to do. Only there was a closer correspondence between brain and fingers with some people than with others. Now," she went on tutorially, "could we give that quality a name? How about dice sense?"

"How about control?" I suggested.

"No," Billie said. " 'Control' is conscious. Almost cheating. This is something everybody does, and what enables some people to do it better is . . ."

"Dice sense, then," I conceded.

Billie resumed her discourse. I listened more and argued less and asked questions only where I needed clarification. Just as dice sense varies sharply from person to person (her theory ran) so it could vary sharply within one person from time to time. One man might be able to exercise a greater degree of influence over the action of a pair of dice when sober than when drunk; another might need alcohol in his blood stream to improve the connection between head and hand. One might suffer a loss of his power when fatigued; another might normally be too tense to transmit the subconscious impulse with sufficient force to affect his throws until fatigue caused a relaxation of tension. And just as rest or drink might sharpen or diminish dice sense, so might the acts of taking nourishment or of sexual intercourse. (This last, Billie pointed out, represented another point of possible correspondence between science and religion by providing a rational basis for the ancient gamblers' adage that advises those wishing to change their luck to fornicate and names the race of the party of the second part.)

"But you're talking about Army craps," I pointed out.

"Of course," Billie agreed. "If they played the game that way up here—short roll, soft blanket, flat wall—the players would own the hotels."

But what had happened had happened here in Las Vegas. I began to chide myself for having allowed myself to believe

Billie could explain, in rational terms, something that, if it had any explanation at all, had only an irrational one.

"It's a difference of degree," Billie was saying. "In an Army game, the shooter wants eight, and his wanting it gets through to the dice often enough so he makes his eight more than half the time, instead of only five times in eleven. Up here, they lay seven-to-six against the eight to all the world, six-to-five to the line bettors, and the house wins more often than it loses. But they don't do away with the shooter, and he still wants to make his point. In fact, he wants it more here than he would at Fort Dix, because he sees a full rack of chips at the table, and he knows the house will refill that rack if he can clean it out, and refill it again if he cleans it out again, so he can win all the money in the world instead of just what's in the other players' pockets. And neither the house nor the shooter can keep the wanting from running down the shooter's arms and into his hands; all they can do is minimize the effect. *Minimize,* that is, not eliminate. Unconscious control becomes *difficult,* not impossible. The dice must go a long way on a hard, smooth table; they must hit the far end and bounce back; and the far end isn't a wall but a pile of crazy corners and angles that throw the dice off course, and you'll never hit the same angle twice. So the effect of the wanting—the effect that wiped out a ten-percent edge in the Army—isn't enough to wipe out even a one-point-something-percent edge here. But it exists, Lew. The wanting exists, and the effect exists. Believe me."

"What difference does it make?" I was getting impatient. "The games still win; the players still lose."

"On average," Billie said. "The average player loses. But he's an idiot anyway. He makes random bets and goes against the maximum percentage; or he makes the bets that will get him the money he needs with the stake he's got, screw the percentage; or he doesn't care about winning or losing just so he stays in action long enough to pick up something with silver hair and pointy tits out of the show. So the average player loses; and the bad player loses; and the players, all of them, average, bad, and good, the group loses. And the good players?" She turned on the bench and looked squarely at me. "What about them? The players who know percentage, and make the right bets to keep the percentage down. What about them?"

"They lose," I said flatly. "They lose slower than the others, but they lose."

"Always?"

"Not always. On balance. Over a period of time. They lose more often than they win." I thought that over and corrected it. "They lose more money than they win."

"But they do win sometimes. They get hot."

"Of course."

"When?"

"When the dice get hot."

"Not the dice, Lew," she said earnestly. "Not when 'the dice get hot.' When *they* get hot. A sound bettor, *when his dice sense is strongest—*"

"Will win?" I was outraged at the notion.

"Not always."

"More often—"

"More often than he'll lose."

I saw the catch. "Afterwards, you can see this," I said. "When a man's had his hot roll, you say his dice sense was working full blast. But the trouble is you have to bet before the dice are thrown."

"Sometimes you can tell before."

"Never."

"Are you sure? Didn't you ever see a shooter pick up the dice and feel winner-winner going through you?"

"Oh sure," I admitted. "And I was right a little less than half the time."

"Then you haven't got it."

"Got what?" I asked. "Dice sense?"

"What Lisa has."

"Which is."

"People sense."

Again I felt myself divide. Half of me listened as Billie explained and amplified what she meant, while the other half noticed that the clock behind the departure desk had two hour hands, one black, one red, and that the black hand showed *Las Vegas & Calif. Time,* which was 3:41, while the other showed *Nevada Time,* which was 2:41. The clock-studying half decided that Las Vegas, like me, had an unusual ability to divide itself, using California time when, if the area were actually in California, and subject to California law, the city that filled the area would never have been built. And then, suddenly, the second, clock-studying half of me no longer existed; and I knew it would never exist again, knew the division would never recur, knew this with all of me, both halves, except that there were no longer two halves but only me, Lewis Eldon White, and all of me was listening to Billie who, I sensed now, had only a little more to say.

"You've seen them at blackjack tables," she was saying. "Guys who play cozy, never hitting when they have twelve or more, hour after hour, and then, suddenly, for no reason at all, they'll hit fourteen and take a seven right off the top of the deck. Ask one of them why he hit that time when he didn't hit thirteen the time before. If he tells you anything, he'll say he *felt* it was time to hit. And that's all he knows. The fact is that the deck was loaded with sevens and sixes and thin on tens at that moment, but he didn't know that. He responded to what he did not know, responded subconsciously, unconsciously. I can't prove it, but I think it can go further than that. I'd swear I've seen moves in blackjack games that happened because the player sensed the order the cards were coming off in, anticipating the results of the dealer's shuffling patterns, feeling the variations that you couldn't observe if you wrote them down and studied them for the rest of your life, the player knowing without really knowing that the seven would follow the ten because the three cards that came between the seven and the ten last time through the deck had shown, without being able to name those three cards, not knowing what he was doing, not even aware that he was doing anything, just feeling that the seven was coming. Card sense. And like dice sense, Lew," Billie said, slowing down, speaking with painful emphasis, "it comes and it goes."

I began to grin. It was coming clear and, in coming clear, gave me cause to grin. A seedy flock of tourists from an incoming bus padded down the aisle next to the benches, and I continued to grin at Billie until the noise of their passing subsided.

"Poker and horses," Billie resumed, "are a little different, because they're basically games of skill with added elements of chance. So the good poker-player wins, if he doesn't get atrocious cards, and the good horseplayer has a chance, depending on what percentage is being taken out of the tote; and each wins more and loses less when he's turned on, when he feels right, when he bets his cards according to what's in his hand nearly all the time, throwing in a little variation now and then so the opposition can't read him, but not often enough to make his play loose. But card sense is a part of poker, too. I don't mean counting what's out and figuring your chance to get what you need; that's just poker. I mean the little moves you make without knowing why. I remember a man letting a five-dollar bet drive him out of a draw game with a hundred in the pot and four good hearts in his hand. I asked him why, and he said the deck "didn't feel right" to him. I rabbit-hunted through the rest of the deck, and there wasn't a heart in it. He didn't *know* that; he wasn't a cheater. He just sensed it. Maybe a corner of his eye and a tenth of his brain somehow registered the fact that the hearts all showed early the hand before and that the shuffle reversed the deck, and the cut put them back on top, but he didn't get that message. He just *felt* the conclusion: fold. Card sense."

"I know." And I did know. At that moment, I knew exactly what Billie was talking about, and I was beginning to see how it related to Lisa. "Way back on the Nebraska wheel," I reminisced, "I was following a horse named Berendo. This was a plater that wanted plenty of distance and cheap company, and he was dropping down and stretching out every time he was winning, and I was laying off, waiting for the spot. Then, one day, there he was, in for $1,500, a mile and a half. I went out to the track to bet him. But during the post parade I got the feeling he wouldn't make it. I put my roll in my pocket, and bet a ten-spot so I wouldn't feel too bad if he won, but I knew he wouldn't, and he didn't. Then I ran into the trainer—he knew I was waiting to bet the horse—and he said he hoped I hadn't got hurt too bad; and I said, no, I hadn't, that I hadn't liked the way the horse went to the gate. And he said: Oh, you noticed? But I hadn't noticed anything. Not really. But it turned out Berendo'd been holding his head high that afternoon, which, for most horses, is a good sign that means they're frisky and ready to run. But Berendo'd never run well on days when he'd held his head up. When the trainer told me that, I said I didn't know that, and I was telling the truth, as far as I knew. But part of my mind must have picked it up and stored it away, not exactly remembering, but not forgetting either. So, when Berendo went by, that part of me said *no, not today. Horse sense.*" I laughed. "Horse sense?"

"We can't call it horse sense," Billie pointed out. "Horse sense is what tells you to stay away from the track in the first place. Horse-race sense?" she proposed. "Horse-race sense, card sense, dice sense." Billie swung into her peroration. I knew what it would contain, but I listened patiently, just the same. "They vary from person to person and, in one person, from time to time. Nobody knows if he's got it, if he had it yesterday, if he'll have it tomorrow, or, worst of all, if he'll have it in the next minute when the dice come around to him. But," she added quietly, "there's always Lisa."

"And Lisa knows," I said.

"And Lisa knows," Billie echoed. "How or why she knows, she wouldn't tell you if she could, and she can't anyhow. But she knows. Beautiful Lisa. Charming Lisa. Refined Lisa, who wouldn't say shit if she had a mouthful. Lisa knows. The man who draws to fourteen can't say why. He just draws. You didn't know why you didn't bet Berendo. You just didn't bet the horse. All right, you didn't like the way he went to the post. But you don't mean you'd prefer to bet on a horse that walks with its head down like Sparkplug. No, but there was something that told *you,* not everybody, *you,* bet, don't bet, send it in, wait, not this one, that one, and that something, as long as it's happening, gives you an edge. And if you know enough, if you're good enough, smart enough, patient enough, while that something is going on, you'll win. The groom down in Kentucky that liked to have a little bet every day, because otherwise a man might be walking around lucky and never know it, had something. If a guy had it—horse-race sense, card sense, dice sense—maybe a little bet would be a good way to see if it was operating."

"It wouldn't work," I said.

"Probably not," Billie agreed. "Probably there's no way to find out when it's working. No way for me; no way for you. But Lisa doesn't need a way. She just knows. She arrived when you started winning, and she left when you cooled off, and you were afraid it was cause-and-effect, and you were right, it was. But there was nothing to be afraid of. You had it backwards. You were the city boy looking around the farm and wondering whether it made sense to use all that electricity just to turn the windmill. She didn't bring you to life; your coming to life brought her around. She didn't make you go cold when she left; she left when you started to go cold. She's not Lady Luck. She's a winner's girl. Believe me."

"I believe you." I had a sudden, unnatural sensation of clarity, of well-being. It was as if I had previously been looking, not at a bus station, but at a motion picture of a bus station, projected so slightly out of focus that the distortion had not been noticeable; but now the projectionist had brought his lens to its proper position and the new image, by its sharpness, made me aware of what had previously been dim and fuzzed. People were beginning to gather in front of the gate as the departure of the Winnemucca bus grew imminent. As if seeing their kind for the first time, I found myself noticing the red-eyed, gray-faced men, the frizzle-headed woman, their cheeks unhealthily red in the harsh light; not a winner in the lot, I decided, which was a fairly sound surmise, since very few players leave Las Vegas winning, and of those, nearly all leave from the airport; and to that fraction of a minority, the winners who depart by bus, the 4:15 to Winnemucca would hardly be an attractive proposition.

The public address system crackled out the news that the Winnemucca bus was ready for boarding. Rabbit woke, grinned at me, rose, stretched, and came around the corner of the bench and took Billie's hand, and murmured an apology for having slept so long.

"They're all the same," Billie said, taking her hand from Rabbit's, turning back to face me. "Kiss a loser's girl goodbye?" she asked.

I kissed her warmly, tenderly, but without passion. There was, I knew, no passion in me at that time. "Thanks," I whispered, my lips close to her ear.

"You understand then?" she asked. Without waiting for my reply, she answered her own question. "You do. I told you about the magic. Now you understand. I wish Andy did. I wish I did."

"Come on," Rabbit said impatiently. "You want to miss the whole bus?"

"O.K." Billie stepped back out of my embrace. "Write to me," she said. "General Delivery, Winnemucca."

"I will." I was lying. "And you send me a card when you open up your place on the Utah line."

"We'll send a cab for you," Rabbit promised.

I watched as Rabbit and Billie walked, hand in hand, to the doorway marked *Platform One*. Even after they were out of sight, I knew there was still time to go after them, to borrow the price of a ticket from Rabbit, to accompany them to Winnemucca, and I was considering doing just that, telling myself there were still questions Billie could answer in the long hours as the bus rolled across the desert, perhaps even questions she might ask that I might answer. Then, almost in the same moment, I knew there was only one question that would matter if I went through the gate: Where is this bus going? And I knew the answer. Reno, Winnemucca, and Nowhere. Nowheresville, the heart of downtown Nowheresville; and I had been there long enough to run for Mayor, but I was there no longer and I was never going back. And I had three other questions that I needed answers to, and three other trips to make. If the three trips produced three answers, that would be best; but if I ended the third trip with no answers, or with one or two, I would have a long time to think about the missing answer, or two or three.

Trip Number One: from the bus depot to the Silver Hotel. Question Number One: how had Billie known?

I walked the four blocks, looking at the neon and electric signs again, seeing them differently this time, not as invitations directed to me personally, nor as warnings, but merely as informative, explaining to all who passed by what went on inside the buildings and, simultaneously, what paid for the buildings and the signs. The Lucky House displayed a red-and-green frame which was filled successively by an overlapped ace-and-queen, a pair of dice that whirled in limbo and stopped with four-trey facing the viewer, and a spinning roulette wheel. I smiled, not knowing at what, then smiled again, now knowing at what, aware that I now saw the ace-queen in the dealer's hand rather than my own, that I saw the four-trey, not on the come-out roll, with the stickman shouting winner-natural-winner-winner, but on the ninth roll of a long hand, with the back line loaded up, setting off the stickman's elegy: went away/ with a four and a trey/ now a new shooter/ the other way, that the roulette ball, when it fell (the sign only showed it spinning; the blackjack display came up as the wheel started to slow down) would not fall into 14, 17, 20, or 23, these being the numbers I always played because one number is as good as another and these four are squarely in the middle of the layout and thus always within reasonable reaching distance, but would fall elsewhere, perhaps even in the zero or double-zero slot.

I turned away from the Lucky House, waited for the crossing signs to switch from DON'T WALK to WALK, crossed the intersection diagonally, and went in the corner entrance of the Silver Hotel.

Answer: Billie had eyes in her head and the vision to see all possible explanations and the sense to choose the only one that matched the facts without incorporating the supernatural, the mythological, the unreasonable, the magical.

I found the pit-boss and told him what I wanted. He took me to the casino manager. "I wouldn't want to vouch for the figures," the pit-boss told the manager, "not without checking with the dealers, but he gave us a hell of a lot of action, and he tapped out, that much I know." The manager took me into his office.

"L. A.?" he asked, sitting down behind his desk and moving various objects around on top of it. When I made an affirmative noise, he filled out a page in a pad of forms he had found and slid the pad across the desk to me, rising, leaning across to indicate the line I was to sign, handing me a ball-point pen marked *Keep Nevada Green . . . Bring Money* to sign with.

"Forty dollars," he said. I looked at the document. It was a receipt indicating that forty dollars had been paid to me by "Casino Ops" for "C.R." "Customer Relations," the manager explained. "We buy you drinks while you're playing. You want to see a show, we'll make the reservations. Our place, or some Strip hotel, no matter. For a good player, we'll pick up the tab. All C.R. So is getaway money, though we don't like to talk about it." He produced two twenty-dollar bills and laid them on the desk. "Plane fare to L.A. is about twenty," he went on. "The other twenty'll get you to the airport, buy you a meal if you wait for a flight, and get you from the L.A. airport to wherever you're going." I reached for the money, but the manager covered it with his hand and nodded toward the receipt. I signed it and passed it back across the desk. The manager's hand was still on the bills. "If you want," he proposed, "I could send you out to the airport in the hotel limousine, have the driver buy your ticket and give you whatever's left at the gate."

"Would he wait till the plane takes off to see that I don't come back?" I asked.

"He might," the manager admitted. "It's up to you. This isn't a loan. It's a service. The receipt is just so I can prove my own accounting. Also, we send your name around to the other places that offer the same service."

"I understand," I said. "I'll take the cash."

The manager handed me the bills. "Come see us again sometime when you're feeling lucky," he said.

I stuffed the bills in my pocket and thanked him. He and I both knew that, in accepting the cash, I was subjecting myself to a test. I—and not he—knew it was a test I would pass.

Trip Number Two: Silver Hotel to McCarren Field. Question Number Two: Why had Billie told me what she knew?

The dawn came suddenly, as dawn always does on the desert, the sky turning from dark blue to milky white in the five minutes it took my cab to roll through the empty streets from the Silver Hotel to the fork that marks the corporate limits of Las Vegas and enter the township of Paradise Valley, more often called the Strip. The marquees outside the Strip hotels seemed pallid in the daylight; in some, the electricity had been turned off. I looked at them as they flashed by and saw the names of the entertainers—Joe E. Lewis, Louis Prima, Harry James, Peggy Lee, Judy Garland, Benny, Sinatra, Durante—and smiled. I remembered the advice given young Lord Chesterfield by his father who, having taken the boy to the races, pointed out the structures erected by the association to contain the spectators and the immense expanse of arable land given over to the course itself, and cautioned the boy to take note of the enormous investment involved and to reflect that it was not made for his benefit. The validity of Chesterfield Senior's argument was apparent to the young English boy; the smallest Las Vegas hotel represents a capital investment exceeding that of the largest British racecourse; the operation of a casino for an hour is more costly than the operation of a British track for a season. What does all this say, I wondered, of an adult who fails to draw, from the more dramatic illustration, the lesson the boy drew from the other? And then I stopped wondering, stopped berating myself, and was smiling again, because I knew that, in asking myself the question, I had shown that I saw what I had not previously seen.

Answer Number Two: Billie told me what she knew because she liked me, because I had been decently kind and considerate to her when I was winning and most winners treat losers' girls with the same contempt they visit on losers, and because she hated Lisa, Lisa being a winner's girl, it being in the nature of the one to hate the other; or for a combination of these reasons, perhaps mixed with others; and I would never know the exact proportions of the mix, nor would I ever be sure of all its elements; and it didn't matter.

The fare on the meter read $3.25 when the cab reached the airport. I gave the driver one of my twenties, asked for green money, got three crumpled fives, asked for another seventy-five cents, and got it, the dollar tip a token of my fairness, it coming to nearly 30 percent of the fare but the driver would have to dead-head back to Las Vegas, and the seventy-five cents a token of my return to a world in which sums of less than a dollar were not meaningless, to be stuffed into slot machines or handed to washroom attendants; where three quarters would buy forty cigarettes and ten cents change, where even the dime would buy something, where buying something was what money was for.

Inside the airport I went past an island of slot machines over which was a sign reading *In Case of Air Raid, Crawl Under Machines. They Have Never Been Hit,* down the row of ticket counters, checking the lists of departures, finally finding one that had a flight to Los Angeles leaving in less than an hour and buying a ticket on it. With the ticket and seventeen dollars in my pocket, I returned to the slot machines and obtained three dollars in dimes from the young lady who strolled around them, making change and (presumably; I never saw her do it) paying off jackpots. Then, to her obvious surprise, I walked away from the machines to a row of telephone booths. I dropped a dime into a phone, got the operator, and gave her Kathy's number.

Trip Number Three: McCarren Field, Las Vegas, to International Airport, Los Angeles.

Question Number Three: Did I, as Billie had said, as I had believed, really understand about the magic?

There was haze over the desert floor when the plane took off, and a white blanket of it covered the mountains so that I could only sense their presence from the plane's ups and downs. The first land I saw was flat and green. I knew we were over California. Somewhere in the vast plateau below would be the site of Max Rosenberg's real estate development. I hoped it was good land, that the water supply would be adequate, that the small speculators who would buy plots from the Rosenberg organization would find smaller speculators on whom to unload their parcels, because I was going to be a part of the operation, because Kathy would meet me at the airport and drive me to the Gardena Motel where I would dress and shave for the last time in those premises, because I was going from there to Rosenberg's office. This was Tuesday, and by noon I would have an office of my own; I would be genuinely, gainfully employed, and be no longer the broken gambler I had been when Labor Day weekend began, nor the genuine gambler I

had become when (or, more accurately, I corrected, just before) four diamonds were played for a diamond flush, but L. E.
White, age forty, occupation sales manager, not much for a
man who had been salutatorian of his high school class, but a
cut above L. E. White, house-player.

The plane was flying smoothly now; the FASTEN SEAT BELTS
sign, which had been lit since before takeoff, blinked off. I was
suddenly sleepy, unreasonably so, I thought, since it was not
yet twenty-four hours since I had slept, and a day without
sleep, to a gambler, is like an hour without water to a camel.
But then, I reflected, I was no longer a gambler, and perhaps
even my body . . . I looked for the stewardess who would
give me a pillow; not seeing her, I fell asleep.

Answer Number Three: The magic was what the winners
had, the attribute that enabled Bolton to do what he had done
in the Americana Club in Steubenville a thousand years before,
that I had possessed at Caliente, at Del Mar, in Las Vegas
before I lost it, the power I once had to have, the power I once
had to show I had, that I could only show by first establishing
that I was rational, and then doing what no rational man would
do unless he had the power, betting higher and higher, until I
stopped the action in the Silver Hotel, proving the power by
creating the moment when nothing existed for me, for Lisa, for
Billie, for Andy, for the players and the employees of the pit
except me, my hand, my cards, and the moves my hands made.
But there was no magic; there was no power; there was, at
most, only an involuntary coupling of brain and hands, an
unnatural ease of reflex, a subconscious evaluation of past
events, an unwilled control of ivory cubes across a green baize
surface. And none of this mattered because there was nothing
to prove.

I woke suddenly; the plane was on the ground, taxiing; I
waited for it to stop. Then, as befitted the solid citizen I had

become, I waited for the engines to be turned off, unfastened
my belt, moved into the aisle and waited for those ahead of me
to leave. As I reached the door, as I stepped out onto the
slightly shaky ramp, I could see Kathy, standing just outside
the gate. I waved and saw her wave back, saw the sunlight
glinting off her hair, saw the briefcase under her arm, and
knew, suddenly, that everything I had done up to that moment
was part of a wrong pattern, and that what I was about to do
would be right.

I hurried down the steps; Kathy came through the gate
toward me, both of us walking, then both of us running; then
both of us with our arms wrapped around each other, both of
us laughing and crying and saying words that made no sense
all at once.

The man stands in the doorway of the house now. The
house, behind him, is nearly dark. Just outside the door, he
checks his pockets to make sure he has his car keys, his wallet,
his silver dollar, and his chip. Then he starts to close the door.

With the door half shut, he seems to change his mind,
glances at his watch, and goes back into the house and stands
in the dark entryway.

Forty-five minutes to plane time. I can get to the airport in
twenty. The sooner I leave, the more time I must spend at the
airport. The more time I spend at the airport, the more risk
that someone will see me. I don't have to leave yet.

You don't have to leave at all.

Let's not start that again!

Still trying to prove what you've proved can't be proved?
No.

Still trying to prove you're smarter than Mrs. Willie?

Mrs. Willie. Willie's wife. Remember?

I haven't thought of Willie's wife in years. I don't even remember where I encountered her, but it must have been in some gambling house back in Ohio. I remember I was on my way from the crap table to the cashier, and my hands and pockets were empty, so I must have been on a losing streak and on my way to cash a check.

"Willie, come here." There was something about the voice that commanded attention; that, and the fact that I was in no hurry to cash a check and get started gambling again, must have been what made me stop and look in her direction. She had a pinched face and badly dyed red hair. "I've been watching this game for an hour and I've got it figured out," she was telling Willie—I never did see him. The game she referred to was craps. I backed up toward her. I had been watching and playing craps far longer than an hour, and I hadn't figured it out.

"They just count the numbers on top," she said. "And they add them together."

That was what she had figured out. Oh, you're so right, lady, I thought. They say eleven because one die has a six on top and the other has a five; and if you start using the numbers on the side, or on the bottom, you never will catch on.

But why should I think of her now?

She is stupid. She is even more stupid than the people who bet horses to place and who continue to do so even when you point out to them that twice as many horses place as win but that they pay, on the average, less than half as much.

Question: Why do I think of Mrs. Willie?

Answer: Because she is stupid, and she must lose, and unless I win I cannot distinguish myself from her and must admit that I am stupid, but I am not stupid, so I must win, but if I do not play I cannot win, and therefore I must, now or in the next few minutes, go out to my car and get in it and drive it to Burbank and go directly to the point from which the Champagne Flite departs, and buy my ticket, and go on board the plane.

Question: Does the above conclusion follow from the above premises?

Answer: It does not. As Billie said, the good players, on average, lose; they lose more slowly than the bad players, but they lose. I can prove that I do not belong among the Mrs. Willies, among the place bettors, among the stupid ones, without winning. I can prove it by losing more slowly than they lose. Or by not playing.

When I have told myself there was nothing to prove, I have been mistaken. There is something to prove. But there is more than one way to prove it.

The door opens and the man comes out. This time he does not shut the door, but leaves it partway open. He moves across the lawn to the street, and walks down the street to a point where no house intervenes between the street and the hillside below, a tangle of scrub oak, mesquite and weeds. He takes the chip from his pocket and looks at it. Then he cocks his arm.

But he does not throw the chip down the hillside. Instead, he stops for a moment, with his arm bent, ready to throw. Then he lowers his hand.

He walks back quickly to his own house and goes into the garage and opens the right-hand front door of his car, then opens the glove compartment and puts the chip in it. Then he closes the glove compartment, closes the car door, leaves the garage, closing the door after him, and goes back into the house. Behind him, the front door closes.

He is not going to Las Vegas.

Not tonight.